BONE DRY

KATHLEEN KARR

BONE DRY

HYPERION BOOKS FOR CHILDREN   NEW YORK

FIRST EDITION
1 3 5 7 9 10 8 6 4 2

Printed in the United States of America

Map art by Alfred Giuliani

Library of Congress Cataloging-in-Publication Data on file.
ISBN 0-7868-0776-8

Visit www.hyperionchildrensbooks.com

For Donna Bray

Both the man of science and the man of action
live always at the edge of mystery. . . .

—*J. Robert Oppenheimer*

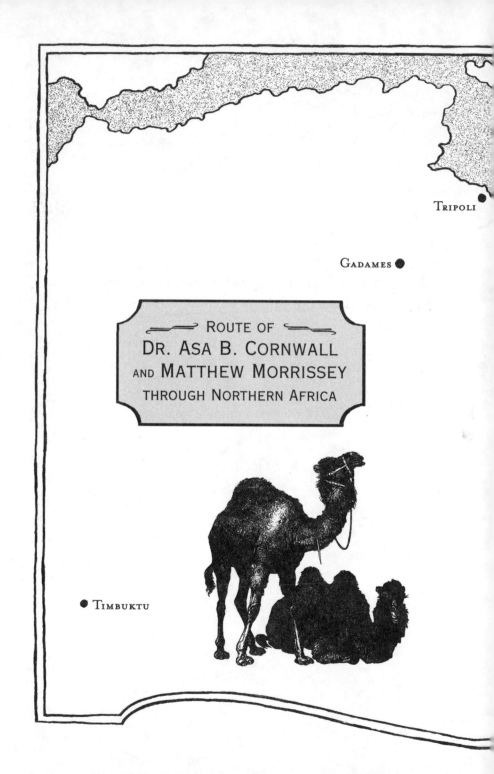

TRIPOLI

GADAMES

ROUTE OF
DR. ASA B. CORNWALL
AND MATTHEW MORRISSEY
THROUGH NORTHERN AFRICA

TIMBUKTU

MEDITERRANEAN SEA

ALEXANDRIA

CAIRO

The Qattara

SIWA

ZUILA

NILE RIVER

- - - = ROUTE
★ = ATTACK BY TUAREG, CHANGE OF ROUTE
● = MEET SLAVE CARAVAN FROM TIMBUKTU

THERE WERE NO MAPS. IT WAS UNCHARTED TERRITORY.
Matthew Morrissey sat astride his camel, willing his body to ease into the stumbling gait that was like nothing so much as riding an earthquake. Not that he'd ever experienced an earthquake, but at this point in his fourteen years he firmly believed it to be one of the few things he had not yet experienced. That, too, might come. The feeling was inescapable.

Ahead of him their Arab guide, Hussein, blazed the trail. Beside him his dog, Gin, loped through the sand. Behind, Asa B. Cornwall, in a state of perpetual panic, clung to his own camel. Bringing up the rear of the caravan were a dozen camel drivers and guards. All had impressive swords slung from their shoulders and myriad daggers hidden beneath their robes. Surrounding them was nothing and everything: the Great Sahara.

Another fine mess he'd gotten himself into. Where had this one begun? On the ragged cliffs of St. Helena, where he and Dr. Cornwall had tried for Napoleon's skull, or much earlier, back in a New York cemetery, where he'd had his first glimpse of the body snatcher? Matthew mulled over his strange fate, trying to probe its deepest roots.

So enmeshed was he in memories that he never noticed the vast sand dune their small caravan was approaching, never noticed something curiously marring its pure silhouette: the telltale glint of hot sun reflected from burnished steel. . . .

Alexander the Great

CHAPTER ONE

PERHAPS IT HAD BEGUN IN PARIS, ON THE BOULEVARD du Crime. Begun with the flaming torches . . .

Higher and higher Matthew tossed the torches into a crisp blue spring sky. Balanced confidently on the shoulders of the acrobat beneath him, he reveled in the gestures that had come so easily to him in these past few months under the training of his new friends. He felt again the emotion that had made the skill irresistible to him from the start. Juggling was a kind of resurrection. It was a

1

game that freed his mind, taking him far above the depths of the graves in which he'd spent too much time. And juggling with *fire* felt like making an offering to the sky and heaven above it. It was a little moment of pardon asked—and forgiveness granted—for the profession he practiced with Dr. Cornwall.

A carriage paused among the throng before him, its matched pair of horses tossing their fine heads. Matthew flung a last round into the firmament, then caught the torches one by one. He blew out the first, then another. But the third flaming torch was his finale. Instead of extinguishing it, he drew the flames into his mouth, then spewed them forth in a stream of fire that almost reached the crested door of the carriage. Still balanced on the strong body below him, Matthew swept into a bow. The carriage window came down. There was the brief glimpse of a lightly veiled face: the countess who came often to admire his new skill. She tossed up a coin. Matthew caught it and bounded to earth with another bow. The carriage moved on.

"It's gold!" He flipped it to his partner, Étienne.

"*Merci*, Matthieu. But your share?"

"It's all yours today, *mon ami*. A present for teaching me your art." He hesitated, unwilling to admit even to himself that he'd soon have to leave this place he'd come to love. He glanced down the grand avenue lined with panoramas, theaters of melodrama and pantomime, food stalls, puppet shows, acrobats, and musicians—all lustily plying their trades to the passing crowds. The bright sun added another level of gaiety to the scene, making it even harder for him. This had been his true home during the months Dr. Cornwall had been closeted in their hotel suite, finishing his phrenological *magnum opus*. Matthew swallowed hard. "I have to go away for a while."

"Matthieu—" His friend's face turned crestfallen. "Do you go very far away?"

To *Siwa*, wherever that was. Dr. Cornwall had made the announcement this morning. Just the one word. To Siwa, in search of Alexander the Great.

Matthew clapped Étienne's shoulder. "Very far, I fear."

"You'll return?"

"God willing, Étienne. But now I must make the rest of my farewells. *Au revoir.*"

Matthew turned away quickly. Partings were painful. Nearby, his dog barked once, reminding him how patiently Gin had been waiting through the entire performance. He deserved a reward. Matthew grabbed for Gin's leash and moved toward the nearest stall.

"*Ça va,* Monsieur Lacenaire?"

"*Ça va,* Matthieu." Jacques Lacenaire readjusted his beret and leaned over the counter of his booth to point below at the newly painted image of a fat, laughing pig.

"Ah," said Matthew admiringly. "*Quel beau cochon!*"

The proud proprietor beamed. "*Un saucisson pour Jeen?*"

"*Mais, oui.*"

Matthew passed a coin to Lacenaire, and presently Gin was wolfing down a very large sausage. Gin ate his way along another length of the boulevard, until the two stood before the Théâtre du Vaudeville, where the magician Robert-Houdin sometimes exhibited his skills.

Matthew found Robert-Houdin backstage, pulling bouquet after bouquet of brilliantly colored artificial flowers from the sleeves of his frock coat.

"*Bonjour, monsieur.*"

"*Voilà, est-ce vous, Matthieu?* Just in time. I was about to practice *The Aerial Suspension.*"

"I haven't time to float in midair today, *monsieur.* I'm on an errand for my master."

The magician focused on Matthew, another bouquet suspended halfway out his cuff. "So. His book is complete at last and he returns to the world?"

Matthew nodded. "*Dr. ABC's ABCs of Phrenology: From the Skull Out.* It goes to press tomorrow, and soon we'll be off to faraway places again."

"*Quel dommage.* You showed promise, young man."

"*Merci, monsieur.* It's been an honor to learn from you. You'll have your own theater soon, I'm sure. People will be clamoring to buy tickets to see the great Robert-Houdin, just as they do now for Deburau the mime."

The magician raised an elegant eyebrow. "*Peut-être.* When I've perfected my *Fantastic Orange Tree*—"

"You will, *monsieur.*"

Robert-Houdin nodded acceptance of the inevitable. "Give your master my regards. I look forward to reading his great work."

"I shall. *Adieu.*"

Regretfully, Matthew hauled Gin from the avenue of so many pleasures and temptations. They wandered through narrow, twisting streets, arriving finally before the bookshop where he'd spent his other free hours since he and Dr. Cornwall had returned on the flotilla bearing Napoleon's body in state. It was a fascinating hole-in-the-wall, crammed from floor to ceiling with the most exotic books in the strangest languages.

"*Librairie du Monde.*" Matthew read the sign aloud

with satisfaction. Even its name was evocative. "Come along, Gin. It's time to pay our respects to Monsieur Baltone."

The inside of the shop was as dark and cavelike as ever. Its elderly proprietor sat bent over one of his books, mumbling words aloud as his finger ran down a page. Matthew cleared his throat.

"*Qui est-ce?*" The gray head jerked up. "Matthieu. What can we share this afternoon?"

"Siwa, *monsieur?*"

"Ah, the desert. The Sahara."

"So there aren't any maps. Or any books, for that matter." Asa B. Cornwall was testy. "That means we begin with a *tabula rasa*. That's Latin for 'empty slate'—"

"I know, sir. I've been studying Latin in your absence."

"My absence?" Cornwall tugged at his rumpled velvet jacket. "Where've I been, I'd like to know? Right here! Under your nose since January!"

Oatmeal, Matthew said to himself. Time to get Dr. Cornwall back on a diet of oatmeal. Months of rich French sauces weren't helping matters any. Aloud, he continued, "But it seems I should have been studying Arabic the whole time instead. That's what Monsieur Baltone recommended. Even found a primer for me—"

"What about Berber?" snapped Cornwall. "Or the other dialects of the Bedouins? Did he find you primers for them, too?"

"It didn't come up—"

"Of course not. And a dictionary of the Saharan tribal languages probably doesn't exist anyway. That's how much your fine Mr. Baltone knows about Northern Africa!"

"He did have a few things to say about the recent French occupation of Algeria—"

"Bah. We're not going to Algeria. And the rest of the upper African continent is blank. Blank, I tell you! We'll have to begin in Cairo, and our French should be useful enough there. Ah, Alexander the Great!" He patted at his wisps of hair and calmed himself with thoughts of the challenge before them.

"After Napoleon, Alexander was the other supreme military genius of recorded history. He should be worth a complete volume in my phrenological works all by himself!" Cornwall chuckled, then became serious. "We need to pick up his trail where Alexander himself began, in a manner of speaking. On the sands of the great desert of Egypt—"

"But surely he's not buried in the desert, sir," Matthew interrupted.

"Of course not! Siwa is an oasis, hidden deep in the dust of time. It's the site of the oracle of the Temple of Amun, where Alexander went in 331 B.C. to confirm his divinity before setting forth on his conquests. It will inspire us, too!"

"Wouldn't it be easier just to head for the place where he died?"

"Babylon? But he's not buried there, either. We're off on a quest of *understanding*, lad. When we finally meet his skull—presumably in Alexandria, where a great mausoleum was erected in his honor—"

"So it's as straightforward as that?" Matthew asked. "We could just take a boat to Egypt, walk up to his mausoleum, and—"

"Of course it's not as straightforward as that," barked the doctor. "Nothing's that easy!" Cornwall wandered to the nearest window to stare out into the Parisian night. "Alexander's mausoleum disappeared centuries ago. It's going to require some creative research to relocate it. But when we do"—Cornwall spun around to focus on Matthew—"when we do, I want to be able to read more than the bumps on his skull. I want the *subtleties*, too." Cornwall began pacing around their sitting room. "First thing in the morning, do some research on camels."

"Camels?" Matthew asked.

"Yes, camels. And begin buying up all the quinine to be found in the local apothecaries."

"Quinine?"

"Malaria, lad. Africa is vicious with it. As for me, the moment I've finished with my publisher, I'll head for the Louvre and its Egyptology collections. Must see what the papyrus scrolls have to say about possible antidotes for scorpion bites—"

"Scorpion bites!" Matthew gulped.

"Stop parroting me, boy. We're going where no American—or European, for that matter—has gone before. At least for the last few thousand years. I like to be prepared."

"Yes, sir." Matthew glanced down at Gin. "What about him, Doctor? Can he come with us?"

"Never heard of a dog getting malaria, have you?"

Matthew grinned. "No sir, I haven't."

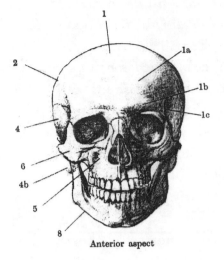

Anterior aspect

CHAPTER TWO

"WE'RE LEAVING HENRY BEDLOW?"

Matthew had begun packing, but found himself distracted by the row of skulls marching across their sitting room's mantelpiece: Henry Bedlow, Aaron Burr, Nicholas Mordecai, Jean-Jacques Rousseau. It was a rogues' gallery of his recent past, more chilling than all the museums of waxworks on the boulevard du Crime.

"We've got to travel light this time, lad."

"But Henry Bedlow? He's always been our

touchstone, always given us our motivation for greater things—"

"And so he still shall," allowed Cornwall. "But he'll do it from a continent's distance, in storage with the rest of our collection."

Matthew patted Henry's varnished cranium for old times' sake. He was rewarded with the usual gaping, ironic smile. "It doesn't seem right. . . . Does that mean you're also leaving your phreno-logical instruments behind?"

"Don't be absurd!" The doctor was currently stuffing a freshly printed copy of his *magnum opus* into his ratty old leather satchel. "I'd feel naked without them when we come head-to-head with Alexander. Pack the calipers and craniometer," he ordered, "but leave the phrenological bust and charts. Push comes to shove, the tools could prove useful beforetimes, too. And they don't take up much room."

"True," Matthew agreed. He opened an empty trunk and began carefully shrouding Bedlow for his interim entombment.

They departed Paris for the southern port of Toulon, carrying only the clothes on their backs, two personal satchels, and an emergency medical bag filled with quinine and other nostrums that

11

the doctor had decreed necessary for their well-being in unknown territories. They also carried—on their persons—the final gold coins from their war chest, along with a letter of credit to a financial establishment in Cairo.

Through the coach window Matthew cast a last long glance at Paris disappearing behind them. Then he laid a hand atop Gin's head for his own reassurance. "What happens if we run out of money, sir? Bribing all those French bureaucrats for passage to St. Helena took a heavy toll on our resources."

"Eh?" Cornwall's head popped up from his *magnum opus*, which he was rereading for the umpteenth time. Its hand-cut pages were already beginning to show wear. "Money? One of my new rules, Matthew, is never to worry about money. We have sufficient for the needs of our current expedition."

"After that?" Matthew pressed. "What then?"

"Providence will provide, lad. Always has." Dr. ABC returned his nose to his book, mumbling, "Quite a cogent point I make here regarding Napoleon's sanguine physiology. . . ."

The worries were left to Matthew, as usual.

Matthew's anxieties evaporated long before they

reached Toulon. Worse came to worst, he decided, he could always keep the doctor and Gin fed with his recently acquired juggling skills. There were other uses for these skills, too, he soon learned. A few hours out of port he stood in the bow of the ship inspecting the Mediterranean Sea spread out before him as he absently kept three oranges suspended in the air.

"How wonderful!"

Matthew automatically caught the falling spheres as he spun. It was a girl. No, a young lady. A very pretty young lady. He gave a bow worthy of the countess of the boulevard du Crime. *"Mademoiselle—"*

"Please don't stop. It's the nicest thing I've seen all day."

"Not the sea?" The oranges sprang to life again. The sea was as deeply blue as the young lady's eyes, Matthew noted.

Those eyes veered from the view. "After making this voyage so many times, the sea no longer impresses me."

"Why would you make such a long voyage so many times?" Matthew feigned a slight indifference as his hands continued their gravity-defying work.

It all came out, then. Her father was Egyptian, her mother French. Her family shared each year between two homelands, but she felt secure in neither. What also came out was her name.

"Nathalie."

Matthew pocketed the oranges to run fingers through his windswept hair. It was as black and curly as hers. "Matthew. Matthew Morrissey. Perhaps we can be some company to each other on this particular voyage."

"Nathalie!"

A hunted look entered her eyes. "It's Papa. I must go."

As she disappeared, Matthew thoughtfully set his oranges spinning again.

Matthew and Dr. Cornwall shared dinner in the salon that evening with Nathalie and her father. Her mother did not make an appearance then, or during the entire voyage. Abdullah Abed chose not to remark upon her absence. He was a modern Arab businessman, dark and sleek, clean-shaven and richly attired—from his tailored black tailcoat to his silk waistcoat with pearl buttons, right up to the gold-embroidered fez upon his head. He and the doctor began an animated conversation about Alexander's role in the history of Egypt that continued throughout the meal. But try as he might, Matthew could not accomplish the same with Abdullah Abed's daughter. She sat across from him, her eyes modestly focused on her plates and utensils through the entire course of the meal. It was not till afterward, when Matthew stood alone under moonlight and sails, that he discovered the reasons.

She materialized out of the shadows, all mystery. "Nathalie!"

"Papa may appear modern"—she clung to the railing, her grasp tense and tight—"but he prefers to treat Maman and me as his private possessions, keeping us cut off from the dangers of the world."

Matthew was too enchanted to pursue her complaint. It was enough that she was here beside him.

From that moment the two were inseparable during discrete periods of the journey. Their hours together were regulated by her father's quirks. He slept late; napped away most of the afternoon; retired early to work on business affairs. Matthew and Nathalie shared these secure interludes. He showed her the Arab primer he was struggling with, and she tutored him. She was a patient teacher, and he a quick student. The weeks of the voyage flew past.

Asa B. Cornwall's friendship with Abdullah

Abed proved fruitful as well. When their ship docked in Alexandria at last, it was Abed who smoothed their way; Abed who made room on his private *felucca* for the much shorter voyage up the Nile to Cairo. And it was Abed who opened his palatial home to Dr. Cornwall, Matthew, and Gin while preparations were made for their expedition to Siwa. Finally, it was Abdullah Abed who secured for them the services of a general factotum and guide into the desert. That is how they came to be under the protection of Hussein.

"Lie down, son of an asp!"

Hussein solidly thwacked the rear end of a camel. Its head and long neck lunged for Hussein's body; but its teeth caught nothing but the hem of the man's robe. Groaning with frustration, the camel collapsed joint by joint onto the dirt of the stable courtyard.

"You." Hussein pointed at Matthew. "Approach and mount. But be vigilant. Ali is a scoundrel. He cares for nothing but the taste of human flesh."

That was not a ringing recommendation. Matthew edged up to the beast warily and lifted a leg to straddle the rug-covered wooden saddle atop Ali's hump.

16

"Stop!"

He jumped back. "What did I do wrong, sir?"

"I am not some fine infidel, *sir*," growled the wiry bantam cock of a man. He was shorter than Matthew, but when he puffed out his chest, he overcame the difference. "I am *Hussein*, follower of Allah, master of camels and men!"

"Absolutely, sir. I mean, Hussein—"

"You must remove your shoes and stockings. A proper Arab guides the camel with his toes."

"Barefoot?"

"You wish to go into the Western Desert? You wish to survive more than a few days in this desert?"

"Yes," breathed Matthew.

"Then you will learn our ways." Hussein waved toward a pile of robes lying nearby. "You will dress as an Arab, wearing the *gallibiya* on your body, wrapping your head as I do. You will go barefoot. If not, the desert raiders will see you and your master as the Christian pigs you are. And then—"

"And then *what*?" Matthew whispered.

Hussein made a slitting gesture across his throat. "You will reach your Christian paradise sooner than you might wish."

Matthew sank onto the ground next to the camel and made short work of removing his

17

boots. "You might have the right idea after all, Ali," he murmured to the creature. "Certain human flesh cries out for biting."

The camel whickered understanding, and when Matthew climbed upon his back at last, Ali rose without protest. The two were companionably circling the courtyard when Dr. Cornwall appeared. He had come from the arcade that paraded through Abed's walled gardens, linking his fortress of a house to the stables beyond. Gin was at his heels and stopped cold, sniffing the alien smells, while Cornwall squinted through the sun.

"Coming along swimmingly, I see, lad."

"Positively, sir. Now it's your turn for lessons." Matthew chuckled with hidden glee. This should be sport worth watching, he thought.

"Remove my shoes? My good Hussein, these shoes have not been removed in daylight since the cobbler set them upon my feet! . . . Retire my coat for a nightgown? Surely you jest!"

To prove his lack of humor, this time Hussein flourished a dagger to illustrate his point about desert raiders. Then he turned conciliatory.

"For you, *effendi*, I have a pearl of a camel." He beckoned to a stable boy who led forth a second of the animals from the inner stalls. "She is called Fatima, and her nature is as gentle as the flow of her name."

By this time jacketless and hopping painfully from one bare foot to the other to avoid the blistering heat of the earth, Cornwall seemed less than convinced. Fatima lowered herself gracefully and the doctor heaved himself atop her hump. Then she rose.

"Whoa! Wait! Stop!" Asa B. Cornwall clung frantically with every piece of his anatomy till the camel had reached her full height and the doctor dangled six feet above the ground. "No! Matthew! Help!"

Across the courtyard Matthew roared with laughter. He bent to pat Ali's neck. "Are we still going to Siwa, sir? Or—"

His face livid, Cornwall made a supreme effort to master his situation. Legs and arms untangled themselves till he was perched lopsidedly atop his camel. He took a deep breath, then made the fatal error of loosing the death grip of one hand to swipe at his rapidly reddening pate. Fatima chose this moment to move.

"Matth-eeew!"

And Cornwall lay in a pile on the dirt.

"Doctor!" Matthew vaulted over Ali's head and rushed to his side. "Are you hurt? Is anything broken?"

Limb by limb, Cornwall gathered himself together. "Only my pride. Lend me an arm, lad."

Asa B. Cornwall remounted his camel.

Hussein stood back, observing everything. He spoke at last. "*Effendi* truly desires to broach the desert."

"*Effendi* truly does," Cornwall replied with dignity.

"Then it shall be done."

Matthew shook his head and turned back to his own camel. He found Ali resettled in the dust, nose to nose with Gin. He watched his dog fastidiously lick the camel's muzzle, and Ali's huge tongue flick out to return the favor. The heat of the midday sun fell more lightly upon Matthew's shoulders. East could meet West.

Matthew wandered in the gardens under a crescent moon, reveling in the cool night breeze. He paused by the fountain to plunge his fingers into the flowing water.

"Matthieu."

He became a statue, frozen in place. But his voice still worked. "I missed you these past days and hoped you would come. We leave before dawn."

"Papa has had me locked in my room since our return to Cairo. Since he discovered our friendship on the voyage. But I bribed my maid to let me out tonight."

At the satisfied smile in her voice, Matthew's limbs unfroze. He turned. "How could he do that to you, Nathalie?"

"You don't understand the ways of the East yet, Matthieu. In Paris, I am almost free. But here—" She stopped. "At least we are not forced to wear the veil, my mother and I. And Maman also saw to it that I was educated." Her words turned bitter. "Such a magnanimous gesture from my father, when he knows he'll never allow me the liberty of using my education. He almost treats me like one of his—"

"What?" Matthew asked. "Like one of his servants?"

"No. Much worse." Nathalie came close, very close. She reached up to Matthew's face. "This scar. Shaped like tonight's moon. Tell me about this scar. I've wanted to touch it since first we met."

Matthew froze again. "It—it's a very long story, from a time in my life I'd rather forget."

"But it is an honorable scar."

"Yes." He stood taller. "A very honorable scar."

"I knew this. You will be an honorable man . . . if you survive the desert. It is bad enough in winter, but in summer when few wise men go . . ."

Matthew reached for her hand and brought it down to touch his lips. A slight scuffling sound from the edge of the garden made her pull away.

"Be on guard every moment in the desert, Matthieu," she whispered. "There, nothing is as it seems."

Nathalie evaporated into her natural place, the shadows, leaving Matthew to finger the souvenir the body snatcher had left on his cheek.

· Chapter Three

MATTHEW GASPED.

The rays of the rising sun struck the dim shapes they'd been riding toward since leaving Cairo in predawn darkness. Gloriously erupting from the flat landscape were the Sphinx and the Great Pyramids of Egypt.

"Doctor! Look!"

"Yes, Matthew. One of the Seven Wonders of the ancient world. These Egyptians really knew how to go out in style!"

The camels had stopped of their own accord. Perhaps they were overwhelmed by the sight as well. Matthew was spellbound, thoughts of beauty, and tremendous age, and history singing in his head.

Cornwall managed to nudge his camel forward next to Matthew's. "It occurs to me, lad, that the mummies of the pharaohs—Cheops, Chephren, the whole lot—might make a very interesting phrenological study once we've dealt with Alexander."

The bubble burst. Matthew toed his camel's neck in frustration, and Ali strode forward. "Hussein!" he shouted ahead. "Where do we meet the rest of our party?"

"Just beyond the Pyramids, *nasrani*. They wait."

Nasrani, Matthew grumbled to himself. That's what Hussein had taken to calling him, and the term was another aggravation. Unlike *effendi*—the title of respect given an educated man—*nasrani* was Arabic for "despised stranger," and was used almost exclusively for Christians. Not that Hussein was aware of Matthew's knowledge. He'd been listening to bits of conversations, keeping his Arabic to himself, thinking it was one of those skills best saved for emergencies. He would swallow the insult, bide his time, and see.

Ali shook his head in protest, distracting Matthew from his grievances. "Sorry, Ali." He loosened his tight grip on the reins that threaded through the camel's nose ring. Ali continued to delicately pick his way through the sands around the Pyramids.

"A rough-looking bunch, I fear," Asa B. Cornwall commented. "Nothing compared to your body snatcher, of course, but still . . ."

The rest of their expedition spread out before them in a long, drunken line facing west and the waiting dunes. Matthew counted twelve men, heavy curved swords slung across their robed shoulders bandolier-style. The faces beneath their white turbans were swarthy, blackened by the sun between wisps of mustaches and beards. These were the camel drivers and guards that Hussein had deemed absolutely necessary for their undertaking to succeed.

"One does not enter the desert without protection, *effendi*," he'd declared during one of their planning sessions.

"But, confound it all," Cornwall complained, "first I'm told no one ever goes into the desert. *Ergo*, it is empty, devoid of human population. Next I'm told any foreigner who does go into the desert is signing his death warrant. It's not logical. If the desert climate is as terrible as the tales told, who in his right mind skulks about in it, waiting like a hungry lion for the odd Christian?"

"Not only Christians, *effendi*."

Hussein refused to say more. Over dinner that evening, Cornwall had broached his complaint to his host, Abdullah Abed.

"But my dear doctor," Abed explained, "there is emptiness, and *emptiness*. Caravan routes have stretched across the Sahara for millennia."

"Then why haven't Europeans heard of them?" Cornwall snapped.

"And why should Europeans—or Americans, for that matter—care about our simple trade routes for transporting salt? Salt is, after all, one of the most basic needs of man." As if to prove his point, Abed spread a pinch of salt over his fish. "None of us can survive without it. No need for you to concern yourself, doctor. Simple precautions are all that Hussein is suggesting. How do the British put it? An ounce of prevention—"

Now Matthew was studying their ounce of prevention. Besides the men there were additional camels: at least twenty riding camels for relief, and several dozen more pack animals, all tethered nose-to-tail and groaning under their loads. Matthew whistled. "All this for just the two of us?"

"What's that, lad?"

"Nothing, doctor. I think Hussein is calling for us."

He was. And soon the caravan was setting off into the Western Desert, the Pyramids and all of civilization disappearing under the scorching blue sky.

"Ooooh."

Cornwall groaned as Matthew helped him off the camel at the end of their first day. "I'll never walk again. I'm too stiff. And my toes! Look— they're blistered from the sun!"

"Here, sir." Matthew handed the doctor a pair of sandals.

"What's this?"

"Apparently sandals are allowed when not riding."

Cornwall glanced suspiciously at their retinue busily unloading camels for the night. "Hah. So they are wearing them. I thought maybe desert Arabs were just naturally born with cast-iron soles."

"Evidently not, sir. They do in fact seem to be human. But most of them also seem to be Bedouins, nomadic people accustomed to the rigors of the desert, rather than Arabs—"

Cornwall bent to struggle into his sandals. "I

haven't the strength for anthropological distinctions at the moment. What must we do next?"

"I think we wait for dinner, sir."

"Berr-uuuup. Ah. *Hamdullah."*

Massive burps exploded like gunfire from the circle of men surrounding the tiny fire. Matthew surreptitiously wiped his fingers, greasy from the lamb and couscous dinner, on his robe and turned to Cornwall beside him. "First no forks," he whispered. "Everyone just sticking their fingers into the pot. Now this—"

The doctor had enjoyed his meal, vying good-naturedly with the camel drivers for the most succulent morsels of meat. He eased back on his haunches and beamed. "Eructation seems to be one of the social graces around here, Matthew. When in Rome—" and he proceeded to produce a monumental belch.

"Effendi enjoyed his food!" murmured the men with approval. Then they stared at Matthew expectantly. It was Hussein who asked the question. "And *nasrani*?"

It had been a long time since Matthew had had flashes of his dead family, but now the memories returned with piercing clarity. The long dinner table in his New York home was strewn with the remains of a huge ham and potatoes, crisp green beans, and thickly sliced bread spread with fresh butter. Amidst the bounty was a much younger Matthew, elbows firmly planted on the table's polished boards, engaged in a spirited burping contest with his little brothers. Raucous laughter filled the air, until his mother systematically cuffed each and every one of her boys.

"Not in my kitchen, at my table, young sirs! I'll teach you all to be gentlemen yet, if I have to beat it into you!"

But the cuffs weren't very hard, and Matthew caught his father grinning into his mug of beer, and his sisters giggling—

Cornwall poked him out of his trance. "They're waiting for an answer, lad."

Matthew felt every eye upon him. His response would have significance. Something churned deep in his belly. He reached for it, coddled it, then brought it forth. The result was the most spectacular of belches, a veritable masterpiece. It took even his breath away as it shook the night sky.

"*Bismellah!*" It was a very awed "In the name of God," and the utterance came from many lips.

"*Hamdullah!*" The "Thanks be to God" was equally awed.

Matthew, victorious, glared across the fire

29

directly into the eyes of Hussein, daring the man to bait him again.

"It is good *nasrani* enjoyed the food," Hussein blandly replied. "It will be the only fresh meat till the first camel dies."

Hussein had bested him. Matthew's stomach cramped with chagrin at Hussein, with loss over his family. He clutched at it until tiny cups of very strong, very sweet tea were passed around. The complete blackness of the desert night overcame him, until not even cup after cup of the hot brew could keep the sudden chill of loneliness from his bones.

The groaning of many camels woke Matthew the next morning. Cornwall was still wrapped in blankets atop his mat, blissfully snoring, so Matthew climbed over the doctor's form to poke his head out the tent flap. A gust of frigid wind sent him back inside for his robe and turban. But even they did little to warm him when he reemerged. He stood hugging his clothing to his body in the half light, wondering how the desert's temperature—which surely had soared well over a hundred degrees only yesterday—could suddenly plummet below freezing with the dawn.

"Tea, *nasrani*?"

Amir, the potbellied expedition cook, handed him the usual thimble-sized cup. Matthew downed it in one gulp. "Thank you." He reached for the gourd being offered. Undoubtedly breakfast. It proved to be a thin millet gruel, bringing back memories of his early oatmeal days with Cornwall. He swallowed gratefully. His shivering slowed, and with the brighter light dawning, he suddenly realized why the camels were making such a god-awful racket. They were on their knees, being loaded for the day: bales of hay, skins of water, the folded tents of the workers. The creatures weren't happy about the situation, and they meant to let the world at large know.

Matthew wandered over to Ali, who was being saddled. Gin was at the camel's side, whining in sympathy. Gin, in fact, had rarely left Ali's side since making his acquaintance. The two animals seemed to share a friendship Matthew had not yet fathomed.

"Good morning, fellows." Matthew bent to ruffle Gin's fur, then pat Ali's nose. "Have you boys had your breakfast gruel?"

"Hussein!" yelled Cornwall around noon of their second day. "When are we stopping for a meal?"

"Tonight, *effendi*."

"Tonight! But I'm hungry now! And by all that's holy, I need to get off this blasted camel to stretch!"

"You may descend to walk at any time you wish, *effendi*."

Cornwall stared at his sunburned toes, then at the scalding sands around him. "But walking would be even hotter!"

"This is true, *effendi*. You show great judgment."

In line directly ahead of Cornwall, Matthew snickered.

"I heard that, Matthew Morrissey!"

"Heard what, sir?"

"Heard—oh, never mind." Cornwall yelled to their guide again. "But what *about* food?"

"Amir will pass some dried meat by and by."

"You mean to say *no one* stops for luncheon?"

"You observed how long it took to prepare the camels this morning, *effendi*?"

"Forever," Cornwall grumbled. "That's how long it took."

Hussein nodded. "Consider, then. The camels have now found their pace. They could walk thus through day, night, and into morning. If we stop them, we must unload them—"

"About two hours to unload, another two to

reload," Matthew contributed from his position between the men.

"*Nasrani* speaks truly. Therefore," Hussein threw back to the doctor, "you must decide. You are the master. For your comfort we will halt. But if you wish to arrive in Siwa during this life-time . . . I await your orders, *effendi*."

Cornwall mumbled to himself for long seconds. "Fine!" he burst out at last. "We'll continue." Then he added, so only Matthew could hear, "But if I ever take my calipers to that one's head, you can bet I'll find his Approbative Center as shallow as one of these *wadis* we're forever stumbling through. The man doesn't give a fig for what anyone thinks of him or his ideas."

Matthew chuckled. "Wouldn't that be the sign of a person totally comfortable with himself? He knows his strengths and weaknesses and accepts them. In short—"

"A wise man?" growled Asa B. Cornwall. "We'll see."

The days passed in a succession of sameness. Matthew rose before dawn to watch the men at prayers, the breaking of camp, and the loading of camels—a process that even with repetition never took less than the expected two hours. This was followed by a nonstop march till late afternoon, the camels managing about twenty miles each day.

The route they followed was never evident to the untrained eye. The first several days beyond the Pyramids were filled with low, shifting sand dunes and a constant hot, dry wind that erased their footsteps almost as soon as they were made. Next came the *reg*. This was a gravel-covered plain stretching beyond the horizon that Matthew embraced with relief. The emotion was short-lived. The rocky debris was brittle and sharp, making any movement upon it an agony. At their first campsite on the *reg*, Matthew noticed Gin limping.

"What's the matter, boy?" Matthew worked his hands down each of the dog's legs, then examined his paws. The pads of Gin's feet were cracked and bleeding. "Poor fellow! You've been trying to keep up with Ali, but forgot you weren't born a camel!" Gin hung his head in Matthew's hands and whimpered softly, admitting his predicament. As Matthew examined another paw, Amir wandered by.

"There is trouble, *nasrani*?"

"Look here, Amir. What am I to do?"

"Ah," the cook bent low for his inspection. "Allah be praised, the trouble is not great. A little of my lamb grease and some special shoes will cure your noble animal."

By nightfall, Gin was liberally anointed and comfortably padding about in specially stitched camelskin booties, apparently quite satisfied with the solution to his problem.

But other trouble arose, and this time not only Gin, but the entire caravan, was affected. After a week upon the never-ending *reg*, Matthew noticed that his water rations were being cut dramatically. Then one morning he woke to find no tea waiting. He'd grown unaccountably partial to the curious brew, and found it hard to imagine starting the day without it. He went to consult with Hussein.

"About the tea business, Hussein—"

"*What* tea?" snapped the usually calm guide.

"Exactly. Have we used up our tea provisions?"

Hussein pointed to a sack in the process of being loaded. "There is tea enough to see us to Timbuktu, *nasrani*."

"Then why—"

Hussein pointed to another bag, this time a *guerba*, the tarred goatskin water container. "Look upon that *guerba*. Look upon all the *guerbas*. Do your eyes not see?"

Matthew looked. The once plump water bag had turned flaccid, settling hollowly in upon itself. Almost as if it were . . . empty. He spun to check the others. The look was the same. How could he not have noticed? Panic hit him. "There's no water? How can that be? How can we survive in the desert without water?"

Hussein shrugged. "I follow the route of my fathers. I study the stars by night, the sun by day. The wells are not where they have always been. Or they are empty. This *reg*—sometimes it is more deceitful than the sands." Hussein hawked to spit, but nothing came from his dry throat.

"How long . . . how long," Matthew asked, "until there is no water at all?"

"Two days," Hussein answered. "The camels can walk another three beyond that. Then they will begin to drop."

Matthew didn't want to ask the next question, but he had to. "And for us? How long is there for us?"

"We will drop long before the camels, *nasrani*."

Chapter Four

MATTHEW SPIED SALVATION AT NOON. JUST BEYOND A low slope it spread out before the caravan like a dream in the midst of desolation: a wondrous lake! Surely no more than a few miles ahead, it filled the complete length of the horizon, and from his position atop Ali, Matthew could see the ripple of low waves being driven by the constant wind. He rubbed at his cracked and swollen lips and swallowed painfully. The half cup of tepid, tar-flavored water Amir allowed him at midmorning had barely cleared the grit from his throat. It hadn't come near to quenching his thirst. Now that thirst was raging again. But it didn't matter anymore. He could survive another hour or two of discomfort until they reached that marvelous, unbelievable lake. How he would wallow in it! No more of this polite sipping nonsense. He'd dive straight in, robes and all—

"Matthew! Hussein!"

Matthew twisted his body to grin at Cornwall's dawning excitement as he sleepily blinked his eyes wide on the extraordinary view. "Have a nice nap, sir?"

"What nap?" the doctor protested. "It's impossible to doze off on a camel. Especially with grit in every pore of one's body—worse than any medieval hairshirt!" Cornwall twitched evocatively. "But that's the least of my concerns at the moment. Do you see what I see? Is it possible?"

Matthew opened his mouth to shout a joyful *Yes*, but Hussein killed the word in his throat.

"No."

It was a very definitive no.

"What do you mean?" Cornwall bleated pitifully. "I can almost taste it. How could my eyes deceive me? It looks like water. Enough to float a ship in! What else could it be?"

"A trick," Hussein replied. "The heat, the light—"

"An optical illusion?" wailed the doctor. "How could that be?"

"The desert has many tricks. The mirage by day . . . the *jinn* by night."

Matthew studied the lovely lake that seemed to be growing closer with every step of his camel. Reality was a hard pill to swallow. "Are the *jinn* as heartbreaking as this mirage?" he asked.

"Worse," Hussein gruffly replied. "The mirage plays with your thirst. The spirits, the *jinn*, play with your very sanity."

Suddenly Matthew was not looking forward to the coolness of the night.

They dined that evening on dates, flies, and another half cup of water apiece. The flies were not part of the official menu, but they appeared the moment the caravan stopped, covering everything. Matthew began with a mad jig of slaps, then noticed the stoicism of the Bedouin men. They'd experienced such a plague before. He calmed himself to the point of merely brushing them off his hands and face and providing the same service for Gin. It hardly mattered, because the swarms returned instantly. They were implacable, unchasable. The flies bit, too, leaving nasty welts on every inch of exposed flesh. But with the setting of the sun, the flies disappeared. There was a glorious ten minutes of peace before the next menace descended upon the diners.

"Mosquitoes!" yelped Cornwall. "Where in heaven's name do they hide in this godforsaken wilderness?" He smacked vigorously, impotently, then turned to Matthew. "Do you suppose Alexander had to put up with all of this to gain his horns of divinity?"

"Subtleties," Matthew replied through clenched teeth. His teeth were clenched to keep from swallowing mosquitoes on top of flies. Consume enough of them and they'd be holding a war in his stomach. He waved away another cloud of the bloodsuckers. "You wanted the subtleties, sir. What formed Alexander the Great's mind . . . what gave him his drive." He paused to sift a breath of air through his teeth. "If Alexander could survive the flies and the mosquitoes, hordes of barbarian armies probably meant nothing to him."

Having said his piece, Matthew cautiously inserted another date into his mouth and began to chew. Before he could swallow, a harrowing scream filled the night air. He spat out the date. *"Jinn?"*

Hussein unfolded himself from his usual spot across the fire in one quick, fluid motion. "Not the *jinn*. A different scourge of this country Allah has forgotten."

The small group raced to the tent of the camel drivers as the scream slowly faded. Hussein parted the flap and thrust a burning stick he'd grabbed from the fire into its blackness. "It is Mustafa." He stepped inside, bent next to the prostrate body, and removed something from beneath the man's bare foot. He held it to the small flame. "Scorpion." Hussein spat and consigned the remains to the fire. "We will have one less camel driver by morning."

"A scorpion bite?" Cornwall, suddenly enthusiastic, pressed his way into the closeness of the tent to kneel before the writhing man. "Fetch the medical kit, Matthew. Immediately. Here's my golden opportunity to learn if the methods described in those papyrus scrolls at the Louvre really work!" He rubbed his hands. "I could give Pliny the Elder's poultice cure a try, too!" He turned to Hussein. "Give me your knife, man. Quickly."

Matthew lingered long enough to watch in fascination as Cornwall slit the swollen welt on Mustafa's foot, then bent his head to the wound and began sucking out the venom.

"Amazing, sir!" Matthew breathed. "Who'd think to treat it like a snakebite—"

Cornwall spat blood. "Don't stand there gaping, boy. The kit!"

Matthew ran.

By morning's light Mustafa was shivering as if with fever, but he was still alive. The rest of the men treated Cornwall differently. Their veiled condescension disappeared before a new respect. Through sheer curiosity, Asa B. Cornwall had become a healer, a real doctor at last.

No one in the caravan had any desire to remain in that pest-ridden campsite a moment longer than necessary. When the packing was complete, Mustafa was unceremoniously slung across the back of a camel, and the animals plunged forward in their tethered line with something akin to enthusiasm. Or maybe it was only desperation. Matthew sat astride Ali watching the camel's nostrils twitch in a new way. He glanced down at Gin.

"Do you suppose Ali is searching for water like the rest of us, Gin?"

The dog, who'd shared Matthew's miserable water ration that morning, looked up at his master and gave a dry bark. That worried Matthew even more. If Gin began to lose his strength, he'd have to be carried slung atop the saddle, like Mustafa, only with Matthew caring for him. It would be harder for Ali. Alternately, Matthew could switch to one of the fresher relief animals. But that was almost inconceivable. The same rapport just did not exist between himself and the other camels.

Matthew bent to stroke Ali's neck, shifting his weight on the hump beneath him. The motion stopped him. Was it possible Ali's hump had shrunken overnight? Its solid buoyancy was gone. He wiggled on the saddle to verify his observation. "Definitely less hump," he mumbled. The camel's reserves were being consumed, too. And there was nothing new on the horizon but more *reg*.

Matthew peered ahead hopelessly. Then he bolted upright. Could it be?

"Hussein!"

"Nasrani?" The guide's tone had a certain quality of despair about it.

"Off to the west, northwest. Something looks different."

"It is the end of the *reg*."

"But that's wonderful!"

"It is also the beginning of the Qattara." Hussein shrugged. "The finish to one hell, the start of another."

"But water," Matthew tried. "Will there be water in this Qattara?"

"There will be mountains. And rocks like you have never seen. Rocks made by *jinn*. And caves.

As for water—" Hussein shrugged again. "Rain has not come to the Qattara in living memory."

Matthew shivered through the blistering heat. "Must we go there?"

"Siwa is beyond."

The camels stumbled on. Matthew clung to Ali with all the strength left in him. He felt himself weakening fast as the hours passed. Occasionally he raised his eyes to peer into the distance. He'd learned to rub charcoal from the cooking fires on his cheekbones and below his lashes each morning; learned how to make his eyes into slits—all to cut the sun's merciless glare. He'd learned much about the desert. Most of all he'd learned that he was probably going to die in it.

He and Doctor Cornwall and Gin would die. Amir and Mustafa and the other men—even Hussein—would die as well. The sun and the wind would leach the final moisture from their bodies and they would become nothing but dry bones littering the Sahara. All because of Dr. ABC's wild-goose chase after Alexander the Great.

Matthew shut his eyes to the eternal glare and considered the hopeless situation. Did he blame the doctor? . . . Not really. What was life without a quest? His only regret was that he wouldn't live longer. Long enough for more quests. Quests that would find the answers to changing the world, because Cornwall truly believed that what they learned from his expeditions *could* change the world. Could make it a better place. He wasn't just a silly, plump, balding phrenologist. Beneath his uninspiring façade, Asa B. Cornwall was a man of vision and drive. Like Alexander the Great himself. It was just different worlds the two had been trying to conquer.

Matthew's affection for his master, his teacher, his friend—for the doctor who had so competently dealt with the scorpion crisis only last night—grew till his chest tightened with the emotion. He turned to say something kind. Something that would give Asa B. Cornwall heart before it was too late. To say the words he'd never had the chance to say to his dying family—

"Doctor!"

Cornwall was slumped over Fatima's neck, head lolling, arms splayed.

"Hussein!" Matthew choked out. "We've got to stop! We've got to help Dr. Cornwall!"

But Hussein wasn't listening. Matthew watched as the guide, suddenly alert, pulled a dagger from beneath his robes. With one efficient chop, the man sliced the rope connecting his camel to the train following. Then he kicked his mount and went loping off into the distance, toward the hard, jagged mountains of the Qattara, toward—

Matthew stiffened on his saddle. He squinted fiercely at the remote crags in the distance. There was something waiting in the foothills that seemed slightly out of place. Something just a little different from the usual mounds of rubble stone and scree. . . .

"A well!" All around him the hoarse shout rose from strained throats.

"Water!"

Belled harnesses jangled as every camel lifted its head. Ali picked up his pace, while behind Matthew, Cornwall managed a croak.

"Water? God bless us all. Did someone say *water*?"

"Yes, sir!" Matthew replied. Then he felt a curious sensation, as if his heart were dropping into his stomach. "Unless it's another false alarm. Another dry well."

But Ali apparently believed otherwise. He trotted off in pursuit of Hussein's mount, dragging the caravan behind him. In short order a roped bucket was being lowered into the questionable hole. Water came forth.

"Hamdullah." When his turn arrived, Matthew broke his enforced silence in Arabic. Then he sluiced another gourdful of water over his head and repeated the word. *"Hamdullah."* It was a good word. Absolutely the right one. God was God in any language, and Matthew was overjoyed to give praise where it was due. The murmurings around him repeated the thanks again and again. And then it was time to unload the camels and give them their share of the blessing.

The watering went on long into the night. Matthew took his turn at dropping the big leather bucket more than thirty feet through the mouth of the stone well into the depths of the desert floor. Then he laboriously hauled the rope hand over hand till the sloshing bucket could be spilled into a trough for the waiting animals. It was such an insignificant-looking thing, this well. Not much more than several yards in circumference, it could have been missed so easily. But Hussein had not missed it. Matthew pulled at the rope, thanking God once again.

Slowly his normal perspective returned. Long before the bucket reached the lip, the prayers in Matthew's mind were replaced with a new image: pulleys. How incredibly useful a block and tackle with two pulleys would be for hauling up the water. Pulleys sped through Matthew's mind until at last he tipped the water into the trough and handed the bucket to the next man. Then he stood, rubbing his strained muscles, wondering anew. This time it was over the quantity of water camels were capable of drinking. He watched one animal after another take its turn. Those still waiting filled the night sky with their groans of impatience. And when Ali's chance came at last, it almost seemed as if Matthew could see the camel's hump expanding and solidifying before his very eyes.

"Keep drinking, Ali. There's still a lot of desert ahead of us."

"Very true, *nasrani*." Hussein walked up to Ali and gave him an unexpectedly fond pat on his rump. Ali was too busy drinking to snap. "But tomorrow we rest. We will need to regain our strength for what lies ahead."

"The Qattara?" Matthew asked.

"The Qattara—and its *jinn*."

Matthew found it necessary to drink another quart of water to chase the new queasiness from his stomach.

Chapter Five

The Qattara was another world. Or maybe the moon. Matthew's thoughts ran as wild as the landscape. Maybe the entire caravan had been scooped up by *jinn* in the middle of the silent desert night and plunked down on the moon. But wouldn't it be cold? And would it have this never-ending wind? Matthew reached for his water gourd and splashed some liquid into his mouth. There was enough water now, to be sure. But it seemed to evaporate from his throat as soon as he swallowed.

He felt dry as paper, as if he could be crinkled into a ball. Crinkled and tossed aside into one of the canyons bisecting the narrow passage they'd been descending through sheer cliffs since they'd left the *reg*. When Hussein finally halted the caravan for their first night in the Qattara, Matthew wanted nothing more than to retreat to one of the shadowed caves whose mouths gaped on every side. He wanted to hide from the wind and the sun; to find a complete silence.

"Dr. Cornwall?"

Asa B. Cornwall was by now capable of dismounting under his own steam, and he was standing next to his camel, Fatima, alternately pouring water down his own throat, and sprinkling the camel's head.

"What are you doing, sir?"

"Anointing Fatima, lad. She's an amazing creature, I've come to believe." He bent to pat her nose and the camel licked his hand. Cornwall beamed. "I've been seriously contemplating unpacking my craniometer and doing a few measurements of her skull. Figure out how she endures so well. But I thought I'd wash some of the dust of the road off her first—"

"Sir." Matthew gently pulled Cornwall away from the camel. "I think maybe you've had a little too much sun today. Let me get you comfortable in the shade. You can rest while I do some exploring."

"Explore? In this maze? By yourself?"

"You want to come with me?"

"After the whole day? The entire past several weeks? Surely you jest, lad!"

After Matthew had carefully checked crevices for hidden scorpions, Cornwall allowed himself to be settled within a rocky overhang. Soon he was nodding off. Matthew stood protectively over the man for a long moment. Then he shook his head and strode toward the nearest gap in the cliffs surrounding them.

The first and most accessible cave was a disappointment. Its interior had been hollowed out only a few feet. Matthew pulled away from the opening and stood back to assess the wall of rock towering over him. If he were to scale it just a dozen yards or so there might be other openings, more interesting caves above. Just interesting enough to take his mind off the doctor's upsetting behavior, to find some solitude from his other caravan companions. If nothing else, to capture the view from above. He made a try for it, but shortly discovered that sandals were not designed with rock climbing in mind. He removed them to make the attempt barefoot.

"Yipes!"

Matthew dropped the six feet back to earth. The wall of rock was still lit—and heated—by the afternoon sun. Digging in for toeholds with his bare feet was akin to walking across burning coals. He turned to find Amir the cook watching him.

"What is this you do, *nasrani*?"

"I mean to climb this rock, Amir."

"Why?"

"To see what's on the other side."

Amir shook his head. "Only more of the same, *nasrani*. Except that the other side belongs to the *jinn*. You will displease them."

"Nonsense." Matthew was already rooting through his pannier, recently unloaded from Ali. "There!" He smiled with satisfaction. "My boots. They'll do the trick."

"Trick?" Amir stepped back. "You mean to play tricks on the *jinn*?"

"I mean to play tricks on no one, Amir. And this *jinn* business is only a silly superstition. I just need a little exercise. I've been doing nothing but riding for days!"

Amir retreated another pace, holding a protective hand before his face. *"Yak, balak!"*

Forgetting himself, Matthew responded, "No

evil will come to me, Amir. But thanks for the thought all the same." His boots firmly knotted, Matthew set off once more for his explorations.

The first twenty feet were easy. After that, Matthew had to concentrate hard for his holds. Sixty feet above the camp, he rested on a ledge and glanced down. It was a sheer fall to solid bedrock below, but the height didn't bother him. Instead it filled him with exuberance. The sort of exuberance he hadn't felt since the last time he juggled with the torches back on the boulevard du Crime. He balanced in his niche, remembering Étienne. How his acrobat friend would enjoy this climb! Remembering the countess. Then his mind soared from Paris over the Mediterranean to Nathalie. Was she still locked in her ivory tower in Cairo? Wouldn't it be lovely to have her beside him now, to show her the world spread out in all directions—

"*Nasrani!*"

Another bubble burst. This time it was Hussein doing the bursting.

"Descend at once! . . . I order this!"

Hussein's voice floated up with the wind like the wings of a hawk. Matthew made an instant decision to ignore the summons. He continued his climb. Another thirty feet, and he attained the rough outcropping of the cliff's summit. He lunged over the top, paused to give a wave to the camp below, then turned to find yet another world.

It was no longer the moon. Perhaps this was another planet. The valley opening before him was peopled with giants! Matthew whistled long and low.

"Not giants," he murmured, "but near enough to."

Hundreds of pillars of rock writhed and twisted toward and away from each other in an ungainly dance that continued far into the distance. The sun colored them with reds and pinks—even greens and blues. It was the most color Matthew had yet seen in the desert. He covered the few yards to the far edge of his narrow peak to get a better view, then found a steplike path down, cleft by nature into the very cliff side itself. He descended a few feet, eyes still focused on the pillars, when the sun's rays shifted slightly, illuminating and drawing his attention to the wall beside him. Knees buckling, Matthew sat.

"I don't believe this!"

Etched into the wall beside him were animals. He stretched a finger to touch the designs. "Giraffes," he whispered. Huge giraffes towered over him, nearly half their true size. "Elephants and deer." He followed the trunk of an elephant down to the next step. . . . "An odd sort of bird." It had a very long, ungainly neck perched atop a fat, feathered body and stood balanced on spindly legs. . . . "And people!" Not people as in a proper painting. More like scarecrow people, drawn like sticks. Lots of them. They were chasing after a horned rhinoceros with spears in their hands.

Matthew traveled halfway down the far side of his cliff until the etchings and the sun gave out at the same time. He glanced up and saw the darkness coming. It would arrive soon and with an awful suddenness. He scrambled back up the steps.

"There were pictures of people, I tell you!" Matthew was trying to explain his experience to the dubious men during dinner. "And that bird—"

"An ostrich, from your description, Matthew," Dr. Cornwall offered. His mind was sharp again after his nap. "The Boers have described them in South Africa. Huge, awkward, nonflying birds almost eight feet tall, by all accounts. But there couldn't have been giraffes and elephants—not to mention these other creatures—anywhere near the Sahara for more than ten thousand years!"

Matthew looked up from the flickering flames of the campfire. "What does it all mean, sir?"

"It means the Sahara wasn't always dry, lad. People once lived here—"

"It means only more work of the *jinn*," growled Hussein, still in a snit over Matthew's disobedience. As if to prove his point, wild laughter abruptly echoed down the canyons of rock through the darkness surrounding them. Evil laughter. Hussein nodded almost approvingly.

"Hyenas," Cornwall proclaimed. "Leo Africanus mentioned them in his sixteenth-century history of the Sahara. Called them abject and silly creatures."

The wicked sound repeated itself. Instead of remaining companionably about the fire telling stories, as they'd taken to doing after the evening meal, one by one the men slunk off to their tents, swords hefted in protection.

"Hyenas?" Matthew asked. "But we've seen no animals at all this far—"

"Nocturnal creatures," Cornwall amplified. "They live on carrion."

"What carrion?"

"Maybe us," Hussein muttered as he joined his men.

"I do appreciate Hussein's consistency,"

Cornwall chuckled. "The man's a pessimist through and through." He tossed a forgotten twig on the fire and settled back to enjoy the night.

Matthew looked upon the hard rock of the Qattara with new eyes the next morning. He'd slept well the night before—slept well despite the constant hysterical laughter of the hyena and the howls of something else that Cornwall had also named before they'd left the embers of the fire for their tent: the Saharan cheetah. There was something marvelous about giving a name to the unknown. With the naming, the terrors disappeared. Every Arab and Bedouin in their party had staggered from his tent bleary-eyed and wan from the same night's entertainment. But for Matthew, the *jinn* had ceased to exist. What he wanted now was to find more of the incredible messages left by a forgotten people.

Matthew spent the next several days of the journey atop Ali staring hard at every foot of smooth-walled rock they passed. He stared so hard he became dizzy from the effort. But there weren't pictures in plain sight for anyone passing to see.

He developed a theory that perhaps these images
had been hidden by their makers on purpose—for
what purpose he wasn't sure. But as soon as the
day's halt was called he went exploring again, poking into nooks and crannies, clambering over
boulders, and climbing megaliths and cliffs.
When Hussein and the other men saw him setting
off, they made the automatic sign against evil, but
they gave up their attempts to stop him.

It was during the afternoon of his third day of
searching that Matthew made his next discovery.
It was also by chance. In fact, it was made through
clumsiness. He'd forced his way through the tight
space between a group of monolithic stone towers, staggered into an unexpected opening
beyond, and landed flat on his face. Nose to the
gravel and dirt, he sighed, when something
caught his attention at ground level.

"What in the world . . ."

Matthew inched closer, propped himself on
an elbow, and examined the pile of debris
before him: fractured bones; bits of charcoal;
something else, too. He delicately extricated a
fragment of shaped stone from the rubble, then
sat up to examine it more closely. It was flint.
An arrowhead! He dove back into the pile and
soon had several more shaped stones before
him. He fingered the carefully hewn edges,

feeling the sharpness. Images of people crafting these tools swam before him. He could almost see them sitting around this very hearth, chipping usefulness into the stone. Then they would be ready for the hunt. Off they'd go to lie in wait for a herd of grazing deer, or one of those ostriches.

This closed circle of stone he'd stumbled into was the campsite of ancient people. There was no question in Matthew's mind. What else had they left behind? His eyes traveled up the smooth insides of the monoliths. Here were his pictures again. But this time they were different. Rather than being lightly etched into the rock, these images had been carved. Animals and people stood out boldly in a long bas-relief of action that completely surrounded him. And there were new animals. Hippopotami. Crocodiles. Creatures of the water in the midst of the Sahara! Dr. Cornwall must see these things.

Matthew scooped up the arrowheads and tucked them in a pocket beneath his robes. He'd run back to camp and rouse Cornwall from his afternoon nap. He'd make him come and see the site. He'd personally shove and squeeze the doctor through the tight opening. Maybe Cornwall had some drawing materials in his bag. Even just a few scraps of paper. These pictures needed to be copied. Needed to be shown to the world. They were so much more interesting than any dry old skull. Even the skull of Alexander the Great! The people carved in this rock seemed almost alive. They were different from his earlier discovery in other ways, too. These people had fuller bodies and were wearing clothes. At least, loincloths. And some kind of headdresses. . . . Matthew squinted at the line of reliefs. No, they were masks. *Cat masks.*

The discovery was entrancing. How different everything was in the desert now, yet some things were the same. Those masks could represent a cheetah, like the one heard on the prowl the last few nights. He sat back on his haunches, unable to tear himself away from the mysterious images. Why were these people wearing the masks? In honor of the huge cat? To try and capture some of the magnificent creature's strength for their own hunt? Or could there be other reasons? Reasons he would never understand?

The hairs on the back of Matthew's neck rose suddenly. Then the hairs on his arms. The very air had changed within the circle. It was charged with some kind of life, some kind of power. He froze, willing complete stillness to his body. Someone— or something—had entered the ancient space he shared with the carvings and the bones.

An eternity passed with eyes drilling into his back. Was it some ghost he'd called up by entering this long forgotten sacred place? Was it the *jinn* he'd so casually dismissed? Matthew could stand the sensation no longer. With infinite caution, he turned. And bit back his own gasp. Perhaps he'd unwittingly beckoned them all. And here they were, in the form of—

A *cheetah*!

The cat was enormous. Bigger than a leopard. Almost as big as a lion. It was terrible and beautiful. And it crouched on its haunches, inspecting him.

"Your howl is mighty, my friend," Matthew murmured. "Remind me to be frightened the next time I hear it echoing through the night."

The cat blinked. Its fur was a tawny golden color, short and sleek.

"Awed, if you prefer," Matthew added. How had the cat found its way inside the circle? There was only one opening, and that hardly large enough. Yet there it waited, all coiled energy, a wall of sheer black stone behind it, only himself before it—

The cheetah bared its fangs.

"Definitely awed," he whispered.

It sprang.

There was no time, no way to escape. Matthew

shut his eyes and prayed. He waited for the collision of bodies. For the gashing of claws and the gnashing of fangs. For the pain and oblivion. And waited.

He opened his eyes.

He was alone.

"Hamdullah." His breath returned. "Oh, yes. *Hamdullah."*

Matthew shakily rose to his feet. Had it been a dream? He waited for his heartbeat to slow, for the tremors running through his body to stop. Then he studied the dust near his boots. No. Not a dream. There were the tracks. That's where the beast had crouched. Here was where he'd sprung. Then nothing. Nothing at all.

Matthew shook his head in a clearing motion. He nodded to the masked hunters surrounding him.

"You win."

He carefully retrieved the arrowheads from his pocket and laid them out in a row before the pictures. He bowed.

"I give you peace for another ten thousand years."

Matthew left the secret circle.

"Any new finds this afternoon?" Dr. Cornwall inquired during dinner.

"Nothing worth mentioning," Matthew answered.

"A pity. Hussein tells me we leave the Qattara tomorrow. I was rather hoping to see some of your pictures."

"Maybe in another part of the desert, sir."

"We reach Siwa soon," Hussein announced from across the fire. "There are only a few days of the Great Sand Sea to journey through." He smiled with satisfaction. "And we will arrive." He spat out a date pit. "I think maybe we travel home a different way. Straight north, then along the coast. That way has no *jinn*—only pirates."

"Pirates!" exclaimed Cornwall. "You prefer real pirates to some fantasy of danger?"

"Yes," said Hussein.

"Hussein might have a point, sir," Matthew offered. "Hussein knows best. Has the tea finished brewing yet, Amir?"

Chapter Six

THE CARAVAN WAS BACK IN THE LAND OF THE *erg*, THE shifting sand dunes. But these dunes had little relationship to the lower mounds they'd crossed beyond the Pyramids of Giza. Hussein had called this the Great Sand Sea, and now Matthew knew why. These dunes were enormous. They were mountains of sand that billowed on and on like the waves of an ocean, seemingly forever. Half a day out of the Qattara, and Cornwall's expedition was wandering between the troughs and

64

heights of these incredible shimmering mountains, enveloped within the alien beauty.

"Hussein," Matthew called. "How can you
possibly find your way through this?"

Their guide was unperturbed. In fact, he
seemed rejuvenated since leaving the Qattara and
its hidden threat of *jinn*. He twisted around on his
saddle to actually offer Matthew a smile, exposing
tea-stained teeth. "The sand has colors, *nasrani*. It
has textures. You learn to tell the good from the
bad."

"How?"

Hussein shrugged. "The most famous guide of
days gone by was completely blind. He would
navigate by holding the sand in his hand, feeling
its coarseness, sniffing its aroma—then point the
way. . . . It is something born to a desert man. In
his bones. You would not understand."

Matthew wanted to understand, but Hussein
declined to elaborate, returning instead to his
solitary cocoon. So Matthew watched the directions their guide took. He learned to distinguish
between the lighter and darker shades of tan, and
slowly began to perceive a pattern between the
harder sands and the softer, more dangerous
areas. There was a pattern to the dunes themselves,
too. There were gently sloping ridges with smooth,
rounded summits that looked like nothing so

much as beached whales. There were cascading, pyramid-shaped sand hills. And there were the crested dunes the men called *seif*, the Arabic word for sword. They all ran in long fields precisely north to south, perpendicular to the caravan's route.

As the afternoon wore on, they approached a particularly enormous *seif*. Matthew studied its crescent shape, then absently rubbed at the scar on his cheek. He hadn't thought of the scar for months. Not since Nathalie's touch in her perfumed midnight garden. Had it been months, or only weeks? . . . Or had it been years? His entire sense of time had been skewed by this strange land. So had his sense of reality.

What incredible things he and Dr. Cornwall and Gin had survived in this chartless desert since that night under the crescent moon. He'd learned new kinds of endurance, new kinds of fear. Experiencing the desert could make even the tribulations of the body snatcher's vengeful pursuit seem insignificant. What was one man compared to a phenomenon like this?

Only a few more days and they would arrive safely in the oasis of Siwa at last. They would achieve the first part of their strange quest for Alexander the Great that had begun in Paris—or maybe on the jagged cliffs of St. Helena lifetimes ago. Only a few more days of stifling heat that seared one's very lungs with each breath taken. Only a few more days of putrid water and sand-dried dates and tea, and Ali's queasy gait as the camel climbed each succeeding dune—

"Ula-la-la-la-la-la-la-la-la-la-la-la—"

Matthew jerked away from his thoughts at the ululating wail. It was a sound like nothing he'd ever heard. Neither had he seen what he was seeing now. Before his eyes was a sight to freeze the very marrow in one's bones: swarming over the rim of the dune ahead were hordes of men—*blue* men! Huge blue men completely swathed from head to toe in indigo-blue robes. They sat high upon their camels and were ferocious to behold. The swords glinting in the sun were like extensions of their bodies. And those swords were closing in on Hussein and himself. On the entire caravan. The ululating cry continued. Matthew strongly suspected that the intentions of these blue men were neither honorable nor pacific.

Battle raged around Matthew and Dr. Cornwall, the only two among their party who were unarmed. From atop Ali, the deceitful air and light of the desert played games with Matthew's perception. His ears were filled with Ali's nervous

groans, Gin's howls, and men's shrieks. His eyes
seemed to be seeing the action of the raiders in
slow motion. The assault of the blue men proceeded in a dream of scattered sand: the wild
onslaught; Hussein's guards tardily pulling curved
swords from their shoulders; blades being raised;
blades slicing down; red blood coloring golden
sands; men on their knees, alternately begging and
praying; swords rising again.

No mercy.

Then it was Matthew's turn, and Asa B.
Cornwall's.

Matthew was swept to the sand with one blow.
Blue hands ripped off his turban. Blue fingers
hauled him to his knees by his hair. A sword still
dripping redly hovered above him—

"Stop!"

The bloody dream changed to real time.
Matthew looked up. The voice belonged to the
largest of the veiled blue men—their leader, their
sheik.

"See his mark." The voice was harsh and gut-
tural, coming from deep within the seven-foot
frame. "It is the crescent moon of Mohammed
himself. Spare him."

Hamdullah. Matthew bent his head to the sand in
the gesture of prayer and thanks he'd watched
Hussein and Amir and Mustafa and the others

perform every morning and evening of their journey. Hussein and Amir and Mustafa. All gone now, forever. His throat tightened. He raised his head to search for Dr. Cornwall. Was it possible he was still alive? . . . Yes, but not for much longer. There, next to his camel, the doctor knelt under a sword ready to sever his quivering head.

"Stop!" Matthew roared the same Arabic word. "He is a sorcerer! A *Maghribi*! A healer, also. Dead, he will call disaster upon you. Alive, he will bring you much luck!" He stared boldly up into the eyes of the sheik. It was all of the veiled face that was visible. And those eyes were black and cold. Matthew held his breath as the eyes glinted, then watched the blue hand rise to signal a halt. The raider above Cornwall hesitated, then lowered his sword, leaving Cornwall to disintegrate into a puddle of jelly upon the sands.

"Prove this thing—"

Matthew's attention shot back to the leader.

"—and you will live to be a slave. You and the old man. If not, you will join your comrades."

Slave, or dead? The decision was easy. Matthew made a motion begging leave to rise. Permission was granted.

"Dr. Cornwall?" He stumbled on rubbery legs the few yards to his friend and knelt next to him.

"Sir. You've got to pull yourself together. Where have you packed your calipers and craniometer?"

"Calipers?" Cornwall mumbled. "Craniometer?"

Matthew grabbed his master by the shoulders and shook. Cornwall's body lolled like a rag doll. "Come on, Doctor. Don't let me down. Don't let either of us down. You're about to give the performance of your life. For your life."

"But Hussein . . . the guards . . ."

"Dead, sir. Every last one of them. Slaughtered trying to defend us. If you want your bones to join theirs—"

Cornwall snapped back to alertness. "No, no. That won't be necessary." He staggered upright and began dusting sand from his robes. "The instruments are packed in my satchel, inside Fatima's pannier."

Matthew turned to the leader. "He needs his magic tools. May I get them?"

"Later," the sheik pronounced. "When the labor is finished."

The sun set before Cornwall was given his opportunity to save his life. The blue men had decided to camp just beyond the crown of the *seif* that had hidden their dastardly ambush, leaving the scene of carnage behind them.

Matthew was ordered to do the final dirty work: to strip the bodies of his friends naked in search of any hidden valuables the blue men might desire. It was one of the saddest tasks he'd ever had to perform.

"Ibrahim," he murmured, turning over a body. "You were kinder than most to the camels. . . . Mustafa. Dr. Cornwall couldn't save your life a second time. . . . Amir." He stopped to swipe at his eyes. "Amir. You loved Gin. You were a friend to me. And you made fine tea."

Matthew worked his way through the scattered bodies, collecting their robes and pitifully few personal possessions, then doing his best to cover them with sand. He knew the protection would not last long. The desert winds would soon expose the bodies to the merciless sun of another day, of endless days to come. But the small gesture of respect gave him some comfort.

Then he came to the final body. This was the one he'd been studiously avoiding, trying to postpone the inevitable. It was inconceivable to him that Hussein could truly be dead. How could their proud, wise, feisty little guide be dead? Matthew turned the body over tenderly, reached to wipe the sand from the man's eyes a final time—

"I see you, *nasrani.*"

Matthew jumped back. "Hussein! You're

alive!" He retreated another foot. "Or is it *jinn* deceiving me?"

"So, you believe at last?" came the dry whisper.

"Oh, yes. I believe." Matthew crept closer. "But how could you be alive? The blood—"

"Is that of my camel." Hussein stirred himself to half rise on an elbow. It was a painful process. "But my head is not well. The hilt of a Tuareg sword struck me a mighty blow. I could fight no more." He fingered his swollen brow. "Then forgetfulness overwhelmed all until you came."

"Is that who these blue men are? Tuareg?"

Hussein nodded, wincing with the effort. "The most feared raiders of the desert. They live by pillage and trade in forbidden things. . . ." He closed his eyes a long moment. "Gold, ivory . . . but above all human beings. Slaves." Hussein fell back onto the sand.

"Hussein," Matthew begged. "Don't leave us now! Dr. Cornwall and I alone have been spared—but only for the moment."

"I am as good as dead anyway," mumbled Hussein. "The Tuareg will never take me with them. They want only the camels and their loads. Prisoners are too much trouble if they are not the black men desired by the slave trade—or the occasional healthy infidel."

"Here." Matthew reached for his water gourd.

He uncorked it and held it to Hussein's lips. "Drink while I plan. My master has his own life yet to save. I think it will be the evening's entertainment. . . . If he succeeds, we can beg a favor—"

"What favor can you ask of the blue men?"

Matthew gently set down Hussein's head. "Your life." He corked the gourd, leaving it beside the guide. Next he gathered his sack of booty. "Lie here and rest. I'll return for you before morning, Allah willing."

Hussein gave one of his old shrugs. *"Kismet."* He sighed. "I will receive my portion as fate wills."

"Fate has nothing to do with it," Matthew growled. "But Dr. Asa B. Cornwall does."

The night sky was filled with a million stars, but no moon. Matthew and Dr. Cornwall had been fed a bowl of camel's milk and a pasty lump of something totally indistinguishable. They ate the offerings without question or complaint. When the meal was completed, the leader of the blue men crossed his legs upon his pillow of office and addressed them.

"I, Sheik Ibn er-Rakik, am ready. Convince me that the old one deserves to live."

It was time to begin.

Matthew realized that, to succeed, Dr. Cornwall's

performance required three things: light, ritual, and a sense of mystery. Light was perhaps the most difficult of these requirements. He'd been puzzling over the solution since clearing the killing field. Now he spoke to the sheik.

"May I be allowed to complete preparations for the great magic?"

Ibn er-Rakik nodded magisterially. While his men settled at a suitable distance to watch, Matthew fetched his props. Wood was the great problem of the desert. There was none. He'd had to gather the slats of broken camel saddles, find Amir's supply of lamb grease, and cobble together torches. Now he approached the small fire of dry camel-thorn that Rakik sat beside and carefully lit and buried a torch to either side of the leader. He glanced back at the doctor, fidgeting with his equipment. "Are you ready, sir?"

"As ready as I'll ever be. Although I must say, I usually have better results with live heads when my subjects are women—"

"Rakik is veiled, Doctor. That will have to be inspiration enough."

Cornwall snorted. "About that bloody veil and headdress. How am I supposed to take my measurements with yards of cloth in the road?"

"Improvise, sir. You saw how attached these

Tuareg are to their cloth. They wouldn't remove it even for eating."

"Improvise! I've never improvised on science in my life! Phrenology is sacred to me, Matthew Morrissey—"

"So is your life, I hope. If you can't improvise, lie. Just make it dramatic. For both our sakes."

"What is being said?" barked Rakik.

"Nothing of import, O Great Sheik."

No more interruptions. They'd have to start the performance. Matthew thrust his remaining three unlit torches into the fire, praying he was skillful enough to handle the unmatched weights. As he began to juggle the flames, he made his introductions in Arabic.

"The all-mighty Asa B. Cornwall hides many things within his simple form. He is a sorcerer of power and strength in faraway lands. Tonight—as a sign of utmost respect—he reveals to you his secret name. It is a name that carries enormous potency."

Matthew paused in his commentary for a sign of interest from Rakik. He received it in one raised eyebrow. The torches spun higher into the sky, flaring up to the stars.

"The name—oh, cringe with fear, all you who hear this secret—the name is . . . *Dr. ABC!*"

A soft sigh rose from the men gathered in the shadows.

"The name signifies the beginning of the alphabet, the beginning of words, the beginning of all knowledge known to man . . ."

Matthew madly embroidered his introduction, suspecting that style was more important than the content itself. He'd listened to Hussein's men tell tales around their own night fires. Long yarns of Scheherazade and the thousand and one nights of endless stories that kept her alive. He'd have to develop some of that same ability if he and Dr. Cornwall were to survive this night.

His torches wheeled into the sky, floated back, were captured, and released again. *Resurrection.* He needed it now more than ever.

". . . And now Dr. ABC will share this knowledge with you. With you, alone, Ibn er-Rakik, because you are the mightiest of desert sheiks. You are the scourge of infidels, the pillager of both high and low. You are a god among men, because you bring unto man a gift only a god can bestow—the gift of death."

Matthew glanced through the flames to note how Rakik was taking his exorbitant flattery. Apparently well. The villain was nodding with pleasure behind his veil.

"But," Matthew continued, "as the giver of death, as the messenger who sends so many men to the Gardens of Paradise, you can also bestow another gift when you choose. Only if you choose." Matthew caught first one torch, then another. He blew them out. He snatched the third torch from the sky, brought it to his mouth, swallowed, then spewed the flame—the great flame the countess had loved enough to bestow gold upon its giver—toward Rakik.

The tongue of fire shot so close to Rakik, Matthew thought his veil might ignite. He held his breath. The flame hesitated a hairsbreadth from disaster before dissolving into the night. Rakik never flinched. Matthew gasped for air to refill his lungs. He finished his piece.

"Choose the gift of life, O Greatest of Sheiks. For sweet though the Gardens of Paradise be, there is also sweetness to be found in living under these stars." Matthew bowed.

"Dr. ABC will now approach to perform his greatest magic upon you. It is not the magic of illusions, which any fakir could perform. Oh, no . . . it is something much greater. It is the magic that will open your mind that you may truly know yourself."

"Masterly, lad," Cornwall whispered as he neared the sheik with his phrenological tools held high. "Didn't understand a word, but the presentation was masterly. If I don't survive the night, remember that I'm proud of you. As proud as any father for his only son."

Warmth spread through Matthew as he bowed again, this time in respect and love for Asa B. Cornwall. "Thank you, sir. I'll remember."

Now Dr. ABC stood poised before the sheik. Taking a lesson from Matthew's dramatics, he raised his craniometer and calipers to the stars in offering. Next he set aside the calipers to run the craniometer's glinting silver through the flames of each torch in turn. Finally he suspended the instrument over Ibn er-Rakik's turbaned head. "I ought to tighten the screws," he intoned, "till I squeeze the brains from your ugly skull, you sorry excuse for a human being, you caveman—"

Matthew took his cue. "Man of the caves," he chanted. "You who were birthed in the sacred confines of the Qattara, with *jinn* blessing your arrival. O, you ancient one of beetled brow and strength of ten. You who are the forebear of the mighty sheik Ibn er-Rakik, inspire Dr. ABC with his analysis. Give Dr. ABC the power to make Ibn er-Rakik understand the innermost thoughts that emanate from his broad and low skull, a skull worthy to be counted as brother to the fabled body snatcher himself—"

Cornwall lowered the craniometer and gently

screwed it to Rakik's headdress. He squinted
through the flickering light. "Base of the brain d
to e, f over f . . ." Through the hushed silence of
the desert night, Asa B. Cornwall charted Rakik's
lumpy turban.

CHAPTER SEVEN

"Wake up, Hussein!"

Hussein groaned and rolled onto his back. His eyes blinked open to the fading stars, then to Matthew. "*Nasrani* . . . by the beard of the Prophet! You have returned as you promised! With my life, or—"

Matthew grinned. "With your life. But—"

The guide struggled to a sitting position. "I fear this *but*. Explain."

Matthew's grin spread. "*But* you have been

80

consigned as personal slave to the great Dr. Cornwall."

Hussein hacked and spat. "So nothing changes after all."

Laughter bubbled up from Matthew's chest. "You may be right. Here—" He offered his arm. "Let me help you over the dune into the land of the living."

Hussein accepted the assistance, but only as far as the rim of the *seif*. There he shrugged away from Matthew and entered the Tuareg camp on his own two feet, as cocky as ever.

Sheik Ibn er-Rakik lounged on his embroidered pillow during breakfast. On a small, brightly colored rug next to him sat Gin, tethered securely by his side. Rakik carefully filled a bowl with camel's milk and offered it to the dog. Matthew, sitting cross-legged in the sand between Cornwall and Hussein, watched him lap it up.

"Traitor," he muttered.

Gin whimpered guiltily before returning to the milk. Rakik caressed the animal, then drained his own bowl. At last he set about explaining the new order of things.

"The sorcerer shall ride behind me at all times. His slave shall ride behind him. At night the sorcerer's tent will be raised next to my own. You—" He stabbed a finger toward Matthew. "You and the holy *Maghribi*'s slave will sleep outside his tent flap to protect him. And," he concluded, "his secret name shall not be spoken, upon pain of death." Rakik carefully selected several of those odd, pasty balls of food from the brass platter placed before him. He tossed one to Gin, who snapped it up, and pressed the other on the doctor.

"What's he saying?" Cornwall asked. "And what is this foul concoction? It's the third one he's made me eat."

"Ground locust meal," Hussein explained. "Moistened with soured camel's milk. A staple of the Tuareg diet. Very healthy."

"Bugs?" choked Cornwall. He blanched. "I'm eating *bugs*?"

"And you will continue eating them," Matthew broke in. "With a polite smile and even a *Hamdullah* thrown in for good measure . . . if you choose to remain the apple of Rakik's eye. He's saying you are to be his shadow. His *protected* shadow."

"After the analysis I made of him last night?"

"Remember that I interpreted that analysis, sir."

"True. I wish I could have understood even a little of what you were saying." Cornwall forced a nod at Rakik, whispered a plaintive *"Hamdullah,"* and bit into his locust treat. After a moment he regained control again. "But oddly enough, Matthew, even wrapped as it was, I could tell the man's head was not broad and low. It's actually quite aristocratic in shape. I suspect vastly enlarged organs of Acquisitiveness and Destructiveness beneath all that blue cloth, though."

"It's common sense, sir," Matthew said. "Phrenology does seem to be based on common sense. Not all brutality is mindless, as was the case with our body snatcher."

"How perspicacious of you, lad. I suppose I suspected, but never truly *believed* that evil could be rooted in intelligence gone bad. I must reread Milton's *Paradise Lost* at first opportunity—"

"Silence!" growled Rakik. "You—" He pointed at Matthew again. "I could order chains set upon your neck and ankles and force you to march, but we have camels enough and they need tending. You will work with my men until we meet the caravan from Timbuktu." He gave Matthew an assessing stare. "If I keep you healthy, you will bring more gold from its slave master."

This was not news—neither the fact of slavery, nor his possible price. It only verified Hussein's comments about the desirability of white slaves.

There wasn't much point in worrying about any
of it now. Survive one day at a time. Matthew rose
with dispatch and bowed. "I thank you for your
consideration, O Great Sheik." Turning, he ran
smack into a vast blue man who grabbed him
bodily and tossed him toward the nearest camel.
The honeymoon was over.

By the time they were en route for the day at last,
Matthew began to truly understand the new order
of things. He sat slumped in exhaustion on an
anonymous camel near the rear of the caravan.
Not only was the view not as fine as from the
front, but as the wind rose, he found himself
nearly overcome with dust and odors from the
progress of several hundred camels in front of
him. He stretched his aching muscles. He wasn't
used to hard labor, either. Loading camels was
the least of it. Much harder was urging recalcitrant animals to rise, then being kicked and
whipped by the Tuareg when he refused to use the
same violence on the poor beasts of burden.

Matthew groaned a groan worthy of a camel.
He knew now why they bit. With all his bruises
settling in, he was ready to bite his keepers, too.
These men enjoyed giving blows.

Was there any way to improve his situation?

Only in the little things, he was certain. He began by rewinding his turban cloth Tuareg style: ends wrapped around his nose and mouth, giving him some protection from the dust. If the cloth were blue instead of white, he'd look like one of the raiders himself. That done, he squinted ahead the long distance to the front of the line. Rakik was leading, followed by Cornwall, as ordered. Behind the doctor rode Hussein. Matthew grinned in spite of his discomfort. Not only was Hussein the slave to Cornwall, but he'd been made keeper of the noble dog Gin, too. That meant the dog was enthroned on the saddle in front of Hussein. Now Gin squirmed miserably atop Ali, wanting nothing more than to run freely by the side of his friend. Even Gin had been enslaved to Sheik Ibn er-Rakik.

Little improved by the end of the long, sizzling day. Dazed from the incredible glare of endless dunes, Matthew dismounted from his camel and walked forward just in time to watch Cornwall do the same. But the doctor achieved his solid footing in an entirely novel way. Fatima was already halfway to her knees and Cornwall preparing himself for his usual bumbling descent when the sheik ordered, "Wait!"

Unsure of what to do, Cornwall froze.

"The slave of the great sorcerer will assist him in dismounting," Rakik clarified.

Hussein glanced over in disbelief. He'd had his hands full dumping Gin from Ali's back, and now the camel—obviously blaming Hussein for the dog's long hours of unhappiness—made a mighty lunge with his neck, giving Hussein a great *thwack* before catching the man firmly by the thigh.

"Son of the devil himself!" Hussein slapped at the camel's mouth, trying to dislodge his large yellow teeth. "You will pay for this!"

Matthew arrived in time to stroke Ali's neck and whisper in his ear. "Enough of this, my friend. You're picking the wrong enemy. Set your sights on Rakik, instead."

As if he understood, Ali loosened his grip and swung his neck to eye the blue man, giving Hussein the chance to limp away. But the guide's ordeal was not over. Rakik, now dismounted himself, poked Hussein in the stomach with the hilt of his whip.

"Down, slave. Prostrate yourself so your master may dismount."

Cornwall finally caught the gist of the action, and protested loudly. "My good sheik, that won't be necessary, not necessary at all—"

"The mighty sorcerer," Matthew tried translating, "would prefer to dismount by himself."

His words were ignored. Rakik shoved a foot at Hussein's back, and the hapless man landed face first in the sand. Cornwall gave Matthew a beleaguered look, then attempted to use his human stepping-stone as gently as possible. Rakik nodded once and strode away.

Matthew gave Hussein a hand up. "Are you all right?"

Hussein spat sand and muttered darkly, but before Matthew could offer further support, another huge blue man bore down on him.

"You. Unload the camels."

Matthew sighed. Another two hours of work. Maybe three or four, taking into account the stolen camels whose keepers were all dead. The sigh cost him a sharp lash across the shoulders from the Tuareg's whip. Smarting, he trotted toward the baggage animals. He'd have to learn to move first and complain afterward.

The night brought little rest. Matthew and Hussein huddled outside the flaps of Cornwall's tent, trying to find warmth in their thin robes as the temperature dropped.

"Perhaps you should have left me behind that dune," Hussein said. "Left me to meet my fate."

Matthew shivered in concert with the guide.

"Nonsense," he said. But his heart wasn't completely in the protest. "Things have got to improve."

"They could also get worse," Hussein pointed out. Then he added, *"nasrani."*

Matthew glanced at the man. Hussein's *nasrani* was no longer spoken as an insult. In some indefinable way, the word now sounded like *friend.* In spite of himself, Matthew smiled into the cold night. Emboldened, he snatched at Cornwall's tent flap and drew it around his friend and himself. Together they listened to the doctor's snores until Hussein began adding his drone to the night music. Matthew's shivering slowed and soon his own eyes closed.

On the fifth day of their captivity something changed. Rakik's caravan had been plowing through the great dunes in a steady west-southwest direction, taking them farther and farther from the safety of Siwa, farther and farther into the endless sea of sand. About noon, Matthew woke from a heavy doze of exhaustion to glance over his camel's neck. He rubbed at his eyes, not believing what he saw. Then looked again.

An odd thing was happening to the sand. It seemed to be rising from the surface of the dunes.

In fact, the dunes themselves appeared to be ascending, almost levitating. He watched as the entire horizon ahead rose a yard, two yards, more . . . and with the rising, the usual crisp, clear blue heavens also changed. Before Matthew's eyes the sand formed itself into a red and brown cloud. As he stared, incapable of anything but wonder, the giant windblown cloud grew larger and larger . . . seemed about to obliterate the very sky—

"Storm!" yelled the rider ahead of him.

Matthew peered up the long line of the caravan. At its head, Rakik had his arm raised. He was calling a halt. In the middle of the day?

From that moment there was no more time for wonder. No time for explanations, either. Everything and everyone moved too quickly. The camels were hustled into a wide double circle. Even before unloading, they were hobbled. Men worked like dervishes to erect tents within this circle of shelter. Wind rose to near-hurricane force, sending sand cutting through every inch of exposed flesh, causing sand to bore through the very cloth of one's clothing. Matthew was forced to ignore the discomfort and the fear. The animals still needed attention. But there wasn't enough time to unload them all before the sandstorm was atop the caravan. As visibility was cut to a few inches, the blue men disappeared into their shelters. No one noticed or cared when Matthew and Hussein stumbled into Cornwall's tent for refuge.

Matthew leaned against the tent wall, fighting for breath. As the airborne sand settled to the floor, he began to make out the forms of Cornwall and Hussein through the haze. He tore off his turban and shook pounds of sand from the cloth.

"Water," he gasped. "Did anyone think to bring some water?"

Hussein forced himself up from the pillow-shaped object he'd collapsed against. "Here."

"A *guerba*," Matthew whispered. "Thank God you found one." He crawled over to the bag and bent under the spout.

"Wait!" Hussein's fingers covered the stopper. "We must have an understanding."

"What about?" Cornwall asked. He was on his knees, second in line for a go at the precious stuff.

"Do you hear that?" Hussein's voice rose over the vicious blasts tearing around the tent.

Matthew raised his head. "The wind?"

"The wind," Hussein agreed. "It will rage for three days. If we are lucky."

"If not?" Matthew asked.

"Then it will rage for five days. The *khamaseen*,

the sandstorm of the springtime, lasts five days. Always. Then—"

Cornwall cleared his throat. His words still came out as a croak. "Then what?"

"Then it stops. As quickly as it started. But this storm . . . it began as the *ajaij*, the storm that can come at any season on the desert, making the sands rise up from the dunes."

Matthew nodded. This is what he'd seen.

"But then it became something else," Hussein continued. "Something I have never seen in the summer." He had the full attention of his audience. He continued. "I cannot say how long this storm will last. Three days. Five days. A week or more. It was such a summer sandstorm that covered an entire caravan in the time of my grandfather—"

"And?" Matthew asked, spellbound.

"And nothing of the caravan was ever seen again."

Cornwall tried his voice once more. This time it was a squeak. "So we ration the water."

"Yes," Hussein verified. "We ration the food, also."

"You brought food, too?" Matthew asked. "When? How?"

"While you were tending the camels," Hussein answered.

"Please, don't let it be locusts!" Asa B. Cornwall prayed.

Hussein smiled at last and pointed to several sacks whose outlines were becoming clearer as the air continued to settle itself. "No. I took supplies only from our own pack animals. We should have dates, and olives, and dried camel meat."

"Thank heaven," Cornwall said. "But now, about that water—"

"Now, we may all share a taste of this water."

From beneath his robes Hussein pulled forth a cup. Matthew sat back and waited for his measure. If there'd been any doubt about it before, the situation—like the air—was now becoming clearer. Hussein had grasped for the upper hand and was once more in charge.

CHAPTER EIGHT

SPRAWLED IN A BED AND BLANKET OF SAND, Matthew idly raised an arm to watch the grains trickling from him like an hourglass. "If I kept my arm steady, we could tell the time," he said.

"What would be the point?" Cornwall groused. "It will end when it ends. It feels like months already."

Hussein shoved away from his section of the tent wall and shook his head, spraying more sand. "Two days. It has only been two days. There were two periods of complete darkness, and now is the morning of the third day."

Matthew dropped his arm and listened to the howling wind. It had been raging for so long that he'd almost begun to ignore it. "Gin is surely safe with Rakik, but how will the camels survive this storm, Hussein?" he wondered. "They've had no water or food, and some of the poor beasts are still loaded with packs."

"Those animals will have sand sores come the end of this." Hussein shrugged. "But sores can be cured. Remember that camels were built by Allah for the desert. In every way. They have nose flaps that close during sandstorms—their own kind of protection."

"Protection," Matthew thought aloud. "We ought to rouse ourselves enough to plan for our own protection come the end of this storm. We ought to be plotting an escape from Rakik and his band of blue giants. . . ."

Hussein shrugged a second time. "There is no point. We could leave the caravan at any time, but on foot . . ." He settled back into the sand. "On foot and without water, we would be pressing even Allah's mercy."

The silence within the tent resumed.

It was hard for any of them to goad themselves from the lethargy that had set in. The wind continued to howl, but they no longer heard the sand striking the tent. Matthew pushed himself upright. There must be huge drifts building outside, drifts bigger than from snow-storms in colder lands. He stared more carefully at the tent walls, then at the arch of the low ceiling. The tightly woven camel-hair threads let in little illumination. "You say it is morning now, Hussein?"

"You see me, do you not?" the guide listlessly replied.

"Barely. Why isn't there more light?"

Hussein pointed to the very center of the ceiling. "Because it comes only from there, *nasrani*."

Matthew studied the dim glow of the oval. Something finally registered in his sluggish brain. "We're being buried alive!" he yelped. "That's why we have so little energy. We're using up our air supply! We've got to dig a vent!"

"Don't fuss, lad," Cornwall mumbled. "It will all be over by and by."

"By and by we'll all be dead!" Matthew forced himself onto his knees. "What happened to your collection of daggers, Hussein? I've got to cut a hole, then—"

"You don't want to let in more sand, Matthew Morrissey," the doctor fretted. "You don't want to go into that storm, either. It's not fit for man nor beast out there."

"And the Tuareg have taken my weapons," Hussein finished.

"Then I'll have to dig through from the flap," Matthew declared. And he set to the task with as much energy as he could muster.

Sand dunes were unquestionably different from snowdrifts. Matthew yearned for the cold, clean, compact snow of a New York City winter. He longed for the chill purity of ice. What he struggled through instead was cascading, choking sand. It clung like molasses to every inch of his body, yet it was bone dry. Twice Hussein had to pull him by his legs back into the tent after he had been inundated by avalanches of sand. He crouched inside, hacking grains from his throat and lungs. But he didn't give up. On the third attempt, Matthew broke through.

"Hamdullah."

His thanks were short-lived. Above him a purple sun fought to cut through a mud-brown sky. Around him the sand still swirled in vicious eddies. The wind bowled him to his knees, and he grabbed for his turban cloth to wind around his nose and mouth. There was air, but it wasn't fit to breathe. He made a valiant attempt to search for the other tents, for the camels, but everything was masked by sand. Matthew stumbled backward, searching for his own tent. The few moments spent within the heart of the storm had so disoriented him that he nearly lost his way.

But yes, there it was. There was something else, too. Imbedded in the sand circling his tent were footprints. He bent and squinted through the cutting haze to inspect them. Not ordinary footprints, not his own. They were, instead, the tracks of a giant cat. Matthew blinked, and when he reopened his eyes the tracks had disappeared in a whirlwind. In a new frenzy, he attacked the piles of sand around the tent flap, realized he was making no headway in clearing an air vent, and finally managed to worm his way back inside the shelter.

"Well?" drawled Cornwall.

Matthew lay sprawled on the floor of sand, coughing. At last, words came out.

"Tell me more about the *jinn*, Hussein."

The guide raised an eyebrow in question, but when Matthew only lay there heaving for more breath, he finally spoke. "What is there you do not know already, *nasrani*? They favor ruins and cemeteries. They are shape-shifters, and travel in whirlwinds—"

"Are they always malevolent?" Matthew managed to wheeze out.

"The *ifrit*, the most powerful among the *jinn*, are known to take strong likes and dislikes. . . ."

"I thought as much."

Cornwall cleared his throat. "Superstitious nonsense. All of it. What's it got to do with this sandstorm? What's the verdict from your travels outside, lad?"

Matthew gave one more racking cough and sat up. "Outside? It's hopeless."

Hussein nodded, more than content to change the subject. "What will be will be."

Matthew was not at all happy with this Eastern brand of philosophy, but he had to admit to himself that for the moment he was stuck with both *jinn* and *kismet*.

Precisely five days after the storm began, it ended. The wind just stopped. It took a while before Matthew and his tentmates actually noticed the hush, the absence of sound. Then Matthew burrowed again. He popped his head from the dune like a groundhog, to inspect a reborn world. The sky was crisp, the air was clean. The sand was where it belonged. He pulled himself upright and shook. Around him blue men were emerging from their own buried tents, doing the same thing. In his euphoria Matthew felt a sudden oneness with his fellow survivors. They were human, too. Then one of the Tuareg spied him.

"You!" His whip—already in hand—lashed out at Matthew. "Tend the camels!"

The days that followed the sandstorm should have been a joyous reintroduction to life. Instead, they were just like the days that had come before. The blue men were still in charge. Matthew and Dr. Cornwall and Hussein were still enslaved to them. Gin was the only one who had changed.

Matthew wasn't sure what had happened during the five days his dog had spent sequestered in a tent with Rakik, but some decision had obviously been made within his canine brain. The new Gin adamantly refused to ride atop any camel. The new Gin planted his paws firmly in the sand and bared his teeth at the sheik. Rakik finally gave up and allowed the dog to pad freely next to Ali again. Now he often trotted to the rear of the caravan to keep Matthew company, too. Matthew had little time to give to Gin, but in a few stolen moments at the end of each day, they communed.

"So," Matthew wrestled with Gin as in the old days. "You've remembered who you really belong to after all."

Gin writhed with pleasure and managed to lick his master's face.

"I knew you'd return to your senses one of these days." Matthew hugged the beast. Then he whispered in his ear. "But don't ignore that villain Rakik completely. Keep on his best side just until I figure how to get us out of his grasp for good."

Gin yipped agreement and Matthew shoved his rump. "Back to the sheik, now. Fawn on him. We all have our roles to play."

Matthew pondered his own role very hard over the next week. Now more accustomed to the backbreaking work of loading the animals, he sat atop his camel flexing his muscles when the work was finished for the morning and the caravan en route at last. There were new muscles to flex, muscles he'd never known he had. And with the fresh ease of his body, his mind felt sharp again, too. He began plotting extravagant schemes for freeing himself and his friends from Rakik's clutch. Nothing came of them, of course, until the day their route crossed that of another caravan working its way from the south.

100

The first glimpse of the caravan filled Matthew with excitement. It was not only the excitement of new faces, but the hope of potential liberation from the Tuareg. Surely someone within this new company would be civilized enough to see and understand the plight of Matthew and Dr. Cornwall and Hussein. It was a very long line of camels, after all. It drifted across the entire southern half of the horizon: hundreds of camels, perhaps as many as a thousand. As the string crept closer, though, Matthew noticed something odd. To the far side of the camels was another line. This one was black against the sand, and appeared to be shuffling along on foot. Coming ever nearer to each other, a curious new sound was added to the animal noises, the chanting of the drivers, the harness bells of the camels. Matthew cocked an ear to try and distinguish the sound. It was a kind of clanking, a grinding of metal upon metal—almost like . . .

Chains!

His body stiffened as the day's halt was called. But before he dismounted, he peered more closely across the distance. The walkers were staggering closer to the meeting point. The column as long as the camels was made up of Africans:

black Africans completely naked save for the heavy iron collars encircling their necks, and the shackles binding their ankles. As the sight fully registered, the horror of a practice he'd only partially fathomed washed over him. Matthew's ideas about right and wrong—good and evil—exploded. Sheik Ibn er-Rakik's caravan had rendezvoused with a true slaver.

Nausea overcame Matthew as his camel knelt. He stumbled off the animal and bent double over his racking stomach. What did he know of slavery until this moment? *Nothing.* The heaving began again as a new thought struck him. This could be the caravan Rakik had been seeking. The caravan to whom Matthew would be sold for his price in gold. Too soon, he himself could be added to that chained line of lost souls. Was there no solution to this terrible predicament?

The sharp slash of a whip across his shoulders was almost welcome. It brought Matthew back to his senses and cleared his mind admirably. *Work now. Change the world later.*

The meeting place was a hollow between dunes that held one of the Great Sand Sea's hidden wells. The well itself would have remained an absolutely innocuous hole in the sand if not for what surrounded it. As Matthew led the first of many camels to be watered, he stopped cold. Even the camel's thirst for the water couldn't move him. The well itself had no walls built of stone, but it did have a halo—a broad rim decorating its perimeters. This was made of *bones*: tens of thousands of weathered bones that had grown into an undulating hill. As his camel lunged vainly for the water trough, Matthew picked out a few camel carcasses in the pile. But the rest were human. He had the experience to know. Countless human skulls and bones had been piling up in this place over how many years?

Matthew was prodded from behind. "Move, *nasrani*. The beasts are thirsty."

"Hussein?" He spun. "How long have the slavers been coming to this well?"

"Many years. For centuries."

"This business has been going on for centuries?"

Hussein made a sharp motion of caution. "Water the camels and see nothing. Say nothing. Only pray to Allah that your own bones are not added to that pile."

CHAPTER NINE

THE NEW CARAVAN HAD COME OUT OF TIMBUKTU, AND its leaders were not Tuareg, but Arabs. When his work was finished, Matthew skulked around in the twilight before nightfall, trying to learn more about the caravan's intentions, its destination—and his own future. Rakik was meeting with the Arab captain, whose name even the Tuareg spoke with a combination of respect and apprehension: Muzzafir. The two leaders had been in conference for some time, seated on cushions within Rakik's tent, its flaps propped open to catch the evening breeze. Matthew wished he could be a fly on the wall of that tent to eavesdrop on their conversation, but all he could catch were the sounds of tea being delivered by the Arab's servant, the clink of the teapot against tiny cups, and the low drone of the ritual opening of an official conversation.

Deciding he'd gain little from remaining near the two leaders, Matthew crept outside the boundaries of the camp to where the Africans were gathered. These people were silhouetted against the indigo sky, heaped in piles almost like the bones around the well. He approached them cautiously, wishing neither to alarm them, nor to call the Tuareg's attention to himself. Choosing a man who was less slumped than the others, Matthew slid down onto the sand before him.

"Salâm aleikoum," he tried. "Greetings."

Terrified stares surrounded him, except from the man he'd addressed. This one stretched his chained neck higher. "Good evening," he replied in halting Arabic. "What does the master desire?"

Matthew held up a hand. "I am no master. I am a slave, like you."

Disbelief crossed the man's face. "Where are your shackles? You walk free." The African turned away. "Do not play with me. My spirit has been grieved enough."

Matthew glanced over his shoulder. No one was watching. He inched closer. "The Tuareg—the blue men—captured my caravan. They murdered most of my comrades. They say they will sell me to your masters."

The story caught the man's attention. He turned back. "I have never seen a white slave. I thought only my people were taken into captivity."

"You are their leader?" Matthew guessed.

His shoulders straightened an inch. "In my country I am a chief." They slumped again. "Now my station is of little purpose."

"Here." Matthew reached beneath his robes and pulled out two locust balls. His dinner. He offered them. "I am Matthew. Matthew Morrissey. Perhaps we can help each other."

The African stared at the food for a long moment. At last he gravely accepted the gift. One lump went into his mouth, the other was given to a woman by his side. Matthew watched as she, in turn, divided the ball in two and fed half to a child in her lap before eating her share.

"Your wife?" he asked.

The man nodded. "And my son. There were two daughters once, but their bones are scattered on the sands."

Matthew sat back and bowed his head. "Your sorrow is my sorrow."

"Why should this be?" growled the black man. "He who has not walked in my steps cannot feel my pain."

Matthew raised his head and stared boldly into the angry brown eyes confronting him. "I have walked in your steps. I have felt your pain. My whole family is lost forever."

Some of the anger faded. "What do you want of me?"

Searching carefully for the right answer, Matthew finally said, "Your name, if you will share it."

Emaciated muscles tightened. "I am Yow Asanti Ay. From the green forests of the south."

"Thank you." Matthew rose. He'd pressed enough for tonight. "Tomorrow, at this same hour, I will bring more food. As much as I am able." He turned to go, then paused. He needed to say something else. What? Words came of their own volition:

"As you walk under the hot sun of the day, try to remember the road back to those green forests. One day soon you may be able to lead your people home."

Matthew spent a restless night outside Cornwall's tent. He'd made a big promise—an impossible one—to the African chief. Not the food part. That was manageable, one way or another. What kept him tossing were those other words that had slipped off his tongue so easily; too easily. He'd suggested the possibility of life and liberty for Asanti and his people.

Now guilt racked him. He'd had a need to make Asanti feel better, but implying the potential of freedom? It was too much for Matthew to promise. Too much for anyone.

How had the Africans let themselves be enslaved to begin with? Why had they accepted this enslavement with such docility? He was a slave himself, yes, but the comparison ended with the word. How could Asanti and his people allow themselves to be so cruelly victimized? Matthew's anger grew before he recognized the truth: hunger, for one thing. Being marched naked in chains, for another. He shivered at the very thought of joining their misery, of being stripped and shackled.

Matthew fought past his nausea at the very concept of true slavery, of the way these human beings were being treated. Of the way he could be treated in the very near future. He began to think.

His first realization—which he was finally able to admit to himself—was that he and Dr. Cornwall and Hussein had no way out of their own dilemma without help. They were only three against too many. They needed manpower to overcome the Tuareg, and now the Arabs, too. As weak and sickly as these Africans were, there were so many more slaves than keepers. If they could only be roused and organized. . .

Matthew bolted upright. *We could help each other. We could become allies in an escape attempt.*

But how? He sank into his bed of sand again.

Cornwall's advice would be to use logic on the problem. Logically, Matthew needed to learn what would wake these people. He literally twisted himself into knots over the puzzle, bumping Hussein in the process. Hussein grunted and turned over on the sand. Matthew stared at the sleeping guide, curled up like Gin. . . . What made human beings different from animals? The ability to think, yes. And in thinking, to be able to strive, to aspire to something better in life . . .

Hope.

Hope was the most important thing needed. Didn't he himself need to keep the fires of hope burning? Didn't he need to keep alive the knowledge that someday there would be an end to his personal slavery, an end to the Great Sahara

Desert? For this, it was essential to keep his body strong. Therefore, or *ergo*, as the doctor would say, food was the next critical item. But without the hope, even more food wouldn't help.

Matthew suddenly realized that perhaps his words to the African had been the correct ones after all. They'd been the seed of a great idea. Now his job was to get some strength into Asanti and his family, into as many of the others as was humanly possible. . . . Strength of heart and strength of body. He had an idea about how to accomplish this. But he'd have to be very, very careful. Maybe the promise wasn't completely impossible. He just needed a miracle. But miracles, like *jinn*, had to be believed in before they could come to life. Faith—and a good plan—were all.

Satisfied for the moment, Matthew wound himself into a ball within his robes and slept at last.

Dawn was not Asa B. Cornwall's best moment.

"You want me to do *what*?" He rubbed his eyes and glared at Matthew. The doctor disliked being woken earlier than usual.

"I want you to tell Rakik that a big holy day is coming up. The most important day of the year in your faraway land. A day filled with signs and

110

portents. Be convincing. You need to tell him that you wish to celebrate this festival of *magic* when we arrive at the next well."

"Why would I want to do anything like that?"

Matthew bent closer to Cornwall's ear. "Because you'd like to be free someday. Someday soon. Or had you planned on spending the rest of your life traipsing around the Sahara as Rakik's trained monkey?"

That got Cornwall out of his blankets. "Now look here, Matthew Morrissey, if you think for one moment that I enjoy my current position . . . if you think that Asa B. Cornwall, eminent phrenologist and author of some note, likes being kidnapped, so close to attaining another monumental victory, another pinnacle in his career—"

Matthew clapped a hand over the doctor's mouth. "We're right next to Rakik's tent. Lower your voice, sir. Please."

But Cornwall wasn't finished. He shook off the restraint. "We were so close to Siwa, Matthew. So close to the trail of Alexander the Great!" He flopped back onto his mat, tears of frustration in his eyes.

"I know, sir," Matthew soothed. "But Alexander isn't going anywhere. He'll wait for us. Try to collect yourself. I beg you!"

Cornwall snuffled. Matthew took that as permission to continue.

"Here's the situation. I need to get some food into the Africans—"

"Why you?"

"Because there's no one else! Most of them don't look as if they'll be able to last another day, much less walk all the way north to the Mediterranean for whatever's waiting for them there."

"Slave markets," Cornwall allowed. He rubbed at his nose and hoisted himself on an elbow. "In Tripoli. According to Hussein they'll be auctioned off, mostly to harems in Arabia. Which also means"—Cornwall gulped audibly—"the strongest males will be turned into eunuchs somewhere along the way. Usually at a place called Ghadames. Apparently there's a whole line of ancient fortresses hidden in the sands. First Zuila, then Ghadames, then—"

Matthew broke in. "What's a eunuch?" he asked suspiciously.

In the dim light of the tent Cornwall's face went pale. "You don't want to know, lad. But they end up protecting harem ladies, it seems."

"From what?"

"Umm," Cornwall hedged. He plucked at his nightshirt. "From unwanted male attention to the sultan's women."

"But putting men to guard women like that . . . isn't it sort of like letting a fox into the hen-house?"

Cornwall sighed. "After this little operation in Ghadames, they wouldn't be foxes anymore, lad."

Matthew sank back on his haunches. "Ouch."

"Precisely."

Sweat was rare in the desert, but Matthew was suddenly drenched with it. "Could they do it—this operation—to me, too?"

"Never fear, Matthew. Apparently the sultans prefer black Africans for the job."

"But still . . ."

Cornwall patted a few stray hairs across his bald pate. "You were saying, before the conversation took this unfortunate turn . . ." He raised his voice. "Something about a sudden need to feed the multitudes?"

"*Shhh.* We *need* them. They're part of my escape plan. But they won't be any use at all without some strength in them."

"Ah." Understanding began to penetrate Asa B. Cornwall's eyes.

"Yes, *ah.* The excuse for improving their rations—only temporarily, Rakik and the Arabs are to understand—is that you need them to perform for your mystical festival. A festival that will bring great good fortune to its celebrants.

Emphasize the *great good fortune*. You know how superstitious most of these men are. Give them some nonsense about how the stars require many, many, strong bodies. You should be able to elaborate from there." Matthew considered further. "Find out how far this Zuila is, too. Maybe that would be the best place for everything to happen, after all. Before we get too close to . . ." He paused, afraid even to utter the word. Then he braced himself and did it. "Too close to *Ghadames*. Somehow I suspect that after Ghadames, the game might be over."

"Zuila. All right. But what kind of performance?"

"It doesn't matter! I'll work something out with the Africans' leader, Asanti. Some kind of huge dance that will require their chains to be removed . . ."

"Better and better," Cornwall muttered. He began getting into the spirit of the conspiracy at last. "And at some point the dance turns into an attack against our mutual captors—"

"Keep that thought, sir." Matthew smiled. "So the Africans have got to be fed. For as many nights as there are till our next big stop. Zuila."

"Why don't you explain all this to Rakik yourself, Matthew?"

"I don't want him suspicious. He gives me

enough odd looks as it is. Hussein will have to do the translating. Just make it good."

"Hmmm. An evening something like the Fourth of July, but for magicians . . ."

"That's the idea, sir. Keep thinking." Matthew withdrew to attend to his camels.

Hussein was not happy with his role in the plot.

"What! You desire me to bring attention to myself, attention to the doctor before Rakik and this Muzzafir? In our position it is madness! Allah has blessed us thus far, but to do this thing would be pressing our luck beyond even Allah's help! The healthy slave, the living slave, is seen only when the master wishes him to be seen."

"And do you wish to spend the rest of *your* life in captivity?" Matthew asked. "And what about *Ghadames*?"

"I am too old and too ugly to be made into a eunuch! Allah be praised."

"Are you sure? Absolutely certain?"

Matthew watched the little grain of doubt planting itself within Hussein's brain. When a film of sweat broke across his forehead, he knew he'd won.

"Tell me again this thing you want me to do."

But even goaded by fear, Hussein couldn't seem to arrange an interview for Cornwall with Rakik that evening. Matthew was forced back on his own resources once again. He'd promised food, and he'd find some. Heaven knew the Africans desperately needed it. From what he could tell, they were served only one meal a day: the thin gruel he'd watched being scooped into gourds from huge cauldrons early that morning.

In the end, Matthew borrowed from his old caravan's food supplies while the Tuareg were eating. He could manage only a single sack hidden beneath his robes, but he filled that sack to bursting with dates and dried camel meat. Then he waited for nightfall to haul it outside the camp. Asanti was waiting. He rose from a mound of huddled bodies and motioned Matthew to the far side, out of sight.

"You kept your promise. You came again."

Matthew unhooked the sack from his belt. "I keep my promises to those who will keep theirs."

Asanti didn't answer. Instead he motioned into the darkness. Several men cautiously approached, grabbed the sack, and began to distribute its contents.

"It's not much," Matthew apologized, "but—"

"One date is life to the starving man. It brings the sweetness of hope."

"Yes," Matthew agreed. "Hope is everything." He crossed his legs on the sand and settled in for a conference he prayed would be every bit as productive as that between Rakik and Muzzafir.

Chapter Ten

"W

HERE HAVE YOU BEEN, *nasrani*?"

Matthew collapsed onto the sand in front of
Cornwall's tent. "You waited up for me? Why?"

Hussein propped himself against a tent pole
and stared into the starry sky. "I was worried.
This interest in the black slaves, it will bring
trouble on our heads."

"I've just come from the Africans. No one saw
me. . . . How much more trouble could we get
into, anyway?"

Hussein raised a hand and began counting off fingers. "First, torture. You have not seen what these desert sheiks can do to a man when they feel playful. . . . Next, death . . . and then there's *Ghadames*." He stopped. "*Nasrani* wishes more?"

Matthew shook his head. "What I wish, Hussein, is that you would explain this slave business to me. I just can't understand it."

"But you have slavery in your own country, do you not? The Africans who are not marched north are shipped west, across the sea."

"I guess you're right, but I've never seen it. Never seen a slave before in my life. They don't have them in New York City, thank goodness. Only in the South." Matthew focused on the stars, too. "I don't think I could live in the South of my own country."

Hussein gave one of his shrugs. "It is hard to understand your passion over this subject. For our plight, yes. But for the blacks? Slavery of black Africans has been going on since before Roman times. Forever. The whole of North Africa runs on slavery. The slaves work in the oases, work in the salt mines. The Tuareg profit from this."

"And the Arabs," Matthew threw in.

"Yes, Arabs, too. Without the slaves and the salt they produce, there would be no caravans crossing the desert."

119

Matthew's eyes followed the trail of a plummeting star. "How can you Muslims be so religious, and treat people this way?"

"There must be correct behavior. The Koran itself says this." Hussein spread his hands. "Alms must be given, women must be protected, slaves must be allowed certain rights."

Matthew turned to Hussein. "Do you truly believe those starving, naked people outside of our camp are being given their rights?"

"Those people, they are in a masterless, in-between stage. When they have acquired true masters, they will also acquire the rights due them."

"You mean they're in limbo? What comes next? Hell?"

"*Nasrani, nasrani,*" Hussein sighed. "I did not make this world. I only live within it."

"Well, I live within it, too. And I say that tomorrow it's time for you and Cornwall to beard Rakik."

Matthew turned away from Hussein and the stars and deliberately closed his eyes. Someday he would learn enough to understand the workings of the traffic in slaves. He didn't believe that it just kept happening because it was a centuries-long tradition. Sure, tradition was part of it—economics, too. Everyone was making a little money along the way. But from his own small experience with business he knew that there was usually someone at the top. He needed to know who was at the top of this particular chain. Someone had to be giving orders to the Tuareg, to the Arabs like Muzzafir. Someone was making the decisions, sending the caravans across the Sahara. Someone was getting very rich from this trade in human misery.

Asa B. Cornwall ran a handkerchief over his very damp forehead. "He bought it! I can't believe that Rakik could be dim enough to have bought the entire scheme—lock, stock, and barrel!"

"And Muzzafir, too," Hussein added. "It is Muzzafir who must waste extra food on his slaves."

"I'm not sure he's wasting it," Matthew said. "You know the slaves will bring more if they don't look half dead. Muzzafir would have had to begin fattening them up soon anyway—"

"Of course," Dr. Cornwall commented. "Like livestock."

"Probably at Ghadames, the last oasis before Tripoli," Matthew continued. "He's only agreed to begin the process a little earlier. The idea of entertainment amuses him."

"It was the 'great good luck' that really brought him around, though," Cornwall added. "His piggy eyes bulged and he reached for an amulet tucked beneath his robes."

The Tuareg had been much laxer with them since the rendezvous, but still the three captives remained cautious. They were hiding behind a sand dune in the twilight, Matthew popping his head over the rim every few minutes to watch cauldrons being readied for the unexpected late meal for the Africans. He hadn't visited Asanti's camp this evening. It didn't seem necessary with another round of gruel in the offing. As yeasty smells began drifting their way, Matthew asked the obvious question. "How long is the journey to Zuila?"

"Only ten days, Allah be praised," Hussein replied. "A day or two more of extra food would have been too much to ask. All might have been lost."

"Too true," Cornwall added. "Once he let go of that amulet, Muzzafir was clicking over his abacus like a miser, working out supplies on hand versus distance to Tripoli. I strongly suspect that if our little revolt fails, the slaves will be placed on half their normal rations for the remainder of the trip anyway, traditional fattening in Ghadames or not. Muzzafir isn't a man to put more into his property than he can expect to get out of it."

"But if they fed these people better to begin with," Matthew fumed, "they'd end up with more of them surviving as far as the slave markets!"

"I don't think humane treatment is a concept Muzzafir could ever understand, lad." Cornwall patted Matthew's shoulder. "Probably has some cockeyed idea about the fittest surviving the ordeal."

Matthew edged his head over the dune a final time. "The guards are beginning to pass out the gourds. Asanti has his people lined up. They look like wraiths in the night . . . swaying weakly . . . with just their eyes glowing. . . ."

Cornwall tugged him back. "Don't go all melodramatic, Matthew Morrissey. We've done the best we can for the Africans. We've gotten them their extra rations. Now it's time to work out the details of our little evening of wonder and enchantment in Zuila."

Matthew shook the stark image from his head and lowered himself onto the sand. "Since you mention it, there are a few items I'll be needing." He began enumerating. "Shovels, paint, a coffin—"

"A coffin?" Cornwall burst out. "What in heaven's name do you intend to do with a coffin?"

"Well," Matthew admitted, "any elongated, body-sized box would do."

"But—"

"I've been spending a great deal of time think-ing about Monsieur Robert-Houdin, Doctor."

"That elegant magician in the boulevard du Crime?"

"Exactly."

"Ah." Cornwall smiled a little smile of sudden enlightenment.

"What is this thing, this person you talk about?" Hussein inquired with some dubiousness.

"Get me what I need, Hussein," Matthew answered, "and you'll find out. The box, espe-cially. Surely one of these Arabs in the new cara-van is carrying a chest of some kind?"

Hussein shook his head. "This is not Cairo, where you can find anything you need in the souks. I think paint will be impossible. As for your box . . . mostly the caravan is carrying blocks of salt, and some ivory. But I will search."

"Oh, and one more thing," Matthew added. "I noticed that a few of the Arabs from Muzzafir's caravan are carrying guns—"

"Traded from your American slavers in West Africa," Hussein broke in darkly. "I have watched them play with these new toys. They cause much envy among the Tuareg. Soon the desert will be filled with even more violence."

"I don't like guns either, but that's not the point."

"What is?" asked Cornwall.

Matthew grinned. "Where there are guns, there must be gunpowder. I need you to liberate that, too. As much as the Arabs have."

Hussein groaned. "Too much. You want too much!"

"Only freedom," Matthew answered.

In the days that followed, Matthew met with Asanti each night after the extra meal had been served. A change began coming over the Africans. The extra food helped, of course, but now when Matthew arrived at the slaves' camp, there was a noticeable buzz circulating around the different groups. Asanti had set them to tasks suggested by Matthew, and the feeling of hope was strong in the air.

Matthew still arrived each evening with an extra sack of dates. As he emptied his own caravan's panniers of the food, he'd been carefully refilling the bags with sand so the theft wouldn't be noticed—at least for the moment. He didn't care to speculate on what might occur when the Tuareg finally went in search of dried dates—or the Arabs in search of gunpowder, or all the other little things Hussein was secretly collecting. With any luck, that wouldn't happen before

Zuila. And with more luck, they needn't worry about either the Tuareg or the Arabs after Zuila.

Asanti smiled each time he spied Matthew's food sack. The African chief always selected a few dates, then carefully allotted the remaining treats to his subleaders, and each night there were more men lined up for fruit and orders. To be absolutely certain of full cooperation on the Night of Nights in Zuila, Matthew finally explained the significance of Ghadames to Asanti. He watched the familiar sweat break out on the black man's brow.

"This is a true thing you tell me, Matthew?" Asanti asked. "We will be gelded like animals?"

"I swear it is true," Matthew replied. "Those who survive as far as Ghadames."

Asanti pounded a fist into his palm. "It would be better to die like a man in Zuila."

"I cannot lie, Asanti. Some of your people may die in Zuila. But if you stick together and don't lose your courage, more will live to be free."

Asanti reached for a date. "We become stronger each day. Our courage grows. We will not fail you."

Matthew cleared his throat. "About that other business. The magical box I told you about. Have you chosen the woman who will be my helper?"

Asanti raised his head. "My wife Afua will be the honored one."

Matthew gulped. "But I have explained to you some of the difficulties. I have been studying the swords carried by the masters, but there may be small differences in the curves . . ."

"It will be my wife."

Asanti had spoken. Matthew nodded acceptance and rose to leave. Now the pressure would be even greater. Robert-Houdin had used carefully measured, straight swords for his own onstage effects. Matthew prayed the rest of his memory was perfect on the subject of this particular trick of the great magician.

Five days passed, then six. After Matthew had Cornwall beg for an extra ration of water for the Africans during the middle of the day, when they usually stumbled through the scorching sun and heat dry-throated, chants began rising from the long line. It gave Matthew heart, and that night he asked Asanti what the singing had meant.

"They sing about home. They sing about slavery. They sing about the *razzia*, the manhunt." Asanti raised his head and cried out a few harsh-voiced lines. Then he translated:

"My sons are led from the abodes of men.
Salt and greed make them slaves."

When he sang again, his words sounded softer.

"At this hour,
Now,
'Round the fires our mothers sit.
Their hearts are filled with pain,
For we are stolen from the good green land.
But soon we shall return."

"Will you sing this at the dance in Zuila?" Matthew asked.

"This, and more," Asanti agreed. "The masters have not learned our language. They will not understand."

"Until it is too late," Matthew said.

Yow Asanti Ay smiled. "Until it is too late."

"I found your box, *nasrani*." Hussein sidled closer to Matthew as he unloaded a camel the next afternoon. He lowered his voice to a whisper. "It is filled with ostrich plumes. Very delicate."

Matthew straightened up from his task. "I'll need to work on it tonight. There are only three more days till we get to Zuila."

Hussein shook his head sorrowfully. "I don't see how—"

"You must talk to Rakik again. You and Cornwall. I'll need permission to work by a fire, officially and in the open. I'll be wanting light. I have a few tools in my own kit that should help."

"Always you need more," Hussein growled. "I find shovels, it is not enough. I see where the gunpowder lies hidden within kegs. The box, too—"

"The box is no good to us unless I fix it first, Hussein. You do want to be free of this lot, don't you?"

"It is easy for you," Hussein complained. "You don't have to stand before Rakik and Muzzafir with pictures in your mind. Pictures of bodies being flayed from the neck down, while the victims still breathe. Pictures of this skin being stuffed and used for balls—"

"Thank you for sharing that with me, Hussein. I'm sure it will improve my dreams tonight." Matthew stared the man down. Grumbling, Hussein set off on his odious errand.

Word of the coming Night of Nights had spread quickly through the caravan. Loading or unloading camels, sitting around evening fires, the men

129

spoke of little else. As anticipation grew, it seemed there was nothing Rakik and Muzzafir were unwilling to contribute to the upcoming festivities in Zuila. As Matthew worked on the box between two fires that night, the Tuareg and the Arab sprawled on their cushions in close attendance to his every move. He tried to ignore their sharp interest, but it was hard.

Matthew had packed his own bag carefully back in Paris. He'd packed it anticipating a close encounter with the skull of Alexander the Great. Earlier encounters with the likes of Voltaire and Rousseau had suggested the usefulness of a crowbar. Since a crowbar was too heavy and unwieldy, he'd substituted a claw hammer and chisel. Always handy for the odd recalcitrant sarcophagus. As he squinted through the poor light for the marks he'd etched into the wood earlier, he wished he'd thought to pack a small file and saw as well. He made a mental note to add them to his kit for Cornwall's next expedition, then snorted ruefully to himself. If this batch of tricks didn't work, there'd be no next expedition. Matthew aimed the chisel, picked up the hammer and began to delicately carve out the first of the many slim, crescent-shaped holes that were necessary if Robert-Houdin's trick were to succeed.

Tap, tap, tap.

Rakik bent closer. "What is this you do, slave?"

Matthew kept tapping. He had only two more nights to finish the job, after all. "In Zuila, O Great Sheik, I will be the Master of Revels for Dr. Asa B. Cornwall. I help to prepare one of his most marvelous wonders."

"Explain it to me!" Rakik demanded.

"I am sorry, magnificent one, but that is impossible. The magic must be kept secret until the moment of its use during the Night of Nights."

Matthew imagined the petulant scowl now being hidden by the Tuareg's veil. "There will be other wonders as well, splendid captain of warriors and camels," he added. "Such as you have never seen, and will never see again in your lifetime."

He heard Rakik settle back on his cushion, mollified for the moment.

Tap, tap, tap.

"What have you done with my ostrich feathers?"

Matthew spun his head. Muzzafir's voice was high-pitched and whiny. It came from an obese, pampered body. Somehow the man, settled within his folds of fat, was scarier than Rakik. Matthew nodded deferentially.

"The feathers are safe, respected leader. They will travel in this same box until Zuila, and thereafter as well."

"Dust will enter the holes and damage the goods!"

"I will line the box with cloth to prevent that, esteemed master."

Muzzafir glared. "The feathers are worth *your* weight in gold, slave. You will pay—personally— for their ruin." The Arab suddenly giggled with pleasure, obviously visualizing one of Hussein's scenarios of torture.

"Of course, benevolent one."

Matthew turned back to the box. In his eyes it suddenly became a coffin again—quite an attractive one, if you imagined Muzzafir reposing in layers within it. He steadied his shaking hands and got on with the job.

CHAPTER ELEVEN

Matthew was totally dumbfounded when his camel topped a dune about midmorning the next day.

"Where's the sand?"

His yelp of surprise must have been loud, because the Tuareg riding in front of him condescended to answer for once.

"It is the end of the *erg* for now, slave. The Black Stone Desert begins."

It was well named. Matthew squinted into the

horizon at nothing but desolation. No life. A wasteland of flat, cracked, blackened earth and stone cooking under the unrelenting sun. He turned to the golden sand behind him that he'd believed would continue forever. Suddenly it seemed warm and hospitable, alive in its undulating waves. Too late. The caravan slid down the last dune and toiled forward.

By the time a campsite had been selected for the night, Matthew was worried about more than the landscape. He'd had to find Gin's boots and protect the dog's delicate paws once more, but there was no protection he could give Asanti and his people for their bare feet.

"This Black Stone Desert," he asked Hussein at the first opportunity, "how long does it last?"

"I've traveled this way once before in my youth, *nasrani*. It continues all the way to Zuila."

"For two more days, then?"

"Even so."

Matthew began praying for Asanti's people—and his great escape plans, too.

Zuila was a bizarre oasis set within a world of blackness. Their long caravan pushed hard to reach it by nightfall of the tenth day. When the setting sun glinted from the walls rising out of the desert, Matthew was certain he was seeing a mirage.

"*Castles,*" he whispered. "Castles and towers within a fortress. In the middle of such a place?"

But it was real, as real as such a fantasy could be in the ever-changing Sahara. The camels stumbled through arches of tumbling stone, nose rings taut as they strove for the water they could smell within. And that was all the stone walls surrounded: a crumbling castle and several wells hacked out of the hardened earth. There were no palm trees, no groves of figs or dates, not a single sprig of grass within the ancient ruins. There were no people, either. There were, however, lizards—and scorpions to spare. Matthew trod on one of the huge insects just after he'd pulled on sandals and swung off his camel. He cringed at the squish. Around him, the Tuareg were stomping with energy. Matthew tore his eyes from the ground to see Hussein making his way toward him. The guide came to a stop.

"Cornwall has informed Rakik that the stars are not in the correct alignment for festivities tonight. He claims they will not be so until tomorrow. Allah be praised, the masters already planned to rest and water the animals for a full day."

"You mean I have all of tomorrow to finish preparations?"

Another colossal scorpion scuttled by and Hussein efficiently dispatched it. Then he nodded. "As Master of Revels, you are to be excused from other labors tomorrow."

"Rakik would allow this?"

"Rakik and Muzzafir are both as consumed with curiosity as their men. They would do nothing to keep you from performing this role you have assumed."

"Hamdullah!"

"Save your thanks till after we survive this scourge of vermin, *nasrani*." Hussein studied the six-inch bug he'd just flattened. "They have grown since my last visit." He glanced at the surrounding walls as shadows fell with heavy finality. "Zuila has always been a place of mystery, never of comfort."

Hussein decamped, leaving Matthew grasping his mount's reins, staring at the closest well. The Africans were shoving camels aside as they fought for spots at the watering troughs. The successful slaves were on their knees, heads lowered, lapping water like the animals. The exposed heels of feet protruding from ankle shackles were as cracked as the Black Stone Desert, only these cracks bled red. Would these people be able to dance tomorrow night? Would they be in any condition to fight for their lives?

Zuila was turning out to be vastly different from Matthew's dreams of it. He shook his head and went in search of a vat of sheep fat. Asanti would be needing it.

Cornwall was up late into the night tending to a spate of scorpion-sting victims. Matthew worked beside the doctor, learning how to draw venom from the wounds, then helping to prepare poultices to further the healing. Scorpions were apparently both color- and caste-blind. They struck equally at Tuareg, Arab, and slave. By midnight, when the crisis had slowed for the moment, there were more than a dozen of the stricken lined up on mats outside the castle.

The doctor finally straightened from his labors. "Funny how the thrill of proving ancient medical procedures correct can pall in the light of an epidemic. All one's left with is hard work and perspiration." He studied the victims. "There's little more we can do for these poor souls, Matthew. Morning will tell us where we've succeeded . . ." He sighed. "Or failed."

The sliver of a new moon, a crescent moon, hovered above them. In the light from it and the stars Matthew had the chance to really inspect the place for the first time since the crisis began.

"Where are we, sir?" He pointed at the ramparts, then the towers. "What is this strange place all about?"

Cornwall rubbed his forehead. It glistened with beads of sweat, and he looked worn out. "From the studies I did back in Paris, it seems that the Romans built a string of forts to defend their desert domain from the wild tribes of their time." He shook his head. "But this is not Roman, Matthew. The architecture is all wrong. The ramparts . . . and that dome on the building attached to the castle walls—it must be a chapel— they seem almost Byzantine."

"Byzantine?" Matthew asked.

"The empire that took over after the Romans fell," Cornwall explained. "It was based in Constantinople. I don't know . . ." Cornwall paused again. "But in my readings I did come across reference to a lost kingdom called Ceballa. It was reputed to be hidden deep in the desert of North Africa. It was also said to contain treasures beyond all understanding." Cornwall swiped at his head again. "Curious how fabled treasures mean so little next to life and death."

He tucked a blanket borrowed from his own tent around one of the bloated, moaning Africans, then gave the trembling hand of an Arab a reassuring squeeze. "I must get some rest.

You too, lad. We'll see what we can learn of this place in the light of a new dawn." He stopped, as if remembering. "Big day tomorrow. We've got to be ready for it." Cornwall turned to leave.

"Wait, sir," Matthew called. "Let me check your tent before you lie down. For scorpions."

Asa B. Cornwall smiled grimly. "It wouldn't do for the healer to be stricken, would it?"

Matthew led the way, with Cornwall following, muttering to himself. "Alexander never had to personally deal with any of this. Six-inch scorpions. Eight-inch scorpions. What're a few soldiers more or less when you've got thirty thousand at your beck and call? All he had to do was conquer the world."

After he'd assured the doctor's safety, Matthew found only troubled sleep for himself. He dozed for a while on the rock-hard ground next to Hussein, strange images floating through his head. There were man-sized scorpions, and lizards as big as houses. They appeared to be in competition with each other. The scorpions marched like worker ants with boulders of black stone in their pincers, making their way toward a giant fortress in the distance. The lizards roughly shouldered the stones from the insects, then nosed them closer to the fortress. Atop the fortress itself stood a single man, waiting. In his dream, Matthew seemed to be flying over the two armies, closer and closer to the man. He was a stonemason, and he calmly accepted the rocks, professionally chipped them into neat squares with a few blows from his hammer and chisel, then laid them upon each other, mortaring the seams, building the fort ever larger. When the man looked up, Matthew saw his face. With a start he jerked awake, drenched in sweat.

It was his father.

Sleep gone, Matthew rose as if being summoned. The crescent moon was much lower in the sky. The night had turned cold. He tightened his robes and set off through the slumbering camp for the ramparts that were calling to him.

Matthew fumbled along the inner walls till he came to a circular tower filled with spiral stone steps that should take him to the top. Inside, it was pitch-dark. He groped out blindly for the rounded wall, then mounted the worn steps, revolution by revolution. He began to feel as if the tower were leaning in toward him; began to feel that there *was* no top, no outlet. And then he broke through. The ramparts stretched to either side of him, solid dark lengths that outlined the desert beyond and the stars above. He leaned against the nearest parapet wall, taking in the extraordinary, alien beauty of the spot. On such a night, in such a place, anything was possible. . . .

A faint scraping against nearby stone made Matthew spin.

"No!"

It couldn't be, yet it was. Again. It was close, perched on a broken section of wall not five yards away.

"My cheetah," he whispered.

The cat stared at him with eyes that glinted like molten amber through the darkness. Matthew stared back, mesmerized for long moments. Then the creature casually broke the connection, raised a powerful paw, and delicately began licking it. Matthew remained terrified; too petrified to move. Yet there was a certain fascination. . . . Did he really want to move?

"My *jinn*," he murmured. "My personal *jinn*. Do you bring me luck—or something else?"

Its grooming complete, the cat spared him another glance, and sprang—but not at Matthew. Instead it gracefully glided to the top of the tower, then disappeared into the night.

"Hamdullah," Matthew prayed. "Thank you, God. Once more."

"Give praise where praise be due, and all good things will come to you."

Matthew spun again, this time in the opposite direction, toward the singsong voice. It was an old voice, cracked and rusty, as if it hadn't had much practice for many years, for centuries. The figure Matthew spied was bent and robed, its head cowled within folds of cotton black as the night.

"Who—who are you?" he stammered.

"Father Moses, that be me. Zuila is my watch to see."

"But I don't understand—"

A cackling laughter was his response, until the figure moved closer and grasped out for Matthew's arm with skeletal fingers that had a leathery, scaled sheen—as if the old man had been dining on lizards for eons. Maybe he had. He spoke again, pulling Matthew's eyes from those fingers.

"Young of mind and pure of heart, *you* shall have the victor's part."

"But, but—"

Protests were useless. Matthew was dragged in the viselike grip along the ramparts to the next tower. This he was pulled into and down, down, down. Certainly farther down than he'd ever climbed to reach the sky. Farther still they descended, the constant cackling of the ancient man the only sound penetrating the darkness, aside from the scuffle of their sandals. And farther yet they went, till surely they were beneath the ramparts, beneath the very desert itself.

The apparition stopped. Matthew's arm was released. He waited in total darkness till he heard the sound of flint scraping iron. A spark appeared and was nursed into flame. A candle was lit—but not one alone. The old man hobbled gleefully around the emerging room, lighting torches and candles, one after the other, until a brilliance Matthew had never conceived overwhelmed him.

He blinked, then rubbed his eyes and blinked again. The brilliance was coming from more than the sudden light. It was coming from piles of gleaming objects heaped about the close stone-walled chamber.

"I don't understand," Matthew said. "Gold?"

The cackle returned. "All these years I've kept it true—now the job must turn to you."

Matthew gaped at the madman. For surely he must be that. Yet gold there was. He knew the look of gold. He'd seen it in quantity before, thanks to Nicholas Mordecai. But that was lifetimes ago, in Philadelphia . . . and even Nicholas Mordecai had never amassed such a fortune.

143

Matthew bent to reach for a coin from among heaped thousands. He fingered the unknown face that was stamped upon it. "Who is this?" he tried once more.

"Justinian." The rhyming disappeared with the significance of the name. "Emperor of the World!"

"But that was—" How long ago? Dr. Cornwall would know. Matthew turned to the shining mounds of plates, goblets, urns, and jewelry, all refracting light from each other. His survey was halted by a partially hidden image on the floor beneath the treasure. Drawn to it, he knelt to clear the space. It was a picture, made from gleaming pieces of colored glass. It showed a mighty cat, *his* cat, springing . . .

Matthew swayed dizzily into the image and knew no more.

The pinks of breaking dawn woke Matthew. He stretched, then hoisted himself partially up. Where was he? Atop the ramparts? How had he gotten here? What was he doing here? He rubbed at his eyes. And what a strange dream he'd had. The whole night had been filled with strange dreams. He rubbed some more, then opened a tightly clenched fist. Something dropped from his hand to roll across the rough stone. It spun, teetered, and fell. Matthew struggled to his knees and reached for it. The sun rose another degree in the sky and cast a ray upon the object.

It seemed to be a newly minted golden coin.

Matthew flipped the coin to study a bearded face gracing the obverse side.

"Justinian. Emperor of the World!"

As the words echoed through his mind, Matthew staggered against the rampart wall. Justinian . . . the golden treasure trove . . . Father Moses . . . the cheetah. They'd been real. It had happened . . . and maybe his own father had been the guide to everything. He stared up into the sky.

"What does it all mean? Please tell me!"

He begged uselessly for an answer. The sun only rose another notch above the Black Stone Desert and the ramparts of Zuila.

Chapter Twelve

Matthew found Cornwall in front of the castle with his patients. He was looking pleased with himself.

"Where have you been, lad? Look here, they've all survived! Every last one of our scorpion victims is going to make it! It's a miracle!"

Matthew smiled as he caught his breath from his mad dash down from the ramparts. "No, sir. It's your care. Maybe you missed your true calling."

Hands were reaching out for Cornwall. When

he bent to grasp them, his fingers were smothered with grateful kisses. He blushed. "Medicine? Who knows, Matthew? Life takes strange detours."

"It certainly does, sir."

Cornwall turned to a few loitering Arabs. "Get the patients under cover for the day. Somewhere cool. And keep a guard posted to kill any lurking scorpions!" When blank faces were his only response, the doctor tugged at his robes in frustration. "The language barrier, I keep forgetting. Explain to them, Matthew."

Matthew explained, directed the evacuation of the patients, then had Cornwall to himself at last. Seeing the stricken laid out before the doctor had brought him back to reality once more. It had also made him begin to doubt his recent experiences all over again. "I need to speak to you about something, sir. Something curious, but possibly important."

Asa B. Cornwall swiped at his brow. "Drat, I'm sweating again. I shouldn't be sweating in this dryness. . . . Is it about tonight? Because I think, possibly, that I might have to rest during the heat of the day myself."

Matthew pulled out the golden coin. "I'm not certain what it's about, but you need to have a look at this."

Cornwall looked. "Justinian the First? He was a sixth-century emperor of the Byzantine Empire. Where in the world did you find this?"

Matthew reached to cover the coin in the doctor's outstretched palm as several Tuareg came into view. "Privately. Let's talk privately, please."

Asa B. Cornwall shook his head. "I'd certainly like to see that mosaic you described, lad. Not to mention the other trinkets. But as for the rest—"

Matthew had recounted everything in the privacy of the doctor's tent. Everything except the encounter with his own personal *jinn*. If Father Moses was hard to accept, that cheetah would be impossible.

"—I don't know, Matthew. I'm having a little trouble thinking clearly."

The doctor was sweating again. And occasional shudders had begun running through his body.

"Are you getting sick, sir?" Matthew asked. He wanted to add *Sick today, of all days?* but couldn't. It wouldn't be fair.

"Strange symptoms," murmured Cornwall. "Slight dizziness, the odd tremor, probably a fever . . ." He stretched out flat on his mat. "The only thing I can think of is malaria. Remember all those mosquitoes a while back? My studies in

Paris suggested an incubation period of four weeks. . . . I'm truly sorry. Miserable timing."

Matthew was already rooting through Cornwall's medicine case. He pulled out a bottle. "Quinine. I knew there was a reason we've been lugging it around for so long. We've got to get some quinine into you right now!"

"I hadn't even thought that far—"

Matthew offered a strong dose. "Take this and rest, sir. You've only got to be in good enough shape to put in an appearance tonight. I'll take care of the rest."

The doctor swallowed, not even complaining about the vileness of the taste. "Bless you, lad. I have complete faith in you." His eyes glazed over as his head sank back once more. "Just . . . try to take a minute to check our patients?"

"Don't worry yourself, sir. I will. I'll take care of everything."

Matthew gently unwound Cornwall's turban, then used the cloth to swab at the doctor's dripping face. Finally he sank back on his heels to think. Malaria surely seemed to pick its moments. What could he do? Where to start on everything else? The rock-hard dirt beneath him gave him his hint. *Shovels.* He'd start with the shovels and Asanti's people. Judging by the density of this ground, it was going to take all day for the

Africans to dig a hole big enough for his opening trick.

Matthew had been spinning around like a dervish all morning, setting up props for the evening. He felt as if he were constructing a tower out of cards. One false move and it would all come top-pling down, dashing his hopes for freedom—dashing the Africans' chance at life. His big break came at noon. He'd set Hussein to watch over the trench Asanti's men were digging behind a hastily erected screen of tent cloth.

"Nasrani—" Hussein found Matthew checking on the scorpion victims. *"Nasrani,"* he whispered in his ear, "you had better come at once."

Matthew finished changing a poultice on the leg of a particularly large Tuareg. "What is it?"

Hussein tugged. "Come."

They left the cool, protective rooms of the cas-tle for the solid, living heat of the outer court-yard beneath the fortress walls. This is where the festivities would be held. Hussein led Matthew to the far corner tower, well away from the huddled tents and resting camels. It was the area Matthew had selected as his stage, and it was where the Africans were still digging. Hussein pulled Matthew behind the screen.

"Look!"

Matthew whistled long and low. "What luck!"

Asanti joined them, tall and proud. He was tall and proud because Matthew's first major task of the morning had been to convince Muzzafir to remove the neck and ankle shackles of Asanti and all the men who would be helping him today. It hadn't been easy. Matthew could almost see himself being flayed in the villain's mind before assent was given.

"See what we have found, Matthew." Asanti smiled. "Is it a help to you?"

"I'll say!" He whistled again. At the bottom of the pit the diggers had discovered the roof of an underground tunnel. Strategies for its potential use nearly overwhelmed him, but Matthew shook them off. There was no time to waste on fantasies. First he needed to know where this tunnel went. He jumped into the pit and eased his body through the gap that had been broken through the stone arch of the roof. It was too much to hope for, but he prayed anyway. *"Please let it lead beyond the fortress walls. Let it open into the desert. Please—"*

When his sandals touched ground, he paused only long enough to get his bearings, then scurried through the darkness toward a dim illumination beyond. When he pulled himself up into the daylight once more, he found himself behind a boulder, thirty yards from the fortress walls. Matthew gave a leap of joy, came down hard on an enormous scorpion, and returned through the tunnel with considerably more care. Hussein was waiting to pull him out.

"What did you find, *nasrani*?"

"A miracle." He beamed. "A true, genuine, verifiable miracle! Thank you, Lord. *Hamdullah!*" He bowed his head in thanksgiving for a moment, then turned to Asanti and business.

"Get more men on the job. Clear away the tunnel roof completely. Build a ramp going down into it that a camel can descend upon. I'm certain the tunnel's high enough. . . ." His brain was operating faster than the words could spill out. "Make sure the opening outside the walls is big enough for a camel, too. And make sure none of the masters sees any of this!"

Asanti nodded his head. "For you we will accomplish all of this before nightfall. For you we will do anything."

Hussein stood frowning to one side. "I don't understand these orders you give, *nasrani*."

Matthew clapped him on the shoulder. "Hussein, tonight you are going to see one of the great Robert-Houdin's tricks performed as never before."

Hussein was unconvinced. "What is this trick?"

Matthew smiled broadly. "I'm renaming it, Hussein. I'm calling it *The Mystery of the Disappearing Camel.*"

The afternoon continued far better than Matthew could have hoped. This was mainly because the Arabs and Tuareg were taking their day of rest seriously. A few of them had appeared for midday prayers, but through the blistering heat of the afternoon they all slunk back into their tents for long, comfortable naps. Matthew, Hussein, and the Africans worked straight through. With the wells nearby, they could stop for drinks or to douse themselves with refreshing water as often as they liked, and Asanti's men worked with a will. When Matthew was fairly certain that the tunnel was going to be usable, he sat down with Asanti and laid out his revised master plan. Asanti's eyes grew wider and wider as he digested all of the ramifications.

"How did you come by this wisdom, Matthew? It is beyond your years. Beyond the years of most men."

Matthew shrugged. "I'm not wise, Asanti. Only desperate. And we could still fail—"

"No!" The chief's dark eyes hardened. "Do not speak of failure. It will happen as you say."

Matthew excused himself to finish the remainder of his preparations. Who knew how the night would play itself out? The best-laid plans . . .

All the dirt from the pit had to go somewhere. Matthew decided that rather than trying to hide it, he'd use it. The sun was beginning to set, and the day to cool, when he stood back to admire the small ceremonial mound he'd had Asanti's men create. They'd set some of the stones from the roof of the tunnel into the side of the hill as steps, and several other stones held up a flat slab of rock on the top. Matthew was pleased. It looked like an altar to some ancient god. It would also make a terrific bench for the ailing Dr. Cornwall to rest upon between his necessary parts in the performance.

"I wish to know something, slave."

Matthew started. It was Muzzafir, dressed in fresh robes and looking pink and rested. The villain had waddled up to him with amazing stealth. "Your wish is my command, master."

"Naturally. But what I wish to know is how you— a mere stripling, a cursed infidel slave—how you have caused these blacks to work so hard today."

"Even black slaves may look forward to festivities, master." He paused. Muzzafir was really more than just a little naturally pink. And there was a certain unmistakable odor emanating from the man. Something Matthew hadn't smelled in a very long time. "It helped that you were gracious enough to relieve them of their chains for the work."

"They will be returned soon enough."

"Of course, master." Was it possible? It had to be. The man had been drinking *alcohol*. Matthew decided to take a chance. "But in the meantime, would the worthy master extend his benefactions to the dancers who are to perform tonight?"

Muzzafir frowned with petulance. "Cannot any black dance? Let those already without shackles do the work."

Matthew knew Muzzafir couldn't tell one African from another. "Those who labored for me today and will continue to labor for me throughout the festivities are not dancers. The chosen dancers are others—others quite expert who will thrill you with their performance."

Muzzafir growled, staggered slightly, but reached for the iron key hanging from his belt. "Here!" He tossed it to Matthew. "Remove the chains yourself. I have better things to do. But if a single one of my slaves escapes—"

"Where would they escape to, O most kind and considerate master? Do you see anything but death outside this fortress for any soul on foot without food and water?"

"True," Muzzafir reluctantly agreed. "In the Sahara chains enslave the mind, not the body."

Matthew bowed his thanks. Even intoxicated, Muzzafir might be more intelligent than he let on. He'd need to be watched.

As Muzzafir lurched away, Hussein appeared. Matthew tossed him the key.

"By Allah's beard! How did you come by this?"

"Our master is two sheets to the wind."

"I do not know these words, *nasrani*."

"I thought Muslims did not drink alcohol, Hussein, but Muzzafir—"

Hussein shrugged understanding. "Hidden bottles have been found and opened behind tent flaps all afternoon. It can happen after long months in the desert. There are some unwilling to await the delights of the Gardens of Paradise."

"Others have been drinking as well?"

Hussein nodded, a little embarrassed by the admission. "Many."

"Allah is good indeed, my friend." Matthew grinned. "Get to work with that key, Hussein. Our captors are welcome to totter, but I believe that *all* of Asanti's people should walk tall and proud this Night of Nights."

CHAPTER THIRTEEN

THE CRESCENT MOON HAD GROWN. AS IF REFLECTING the flames below, it shone with a strange reddish hue. Matthew stood atop his ceremonial mound directly beneath the tower and ramparts of the fortress—and this bloody moon. The matching crescent scar on his cheek was boldly outlined by the light of the halo of fires blazing around the mound. He stared for a long moment at the multitude seated before him. Rakik and Muzzafir were settled on opposite sides of the central aisle he'd marked out leading to the dancing circle just below the mound. The blue men were in a block radiating out from Rakik. The Arabs surrounded and spread away from Muzzafir. To the rear were the Africans, bearing unlocked chains that could be cast aside in a moment. They were so silent—their ebony nakedness blending so well with the night—that one could easily forget their presence. This was as it should be. Matthew needed them to remain as unobtrusive as possible until their moment arrived. His survey complete, he spread his robed arms wide.

"I, Matthew Morrissey, son of John, grandson of Seamus, born in the distant, fabled land of America, walker in the golden streets of New York, voyager on the seven seas; I, who have burrowed in the depths after mysteries beyond your ken, who have made offerings to the Almighty on the boulevards of Paris, who have cast the very face of evil itself from the cliffs of the lost island of St. Helena and have now become a wanderer of the Great Sahara—"

He paused to be certain he was weaving the proper storytelling web. Heads were bent forward in interest. He continued.

"I, Matthew Morrissey, young in years but rich in experience, present to you one who has journeyed vastly beyond any of my meager adventures. I present one who understands not only the hidden secrets of the earth, not only the inner mysteries of men's hearts and minds, but also the riddle of the stars. On this Night of Nights, this Festival of Festivals, I present to you the man who will lead us into new realms of wonder, fear, and delight."

Matthew bent to reach for the torch he'd prepared. It was his first signal to Asanti. A single drum sounded.

Tom. Tom. Tom.

The beat began slowly. Matthew lit the torch, flung it high into the heavens, caught it, brought it to his mouth, then spewed forth a stream of fire toward the trickle of gunpowder he'd carefully spread at the foot of the mound.

The drum increased its pace and volume.

TOM-tom-tom, TOM-tom-tom, TOM-tom-tom.

Catch, he prayed to himself. *Catch!*

The flame caught. A thin, bright trail of fire sped down the central aisle of the courtyard to end in a circle around the waiting figure of the doctor. He was swaying, his face preternaturally bright. It was the malaria.

Walk, Matthew silently urged. *Walk!*

The first drum was joined by a second.

TOM-TOM-tom, TOM-TOM-tom, TOM-TOM-tom . . .

159

Cornwall caught the rhythm and began careening toward the mound.

"I give you Dr. Asa B. Cornwall!" Matthew exulted.

The last of the flames flickered at the tail of his robes as Cornwall staggered to the foot of the mound. Matthew reached out a hand to grasp the doctor's and pulled him halfway to the top as the drums reached their crescendo and stopped. Cornwall steadied himself and turned toward the crowd, then Matthew. He blinked.

"I'm not going to make it through the night's events, lad. . . . Malaria is worse than I estimated. Far worse. I just cannot—" He crumpled into Matthew's arms.

Matthew swallowed hard as he faced the audience. *Improvise.* That's what he had to do. Fast. He raised his head high over Cornwall's body.

"The power of the stars is so strong this Night of Nights that the great Dr. Cornwall finds it necessary to withdraw into himself in silent meditation to focus the power—all the power of the universe—over Zuila. He will continue his meditations from the altar of Justinian!"

Matthew mounted the final step as if it were all part of the ritual and laid Cornwall's quaking body on the flat slab of stone. He arranged the arms and legs in a suitable pose, then bent to whisper in his friend's ear. "Don't worry, sir. Rest. Get well." But Cornwall's eyes were already out of focus. Matthew turned away.

"He begins his inner trip to the transcendent stars. Soon the great Asa B. Cornwall will be gazing down on us from the moon itself! Thence from Venus, from Mars, from Saturn and Jupiter—and even farther than the moon and planets, to the very edges of the universe." *But not too far, sir,* Matthew added in his mind. *Don't go so far that you can't return to me.* Matthew raised his arms once more, and stretched his head back to gaze at the moon. A rare night bird flew across its narrow face. The audience gasped.

"An omen!" someone cried out. He was joined by others shouting, "An omen! An omen!"

Matthew riveted his gaze upon the people. "You yourselves have seen the sign! It is as I said. Under the watchful eye and soul of Asa B. Cornwall, we will begin!"

"We will begin" was Asanti's next cue. The first drum started up again, with a different rhythm. Matthew descended the steps from the altar, relit his torch, and directed it toward the tower corner to his right. All signs of digging had been hidden by a tarp spread tightly over the ground of the courtyard.

"Behold the Stage of Illusions upon which our

revels will begin. For your amusement and pleasure, great Sheik Rakik, mighty master Muzzafir,
for the amusement and pleasure of the men who
bravely follow you into the depths of the Sahara,
a special magical trick has been devised. It is
called *The Mystery of the Disappearing Camel!*"

Matthew decorously progressed to the tarp.
"Merely observe the complete solidity of the
stage." He paced across it carefully, hoping his
footsteps would not vibrate and give away the
gaping hole beneath. He made it across, then
planted himself in front and to one side of the
fraudulent surface. He nodded to Rakik. "With
your permission, Sheik Ibn er-Rakik, I will make
one of your camels disappear into thin air from
this stage."

Rakik's eyes glinted above his veil. "Such a
thing is impossible."

Matthew stared back. "Nothing is impossible
on this Night of Nights, great Sheik."

Rakik nodded. "I give my permission. I wish to
see your wonder performed."

Matthew waved his torch like a conductor's
baton. "First we must build the Walls of Magic!"

Several of Asanti's men appeared from the
shadows, carrying more stretched tarps made
from tent poles and cloth. They carefully posi-
tioned these walls upright, behind and to

Matthew's side, almost completely boxing in the area of the covered hole. Matthew feigned disinterest in the proceedings, staring instead beyond the assembly.

"Bring on the camel!" he ordered.

All heads stretched back to watch as a fully loaded camel was led forward out of the darkness by an African. The animal complained vehemently at the injustice of being forced to work during the night. Arab and Tuareg alike chuckled as the camel's neck swung out and its teeth chomped blindly at the nearest humans. Under the cover of this entertainment, preparations were completed behind the false walls. When the camel was halted at the edge of the courtyard stage, two walls had turned into a covered hut with a side entrance. Matthew waved his torch again.

"Enter, O great ship of the desert. Enter into the magical tent! Allah go with you, for who knows what lies beyond?"

He waved once more and the drumbeats, which had become a part of the night, increased in fury as a third, a fourth, then a dozen drums joined in the cacophony. Matthew raised his arms, watching the camel lunge for the bait being offered from within—irresistible bait: a ball of honey-coated grain. As the camel's tail disappeared, he waited for the safe signal from Asanti behind the stage. It came. He brought his arms down, and the drums gave a final crash and were silent. Matthew wheeled back to his audience.

"Now you will observe, great Sheik, a true mystery of the Sahara before your very eyes." He motioned to Asanti's hidden men, and the front wall of the hut was slid open. "Seeing is believing."

A great sigh swept over the audience. Matthew exhaled a great sigh himself. The camel was well and truly gone. All that remained within view was the foreshortened rear wall of the hut. The trick had worked!

"Do it again!" The order came from Muzzafir. "I know it cannot be accomplished another time, slave!"

Matthew bowed, hiding his grin. It was the effect he'd hoped for, planned for. "Your wish is my command, O mighty master."

"I should think so, accursed infidel slave."

Matthew performed *The Mystery of the Disappearing Camel* a second time for Muzzafir. Then in answer to shouts from the drunken crowd he performed it again and again, nearly twenty more times. Rakik and Muzzafir's giddy men couldn't get enough. That was twenty camels, he noted to himself. Twenty fully loaded, fully fed and watered camels. A decent little caravan's worth. It was more than he could have hoped for. It was

enough. Now was the time to move forward
before suspicions were raised. Matthew turned
from the false walls.

"Do you believe, great Sheik? Do you believe,
mighty Muzzafir?" He didn't wait for their nods.
"Then it is time to perform my next trick—magic
so frightening that it will make your very toes
curl!" Matthew strode back to the mound, leading all eyes and attention away from his dangerous hole. He reached for another, fresher torch.
"I present to you now *The Coffin of Death!*

To the throb of drums, more of Asanti's men
carried out the box Matthew had spent long
nights working on. He'd planned to place it on
the altar atop the mound, but as that was currently occupied by Cornwall, he settled for the
area just beneath. He motioned the men to lower
the box. They did so carefully, backing away from
it with fear in their eyes. They'd been told who
was to lie within it. Matthew approached the box
and ran the flames from his torch over it, inton-
ing bits of Latin nonsense. *"Ergo. Ipso Facto. Tabula
rasa—"* Cornwall's favorite. He ended with *"Pro
bono,"* and a heartfelt *"In Deo speramus,"* raised the
lid, and spun back to confront his audience.

"I challenge you, Rakik. I challenge you,
Muzzafir. Come and look into this coffin of
mystery. Tell me if there is anything within that

should not be within. Tell me if there are any secret compartments; any deviousness whatever about this simple box. I desire your true belief in my magic."

Rakik held up his hand, declining, but Muzzafir shifted himself from his pillows and rose in his mountainous majesty to ooze up to the "coffin." It was his ostrich-feather box, after all. He bent over and slowly stuck his fingers into each of the crescent-shaped holes, then, as Matthew held the torch over his head, peered suspiciously into its depths and tapped at all of its surfaces. Satisfied, he backed away.

"Is it as you remembered, mighty Muzzafir?" Matthew asked.

"Yes," Muzzafir allowed.

"Then I would ask a boon, O great master of slaves and men."

Muzzafir's suspicion returned. "Remember that you remain a slave, infidel. No matter your tricks. When we arrive in Tripoli, Rakik, who has been hoarding your services, will sell you at last into my keeping"—he smiled evilly—"and my pleasures."

"It is as you say, powerful Muzzafir." Matthew bowed with great deference. "Tonight I ask only the loan of your sword—and the swords of your men. Many swords. Enough to fill all these holes." Matthew had made dozens of holes. He needed dozens of swords. "Enough to skewer with pain and to inflict death upon the African woman who chooses to lie within . . . if the magic should fail."

Muzzafir's eyes lit with anticipation. The occasion was irresistible. He reached for his sword and offered it to Matthew. "I will grant this boon with pleasure."

Matthew bowed again as he grasped the handle. Then he watched Muzzafir snap his fingers. In a moment, the ground before them was littered with more swords than he could have dreamed of. Swords of pain and death. In his hands, swords of freedom. Matthew rose from his deep bow of thanks as Muzzafir returned to his pillows and snapped his fingers again. "The magic! I will have the magic begin now!" They were his swords, too.

Matthew confronted the assembled once more. "You will have the magic, honored guests. I call out for Afua, Queen of the Green Forests of the South, to fill this box, to partake of this magic!"

Asanti himself led his wife to the box. She had fixed her hair and greased her body. In the fire-light she stood proudly for a moment, god-desslike—and slim enough from her desert march to avoid the sharp blades he must thrust around

her, Matthew fervently hoped. Matthew took
Afua's hand and helped her settle within the box.
Asanti grasped one end of the lid, Matthew the
other. Together they lowered it over the woman.
She gave one frightened gasp; then there
remained only silence. The two stepped away as
the drums sounded again. Asanti took control of
the torch, while Matthew had no choice but to
grasp the first sword, Muzzafir's sword. He held
it dramatically over his head.

"Afua, daughter of grace and life. Afua, wife of
Asanti, mother of Asanti's son—I beg your forgiveness!" He plunged the sword through the
first hole. A scream of fear erupted from the box.
Or was it a scream of pain? Matthew felt sweat
beginning to bead his face. Had he pierced her?
He couldn't know. He must continue. He
reached for the second sword. And the third.
And the rest. Each plunge drew a gasp from the
audience and a titter from Muzzafir. When there
were no more holes to fill, Matthew stood back
and wiped his face. He reached to Asanti for the
torch. The African's eyes were rimmed white with
terror, but he uttered not a sound. Instead, he
evaporated into the shadows.

"Muzzafir!" Matthew roared. "Rakik! Is it your
pleasure to inspect *The Coffin of Death* before the
swords are removed?"

Once more Rakik refused, but Muzzafir returned with even more enthusiasm than before. His eyes glinted as he made a full circuit of the box, looking now like nothing so much as a vast, elongated porcupine. "This is a fine trick. A wonderful trick. I will remember it."

Matthew shuddered at the thought.

When Muzzafir returned to his place, the drums returned too.

"Asanti!" Matthew called. "Your wife awaits you!"

As the African reappeared, Matthew pulled the swords, one by one, from the box. The lid was raised. Matthew held the torch over the opening, afraid to look at what he had wrought. *Please, Robert-Houdin. Please let your trick have worked.* He finally forced his eyes open. Afua lay within, in a dead faint. Asanti gently wrapped his arms around his wife and lifted her out. Her eyes opened and she moaned.

Matthew stared. She was alive. There were drips of blood trickling from her arm and leg. He'd grazed her, but she was *alive.*

Asanti set his wife upon her legs and she stood, hanging on to him for strength.

"She lives!" the crowd exulted. "The woman lives!"

Matthew sank against the coffin as cheers rang

around him. Then he remembered the purpose of the entire exercise. *The swords.*

"Let the dance begin!" he bellowed.

Out of nowhere, masses of unchained Africans surged through the central aisle. Matthew remembered his next effect just in time. He bent to light the gunpowder surrounding the great dancing circle. The black people sprang over the fire like gazelles, carrying drums cobbled together from cooking cauldrons and food vats. The drums began again, until there was a wild frenzy of leaping, singing, writhing, and shouting within the circle. Matthew watched it build. Watched as Asanti and his special followers danced closer and closer to the forgotten swords. *Now*, he thought. *Now!*

Asanti read his mind. Suddenly there were swords raised in the hands of the slaves. Swords being turned on the unsuspecting masters. But there was something else, too. Something unplanned. A wild howl from the ramparts jerked Matthew's attention upward. His cheetah! His cheetah was outlined against the sky . . . leaping down from the walls of the fortress . . . leaping where? Matthew twisted to find Rakik behind him, the curved blade of his sword raised over his head.

"Your magic is nothing but deceit!" Rakik

growled. "You will pay for it with your life!"

Matthew had used up his supply of cleverness for the night. He froze in defeat, his eyes locked on the blade above him as the cat completed the arc of its leap. Onto Rakik's head. As the sheik fell beneath the claws with a shriek of horror, Matthew spun again. This time it was toward the high-pitched squeals of terror emanating from Muzzafir's throat. Matthew stared into the sky above Muzzafir. A huge, hewn rock was gracefully, inexorably tumbling from the crumbling tower toward the rigid slavemaster. As it collided with his skull, Matthew heard a cackle from on high.

"A present I send to accomplish right's end."

Offerings from the *jinn*! From Father Moses! Perhaps a little too enthusiastic an offering from Father Moses. A chip from his present glanced Matthew and he stumbled backward to clutch at his head as the Night of Nights completed its unfolding around him.

Chapter Fourteen

THE BLOODY CRESCENT MOON OF THE SAHARA squinted down at Matthew as he tidied up some of the night's loose ends. He turned from issuing another set of orders to find his great dog loping across the courtyard and into him. Down Matthew toppled. He gently pushed away the enthusiastic wet tongue to sit up on the hard-packed dirt.

"What brought on that hero's welcome? And where have you been all this time, Gin?"

172

"He was assisting me, *nasrani*." Above him, Hussein offered a hand and Matthew accepted it, struggling to his feet. "There was much to do outside the fortress walls. The caravan had to be assembled. Directions had to be given—"

The main purpose of the Night of Nights returned to Matthew. All its vivid drama returned, too. "Asanti and his people—when they slipped away, I had this mess to clean up. The bodies . . . the prisoners. Tell me how their escape went! What happened?"

Hussein grinned slyly. "In the madness of the final moments of your revels, I and a few waiting Africans managed to release another fifty riding camels, right through the main gates of Zuila! Asanti and his people are miles away by now, Allah be praised."

"But how will Asanti find his way?" Matthew asked.

Hussein straightened his wiry frame. "I, Hussein, desert navigator of some renown, set his course by the stars. Your chief need only follow these stars. He must travel by night and rest during the heat of the day. The caravan has water and provisions enough to reach the next oasis. After that Asanti and his people are in the hands of Allah."

Matthew rubbed his head. He'd had to ignore

the ache, but there was quite a large bump hiding under his turban from that fragment of Father Moses' rock. Right over the faculty for Hope. A vision of green, wet forests overcame him for a moment. "The Africans will succeed." He sighed, but not from despair.

"Asanti said one final thing, *nasrani*. It was a special message for you."

"What? Don't just stand there keeping me in suspense!"

Hussein's answer was laced with a certain pride. "Asanti bade me relate to you that his next two sons will be named in your honor: 'Matthew' and 'Morrissey.'"

It was Matthew's turn to grin. "That's a very fine message." As he peered into the night, other questions popped into his mind. "What became of the Tuareg and the Arabs who escaped our trap? I couldn't be everywhere, and I was busy dealing with the dead." He pointed to a dark pile nearby.

Hussein nodded. "We will bury them and the African martyrs as best we can in the morning." He gestured approvingly toward a white-robed, huddled mass at the far end of the courtyard. "It is satisfying to see how your revenge has become more Arabic in nature. How fitting for those slavers to be wearing Muzzafir's shackles."

Matthew smiled ironically. "A sense of humor sometimes helps. But the others? Those who escaped?"

"As for the rest, those not among your captured or fallen . . ." Hussein shrugged philosophically. "When Tuareg and Arab alike accosted me outside the fortress walls, I pointed out to their new leaders one thing."

Matthew bit. "What might that have been?"

"That which is completely evident, *nasrani*. With Rakik and Muzzafir dead, *they* were now in charge. And who was responsible for this unexpected elevation in status? . . . To receive mercy from those with much to gain is sometimes possible."

Matthew laughed, then stopped. "Where does that leave us? You and I and Dr. Cornwall?"

"There were negotiations, you must understand. It was a help that desert raiders are a superstitious lot. They appear to hold you, for once, in a certain awe."

Matthew squared his shoulders.

"I will not ask from whence you called up that giant cat, or the madman, either, but the hidden presence of these creatures—perhaps to strike out once more at your calling—will be a strong reason for the desert men to keep their promises."

Hussein's sharp eyes focused on a scuttling motion near his feet. *Splat.* He glanced up.

"Another piece of vermin no longer with us. . . .
And then there is Dr. Cornwall," he continued.
"Those he saved from the scorpions have chosen
to cast their lots with us." Hussein paused before
adding the decisive fact. "With them to help, and
a small caravan of our own original camels and
supplies, I believe we can safely make our way to
Siwa at last."

Hussein had been as busy as Matthew. The new
revelations were amazing, and it took Matthew a
long moment to register them all and ask his next
question. "When?"

"When Dr. Cornwall recovers from his struggle with malaria. That will give us all a few days to
rest and plan."

"Dr. Cornwall—" Matthew felt his body tense
for action again. "In the press of events I nearly
forgot about Dr. Cornwall! I must give him his
quinine. Where is he?"

"Where you left him, shivering with fever atop
your hill."

Matthew bent to rub Gin's head. "Come on,
boy. Let's go rescue the doctor from his sacrificial
mound."

When morning arrived, Matthew found himself
waking upon a proper mat within the walls of a

tent. It was the first time since he'd caught the glint of burnished steel peeking over the rim of that great dune ages ago. He relished the novel comfort, then twisted in his blankets to find Asa B. Cornwall lying next to him, eyes wide open.

"You're awake, sir! How do you feel?"

"As if I could wring out the fever sweat from my clothing and irrigate the entire Sahara." He propped himself weakly on an elbow while Matthew reached for the next dose of quinine. "Hussein claims malarial bouts go in cycles. Two or three terrible days broken by a few moments of clarity before it disappears to attack as it wills, when it wills, throughout the rest of your natural life. . . ."

Matthew administered the medicine with lots of water while the moment of clarity remained. After relating the night's events to the doctor and making him as comfortable as he possibly could, he emerged from the tent.

It was another clear, hot desert morning. What would such heat do to the pile of bodies resting through the night? Matthew set off in that direction, only to find the dead gone. Where? Surely this rock-hard earth could not have been broached that quickly. When he glanced toward the far corner of the courtyard, he received his answer. Hussein had risen even earlier and was busily directing a crew of shackled Arabs. They seemed to be throwing objects down Matthew's magical hole. He trotted over.

Hussein nodded recognition. "The solution has been found, *nasrani*. The last of the bodies are even now descending into your tunnel. In a moment both ends will be sealed. The burial will be complete."

Matthew watched the final rigid form being lowered. "There were too many."

"It's no longer of import, *nasrani*. Here within the secret passageways of Zuila, Arab, Tuareg, and African alike will share eternity together. Perhaps they will grow in understanding."

Matthew continued to watch as the tunnel was closed and his mound was slowly shoveled back into its original home. Someday other travelers might venture upon the catacomb and wonder . . . He shook his head. So much death. He and the doctor and Hussein had to make it back to civilization. Asanti had to reach his green forests, or the effort would all have been in vain.

Hussein touched his shoulder. "Come, *nasrani*. This is finished, but there is still much to do."

By midmorning what remained of the Arab caravan was wending its way from the gates of Zuila, heading north to complete its journey to Tripoli. The Arabs would be poorer for the loss of the slaves, but still carried impressive loads of salt and ivory. Matthew and Hussein watched the departure from atop the ramparts of the fortress. Hussein was shaking his head.

"We could have had some of that salt and ivory, *nasrani*. It would have made us rich in Cairo."

"No," Matthew disagreed. "We want none of their ill-gotten gains."

Hussein sighed. "Speak for yourself, *nasrani*."

"Besides," Matthew added, "we want to give the Arabs no excuse to change their minds and pursue us to Siwa. Anyway—" He smiled and pulled something from beneath his robes. It was Muzzafir's iron key, the key to the shackles. He flourished it. "It will take a good long while for them to figure out how to remove those chains without this. A few days of such medicine and they may begin to rethink heading south for another *razzia*, another slave raid."

"You are still young," Hussein murmured. "You still believe the world can be changed."

"Yes." Matthew said it proudly. Then he stood quietly beside Hussein and watched as Rakik's old band of raiders, the blue men, slipped from Zuila to head west, farther into the Black Stone Desert.

The fortress of Zuila baked under the hot sun through the course of the long afternoon as the survivors slept. It baked silently, with only Matthew slipping between Cornwall's tent and across its courtyard to the castle to give assistance to the recovering patients. The silence became eerie, and Matthew began to imagine voices from Zuila's past rising around him. The voices seemed to be calling him as something—or someone—had before. He finally surrendered and returned to the ramparts where he had stood that first night. The night he'd had his third encounter with his *jinn*; the night he'd met Father Moses. He stared across the desolation of the Black Stone Desert, then began to concentrate.

He was in the exact spot. His cat had appeared from the tower—*there*. Matthew turned. Father Moses had materialized *there*. Matthew carefully paced the distance to the next tower, took a deep breath, fumbled with the match and candle he'd brought, shielded the fresh flame, and plunged inside. *Absolutely nothing mysterious about all this*, he tried to convince himself. *Nothing mystical.* Zuila just happened to be riddled with underground passageways and secret chambers. He descended.

The descent took even longer than he'd remembered. When he reached bottom, the coolness of the deep earth surrounded him. Also surrounding him was a maze of passageways. Which turn had Father Moses taken? He could get lost in here. So lost that his bones would be keeping company with those he'd watched being buried only this morning. Matthew heard Cornwall's voice. *Think logically, lad.*

He thought logically. Then he set down his candle and removed his robe. He picked at its hem till he'd pulled out a thread. He kept pulling. Soon his robe was shorter, and he held a ball of white cotton string. Matthew retrieved the candle and set off down the first corridor, leaving a trail of string behind him.

The first passageway led seemingly nowhere. Matthew retraced his steps and paused to leave a distinguishing soot mark at its entrance. He entered the second tunnel. When the smell of putrefying bodies enveloped him, he backed out in a hurry. The third tunnel led to the treasure room.

He stooped to duck under the low stone lintel of the gaping doorway and waited a moment, breathing the ancient air, feeling his heartbeat quicken. *More light.* He studiously avoided the center of the room and its contents while he made his way around the edges, lighting the half-gutted candles set into wall alcoves. At last he allowed himself to look at the horde. *It's only metal,* he told himself. *Shiny metal. Magnificently worked shiny metal.* Was it the gold that had been calling him back? Did he really care about the gold? He and the doctor had always managed . . . yet their war chest *was* depressingly low. . . . Would he be steal- ing if he took a few of these lovely things? From whom? Who even knew of their existence, except for—

"I see the gold glint in your eye."

Matthew wheeled away from the treasure. "You!"

Father Moses' humpbacked form had materi- alized out of the very air, from nowhere. But today he was leaning heavily on a stick. His wiz- ened face—the most ancient face Matthew had ever beheld—cracked into a smile. One eye was clouded white, the other still sharp. "I told you true when first we met: the treasure is yours, for good to get."

"But it's too precious!" Matthew protested. "The tales it must tell—the history! It belongs in a museum like the Louvre!"

The old man shuffled a step forward and touched Matthew. When he spoke again, his voice changed. "Then this thing you must do. My days are numbered, this is true—" He coughed hard, then stopped and caught his wheezing breath.

His fingers had a palsied shake to them as he groped for something around his neck and with effort pulled it over his head. He beckoned Matthew closer. When he came, Father Moses formally—as if knighting him—slipped the golden chain over his head. Matthew touched the finely worked gold cross suspended from the chain.

"This belonged to Justinian of the Byzantine Empire," croaked the old man. "Now it is yours." A new fit of coughing overcame him and Father Moses stumbled aside to spit up blood. Matthew rushed to him.

"You should be resting, sir. Let me take you into the castle. Fix some broth for you—"

"No." Father Moses backed away. "Too long from humans I have been. I cannot face them—or their sin. . . . That rock I pushed sapped my strength, but the story—my story—must be told at length. . . . Take the treasure trove. Take as much as you can hold—" The old man collapsed.

"Father Moses! Sir! I need to thank you for what you've done. I want to hear *your* story! Don't go away. . . . There's been too much death already."

Matthew bent over the figure to pick up a skeletal wrist. He applied pressure to ancient veins, but could feel no pulse.

"Father Moses!"

Matthew collapsed to his knees among the useless golden treasures. It was too much. Too much drama. Too much death. Too much of everything. The weight of the past days nearly crushed him. He bent his head and cried.

Chapter Fifteen

MATTHEW HID HIS SORROWS AND HIS SECRETS UNTIL the doctor recovered from his malaria bout. At last, under cover of darkness, he led Cornwall up to the ramparts and to the second tower from the corner. Cornwall was still weak, and paused to catch his breath at the entrance.

"Are you sure you want to drag me down there, lad?" He peered skeptically into the inky chasm. "Are you certain it wasn't all a desert dream? Like your *jinn*? Perhaps a touch of

185

malaria. I can personally vouch for the oddness of fever dreams. . . ."

"My *jinn* wasn't a dream, sir. And you yourself touched Justinian's coin—and my cross." Matthew felt for the heavy cross and chain hidden beneath his clothing, next to his skin, where he knew it would have to remain until they returned to Christian lands. The brief contact gave him courage to plunge into the blackness with only the pinprick of his candle, hauling Asa B. Cornwall behind.

Matthew's first concern after he'd illuminated the chamber was the body of Father Moses. Wanting to do the right thing, he'd laid out the old man with reverence along one wall, placing the gnarled hands across his chest, fingers carefully wrapped around a large golden cross from the hoard.

Cornwall gasped once at the glittering gold, shook his head disbelievingly, and followed Matthew to Father Moses. He knelt beside the body to knowingly feel the old man's skull, only to gently set the head down again.

"The tales this one could tell," he murmured. "Perhaps it wasn't a dream. None of it." He glanced up at Matthew. "Don't worry, lad. I haven't brought my calipers. I suspect the desert has mellowed me. One begins to learn the difference between fanaticism and grace."

He studied the leathery arms protruding from the old man's robes. "I think he was half mummified already when he died. In this chamber the process will complete itself. Who knows? We may be looking at the remains of the last of the desert hermits . . . an unsung saint." Cornwall stroked a hand, then creaked to his feet. "As for his treasure trove—"

"You see, it does exist! But what's to be done with it, sir?" Matthew asked. "Father Moses specifically gave it into my keeping. To do the best good, is what I think he was trying to say."

Cornwall rubbed at what remained of his jowls after the fever. "For starters, I believe it's best that our traveling companions know nothing of this, lad."

"Not even Hussein?"

"Not even Hussein. The average man would be overcome by gold lust. And really . . ." He reached for a small painting set within a jewel-encrusted gold frame, then dangled an earring from his other hand. "This sacred icon of Christ's mother; such jewelry—the only monetary value to be had in any of it would be by extracting the jewels, melting down the gold—"

"Melting down these treasures!" Matthew was outraged. "All the history would be gone! The art and craftsmanship. The stories—"

"Precisely. So we'll quietly pack up a reasonable amount—a selection of the best, as it were—and try to get it back to Paris, and the Louvre."

Matthew heaved a sigh of relief. "I hoped you'd see it that way, Doctor."

"Except for a few of the coins, of course," Cornwall continued. "There are more than enough of them to go around. More than enough to rebuild our war chest."

Matthew struggled within himself, and finally shrugged. Father Moses had willed everything to him, for some unknown reason. Maybe that reason was yet to be discovered and the coins would help.

"And Hussein will be given a decent share when we've safely arrived back in Cairo," Cornwall concluded.

Matthew smiled. "It's all right, then."

Within the silent embrace of Father Moses, the two began making their inventory.

On the fifth morning after the Night of Nights, the last caravan wended its way from the fortress of Zuila. This one headed east-northeast, out of the Black Stone Desert and back into the dunes of the great Sahara, cutting a straight line through the sands toward the oasis of Siwa.

Matthew exulted when the first dune grew large before them. He was astride his old friend Ali once more, with Gin contentedly padding by their side. "Look, Ali! Look, Gin! It feels like coming home!"

Ali delicately placed one foot, then the next, upon the shifting grains. He stretched his long neck and snorted with something akin to camel pleasure. Having paid his respects, he plodded on. Cradled within the old rhythm, Matthew beamed. They'd survived Zuila. They'd made it out of the Black Stone Desert. In a matter of only a week or two they'd arrive in Siwa at last. Never mind the new scars he and the doctor had added to their bodies and souls. Soon they'd be in Siwa. If the oasis answered at least some of the doctor's questions, from there maybe they could even think about going home. To their real home. That stopped Matthew's rambling thoughts for a long moment.

Where might their real home be? Paris? . . . New York? Matthew rubbed the grit of sand from his sun-bronzed face, considering. Did he and Asa B. Cornwall truly belong anywhere? Or had they become eternal wanderers? Matthew's mood darkened with the idea, and he rode on with it weighing upon his shoulders all the way to their night camp. But once in camp he wasn't given the opportunity to stew in his new gloom. Hussein was once more in full command, and glorying in it.

"Why do you sit and stare, *nasrani*? Get off that useless beast and help with the work. There are few enough of us now, and you have learned the ways." The guide stopped as Matthew made no show of moving from Ali. "Or would you prefer I carry a whip like the blue men?"

"No. Definitely not." Matthew slid from Ali with a rueful grin. Maybe Hussein was his family, good-naturedly bossing and nagging him the way his mother used to. Maybe the desert was his true home for now. Maybe he and the doctor would have to remake their home and family wherever they went. Maybe—as their old friend Voltaire used to say—that could be for the best in this best of all possible worlds.

Siwa Oasis was a burst of color and life almost unbelievable after months within the monotones of the desert. As it grew ever larger before them, Matthew's eyes widened. He'd pictured the oasis as being a few wells surrounded by drying palms. Or maybe something just a tad bigger—say, the size of Zuila. But Siwa Oasis spread out for miles. First there were scattered palms, next groves of olive trees. Small springs began popping up, and flocks of grazing sheep. Beyond the sheep a clump of camels ran faster than Matthew believed a camel could run. And in the distant, even greener core were hills dotted with holes, brown crumbling ruins, odd walls of stone. As they progressed ever nearer to the center, mud huts sprang up, people appeared . . .

Matthew gasped. *Women* appeared. Well, at least they were there. As for actually appearing—they were bundled up to the eyes and down to their toes more thoroughly than any veiled Tuareg. But they were women, moving with a grace that Matthew had almost forgotten existed—the grace Asanti's emaciated people had had starved out of them. Children appeared, too. They scampered from the huts to trail after the caravan, jabbering in a language Matthew had never heard.

"Hussein!" he called ahead. "What are these children speaking?"

"A Berber dialect, *nasrani*, known by few outside of this oasis. Siwa is very ancient, and has few visitors. You will hear some Arabic, but badly spoken."

"As badly spoken as my Arabic, Hussein?"

"It is impolite to seek compliments, *nasrani*," the guide shot back. "You know you speak like a native. Allah only knows how you came upon this gift."

Matthew grinned. It was one of the few compliments he'd ever received from Hussein, and worth waiting for. Wrapped in a cocoon of well-being, he rode Ali into the center of the town.

Hussein raised his arm for a halt outside a mud-walled caravanserai. Matthew and their odd complement of helpers had just begun the unloading chores when a slim figure darted from a nearby coffeehouse.

"Matthieu! You are alive! *Mon dieu*, Matthieu—"

That voice— He spun. "Nathalie? Here in Siwa?"

"Yes, yes, yes! Papa had business, so we took a boat, then came the short way from the sea, and—"

Words failed both of them, and they only stared at each other. Nathalie finally spoke again.

"You have changed, Matthieu. You are—how should I say—bigger. Older."

Matthew let out his breath. "And you are even lovelier, Nathalie."

They stared for another long minute. They both opened their mouths for the next words, but they were stillborn.

"Nathalie!"

She froze. "It is Papa, wishing me back under his wing. Why he even allowed me to accompany him on this journey, if I am to be forbidden to show myself, to even speak—"

"Nathalie!" The voice was more peremptory.

"I must go, but we will meet again."

Matthew caught her arm. "Where? When?"

She stared straight into his eyes. "At midnight. Where the oracle lives."

He relinquished her arm, but his hand was still tingling when Cornwall bustled up. "That exotic young lady. She looked the spitting image of Abdullah Abed's daughter—"

"She *is* Abed's daughter."

The doctor beamed. "Splendid. That means her estimable parent must be in the environs. What in the world could have brought him to Siwa in the heat of summer? Well," he rambled on, "nothing for it but to beard the man and find out." And Asa B. Cornwall set off for the doorway into which Nathalie had disappeared.

Matthew watched longingly, wanting nothing so much as to follow. Hussein, however, arrived first.

"The beasts deserve a well-earned rest, *nasrani*. I have arranged rooms for us within the caravanserai, and hired some of the Siwan boys to see to our animals. But first we must transport our belongings. We cannot leave them in the streets, the way we leave them outside on the desert sands."

Matthew roused himself from thoughts of midnight. Certainly a number of carefully selected panniers could not be left in the street. They couldn't be left in anyone else's keeping, either. He began unloading and transporting the golden hoard.

Matthew stood near the walls of the ruined temple under a gibbous moon. The light was eerie, and he could believe that fortunes had been told here, could almost hear the hollow, ancient voice of the oracle of the god Amun prophesying to Alexander. He shoved a hand beneath his robes to feel for the trinkets he'd placed in his pocket. Had it been wise of him to bring them? Would the gift be accepted? Would Nathalie even come?

Then out of the shadows her figure appeared. She'd thrown a cloth over her head, wrapped around her face in the fashion of the Siwan women. Matthew stepped forward.

"Nathalie?"

"Matthieu!"

She floated to him under the moonlight and raised a hand to his scar. "It is still there. That has not changed."

"No." He unwrapped her headdress. "And you have not changed in certain ways, either. I think

194

you hold mystery within you. Do you live always in the shadows?"

She smiled as he touched her face in turn. "After you left Cairo, I was banished to my room for weeks. When I became wan, Maman begged my father to set me free. That is why I am here, but in a few more days—oh! To think our paths might not have crossed! In a few more days the great camel races my father came to attend will be finished, and we will be gone again, to Tripoli."

"So we have just a few days. And I'll be busy digging with Dr. Cornwall." Matthew decided to take the chance. He reached beneath his robes for his pocket. "I've brought you a present. They're very old, but in my heart I heard them cry out to live again—" He paused. He'd gone over the speech so many times in his mind. *Finish it.* "On you, they will live."

The moon shone on the Byzantine earrings in his hand. Its rays made the gold and dangling jewels almost throb.

Nathalie hesitated. "Emeralds?" She reached out and set an earring in one lobe, then the other. She tossed her head. In that instant Matthew felt drawn back thirteen hundred years to Constantinople. He could see Nathalie gliding through the gilded court of Justinian, her head high and proud. Belonging.

195

She smiled acceptance. "But I have no gift for you . . . except—" The young woman leaned forward and offered her lips to Matthew. His heart stopped beating for a precious moment. Then she spun and fluttered off into the shadows once more.

"Nathalie!" But she was well and truly gone.

Idiot! he chastised himself. He'd let her disappear again. And he'd learned little more about her, or if he'd see her again. All he'd really learned was that he was smitten. Hopelessly. He turned to stare at the ruins behind him.

"Prophesy, O Oracle. Tell me what's to become of this affair!"

Matthew could have sworn he heard an answering chuckle. But maybe it was only the scuttling of lizards across ancient stone. He sighed, and slowly made his way through deserted streets back to the caravanserai.

Chapter Sixteen

In the half light just before dawn, Matthew noticed something he'd missed in his first exuberance over arriving in Siwa. He'd missed the skulls. Donkey skulls. After spotting the first one, he discovered they were everywhere about the town: hiding in the byways of crooked alleys; mounted over gates; leering down from mud walls. Donkey skulls impaled on long sticks. He shivered and turned to Hussein, trailing behind him.

"These skulls . . ."

Hussein rubbed blearily at his unshaven jaw. "Against the evil eye. Siwans take no chances."

Perhaps it was only the chill of the early hour, but another tremor passed through Matthew. Skulls might be his business, but not this kind, used in this way. He avoided the next one and increased his pace to catch up with Dr. Cornwall.

Asa B. Cornwall wasn't taking any chances either. He'd finally made it to Siwa, and he was going to do his job right. Shortly after dawn he and Matthew and a crew of Siwan men under Hussein's direction were already working at the Temple of the Oracle of Amun. Cornwall stood back to oversee the beginnings of progress with a proprietary air.

"This is not at all like skulking around cemeteries in the old days, eh, lad? Here we've got the headman's permission, and plenty of men eager to work for their wages. Amazing what a little *baksheesh* will do." He rubbed his hands with enthusiasm. "We're going to excavate until we find something, Matthew. I can feel it in my bones. Someone's here."

"But the missing mausoleum in Alexandria—" Matthew tried.

"Tosh. Alexander's remains were moved so

many times, everyone finally lost track of them. And what better place for him to end than where he began?" Cornwall beamed as the first load of dirt was carried past them in a great basket on the head of a laborer. "Yes, indeed. Beginnings and endings. I truly believe Siwa is going to answer all of our questions."

"I hope so, sir. I truly do." Matthew left the doctor to his dreams and went off to inspect the acropolis in the light of day.

All work stopped for lunch and rest during the worst heat of the afternoon. Cornwall was propped against a mighty stone column in the shade of what remained of the temple roof. He was gently snoring. Matthew brushed a few flies from his face and braved the sun to continue his explorations. He climbed to a pinnacle above the ruins to get his bearings. Behind him was the dozing town, while past the temple mound in the plains below were groves of date palms that ranged as far as a line of distant parched hills. The mountains rising beyond were the limit of the horizon, the limit of the oasis. The sun was so fierce that the sky above everything was bleached white, rather than blue. Matthew squinted through the glare, searching for he knew not what. Not far off, his eye caught a glint. Water? One of the many springs of the oasis?

What he discovered was a deep pool of bubbling water nestled within the palms.

"Eureka!" he crowed, scaring away a few perching birds. In moments he'd flung off his clothing and was blissfully submerged in the pool. This is what he'd dreamed of all those long days journeying across the sands. *Water.* And here it was. Not exactly enough to launch a ship in; not even enough for a good swim—but enough. He plunged under its coolness again, then regretfully pulled himself out to return to the temple. By the time he arrived, he was hot and dry again, his momentary euphoria dissolved in the heat. It didn't help that when he found Cornwall in the same spot—still snoring—he found something else as well.

"No!"

His exclamation woke the doctor. "What is it, Matthew?"

"There. Right above your head!"

Something had been added in Matthew's absence. It was another of those impaled skulls.

"Well, well," Cornwall commented. "The word does get around. Someone has discovered we're searching for skulls. A kind thought, but not the correct mammal, I fear."

"But sir, this has nothing to do with Alexander—"

"Be kind enough to rouse the workers, lad. Time is marching on, and we've much to accomplish."

Three days passed excavating the depths of the oracle's temple. Three days passed without another sight of Nathalie. The only discoveries were new donkey skulls mounted around the dig each morning. The Siwans might be hungry for their wages, but they still weren't comfortable with unearthing the dead. Matthew became increasingly uneasy. His experience with *jinn* had taught him that not all superstitions were foundless. *Something* unpleasant was in the offing. Cornwall, however, was oblivious to everything but his quarry.

"Did I ever mention Plutarch's comments in his life of Alexander, Matthew?" He didn't wait for a response, just chattered on over the sharp thuds and clinks of dozens of men wielding shovels and picks against dirt and stone. "Alexander could be munificent. He gave away a hundred fortunes to his soldiers. Then again, he also speared his best friend Clitus through the heart in a drunken rage."

"Who needs a friend like that?" Matthew

asked. Try as he might to equal the doctor's enthusiasm, his patience was wearing thin on the subject of Alexander the Great.

"An ignoble thought, lad. Majesty always has its little quirks." Cornwall gazed off across the distant plains as if summoning up visions of his hero. "Alexander would footrace only with kings, yet he said that if he were not the lord of the known world, he'd choose to be like the penniless Greek philosopher Diogenes. You remember, he's the one who wandered around the streets looking for an honest man."

"And lived in a tub," Matthew added. "I really can't see Alexander the Great living in a tub."

"Perhaps not, but never forget he was a man burning with ambition, grappling with his demons like the rest of us—"

"*Effendi!*"

The shout ended Cornwall's musings.

"*Effendi!* Something has been found!"

The doctor gasped, then sped toward the excitement. Matthew trotted after him.

The laborers had opened a gaping hole on one side of the temple sanctuary. Cornwall himself had chosen the spot in which to begin because of the curious markings worn nearly smooth on the stone pavers of the floor. Now the paving stones were cast aside, and one of the Siwans was eight feet down, bending over a dark pile of encrusted rubble beginning to emerge from the earth.

"Out of the pit!" Cornwall commanded. "The discovery could be fragile. I'll deal with it myself." Hussein translated the order, and in a moment the doctor was deep in the hole himself, yelling to Matthew. "Hand me one of those brushes! A soft one. And a spade!"

Matthew sent down the tools, then hunkered over the edge to watch the progress. Around him, curious Siwans did the same. Cornwall fastidiously chipped and brushed, chipped and brushed, till at last the shape of the objects before him emerged.

"It's a cache, Matthew!" he shouted. "A cache of weapons and body armor. The kind that would have surrounded the burial of a great warrior!"

Matthew felt the sharp intake of his breath. His earlier indifference disappeared with his excitement. He tried hard to keep that excitement within bounds. "Are you sure, sir? Could it really be Alexander at last?"

"Who else would be buried here besides the oracle? And the oracle would be surrounded by graven images, not weapons. Still—" Cornwall wiped sweaty hands on his robes, leaving damp brown streaks on the cotton. "It's going to take hours to ease out these finds without doing damage to them. Come nightfall we should have the answer."

Matthew leaned closer. "I hope so, Doctor."

Hussein and the laborers had long since grown bored with watching Asa B. Cornwall's tedious work. They'd decamped for their suppers, and the sun was rapidly setting over the oasis before Cornwall was sitting in rapture over the bits and pieces that he'd finally allowed Matthew to cart from his pit.

"Look at this, Matthew!" he exclaimed for the hundredth time. "A piece of a scabbard! Of the correct period! And a sword, hilt and all!"

Matthew, too, had grown a little dubious with the passing of the hours. "But they're all green and nasty, sir. Nothing like Father Moses' treasure."

"Bronze. That's what happens to ancient bronze. Almost like rust." He rubbed at the sword's hilt and scabs fell away. "You see! There's a design underneath, a raised design." He rubbed some more. "Good heavens! It appears to be . . ." Cornwall peered more closely. "*A ram's horn!* Matthew! That was the sign of Zeus-Amun, the symbol Alexander took as his own after meeting the oracle! This very sword could have belonged to Alexander the Great! And this—" He picked up a larger bit. "Almost half of a shield. This, too, might have been held in his very hands!"

Matthew's stomach rumbled. He was anxious to return to town for the evening meal, true. But he'd also had in mind prowling around the walled compound where he now knew Nathalie was staying with her father's entourage. Somehow the pull of the very alive young lady was becoming stronger than that of a long-dead world conqueror. "Aren't you the least bit hungry, sir?"

"Food? Who can think of food at such a time! Find me some lamps or torches. We're proceeding without the workmen. Even if it takes all night." And with that, Asa B. Cornwall threw himself back into the artifacts pit and began scrabbling in the dirt.

"Sir? Doctor?"

It was no use. Matthew had long since learned that a phrenologist in the heat of discovery couldn't be reasoned with. He headed for the equipment pile to fetch a lantern. He'd barely gotten it lit when the sun seemed to blink, then completely slid below the horizon.

"Light!" Cornwall yelled. "Where's my light?"

"On its way, sir."

Grumbling to himself about the endless day, his empty stomach, and his frustration over

Nathalie, Matthew delivered the lantern. Cornwall snatched for it and hauled it into the pit. Bent again over his task, the doctor and the light both disappeared. Matthew sighed. He really ought to bring another lantern. No sense in the doctor working half blind.

En route to fetch it, he passed the small pile of ancient objects Cornwall had been gloating over. Matthew bent for the sword—Alexander's sword?—and raised it above his head. It was cumbrous and heavy, not at all like the balanced swords of modern Arabs. And its fighting surface certainly couldn't compete with curved blades of burnished steel.

Matthew slashed the weapon through the air, then brought the tip closer to flick off more effects of the ages. He fingered the results. Amazingly, the blade's edge was still sharp enough to prick him. Matthew set the sword down to rub a little sand over the cut, the way the Tuareg did. That's when he heard the sound.

Leaping to his feet, Matthew spun in its direction. Camels were coming from the town. They were only dim shapes in the deepening twilight, but he made out two of them. Who could it be?

"Company coming, Doctor."

"Eh?" Cornwall's head popped out from behind a column. "What?"

"Camels headed this way."

"Make them go away. I don't want to see anyone. Don't want anyone messing with my discovery, either." He popped back out of sight. "Tell them I'm not here . . . absolutely no disturbances . . ." His mumble faded away.

Matthew obediently stood guard before the steps of the temple, waiting for the unwanted visitors.

Almost as suddenly as the sun had set, the moon rose. Tonight it was full, and its bright light fell squarely on the procession of two.

"Mr. Abed!" Matthew gulped. It was Nathalie's father, looking none too pleased. And behind him on the second camel was Nathalie.

Abed prodded his camel to its knees with the hilt of his whip and decorously dismounted. He'd traded his usual fez and Western clothing for the turban and robes of the desert. He wore them well, looking every inch the powerful man beneath them. He advanced on Matthew, his whip brushing him aside like an insect.

"Where is your master?"

"Dr. Cornwall?

Abed deigned to stop and turn back toward Matthew. "Of course, Dr. Cornwall. Where is he, boy?"

It had been a long time since anyone had called him *boy*. Dr. Cornwall's endearing *lad* he'd never minded. Yet Abed's *boy* raised his hackles alarmingly.

"He's not here."

"Then why are you?"

Matthew stiffened his spine. "I'm guarding the site."

Abed stared up and down Matthew's form, the whip in his hand trembling with some unknown fury. "Then it's you I'll deal with directly. I'll tend to the doctor later." He turned. "Nathalie! Dismount and approach!"

Matthew watched Nathalie do her father's bidding. As she crossed the courtyard before the temple, the rising wind blew her loosely wrapped head scarf to her shoulders. Dark hair swept down her back, and the earrings—his earrings—glinted in the moonlight. As she tentatively paused, Matthew involuntarily felt his chest tighten anew at her loveliness. He had to remind himself to breathe.

"Come forward, daughter!"

Nathalie moved again, a puppet under her father's control. Abed grabbed her arm. He pointed at an earring. It jangled evocatively to its own music. "This discovery I made tonight." He ripped the earring off and thrust it in Matthew's

face. "*Where* did this come from? Are *you* responsible for this demeaning of my only daughter?"

"Demeaning?" Matthew stepped back in shock.
"How could a gift, such a gift—ancient jewels from
the Byzantine court of Constantinople—" He had
to swallow back his hurt and rising anger. "How
could such a gift demean your daughter?"

Abdullah Abed's whip lashed out, just missing
Matthew's face, but striking his shoulder. Hard.
He refused to flinch.

"She is not yet of an age to receive gifts. And
when she is, *I* will be the judge of who is worthy
of giving them. You have dishonored my only
child! You have impugned her honor!"

"Papa—" Nathalie finally spoke up. "Papa, I
told you it was completely innocent—"

"How could such jewels, such gold, be innocent?" raged Abed. "Your reputation has been
besmirched, *ruined,* by this infidel nobody! I
won't be satisfied until I learn of their source."

"But, sir—" Matthew glanced toward the temple where Cornwall was hidden, oblivious to the
turn of events. No point in seeking help from
those quarters. He tried again. "The treasure of
the Emperor Justinian is untainted, like your
daughter. I would never—"

Abed's eyes flicked. "Aha! You admit the treasure! You admit there's more!" He discarded his

daughter, to raise the whip again. "Tell me, slave. Where it came from. Where you've hidden it. Confess, or you'll regret it. Every bone in your body will regret it."

Now Matthew was really angry. He glossed right over the threat of bodily harm. "*Slave?* I'm no one's slave! Not even Sheik Ibn er-Rakik could keep me enslaved. I'm a free man, an American citizen—" Matthew stopped. The word had come entirely too easily to Abed's lips.

The whip slashed down again. "If I say you are a slave, it becomes so. Have not my ancestors, have not *I*, enslaved half the continent of Africa already?"

"*You!*" The experiences he'd survived in the desert rushed back to him. Answers to questions born with Asanti and his people were at hand. Matthew moved forward, on the offensive at last. "You're on your way to Tripoli, to the slave markets—"

Abed barked out a laugh. "It's unnecessary to dirty my hands at any slave market. The profits are brought to me. I need only issue a few orders, keep an eye on my employees. Make certain that their greed does not exceed its bounds. My web of power stretches everywhere."

Matthew stood eye to eye with the man. "You're more evil than Muzzafir."

Abdullah Abed smiled. "One of my best lieutenants."

"Not anymore," Matthew boldly informed him.

"What do you mean?" This time Abed took a step back. Then he dug in. "You evade my question. What of the treasure?"

"So it's not your daughter's honor that really concerns you, is it?" Matthew brazenly asked. "You're using Nathalie—"

The whip slashed out once more. "*Never* speak my daughter's name again! What of Cornwall? You are protecting him. He is never far from you. Produce him at once! Cornwall will tell me the truth of this matter. Cornwall could *never* lie to me."

He surely couldn't, Matthew thought. Not once Abed had tested his tortures on the doctor. His ear caught the soft clink of spade against something hard. He needed to distract Abed before he heard Cornwall's labors too. He needed to protect his friend.

Enough confrontation. Now it was time to consider defense, as well as a diversion. Matthew edged away from whip distance to trip over something. Without missing a beat, he grabbed it and sped toward the camels.

"Stop!" Abed cried. "How dare you—"

Matthew slid onto the saddle of the first camel, begging it to rise.

"Good fellow. Up now."

He stroked its neck, continuing his endearments, using the voice Ali loved. The camel responded. By the time Abed had pursued him to the second animal, Matthew was already urging his camel past the ruins of the oracle, down onto the plains spread out below, clutching to his chest the sword of Alexander the Great.

Abdullah Abed followed, abandoning Nathalie to the moonlight and the ghost of the oracle of Amun.

Matthew risked a quick glance over his shoulder. His heart dropped. Abed was almost upon him. And he'd had such a start on the villain. How could that be? . . . Nathalie's passing remark from his first night in Siwa returned to him, and finally made sense. Abed came to Siwa for the races. . . . He trained racing camels. . . . The man must be riding one of them now. That meant there was a chance he was, too. Matthew gave his beast a sharp prod. As if by magic, it broke out of its careful plodding gait to lope, then gallop, across the landscape.

Matthew laughed into the wind. The silhouette of the town was to his left, its minarets rising toward the stars. The ridge of mountains was to his right. And he was racing through the plains between them, going he knew not where. But he was going *fast*. He had a chance. Asa B. Cornwall had a chance.

His elation was short-lived. Abed's camel began gaining on him. Matthew kicked his mount in a new direction, off toward the nearest hill. As it grew larger in the moonlight, he saw strange holes tunneled into its slope. It was the necropolis of Jabal Almawta, the mountain of the dead. Hussein had spoken of the place. If he could make the distance, Matthew knew he could hide in one of the tombs. There were thousands carved into the stone. Abed could search days for him.

With the tombs looming ever closer came thoughts of his *jinn*. If ever there was a moment when his personal *ifrit* would be welcome, it was now . . . too late. Too late for the thought. Too late for the wish. The clatter of pursuing hooves grew louder. Abed was overtaking him.

Matthew turned to see Abdullah Abed speed ever closer. Twenty yards . . . ten. At five yards his whip flicked out. Matthew watched, mesmerized, as it curled past the face of the moon, undulating like a snake. Waited for its cutting lash. . . . But Abed hadn't angled for Matthew. Instead, he'd cleverly aimed the length of braided leather for the neck of Matthew's mount. The camel gasped, groaned, and came to a choking halt. Matthew stared at the necropolis almost before him in despair. The unwinking black holes gaped back at him. The dead would not be helping him tonight.

Too soon, Matthew felt the sharp edge of steel against his throat. Abed's dagger.

"Dismount, *slave*," he ordered. "*No one* turns his back to Abdullah Abed. *No one* steals his prize camel. *No one* refuses answers to his questions. Your chance at life flew with your escape attempt. After you've revealed all, you'll have the pleasure of bleeding your last drops of blood under the desert moon."

Matthew moved to obey, and the dagger's pressure let up. Alexander's sword was still in his lap, unseen, nearly forgotten. It set off a strange heat, and it almost seemed to be humming. No, it was a different sound that came to his ears: the deep purr of a great cat working up to a mighty growl. The growl came forth, ringing through the night. It became a cry emanating not only from the sword, but also from the necropolis before him, and the desert surrounding him.

His *jinn* lived.

Casting despair to the winds, Matthew exulted in the strength-giving roar, the fortifying vibrations. He firmly grasped the sword of Alexander the Great and in one fluid movement swung the blade through the sky in a circle that encompassed Abdullah Abed—

Nathalie was waiting when Matthew led the two camels back from the plains onto the temple mount.

"Papa, have you come to your senses? And you too, Matthieu?" She ran up to the animals. *"Papa!"* Her long shriek filled the night.

Abed was slumped over the second camel, motionless. Matthew urged his own animal to its knees. Wearily he stumbled back to the solid earth. "Nathalie . . . your father . . ."

"Papa! Speak to me!" Nathalie frantically prodded her father's lifeless body. Then she turned on Matthew.

"How could you? I trusted you, Matthieu!"

"Nathalie," Matthew tried again. "He gave me no choice, Nathalie—"

Unhearing, she flailed out in fury with fists and nails. "He's dead. You killed him. *Pig of an infidel!* You murdered my father!" Tears streamed down her cheeks as she furiously slashed at Matthew's face. "*Honorable* man. This is the return you give my father's hospitality! This is your thanks! I'll give you another scar that you'll never forget. I'll gouge out your eyes—"

Matthew caught her raging hands at last. "He cared nothing for you, Nathalie. It was the treasure he was after. He tried to murder me. For the treasure. He had his dagger to my throat—"

"*Pig! Lying pig!*"

Matthew grasped her more tightly. "He treated you like a prisoner, Nathalie—"

She pulled away to rip off the last earring and throw it to the dirt. She stamped and ground the gold and jewels into the earth. That done, she spat in Matthew's face for good measure.

"You know *nothing* of my father, Matthieu. His greatness was beyond your understanding. I'll prove my usefulness to him! I shall continue his work."

Her fury vented for the moment, Nathalie turned and defiantly marched to the first camel. Shortly she was upon its saddle, urging it to rise, leading her father's body back to town.

Matthew slowly wiped spittle and blood from his face. Then just as abruptly as Nathalie, he spun and headed for Asa B. Cornwall's hiding place.

"Dr. Cornwall, sir, I think it might be best if—"

"Matthew! Where have you been? You missed the momentous moment! The crowning achievement of my career and life! After Napoleon, of course." In the flickering light of the lantern, Cornwall proudly displayed a dirt-encrusted skull. *"Alexander the Great,"* he intoned.

"Perfect timing, sir." Matthew grabbed for the skull, then the doctor. "Let's just get Alexander wrapped up and be on our way. I strongly suspect we're about to overstay our visit to the oasis of Siwa."

CHAPTER SEVENTEEN

Matthew stood on a ship once more—this time at its stern. He wasn't juggling. He was gazing back at the port of Alexandria as it slowly dissolved into sky and water. Asa B. Cornwall leaned against the deck rail beside him, Gin standing guard over the old satchel by his feet.

"It would seem that we made good on our escape from Abed's minions, lad."

"Yes, sir," Matthew muttered.

"Why so glum? We're returning to Paris with

218

Alexander the Great! Not to mention a full war chest—even after making Hussein the richest guide in Egypt!"

"Yes, sir." Matthew sighed.

"And the Louvre—the Louvre will be the beneficiary of the best collection of Byzantine objects outside of Istanbul. Why, the French might even be pleased enough to award me one of their medals. I'd look well with one of those ribbon things around my neck, wouldn't I, lad?"

"Yes, sir," Matthew mumbled.

"Snap out of it, Matthew! That girl was her father's daughter. Trouble through and through. And besides, you're much too young for affairs of the heart anyway."

"Just because *you* never—"

"Enough." Cornwall fumbled in a coat pocket. "Here. I was admiring Justinian's trove last night, and this turned up in one of those little jewel boxes." He held his fist out to Matthew.

Matthew listlessly accepted the object. Then he looked at it. "Bigger than a coin . . . gold." He turned the medallion over. And gasped.

It was his *jinn*. His cat. Etched in full life: bared teeth, extended claws, springing at a hidden prey. "But—"

"I think you'd best take good care of that, lad. Sort of a talisman, eh? We might need his help when we take off for our next expedition."

Matthew smiled at last. "And where might that be, sir? *Who* might that be?"

Cornwall's eyes twinkled. "I've about had enough of the desert myself. I had in mind something on the order of, perhaps, Justinian?" The doctor patted wisps of hair across his bald pate as the sea wind rose. "Then again, there's farther east to consider as well. Tamerlane? Genghis Khan?"

Matthew grinned. "There's still a lot of world out there."

"And heads," Cornwall added. "Never forget the heads, young man."

Time Was Soft There

Time Was Soft There

A Paris Sojourn at Shakespeare & Co.

Jeremy Mercer

St. Martin's Press ☙ New York

www.stmartins.com

Library of Congress Cataloging-in-Publication Data

Mercer, Jeremy.
    Time was soft there : a Paris sojourn at Shakespeare and Co. / Jeremy Mercer.—1st ed.
    p. cm.
    ISBN 0-312-34739-1
    EAN 978-0-312-34739-0
    1. Shakespeare and Company (Paris, France : 1964–) 2. Booksellers and bookselling—France—Paris—Biography. 3. Bookstores—France—Paris—History—20th century. 4. Mercer, Jeremy. 5. Whitman, George, 1913– 6. Authors, Canadian—20th century—Biography. 7. Paris (France)—Intellectual life—20th century. I. Title.

Z305.S452M47 2005
381'.45002'0944361—dc22

                                                                    2005045289

10 9 8 7 6 5 4 3 2

For Julie

Author's Note

What follows is the story of how I found refuge at a peculiar old book-store in Paris and the remarkable events that occurred there during my stay.

In writing a memoir such as this, the truth becomes liquid. The true volume of all that brought me to France and all that happened at this bookstore would require a far greater capacity than these pages allow. Thus, the events have been distilled and condensed and then distilled again. Minor liberties have been taken with chronology; select inci-dents have been omitted or amended, and the name of one person has been changed at their request.

Otherwise, this is as true a story as can be told at this time.

Time Was Soft There

I.

It was a gray winter Sunday when I came to the bookstore.

As had been my habit during that troubled time, I was out walking. There was never a specific destination, merely an accumulation of random turns and city blocks to numb the hours and distract from the problems at hand. It was surprisingly easy to forget oneself among the bustling markets and grand boulevards, the manicured parks and marble monuments.

On this particular day, a thin drizzle had begun falling early in the afternoon. At first, it was barely enough to wet the wool of a sweater, let alone interrupt this serious business of walking. But later, toward dusk, the skies abruptly thundered and opened into a downpour. Shelter was needed, and from where I'd been caught near the cathedral of Notre Dame, the yellow-and-green shop sign could just be glimpsed on the other side of the river.

By then, I'd been in Paris a month, long enough to hear vague rumors about the legendary bookstore. I'd been intrigued, of course, and had often meant to visit. Yet as I crossed the bridge, with the wind whipping at my pant legs and umbrellas sprouting around me, these rumors were far from mind. My only thought was to escape the storm and idle the rainy minutes away.

Out in front of the store, a tour group bravely posed for one last round of photographs. They used thick guidebooks to shield their cameras and their teeth were clenched into chattering smiles. One woman glared from beneath the hood of a rain slicker as her husband twisted a complicated lens. "Hurry," she urged. "Just hurry."

Through the fog of the shop's main window, there could be seen a blur of warm light and moving bodies. To the left stood a narrow wooden door, its green paint wrinkled and chipped. With a faint creak, it swung open to reveal a modest delirium.

A glittering chandelier hung from a cracked wooden ceiling beam, while in the corner an obese man squeezed rainwater from his turquoise muumuu. A horde of customers circled the desk, clamoring for the clerk's attention in a loud mash of languages. And the books. The books were everywhere. They sagged from wooden shelves, spilled from cardboard boxes, teetered in tall piles on tables and chairs. Stretched along the windowsill and taking in this mad scene was a silky black cat. I swear it looked up at me and winked.

There was a sudden spray of wind as the tour group pushed inside the store. I was bounced forward, past the crowded desk, then up two stone stairs painted with the words LIVE FOR HUMANITY and through into a large central room. Here, tables and shelves overflowed with more books, two doorways led deeper into the store, and a murky skylight was set overhead. Most unusual was what this skylight cast down upon: an iron-rimmed wishing well, where a man on bended knee was clawing out coins of high denomination. As I approached, he glared up at me and quickly shielded his bounty with a crooked arm.

Giving this fellow wide berth, I entered a narrow passage and found myself surrounded by books written in what appeared to be Russian. A wrong turn took me down a dead end to a sink surrounded by stacks of yellowed nature magazines. There was a soapy razor lying on an issue featuring the jungles of Madagascar. A dab of foam added an unnatural spot to a reclining leopard.

Backing up, I arrived at a wall of German novels, then, stumbling slightly, there was another turn and a loose pyramid of glossy-covered art books. To one side was a stained-glass alcove with a bare bulb flickering inside. A woman was crouched there, muttering in Italian and trying to decipher the book titles in this shaky light.

Finally, after stepping through another doorway, I was back in the room with the wishing well. The man who plunged his hand in the coins had vanished, but now the tour group had surged ahead and laid claim to the space. Half-blinded by flashing cameras, I was jostled among wet shoulders as they herded past me and into the very labyrinth from which I'd just emerged.

It was at this juncture that I decided a café would be a calmer harbor from the storm. Making a cautious retreat past the clerk and the winking black cat, I went back out the green door. The sting of rain made me pause to reconsider, and as I stood huddled in the doorway, I noticed a wooden bookcase drilled into the wall beside the store window. The paperbacks were damp and bloated, but they cost just twenty-five francs, a sum even I could afford in those desperate days. A copy of *A Portrait of the Artist as a Young Man* edged out at me. Guessing it would be an inexpensive way to swallow time, I ventured back inside.

When it came my turn to be served, the young woman at the desk gave me a bright smile and folded open the cover of my book. With meticulous care, she stamped the title page with the crest of the Shakespeare and Company bookstore. Then she invited me upstairs for tea.

2.

I used to be a crime reporter for a newspaper in a midsize Canadian city. We liked to say we had a population of a million people, but that figure included farming communities an hour's drive from downtown. For me, a more relevant statistic was the murder rate. There were a steady fifteen or twenty a year, maybe twenty-five if things were particularly good, at least good from a crime reporter's point of view.

Mine was a foul profession. The object was to pry into the dark corners of life and drag out all that was vile and diseased for public contemplation: an infant girl raped with a flashlight, a toddler drowned in a backyard swimming pool while the baby-sitter napped, a young father crushed by a rowdy car of drunken teens. This was the daily routine, a steady stream of sorrow that gradually colored my vision of humanity and dulled my sense of compassion.

As loathsome as it might have been, it was easy enough to justify the work: It's a newspaper's duty to keep abreast of police activity; reporting tragedy helps a community better understand death and human suffering; doing so in an honest fashion dispels the rumors and half-truths that inevitably surround such events. And those wretched evenings when I found myself on the doorstep of a tear-stained mother, urging her to give me the school photograph of her hours-dead son, I consoled myself with the notion that another mother might hug her child more tightly when she saw the dead boy's picture in the newspaper the next day.

The lie was put to these rationalizations whenever murder became a topic of discussion among the crime reporters in my city. Our success was measured by how often we reached the front page of the newspaper or led the evening telecast, and we agreed there wasn't enough home-town crime drama for our liking. We dreamed of working someplace like Toronto, with fifty murders a year. One a week. Imagine that. Once, when a colleague had drunk enough beer to loosen his tongue, he com-plained bitterly that he'd been at an out-of-town wedding the weekend there were an unprecedented four gruesome murders. A pair of which had been performed with a claw hammer and left stalactites of brain on the ceiling. He couldn't believe he'd missed the fun.

At first, I enjoyed the job. The late nights at crime scenes, the treasure hunts for facts and photographs of the dead, the adrenaline of racing against deadline and competing against rival newspapers. It was a chance to muck about knee-deep in the festering side of the human soul. Every-one rubbernecks when they pass an accident; I had the dubious pleasure of standing a few feet from the scorched wrecks.

But I also took to the work for personal reasons. I happened to have my own skeletons, which made me that much more eager to dig into the closets of others. Surrounding myself with darkness and misfor-tune made me feel almost normal.

It was by the grace of an internship program that I got my start at the newspaper. I was in my early twenties and studying journalism at the local university. I'd arranged with the city editor to volunteer over the winter break, when regular newsroom staff took vacation days over the holidays and an eager body could fill important cracks. Sure enough, things quickly became interesting.

On Christmas Eve, one of the paper's senior crime reporters had been sent out to investigate an emergency broadcast that had come in over the police scanner. He called back to the office with two important bits of news. First, there were corpses. Four bodies had been discovered in an apparent case of murder-suicide. And second, this reporter was booked on a flight out of town that very evening so he could spend the holiday with his wife's family. Somebody had to take his place, and after surveying the near-deserted newsroom, the editor gave a what-the-hell shrug and called me over.

At the low-rent apartment building where the bodies had been found, I took the elevator up to the crime scene. When the doors opened, the molasses stink of decomposing flesh made me gag. At one end of the hall, reporters and television cameras gathered behind a string of yellow-and-black police tape. Beyond that tape, a uniformed officer guarded an apartment doorway veiled in protective plastic.

My job was to wait by the police line until the lead detective came out to brief the press. Once the official details of the crime were collected, the crucial task was to discover the identity of the dead family before the rival newspaper did. It was a tabloid, the sort that featured celebrity gossip and photos of almost-naked women on page three, and it had long held the upper hand when it came to the grittier details of death.

Shortly after I arrived, the doors to the elevator opened and out stepped a uniformed officer carrying bags of fast-food hamburgers. When he crossed the police line and peeled back the plastic so he could get inside the apartment, the wave of rotten air forced the reporters a collective step back. Two forensic technicians came out wearing sanitized bodysuits, hair nets, and surgical baggies on their shoes. The bottoms of those baggies were sticky with clumps of flesh. The techs stood there amid the stink and blood, calmly eating their fries and sipping their milk shakes.

The lead detective eventually emerged, tugging a blue hospital mask from his mouth so he could speak. A man had used a shotgun to kill his wife and two young children before committing suicide. It was difficult to determine which child was which because their faces had been shattered by the high-gauge shells. Matters were made worse by the fact that the thermostat had been left on high and the bodies had been decomposing for at least ten days in the overheated apartment. Though police knew the name of the family, the information would not be released until the next of kin were notified. That was it, that was all, now go have a Merry Christmas.

Nobody moved except two cameramen, who rushed back to their stations with the tape of the statement for the late news. The tabloid reporter approached the detective and began scribbling more notes. This same detective turned his back on me, saying he didn't talk off-the-record with reporters he didn't know. Lost, I called in to the paper.

"No names?" I was told to push harder.

I knocked on every apartment in the building, but this yielded nothing but an offer of a Christmas Eve gin from an elderly grandmother left lonely for the holiday. I called back to the office to try the reverse phone directory, but the family apparently had an unlisted number. I even asked the officer standing guard at the apartment for help, pleading that I was a helpless intern, but she shook her head at my presumption.

As for what came next, I attribute it to my deep desire to impress the editor and my manic competitiveness that couldn't cope with getting beaten on the story. Taking the elevator to the lobby, I found the row of cheap metal mailboxes. The box of the dead family bulged with uncollected mail. Car keys easily pop such a lock, and soon I had in my hands electricity bills, parking tickets, Christmas cards, the family's name ten times over. The detective scowled when I told him I had the name of the dead; the night editor was greatly pleased. I neglected to tell either how this information had been obtained.

It wasn't the best Christmas ever, but the feat proved to the paper I had the makings of a journalist, and as a result, I was hired as a stringer, then as a summer replacement, and finally as a full-time reporter. The incident proved to me I was of suitable disposition for the job. As opposed to being sickened by the crime scene, I was intrigued. No further proof was needed than the mailbox. Along with the phone bills and junk mail, I had found a copy of a Victoria's Secret lingerie catalog addressed to the dead woman. I took it home with me for my browsing pleasure.

———

For five long years, I worked like this, the filth and pressure taking their twin tolls. Anytime I saw a middle-aged man with a young child, I wondered if he was a pedophile in the middle of an abduction. On slow news days, I found myself rooting for murder or at least a creatively violent bank robbery so I could worm my way onto the front page. The stress of competing against the tabloid slowly devoured me, and on one occasion I was suspended from work for throwing a chair in the office after getting scooped on the story of a baby girl abandoned in a car under the broiling August sun.

In such a world, things can go bad quickly. My relationship with a good woman began to falter, then broke under the weight of my unhappiness. I couldn't bear to talk to anyone but police officers or defense lawyers or crime reporters, people who worked with the same nightmares as I did. Rather predictably, I started to drink heavily, dousing myself in alcohol most every night.

By the end, it was abundantly clear that I'd become affected by my work, seen too many crime scenes, crossed too many moral lines. There were obvious signs to get out. The drug police were taking an interest in my activities and threatening to press charges against me. I narrowly escaped being arrested for drunk driving. Then there was my shaming involvement in a scandal involving a heart surgeon and a street prostitute. But what truly inspired me to quit that job and that life was a late-night phone call.

It was December 1999, just two weeks before the much-heralded new millennium. I was in my apartment, typing up the transcript of an interview and drinking my way through a six-pack of beer. My phone rang the late side of midnight and thinking it might be an invitation for last call at one of the neighborhood bars, I answered on the first ring.

Instead, it was a thief I knew. In the past, I'd written of his exploits for the newspaper and he'd come to enjoy the celebrity the articles brought him. Sometimes, he would even add an extra detail to make the events more compelling. After several collaborations, we became uneasy friends, drinking the occasional pint together, trading gossip about the detectives, lawyers, and convicts who made up our world.

As a personal favor, earlier that year he'd provided me with explicit details of a $150,000 safe job he'd orchestrated. It was for a book I was writing, and several days before this midnight phone call, that book had been published with some of the facts he'd specifically forbidden me to use, including, most unfortunately, his name. Even though I'd somehow convinced myself I hadn't violated the spirit of our agreement, I was anxious for his reaction. It was pure fury.

He was a man accustomed to violence, a man who'd done time in maximum security alongside murderers and Hells Angels, a man known for his brawling and rages. He'd once hinted at what would happen if I betrayed his confidence: a baseball bat to my knees or some similar agony. He'd even boasted of how easy it would be to arrange, how little jail time a man faced for assault, the dozens of people he knew who were sadistic enough to slip on a ski mask and take care of the business for only a few hundred dollars.

That December night, the punishment seemed destined to be worse. Swearing loudly into the phone, he let me know I had become the most despised of street creatures, a rat, the type who sold out friends to the police, or in my case, the reading public. Out of respect, he wouldn't touch me himself. But there were others, he warned. His last words before hanging up were to watch my back.

I panicked. In hindsight, perhaps it wasn't a real death threat, perhaps I overreacted, but that night I was struck with sweaty terror. After dropping the phone to the ground, I quickly packed a bag of clothes and left for a friend's house. In the course of the next week, I quit my job at the newspaper, moved out of my apartment, broke the lease on my car, gave away most of my belongings, and twitched nervously at each approaching footstep. Then, three days before New Year's, I got on a plane for Paris and left it all behind.

3.

Paris was at its festive best that late December. A rivalry had developed between world capitals to see who could throw the best millennial party, and the city had taken to the competition with passion. Shop windows teemed with bottles of champagne and year 2000 novelty items; the Eiffel Tower had been mounted with sparkling lights and fireworks; the Champs-Elysées was lined with Ferris wheels that had been decorated by artists and sat cloaked beneath canvas until the fateful midnight struck. The lusty glow of optimism was everywhere.

But beneath this glitter, there were murmurs of distress. The historic New Year's Eve was also feared to be an ideal time for zealots and terrorists to burst forth. In the last days of 1999, there were already reports that several dozen men claiming to be Jesus had been expelled from Israel, a carload of explosives was seized at the Canadian-U.S. border, and bottled water and canned goods were being hoarded in preparation for an apocalypse. The world was in an uneasy state of alert, made worse by persistent worries that the Y2K computer bug would shut down telephone systems and knock airplanes from the sky. In Paris, the more conservative sorts were actually leaving the city for fear of riots, and one young woman I spoke with on the metro even tried to convince me to accompany her family on a retreat to the safer shores of Brittany.

Exhausted by my panicked rush from Canada, I didn't feel much of anything. After landing at Charles de Gaulle, I rented a room near Porte de Clignancourt, an African neighborhood at the northern tip of the city. The hotel was down a dog-spattered side street and the air was filled with the ceaseless throb of traffic from the Périphérique. The room itself was a grueling walk up six flights of stairs, and once inside, you could touch all four walls without moving your feet. Still, I couldn't complain. It was fit for modest budgets and provided a perfect place to discreetly regain one's bearings.

There had been scant preparation for my departure, and Paris had been chosen with only minor calculation. Having been hired by the newspaper before completing my final year at the university, I was still one credit shy of graduation. As a self-assured young reporter, I'd never imagined something so mundane as a diploma would be necessary, but now that my future was a gaping void, I thought it a good time to finish my degree. The missing credit was a French-language course, and having convinced the university to let me take lessons in France to meet my academic requirements, I booked a last-minute plane ticket for Paris.

The news that I was abandoning my apparently productive life unnerved my family, though. My parents are the epitome of decent and responsible people, my mother a manager for a technology firm and my father a guidance counsellor at a local high school. My sister and I were raised with devotion in a comfortable downtown neighborhood and were given every opportunity to succeed in life: music lessons, Little League baseball games, family vacations to the lake, and the other trappings of a middle-class upbringing. Yet, as a result of several adolescent misjudgments on my part, I had already subjected my parents to an unwarranted amount of suffering. All they wanted was a normal level of stability for their son, and I couldn't bring myself to tell them of my fresh troubles. Finally, a few days before my flight left, I confessed that I had quit my job and was leaving the country, with no set plans to return. I tried to spin enough lies to spare them worry: The job had become too depressing; I needed to explore the world before the passing of my thirtieth birthday; I didn't want to spend the first hours of the millennium waiting for somebody's holiday to be ruined by death or traumatic injury. There were shadows of suspicion, but eventually my parents accepted my story.

As for the actual cause of my predicament, although I'd survived that last week, there had been one disturbing moment. Just when I'd thought I was taking that midnight phone call a little too seriously, there was a break-in at my apartment. I'd gone back a few days after receiving the threat to gather up my belongings and prepare for the next tenant. Sometime during that day of packing and cleaning, I'd stepped out to the restaurant around the corner. When I returned, my door was ajar, a few boxes were out of place, and the butt of a cigarette was floating listlessly in my toilet. I could have convinced myself I'd left the door unlocked and hadn't remembered the exact position of my boxes, but I knew for certain I didn't smoke. Somebody had paid me an unannounced visit.

By taking a plane to Europe, I'd avoided the physical threat, but there was still a knot of problems to sort out. Foremost was money. I'd earned a generous salary at the newspaper and enjoyed modest royalties from the true-crime books I'd written on the side. Yet somehow I'd frittered it all away. Drinks and meals out most every night, winter vacations to sunny islands, a German car that wasn't really needed, a ridiculous array of computer gadgets, rack after rack of rarely played CDs. . . . For one embarrassing year, I'd even bought disposable plates, forks, and cups just to spare myself the strain of household washing.

With this lifestyle, I'd dug myself into such a hole that when the phone call came, I had exceeded the limit on my credit card and I barely had enough cash money for a bus ticket to Montreal, let alone an escape to Paris. Leaving the newspaper helped sort things out a bit, as I had several weeks in unused vacation time and I was given two thousand dollars as compensation. This got me to France and left me with some money in my pocket, but it wasn't going to last forever, maybe six weeks if I budgeted well.

It was obvious that something was going to have to be done about the future, but it would have to be done on the ground. I'd run and I'd run fast, not wanting to look back at the mess I'd left behind. I had no plans, just the loose thought to stretch my life out and try to understand how I'd ended up in such a dark spot.

By manipulated coincidence, one of my best friends was in Paris when I arrived. I'd met Dave at the university, where we both worked for the student newspaper. Those were heady times and we had become close after discovering we shared a taste for late nights. Now, Dave was taking a year away from his job reporting on the stock market to circle Europe and then snowboard in the Austrian mountains. Having received word of my difficulties, he'd detoured into France so he could greet me that first morning.

We hugged out in front of my hotel and his presence was instantly cheering. Dave was a tall, thin fellow with curly brown hair and an insatiable enthusiasm for life that was contagious. After assurances that he'd help me forget my worries, he bounded ahead, eager to show off the city as he knew it.

"Paris is welcoming you," he shouted, pointing up to where the chronic winter clouds were parting. "I've been here for three days and this is the first time I've seen the sun."

As we walked, I was awed by the consistent beauty. Even the most ordinary of intersections was graced with carved stone doorways, handsome wooden shutters, and sculpted iron streetlamps. Such decadence was a stark contrast to the place I'd left, where the predominant architectural concerns were economy and utility. The sudden change in aesthetic was one more reason to feel transported.

After a maze of these glorious streets, we arrived at the base of an enormous flight of stairs. Dave climbed them two at a time, insisting the effort would be rewarded. Sure enough, when we arrived, Paris dropped before our feet.

We were at the top of Montmartre. Behind us were the chalk domes and stone horses of Sacré-Coeur; before us lay Paris, block after block, until the buildings blurred into the horizon. You could play spot the monuments with the Panthéon, the Louvre, the Opéra, and, if you leaned out along the rails, the iron grid of the Eiffel Tower. Just twelve hours before, I'd been in the frigid snow and ice of Canada, thinking only of making it to the airport and away. Now I stood above one of the world's great cities with the sun on my face and my future a blank canvas. For the first time since that phone call, the oxygen reached the bottom of my lungs.

There was a café halfway along a cobbled side road, and even though it wasn't yet noon, we switched our order from coffees to a bottle of red wine. We sat outside, warm enough in our shirtsleeves, catching up on each other's lives.

Dave bubbled with tales of his travels. He'd been on the road for months and his eyes were wide with life beyond North America. In Sofia, he'd showered with an enchanting young poet. In Madrid, there were nights with a graffiti artist on a wayward quest to tag the great cities of Europe. In Tangier, golf balls of hashish sold for only a few dollars, and for those with Western passports, money could be earned by carrying several kilograms back on the ferry to Spain. Dave had wisely declined the offer.

As we sipped our wine, I mentioned that I, too, had faced narcotic-related temptations but hadn't been as disciplined. At the newspaper, I had done a considerable amount of work on the local medical marijuana network and earlier that year I'd accepted an offer to become a "sponsor." This meant I was one of four people who donated one thousand dollars to pay for the rent and electricity at an indoor grow room. The crop was supposed to yield twelve kilograms and each sponsor was to get one kilo as repayment for his donation, with the rest of the crop funneled back into the network of AIDS and cancer patients. I felt it was noble work and thought of it as a research project for my crime books.

Days before the crop was ready to harvest, the drug police broke down the door. Two sponsors were arrested on the spot, and the police had followed my car to and from the grow room on three separate occasions. The month before I escaped to Paris, detectives came to my office to question me, and it was only the careful work of a lawyer friend that prevented the pressing of charges. It was a black cloud over my head, one that made my decision to leave Canada that much easier to make.

The sun was high overhead now and at some point during the conversation, we'd ordered a second bottle of wine. This now stood empty, as well. We must have been a boisterous pair, for a street artist approached to complain we were scaring customers away and the waiter declined us further service.

We retired to the front steps of Sacré-Coeur and for the rest of the afternoon watched the tour buses disgorge their school groups. Dave had with him a cheerfully wrapped bottle of Christmas gin, a gift from his girlfriend back in Canada. We sipped this bottle dry, too, as the sun set orange over the evening city. At one point, Dave tripped down several steps of the long concrete staircase and was left writhing on the ground. His ankle swelled an alarming purple, but otherwise all was good with the world. That evening, I stumbled back to my hotel room, distinctly pleased to be in Paris.

New Year's Eve was a rabid parade of people, light, and noise. A few minutes before midnight, the clock the city had installed on the Eiffel Tower malfunctioned, so the great countdown was scuttled, but the fireworks filled the sky with lightning and falling stars. On the Champs-Elysées, the Ferris wheels were unveiled, and as they turned, out came soaring acrobats, spinning drums, and thousands of white helium balloons. The crowds thronged and Dave and I were pulled along in a merry chaos of kisses and champagne. Amid this enormous crowd in this foreign city, I felt weightless, drifting on the currents of life, ready for anything. When a party of Hare Krishnas came dancing past and fed Dave and me honey bread from their handwoven baskets, I even felt a tug to follow them into the unknown. In the end, all was peaceful in Paris and around the world. Despite the grim predictions, the millennium arrived with goodwill. I couldn't help but be buoyed by the thought that the happy dawn to this new era might mirror my own new beginning in life.

Then things got a little more real. The next day, there were the inevitable hangovers and a steady gray rain. The Ferris wheels were packed away, save for a mammoth contraption at la place de la Concorde that tourists rode for thirty-five francs. Dave, bad ankle and all, took the train to Austria. Paris settled back to its sober winter routines.

For the first weeks, I did little to address my future. I read in parks, toured the museums, completed my French lessons, attempted a semblance of ordered life. But I knew this couldn't go on forever. The hotel bill needed to be paid and money was dwindling. I thought of finding a job, but I didn't have work papers or any contacts in the city or even an idea of what I could do.

Depression crept over me. One lonely night, I drank a bottle of cheap wine while sitting alone by the Seine and then fell asleep on the night bus back to the hotel. I was roused by the smell of something burning. It turned out to be my hair. Sitting behind me, three large men held up a lighter and smirked wildly. The city that had once shined upon me was turning hostile.

By the end of January, desperation set in. I could afford the hotel room for only another week at most. Day after day, I walked the city, numbing the hours, waiting for something to happen, hoping there would come a sign of what I should do with my life. I was on such a walk when the skies opened in front of Notre Dame.

4.

"Tea?"

"The tea party is about to begin."

The woman introduced herself as Eve. She had a bob of dark hair, a porcelain doll's smile, and spoke English with a wisp of a German accent. Sensing my confusion, she reached across the desk and patted my arm.

"There's a tea party upstairs every Sunday."

She pointed toward the back of the bookstore. Although my first moments at Shakespeare and Company had been decidedly odd, I followed her directions. The storm raged outside, curiosity was beginning to tickle, and, it must be said, it wasn't every day a woman with such a sweet smile invited one to tea.

At the back of the store, just past the stain-glass alcove and beside the German books, there was a wooden staircase. Red-carpeted stairs led up to another book-filled room, this one decorated with a mirror and a bunk bed surrounded by children's books. An antique copy of *Alice in Wonderland* lay open on the velvet cover of the bottom bunk and a pair of slippers were off to one side.

From here, there were two doors to choose from, and I chose the one on the right. It led into a small room with more walls of books, a wooden cabinet, two beds with neatly folded blankets at their feet, and two men hunched over a portable gas burner. One was slicing an onion while the other crumbled instant noodles into a pot.

"Tea party?"

"No, no. Soup. Would you like some?" asked one of the men, proffering a bent spoon.

Too surprised to answer, I backed out of the room and considered the second doorway. Painted over the frame were the words BE NOT INHOSPITABLE TO STRANGERS LEST THEY BE ANGELS IN DISGUISE. This door led into a narrow book-lined corridor that had a window, a metal sink filled with miniature drinking glasses, and a strange wooden cubbyhole with a curtain stretched across its entrance. I paused when I heard the faint clicking of typewriter keys, but a bony hand shot out from behind the curtain and tapped on the handwritten sign pinned beside the cubbyhole. WRITER AT WORK, it read. PLEASE DO NOT DISTURB.

Mumbling apologies, I hurried to the end of the corridor and found myself in the main room on that floor. Here, every wall had a bookshelf that went two books deep; I also noted a writing desk with a typewriter perched on top, a large wooden door with black metal girding, and two more narrow beds. The front window looked down onto the entrance of the store and out across to Notre Dame.

"You're in the library."

Puzzled I hadn't noticed him when I entered the room, I now realized there was a man with short black hair and a frayed wool sweater sitting quietly on the corner of a bed. On his lap were a French grammar textbook and a French-Mandarin dictionary.

"The tea party is upstairs," he continued, pointing to the big wooden door. "Two more floors. Go, go. Many interesting people."

Beyond this door was the common staircase for the building that housed Shakespeare and Company. From above, I could hear the hum of voices mixed with the occasional clatter of plates. Two flights of stairs later, I found a gray metal door that stood ajar, but before I could knock, it swung open and a woman of breath-stealing beauty swept toward me.

"Do you have tobacco? I must have a cigarette."

This woman had deep red lips and wore three layers of skirts and a torn sweater that revealed a most delicate shoulder. I cursed myself for not smoking, sure it would stand as one of my life's great failings. Shaking her head at my impotence, the woman heaved a sigh and fled down the stairs.

The only thing left was to cross the final threshold. I found myself inside a book-lined sitting room with a haphazard collection of furniture and an even more haphazard collection of people. An elegant woman with scarves in her hair sipped tea at a round wooden table while a one-eyed white dog slept at her feet. She was speaking with a man wearing a black trench coat, knee-high black boots, and a scowl of perpetual disillusionment. On a raised red velvet couch, a dapper middle-aged man with a well-kept beard discussed the current political climate in the former Yugoslavia. At a square table beside the window, a couple with matching University of Georgia sweaters were holding glass jars of tea and looking very much bewildered.

"You came!"

It was Eve, and she led me to a second velvet couch at the back of the room. With great authority, she opened a wedge of sitting space and pushed me into it. Then, after placing a jar of hot tea into my hand, she disappeared around a corner.

It was now I who sat bewildered. There were more than a dozen people in the room, a number of whom I would classify as extremely unusual. They were engaged in tumbling conversations, all in English, and all conducted at wild pitches that suggested they wished to be overheard. If a mental asylum had a Sunday tea party where the inmates could dress however they liked, it wouldn't be much different than this.

The books here were well-bound hardcovers and seemed more precious than those elsewhere in the store. There were several volumes of Marx, biographies of the heroes of the Russian Revolution, a history of European socialism. I was inspecting a book by Studs Terkel when I felt a tug on my sleeve. Beside me was an earnest-looking man with a slight paunch and graying hair worn too long at the back.

"I'm a poet," he said.

"That's . . . good?" I offered.

Encouraged, he began to talk. There'd been a divorce back in America, a job in a hardware store in Pittsburgh, where he'd worked night and day for seven years to pay debts, then the move to Paris to chase literary dreams. The man had given readings across the city, including one right here at Shakespeare and Company, and he'd published a book of his poems, which he happened to have with him, if I was inclined to take a look.

While the poet dug in his satchel, Eve returned with a tray of custard cookies. Famished, I took a large handful, but before we could speak properly, she was besieged by other guests. Instead, a man with long greasy white hair, a leather vest, and the stink of alcohol put a stool down in front of me. He looked like a filthy pirate.

"What are you doing here?"

This wasn't asked in a particularly mean fashion, but it wasn't friendly, either. I pointed to my tea and said something about passing through Paris.

"Get out. This city is no good."

Paris was dead, he insisted, dried up and used up. It was full of pretenders now, not like May 1968, which he'd seen personally and could personally say was a hell of a lot better than anything going on today. To mark his point, he took a flask of pastis from his vest pocket and took a wet pull.

Inspired to defend the city I'd so recently adopted, I noted the virtues of its parks, its boulevards, its markets, but the pirate only dismissed me with a wave of his hand.

"Bah, you're too weak to leave. You'll end up here, just like all the rest."

Bristling, I began to argue, but before I could finish a sentence, the man with the turquoise muumuu blundered into the room, grabbed a mound of custard cookies, and squelched onto the couch. The pirate recoiled like the Wicked Witch doused in water, while the man in the muumuu wriggled about beside me to make room for his large frame.

Okay, I thought. Given the poet, the pirate, and all that had gone on below, it'd been a pleasantly unconventional visit, but my jar of tea now stood empty and outside the rain had stopped and a peek of sun had even appeared through the clouds. I excused myself from the couch, much to the disappointment of the poet, who'd finally found his chapbook, and went to thank Eve for her kind invitation.

Around the corner from the sitting room was a most bizarre kitchen. There was another bookshelf, along with a framed photograph of Sacco and Vanzetti on the wall, a wooden table, and then, along with the fridge and stove, row upon row of sticky cans, a jumble of utensils and plates, jars filled with moldy-looking preserves, and, most unsettling, the husks of dried cockroaches scattered across the countertop. Here, I found Eve, who looked happily at home and was stirring an enormous cauldron of tea, her cheeks bright pink from the steam and exertion.

"Are you having a good time?" she asked, pushing more custard cookies at me with her free hand.

It had been an interesting afternoon, I said, though some of the guests were rather . . .

"Strange?" she said, finishing for me. "There are some unusual ones, aren't there? I think George likes them that way."

"George?"

Eve stopped her stirring and peered at me.

"You mean you don't know who George is?"

She beckoned me deeper into the apartment. We entered what appeared to be the master bedroom, which contained a king-size bed, more books, and a collection of photographs lining three walls. Some of the pictures featured Hemingway, Miller, Joyce, and such, while in the rest another man figured prominently. Depending on the year the picture was taken, he either sported a curling goatee and a wild skew of brown hair or tufts of short gray hair and rumpled suits.

"That's George." Eve was pointing to one picture where the man was leaning over a table covered with books, a broad smile on his face. "He runs Shakespeare and Company."

She said this as if it explained everything, but it still didn't make sense. Nothing made any sense: the tourists out front . . . the man at the wishing well . . . the men making soup . . . and the beds . . . there were beds everywhere. . . .

"But what exactly goes on here?" I was gripping her arm a tad tightly.

Eve smiled like a teacher smiles at her student and gently unfurled my fingers. "The bookstore is like a shelter. George lets people live here for free."

She left me alone in that back room, gazing at the picture, marveling at fate.

5.

For the better part of a century, an English bookstore by the name of Shakespeare and Company has served as a haven for artists, writers, and other wayward souls of Paris.

It began with Sylvia Beach. Born in Baltimore and raised in New Jersey at the end of the nineteenth century, Beach was fourteen years old when she first traveled to Europe. Her father, a Presbyterian minister, had been appointed the assistant to the pastor of the American Church in Paris and moved his family to France in 1901. Beach tumbled into love with the city, and after working as a nurse in World War I, she returned to make Paris her home. Always of a literary mind and keenly aware of the need for English books, she opened the original Shakespeare and Company in November 1919 on rue Dupuytren. In 1922, Beach moved her store to rue de l'Odéon, a side street in the sixth arrondissement, near St.-Germain-des-Prés.

This strange nook of a bookstore became the hub for a generation of American and British writers in Paris. The likes of F. Scott Fitzgerald, Gertrude Stein, and Ezra Pound gathered here to borrow books, discuss literary matters, and drink hot tea in the private parlor at the back of the store. In his Paris memoir, *A Moveable Feast*, Ernest Hemingway described Beach's Shakespeare and Company as "a warm, cheerful place with a big stove in winter, tables and shelves of books, new books in the window, and photographs on the wall of famous writers both dead and living." Most notably, it was Beach who raised the money to edit and publish her friend James Joyce's manuscript *Ulysses* when other publishers rejected it as scandalous and sexually provocative.

"There was a tremendous amount of talent in Paris then," Beach wrote later, "and my shop seemed to be a gathering place for most of it."

This original Shakespeare and Company was shut down in 1941 when the Nazis occupied Paris. Romantics say the store was closed after Beach refused to sell her last copy of *Finnegans Wake* to a Nazi officer, while others claim the shop's reputation for creative nonconformity worried the Germans. Whatever the case, Shakespeare and Company was closed for the duration of the occupation and Beach spent World War II in an internment camp. Hemingway himself liberated the premises when he entered Paris with the American troops in 1944, but Beach preferred to retire. She never opened the shop doors again.

A decade later, a similar bookstore opened on the Left Bank, not far from the old shop on rue de l'Odéon. It, too, was run by a rogue American, this time a vagabond dreamer and writer by the name of George Whitman. He'd spent years wandering the world, and after settling in Paris in the 1940s, he devoted his life to the quixotic pursuit of bookseller.

George was born in East Orange, New Jersey, on December 12, 1913, the first of Walter and Grace Whitman's four children. The Whitmans had deep roots in the New World, their family line tracing back through two different sets of relations to the Pilgrims who arrived on the *Mayflower* in 1620.

Grace Whitman was the granddaughter of Joseph Bates, a Connecticut sea captain, and the daughter of Carlton Bates, a prosperous factory owner who manufactured sewing implements such as ivory buttons, knitting needles, and crochet hooks. Grace's father was a determined man with a flair for business. As a fourteen-year-old boy, he began the job of lighting the stoves at the factory; twelve years later, at the age of twenty-six, Carlton Bates bought the factory for himself. George's paternal grandfather, George Washington Whitman, was a Civil War veteran who had fought at Gettysburg; he then went on to become a farmer and seasonal factory worker in Norway, Maine. George's father, Walter Whitman, was a science editor and writer who worked at the American Book Company in New York. In 1916, he resigned that position to take a job as a professor at Salem Teacher's College in Massachusetts. George's father went on to write five high school textbooks and founded the professional journal *General Science Quarterly*. To this day, among George's cherished possessions are a copy of *Household Physics* that his father authored and a letter Albert Einstein wrote to his father about a possible collaboration on a textbook.

When Walter took the teaching position, the Whitmans moved north from New Jersey to Salem, just a short drive from Boston. They moved into a three-story white-frame house with a large front porch, it was just half a block walk from the Atlantic Ocean. The family now numbered four, George's sister Mary having been born in 1915. A few years later, another sister, Margarite, died in the hospital after becoming sick as an infant during the influenza epidemic of 1918. In 1924, George's younger brother, Carlton, was born.

Grace Whitman had been raised with an abundance of religion in her home and she insisted her children embrace the church. She and the three children trundled off to services every Sunday, though George's father hid himself away in his office and could only be convinced to attend on Easter and Christmas. At school, George showed an aptitude for the written word. In the fifth grade, he got straight *A*'s in reading and literature, though he consistently got a *D* in penmanship. Considering he ended up owning one of the world's most celebrated bookstores, it isn't surprising George was a compulsive reader as a child. Each night, he would hide himself under thick blankets with a book and a lamp to escape the wrath of his mother, who was convinced so much reading would ruin his eyes. Sure enough, he could barely open them in the mornings, but he devoured the great novels and read Thoreau's *Walden* when other children his age were struggling with their school primers.

George's father was a risk taker and a promoter, but he lacked a real sense of business. He became a regular player on the stock market but probably lost twenty years of royalty income from his textbooks thanks to ill-conceived investments. These financial dealings were a constant source of worry for Grace, who preferred to put the money she inherited from her family into AT&T stock and the regular dividends this provided.

Walt also yearned to explore the world. As a young man in the 1890s, he got a job on a ship carrying live cows to Europe. He took a bicycle with him, and after the ship docked, he wheeled off to explore the Continent. Later, he accepted assignments as a traveling professor in places like Greece and Turkey. One of the greatest adventures came in 1925, when he took a job at Nanking University and moved the entire Whitman family, save for young Carlton, who was left with relatives, to China for a year. After traveling by train across Canada, they took a boat from Vancouver to Tokyo and then made their way through Shanghai to Nanking. Though his mother had him enrolled in the local Christian Endeavour program, where thirteen-year-old George made complicated maps of Saint Paul's biblical journeys, he was captivated by the more novel aspects of his new life. He kept a journal, in which he described feeding a pig every day on his walk to school, hearing other children brag about seeing a baby cut in two, and playing in graveyards, where he once "put a man's leg bone in my pocket but decided not to keep it." It wasn't an easy transition for the Whitmans. Both George and Mary were called *yang gui zi*, meaning "foreign devil," and were often showered with pebbles by other children as they made their way to school. But George's eyes had opened to the world and they became wider on the way home when the family stopped in Calcutta, Delhi, Bombay, Aden, Jerusalem, Cairo, Constantinople, Bucharest, and Vienna before returning to Salem.

In high school, George was known for the small businesses he ran, his attempts at school newspapers, and his somewhat unruly appearance, which his high school yearbook described as that of a "revolutionary." George was fifteen when the Great Depression struck, and with two of his uncles losing their jobs and the streets suddenly filled with out-of-work men, he became interested in social justice and turned away from his mother's church. But it was at Boston University, where he was studying journalism, that he was transformed. In 1933, in an essay entitled "My Freshman Year at College," George wrote:

> I entered college a devout believer in the Christian superstition and a staunch supporter of the capitalist system and of the military systems which is the tool of capitalist imperialism. For eight months these ideas were subjected to the food for thought and mental callisthenics which are dispensed at the College of Business Administration and at the end of that period my "idea factory" was turning out a wholly different product. In short, I had become a radical—a socialist, atheist and pacifist.

Upon graduating in 1935 with a degree in science and journalism, George received tempting offers. The *Christian Science Monitor* invited him to apprentice for a job and his father urged him to coauthor a science textbook. But George politely declined them both. His new "idea factory" had pushed him in a different direction: He wanted to explore the world and mix with the people.

George headed west, hopping trains, sleeping in hobo jungles, living off the kindness of strangers, seeing America from the bottom up. There were struggles, of course, mostly with local police. He says he was jailed more than fifty times during his travels, courtesy of the strict vagrancy laws. Utah was the worst, he remembers, with police combing the trains for drifters and throwing them straight into jail. In one town, George was jailed for seven days, then driven into the desert. Left there with his sparsely packed bag, he was warned it would be six months' imprisonment if he ever showed face in the county again.

Despite these occasional lumps, the life became infectious and he came up with an even grander scheme: to walk around the world, an 113,000-mile journey, with 30,000 of them on foot. He set out from California in 1936 and walked for months, down through Mexico, where he met Mayans in the Yucatan, then onto Belize, where he met some Caribs. This was before there were roads in many places, and so he clambered through jungles and waded through swamps. Once, he walked himself into such a state of exhaustion that he collapsed under a palm tree, sure he was going to die. But, as George tells it, natives discovered him, hoisted him onto their shoulders, and carried him back to their village, where they resuscitated him with milk from a nursing mother.

"No finer way of life is there in all the earth than this," wrote George at the time. "To wander through the palace of the world on foot, to walk, to dance, to sing, and to read—to read the Book of Life."

Arriving in Panama in 1937, he was lured by the promise that no able-bodied man would be refused work at the Panama Canal. He was given a job at one of the neighboring construction sites and worked as a "powder monkey." From dawn to dusk every day, he scampered across the rocks, drilling holes, then stuffing them with gunpowder so the earth could be blown aside. Staying at the YMCA in Cristobal, George continued his socialist investigations. He wrote of the exploitation of the local population and kept statistics on the death rate among the workers in the Canal Zone. Already an adherent of magazines like *New Masses* and having read all of Trotsky and Marx, George was ready for the next step in his political growth. In a letter he wrote to his mother from Panama, he declared, "I am a communist and I will always be a communist, completely and unequivocally."

When he was ready to move on, George got a job with the Matson Line on the five-thousand-ton sugar freighter *Lihue*, which was leaving Panama for Asia. His plan was to continue his walk in the direction of Moscow, but after union problems led to a mutiny among the ship's crew, the boat stopped in Hawaii. George stayed on the island for months, living on beaches and learning the rudiments of the Polynesian language. But, the momentum of his travels lost, he eventually caught a boat back to the United States and returned to Boston.

After his travels, George was convinced the world order would have to be changed. He took an apartment in Cambridge so he could study Russian at Harvard and prepare himself for the future. "There is only one beacon and lighthouse that will shine undimmed over the stormy seas of the coming years and that is the Soviet Union," George wrote in 1940. To aid the dawning of this new era, he attempted to launch a magazine called *Leftward*, which would feature articles such as "Fascist Tendencies in American Universities," and he railed against the lack of political insight of the average workers and middle-class citizens of his country. He even attempted to recruit his younger brother to the cause. When Carl was a teenager, George would teach him Russian phrases, insisting they were the only ones with any "good ideas."

To earn money to visit his promised land, George worked as busboy, and later he negotiated to join the National Maritime Union so he could work on freighter ships again. But in the meantime, Pearl Harbor was attacked and the United States entered World War II. George was twenty-eight years old when he was taken into the military, and perhaps the commanding officers took his unusual nature into consideration, as he was sent to an obscure military base in Greenland. For two years, George lived north of the Arctic Circle, dispensing medicine to the occasional soldier and, more frequently, to the curious Eskimos. Still, when the war was over, he got his letter from Harry Truman, thanking him for undertaking "the most severe task that one can be called upon to perform."

On returning to the States, he served at the Myles Standish military base in Taunton, Massachusetts, and used the time to set up his first bookshop. Declaring that "not reading is worse than not knowing how to read," George opened the Taunton Book Lounge. His clientele were mainly men from the base, but he also shipped books to soldiers serving overseas. After receiving his discharge, he flirted with the idea of opening a bookstore in Mexico City, even writing the U.S. trade commissioner in Mexico for details on foreign investment. But instead, Europe beckoned. Reading about the need for volunteers in France, George decided to cross the Atlantic.

After arriving in France, George first volunteered in a camp for war orphans, but then he moved to Paris. The city was an attractive place for

Americans to be in those days. Paris was in full romance with its liberators, and the cost of living meant that sparse funds could support regal lifestyles. George was also motivated by other concerns: The rumblings of the anti-communism movement had begun and his kind weren't particularly welcome in the United States.

George ended up taking a French civilization course at the Sorbonne and living in a cheap room at the Hôtel de Suez on boulevard St.-Michel. He scrounged enough to buy up a decent collection of English books, and since these, like everything else in the occupation-weary city, were in short supply, he soon found himself running an impromptu library. Dozens of books would go out every week, and George kept meticulous track of what was borrowed, even noting that Arthur Miller's new play, *Death of a Salesman,* was his most popular book, as it was borrowed on average eight times a month. Early on in his stay at the Suez, George lost the key to his room and stopped locking his door. One day, he returned from class, to find two strangers reading his books. Considering his belief in shared property and communal living, it was a thrilling development. His sole regret was that all he had was coffee to offer, so from that point on there was usually soup and bread ready for those who came.

These were the fragile roots of George Whitman's Shakespeare and Company, this cramped hotel room with a bedlam of books and a pot of communal stew. George hosted most every impoverished expatriate in Paris, including a young poet by the name of Lawrence Ferling, who was getting a doctorate in French literature at the Sorbonne. The poet, who later retook his family's original name, Ferlinghetti, had met George's sister Mary while studying at Columbia University and enjoyed a romance with her. Upon arriving in France, he looked up George and, using funds allocated under the G.I. bill, he began buying books from him, including Gallimard's complete edition of *A la recherche du temps perdu.*

"The first time I saw George, he was in his tiny hotel room with no windows, there were books stacked to the ceiling on three side and he was sitting on the floor heating his dinner over a can of Sterno," Ferlinghetti recalls. "I knew I had found a true bibliophile."

The two became friends, and George noted in a letter home to his mother that Ferlinghetti had been "lionized by a group of French writers ever since he wrote his first novel last Summer." When Ferlinghetti left Paris and headed to San Francisco, he, too, opened a bookstore, the famous City Lights, which to this day remains the sister bookstore of Shakespeare and Company.

As George watched Paris come back to life at the end of the 1940s, he thought it might be time to open the bookstore he'd always dreamed of. First, he tried renting a location in the seventeenth arrondissement; then he tried to buy a property near St.-Germain-des-Prés. It was in 1951 that he finally found the storefront across the Seine from Notre Dame. It had been a small Arab grocery, but the owners had run into financial difficulties and were willing to sell the property cheaply, thinking it would be seized by creditors. George was thirty-seven years old then and had been drifting for almost two decades. Though he didn't have much money, he did have stocks his father had recommended to him, particularly in a company called Bath Irons Works. It was a little more than two thousand dollars, but that was enough to get started in post-war Paris, so he decided to gamble it all on a bookstore. He opened for business in August 1951.

George initially called his bookstore Le Mistral, which was both his pet name for Jacqueline Tran-Van, his girlfriend at the time, and the name of the famously fierce wind that blows through the south of France. The store was tiny, just half of the main floor as it stands today, but George made the best of it. He lived the Marxist creed of "give what you can; take what you need," and with this spirit he built the bookstore. From the first day, he installed a bed in the back for friends who needed a place to sleep, kept soup bubbling for hungry visitors, and ran a free lending library for people who couldn't afford his wares. On the night of August 15, 1951, he gave his first writer a place to sleep, the playwright Paul Abelman, who would go on to write such books as *I Hear Voices*.

"It was exceedingly disagreeable and uncomfortable," recalls Abelman. "But it was generous of George and I had no other place to go."

Paris was in the midst of another glorious literary era then, and the bookstore was its unofficial clubhouse. Henry Miller and Anaïs Nin were constantly about. To this day, the intimacy of George's relationship with Anaïs remains the subject of constant speculation. Richard Wright, who lived up the street on rue Monsieur-le-Prince, gave readings at the store, and eventually his son earned a job working the desk. Alexander Trocchi set up the offices of the *Merlin* literary journal in the back of the store, George Plimpton and the *Paris Review* crowd stopped by regularly, and even Samuel Beckett moped about, though George says the two didn't have much to say and mostly sat and stared at each other.

Then the Beats arrived, with William Burroughs using George's bookstore as a library to research medical deformities, Allen Ginsberg gulping wine to find the courage to give a reading of *Howl* on the front esplanade, Gregory Corso stealing first editions to fuel his various habits, and Brion Gysin and the rest of them stirring up the Kerouac-istical blues just a few blocks away at the hotel on rue Gît-le-Coeur.

In 1963, George celebrated his fiftieth birthday, and a year later he changed the name of the store. He'd long been a devotee of Sylvia Beach and admired the name Shakespeare and Company, "a novel in three words," as he called it. He and Beach met for tea and she even visited Le Mistral on occasion. After Beach died in 1962, George bought her collection of books, and then in 1964, on the four hundredth anniversary of William Shakespeare's birth, he rebaptised his store Shakespeare and Company. Detractors claim he stole the name and profited from the association, but if George were a mercurial sort, he never would have turned his bookstore into a sanctuary for the disaffected and creatively desperate.

Though its name was now more literary, the store became, if anything, more political. George continued to house radicals and writers as they passed through Paris, but he also held a lecture series called the Free University of Paris, ran a long-standing protest against the Vietnam War, and hid the students of the May 1968 uprising among his books. He even teased that Shakespeare and Company offered honorary degrees in LSD, with "Make Love, Not War" buttons as diplomas.

On through the seventies, eighties, nineties, the decades now counted like years, his reputation and his store constantly grew. Room by room, Shakespeare and Company expanded, until it spread over three floors of the building, "a giant literary octopus," as Ferlinghetti described it. With each expansion, George always made sure to add more beds, and the rumor spread to the corners of the world that there was a strange bookstore on the Left Bank in Paris where you could sleep for free. By the thousands they came, and George invited them all to stay, at least as many as the bookstore could feasibly hold. A generation of writers and wanderers were sheltered and fed, and then that generation's children.

By the time I had my cup of tea at Shakespeare and Company in January 2000, George was telling people he'd let forty thousand people sleep in his store, more than the population of his hometown of Salem when he was growing up. After my visit, I was intent on becoming the next.

6.

After the tea party, I felt so exhilarated that I climbed the six flights of stairs to my hotel room effortlessly. For hours, I leaned out the narrow window of my room and watched smoke curl from the clay chimneys on the surrounding roofs. It was long past midnight when I finally tried to sleep, but even then I could only lie awake with the restlessness of a child before Christmas.

From what Eve had told me, George welcomed lost souls and poor writers. I qualified on both counts. Considering the precious little money in my pocket and the scarcity of options before me, it didn't take long to decide that fate had brought me to Shakespeare and Company that rainy Sunday afternoon. For the first time since the threatening phone call, I began imagining a future. I would write a brilliant novel at the bookstore, I would be acclaimed a genius, I would bask in untold fame and fortune. It was absurd, of course, but I reveled in this sudden ecstasy of optimism after so many bleak days. I felt the adrenaline of a gambler who watches the roulette wheel spin with his last chips on the table. Outside the window, the sky was molting from night black to morning gray before I finally fell asleep.

The next afternoon, I washed thoroughly in the bathroom down the hallway from my room and even hung my best shirt outside the shower to smooth its wrinkles. Standing before the cracked mirror, I practiced my smiles and rehearsed my introduction. Nothing seemed good enough. By the time I was ready to leave, I was so nervous that even though the line four metro cut almost directly from the hotel to the book-store, I decided to walk so as to better measure the mission before me.

With each step toward the bookstore, I became more apprehensive, my stomach a sour mix of a thousand first dates and job interviews. Who was I to go live in a bookstore? Would I even be accepted? And that constant nagging worry: What exactly was I doing with my life?

I walked by the African groceries and call shops of boulevard Ornano, then under the iron beams of the elevated metro at Barbès, where men offered gold chains from their coat pockets. Past the Gare de Nord, then the Gare de l'Est, a voice inside wondering if maybe I shouldn't just hop a train and try my luck in another city. Three times, my resolution faltered and I started back toward the hotel. But I always turned and continued on to Shakespeare and Company. There was really no other choice.

In the midst of this anguished walk, I heard my name called out. It was Fernanda, a young Brazilian woman with dark hair and happy cheeks. She was a student from São Paulo who'd saved for two years to come to Paris. We'd met at the language school, and as we were the only people in the class with baguette budgets, when the others lunched in cafés, Fernanda and I ate sandwiches in a park and jabbered in our broken French.

While I had spent my time in Paris in a most aimless fashion, Fernanda was at the pinnacle of touristic efficiency. She went to all the museums and galleries, found discount passes for the theaters and opera houses, knew the metro system better than many Parisians. That day, she was coming from a free exhibition at the Centre Pompidou. Grateful for the distraction, I invited her for coffee.

Sitting in a grim brasserie on rue Beaubourg, we ordered the cheapest drinks on the menu, the tiny café express, and two glasses of water. It didn't take Fernanda long to note my agitated state, and I was happy there was somebody to listen. I explained my money had almost run out but that I couldn't go home to Canada because of the troubling circumstances I'd left behind. I told her of my brooding walks and the miserable emptiness before me. Then I came to my visit to Shakespeare and Company the day before. Fernanda listened with great intensity and asked for several parts of the story to be repeated. After absorbing it all, she sat back in her chair and looked at me with serious eyes.

"This is a sign from God," she said.

Coming from a family of lapsed Catholics, I'd seldom given time to spiritual matters. I was happy enough to use the word God as a noun to explain the mysteries of existence that still escaped modern science, but that was about it. Fernanda, on the other hand, was devout and had worshiped in more than a dozen Paris churches. We'd already spent many an hour talking about questions to which there are no answers, so I only smiled without conviction when she said this. I was just about to launch into another refrain of "God-doesn't-actually-exist-but-is-only-a-necessary-human-invention," but I stopped when I saw the hope blossoming across her face.

"You must go and ask to stay," she insisted. "This is meant to be. I am sure of it."

Then, before I could say anything, she was on her feet, pulling a street map from her shoulder bag.

"I am going to pray that this George man tells you yes," she said, and then rushed out the brasserie's door.

I didn't try to stop her. At that moment, I would take help from wherever I could get it.

Shakespeare and Company sits on the very left edge of the Left Bank. The store is close enough to the Seine that when one is standing in the front doorway, a well-thrown apple core will easily reach river water. From this same doorway, there is an inspired view of Ile de la Cité and one can contemplate the cathedral of Notre Dame, the Hôtel Dieu hospital, and the imposing block of the main police prefecture.

The bookstore's actual address is 37 rue de la Bûcherie. It's an odd cobbled street that begins at rue St. Jacques, runs for one block, hits the public park of St.-Julien-le-Pauvre, then continues on for another two blocks before ending at the square Restif-de-la-Bretonne. The bookstore is on the part of rue de la Bûcherie close to rue St. Jacques, where, thanks to a quirk of city planning, there are only buildings on the south side of the street, which is what gives the bookstore its splendid view.

This end of the street is reserved for pedestrians, but this is only part of the reason it retains a certain calm. There is also a tiny city garden that separates the bookstore from the racing traffic of Quai de Montebello and then the sidewalk widens in front of 37 rue de la Bûcherie to create an almost private esplanade for Shakespeare and Company. For the coup de grâce, there are two young cherry trees on this esplanade and a green Wallace drinking fountain sitting majestically to the side. All this gives the bookstore an air of tranquillity that is shocking in the midst of the frenzy and noise of downtown Paris.

As for the bookstore itself, there are actually two entrances. Facing the shop, the main part of the store with the narrow green door I entered on the day of the tea party is on the right. It is here that one finds the famous yellow-and-green wooden Shakespeare and Company sign and the broad picture window. To the left of the main store, there is a second, smaller storefront. This is the antiquarian room. Along with the shelves of centuries-old books, the antiquarian room has a desk, a lovely stuffed armchair, and, of course, a creaky but thoroughly sleepable bed.

When I arrived after my coffee with Fernanda, it was nearing dark and the streetlights were flickering to life around me. The window of the main shop glowed a soft yellow against the early night, and at the desk there was an elderly man with a rumpled suit and a faraway look in his eyes. From the photographs I'd seen the day before, I knew this man to be George. Taking one last breath for courage, I stepped inside.

The door creaked to announce me, but George kept gazing out the window, deep in private thought. In the store's irregular light, I could see his uneven tussle of fine white hair and the thin wrinkles that lined his face. After long moments, he shook his head as if awaking from a dream and turned to look at me. His eyes were an impossibly pale blue.

"What do you want?" he demanded.

His voice was so gruff that I took a step backward. Stammering, my rehearsed lines disappeared and I mumbled something about being a writer with no place else to go.

"I wouldn't stay for long," I finished. "Just enough time to catch my feet. I've hit a bit of a rough patch."

He stood there, appraising me with those pale eyes, stopping time.

"You've written books?"

I nodded.

"Are they self-published?"

Using a vanity press is akin to buying sex, but more shameful in a way. Visiting a prostitute is at least a private act, while paying to publish one's book is a very public display of creative desperation. Despite my nervousness, I took affront to the question. Though the crime books I'd written were hardly works of great literature, I was proud of what I'd accomplished.

"No, not at all," I replied, trying to keep the anger from my voice. "I'm not saying they're the best books ever written, but I had a real publisher."

George waved the back of his hand at me as if I were speaking nonsense, but a smile crept across his face.

"A real writer wouldn't have asked; he would have just come in and taken a bed. You, you can stay. But you'll sleep downstairs with the rest of the riffraff."

And like that, things changed forever.

7.

The next afternoon, I checked out of the hotel and, my meager bag in hand, I came to the bookstore. George was at the desk, pricing a stack of used paperback novels with a dull pencil. He would pick a book up, look at its cover, read a paragraph or two, smile to himself, then scratch a price on the front page. When I said hello, he didn't seem to recognize me at first, but then his eyes flashed and he chuckled.

"The Canadian writer," he said. "Come with me. I have your lunch warming upstairs."

Putting aside a copy of Malmud's *The Assistant,* George called out to a tall blond woman shelving books at the back of the store. As she came forward to cover the desk, she paused to give him a kiss on the cheek.

"This is my surrogate daughter." He beamed. "She's the only person who ever wrote me a thank-you letter for being invited to my tea party, so I gave her a job in the store."

The woman smiled modestly. "I'm Pia. I hear you're moving in?"

For the second time at the bookstore, I found myself confronted with a woman of such confounding beauty that words vanished. All I could do was nod dumbly until George finally tugged me back to the narrow staircase.

"She wants me to go to China with her in the spring," George said, catching me staring back at Pia. "I don't know if I can take a break. Things are too busy at the bookstore, always too busy."

He took me up past the children's bunk bed, through the narrow corridor with the writer's cubbyhole, and into the front room with the window that looked across to Notre Dame. Here, a young man sat at the desk, banging loudly on the typewriter. He was American handsome with tanned, even features, politely messy hair, and strong white teeth.

"George!" he bellowed. "I'm writing!"

He waited for approval, but George only grunted and fumbled with his keys. Disappointed, he began to eye me suspiciously.

"This is the new man. He's a writer," George said. "He's going to sleep in the antiquarian room, but he'll need a bed up here until that gets sorted out."

The fellow at the typewriter looked perplexed by this news, but before anything else could be said, George dragged me through to the building's common staircase. Instead of climbing to the third floor, where the tea party had been held, he opened a door across the hall and gestured for me to follow him inside.

This was the most curious room yet. Two enormous gilded mirrors reflected our entrance, one over each of the two beds in the room. The walls were papered in red felt, but most of the wall space was occupied by five large wooden bookcases. Three hung precariously over the main bed, looking ready to avalanche books onto whoever slept there. In the back corner, a small doorway led to an even smaller kitchen, where among uneven stacks of cans and a drifting pile of old newspapers there was a hot plate with a pot of soup atop it. The centerpiece of this strange room was a sturdy wooden desk in front of yet another window that looked over to Notre Dame. There was a wooden swivel chair rolled up to the desk, and George pulled it out for himself.

"I'm preparing for the accountant," he said as he motioned me to sit on the bed. "My papers are a bit of a mess today."

This was a gross understatement. There was only the slimmest corner on which I could sit, because the bed, like the floor, the chairs, the shelves, and most every other available surface in the room, was covered with papers—bills, invoices, letters, receipts, account ledgers, and book catalogs, all of them either crumpled or coffee-stained, and sometimes both. Most distressing was the desk itself, where the same clutter of papers was joined by discarded dinner plates, empty glasses, full glasses, bowls of loose change, and a jar with what looked like a slice of lemon meringue pie squished to the bottom. George surveyed the room and raised his hands with slow exasperation. "Things aren't as clean as they used to be. I can't seem to keep up anymore."

I had to agree that things appeared somewhat out of control, but I assured him the tumble and disorder held a touch of romance. To my mind, it was miraculous he was keeping the bookstore running at all. He was eighty-six years old that winter. My own experiences with folks of such an advanced age were limited to my grandparents, and they'd all died before reaching eighty-six and certainly none could have operated a bookstore in his or her later years. Not only had George kept Shakespeare and Company running; he'd created a living museum of books and a hostel for needy writers.

"You think so?" George said with a modest smile, as if never realizing the extent of his accomplishments. "I like to tell people I run a socialist utopia that masquerades as a bookstore, but sometimes I don't know."

There was a sudden blur of black and a cat scampered onto the desk, knocking a half-full glass of cola onto a pile of invoices. George took a swat at it, but the cat only looked at him with indifferent eyes and then leapt across to the second bed, toppling a box of publishing catalogs to the floor. George cackled with laughter and told the cat it was her fault the office was such a mess.

This was my formal introduction to Kitty, the same cat who had greeted me from the windowsill the day of the tea party. George had named her after the imaginary friend of Anne Frank, whose diary was one of his favorite books, and she seemed to be queen of the bookstore castle. Seeing Kitty bent on destruction, George went into the kitchen and returned with a plate of tinned food to pacify her. With the cat occupied, he settled back in his chair and got down to business.

"Did you bring your biography?"

The biography. This was one of the grand bookstore traditions. During the heated days of Paris in the 1960s, when the students rose up, and the Communists carried an uncomfortable amount of influence, at least in the opinion of the French authorities, George became the subject of political scrutiny. It shouldn't have come as too much of a surprise, as he was a member of both the American and French Communist parties and had been letting political radicals and social undesirables sleep in his store for years. But it made life decidedly inconvenient.

As a means of pressure, the police forced George to follow the by-laws governing hotels, and thereby account for everybody who slept in his store. This was an imaginative stretch, since George never accepted payment and considered all his guests friends, but he was required to take down the passport number, date of birth, and other vital information of every person who stayed at Shakespeare and Company. Unlike the tourist hotels, however, George was required to file a report on a daily basis, and not at the main police prefecture across the Seine, either, but at an obscure station a ninety-minute walk from the store.

Yet George forged on. First, he bought a bicycle to facilitate making the journey to file the daily police report. Then he twisted the process into a creative exercise for his guests. Instead of simply noting down dry personal information, he asked people to write a short account of their lives and how they had come to the bookstore. The custom continued long after the police harassment stopped, and George now has an archive of sociological wonders: tens of thousands of biographies written between the 1960s and today, a vast survey of the great drifters of the past forty years. The task of putting one's life in words was a chance at confession for many, and among the overflowing file boxes there are stories of love and death, incest and addiction, dreams and disappointments, all with a thumb-sized photograph attached.

When I'd asked to stay at Shakespeare and Company, George had told me of that tradition, and I was imbued with a sense of the gravity of the assignment. For the first time in recent memory, I was actually nervous about writing.

Working at a newspaper, the art of language becomes obscured by the daily ritual of flushing out a thousand words of copy in less time than it takes to eat a proper lunch. I became a cheap magician who knew that with a bit of dexterity and practice one could conjure up drama. Tragic accidents, grisly deaths, devastated mothers—the hyperbole of daily crime reporting turned writing into a Lego exercise requiring blocks of strong adjectives and simple nouns.

But with both the store's literary history and the desire to impress my new landlord weighing upon me, I seized up. I'd spent the previous night in the hotel room starting my biography a dozen times, only to curse my words as trite and heave them into a crumpled pile. I knew George wanted a sense of my life and my family, so at around four in the morning, with a bottle of cheap Côtes du Rhone for inspiration, I decided to tell of a painful rift with my father.

One of my mentors at the newspaper was a man by the name of Woloschuk. An investigative journalist of national renown, he was a few years older than I. Among the feathers his cap sported were a bestselling book about the feud that nearly destroyed the world's largest french fry empire, a story exposing a museum's prized collection of Fabergé eggs as fakes, and the identification of the Canadian soldier who seduced a fifteen-year-old English girl during World War II and thus unwittingly fathered Eric Clapton.

Shortly after I started at the newspaper as a junior crime reporter, Woloschuk was hired on as a star investigative reporter. By chance, his desk was next to mine, and what began as casual cross-cubicle conversation developed into deep friendship when he recruited me for a dubious assignment. When he'd moved to the city, he'd been duped into taking an overpriced apartment and now he was skipping out on the lease. It was my job to help liberate his furniture in the dead of night so he could avoid the landlord and take a cheaper apartment in my building.

His confidence thus earned, Woloschuk took me under his wing. He was the one who taught me the things you don't learn in journalism school: how to develop off-the-record sources, how to flatter on-the-record sources with well-placed adjectives, how to talk to police so they treat you as one of them.

Woloschuk was also the first to make me fully aware of the internal politics and social hierarchies that rule daily newspapers, and he was the one person who tried to get me to take my job a little less seriously. He'd force me to eat lunch away from my desk, he'd make frequent references to the fate of the horse in *Animal Farm,* and, on the thrilling occasion when I was asked by the editor of the automobile section to test a brand-new Lincoln Continental, he convinced me it was a good idea to drive to a barren stretch of highway and speed it along at 140 miles per hour. At Woloschuk's request, we became informal partners, teaming up on investigations, driving the city to meet off-the-record sources, spending hours sitting in coffee shops and airing out story ideas.

A few weeks before I received the threat, Woloschuk got a tip from a police source concerning a renowned heart surgeon who was also director of an internationally respected heart institute, inventor of an artificial heart, and a standing member of the Canadian Senate. According to the source, this doctor had been arrested for picking up a prostitute on one of the city's filthiest strolls. Because of his reputation, instead of being publicly charged, he was funneled into john school, a program that instructs men on the disease and desperation of street prostitution. This program was supposed to protect the individual's privacy, but Woloschuk's sources were good and some officer obviously wanted the esteemed doctor to take an embarrassing fall.

The newspaper wanted the story badly, so we hit the streets to track down the facts. Our evidence gathered, we went to the hospital where the doctor performed heart transplants to confront him with what we knew. The doctor stuttered and denied everything. When we pressed harder and insisted it would be easier if he told his side of the story, he picked up the phone and told us he was going to call hospital security if we didn't leave immediately.

Woloschuk and I were frustrated we hadn't gotten the doctor's personal confirmation, but we were soon staggered further. After we left the hospital, the doctor contacted one of the country's leading public-relations firms and, on their advice, scheduled a press conference for that afternoon. Then, with his wife and children sitting beside him as he faced a brimming room of reporters and television cameras, he confessed. Begging his family's forgiveness, he concluded by saying that as a result of his indiscretion and the badgering of newspaper reporters, he was resigning as head of the National Heart Institute.

If he had held his ground or resigned from his political post, the country might have shrugged it off as another example of the eminent corruptibility of the human spirit. By stepping down from a position where he saved lives on a daily basis, the battle of public opinion was won. Across the country, talk radio denounced media tactics. Politicians and pundits begged the doctor to return to his post, and even our own newspaper turned its back on us. The editors said Woloschuk and I had acted on our own initiative, and the paper started a petition asking the doctor to go back to work. The argument that it was a health risk for a surgeon to visit a street prostitute and hence a legitimate public story fell on deaf ears.

The worst part of this affair was that even my father questioned me. He is an internal man, not prone to voicing his complaints or disappointments. When it came to my work, he'd never commented on its unscrupulous aspects. I'd once covered a story about a fatal car accident that touched the teaching community at his high school. A colleague told him it was a fair job of reporting and that the family had appreciated what I'd written. This left him with the impression I was a compassionate and perhaps even ethical reporter, and this was enough for him. When my involvement in the doctor's scandal came to light at a family dinner, my father shook his head and quietly wondered how his son could have done such a thing.

When George was done reading my account of this incident in my biography, he nodded and placed it on his cluttered desk. "You need more stories," he said with a dismissive wave. "You need to make it longer."

He smiled, though. And then he reached into his pocket for a ring of keys. Putting them in my hand, he made sure my fingers closed over them.

"Finish your biography here. Stay as long as you need to."

In the kitchen, the pot was now steaming, and George got up to fetch two bowls of pepper soup and a baguette. After pouring us hot milky coffee and stirring our cups with his pencil, he sat down and looked me in the eye.

"You know," he said, "I don't normally ask writers to do anything other than make their beds in the morning, but you . . . I think you're different."

Then, as we ate our soup, he explained the first great task that would be asked of me at the Shakespeare and Company bookstore. It involved the unusual case of an old poet and an unpleasant eviction.

8.

Two months before I'd had a high-profile job with an enviable salary, a sleek black German sedan on lease, an apartment in a fashionable downtown neighborhood, and a collection of not-so-inexpensive shirts and jackets hanging in the closet. Now, there were a few hundred dollars in my pocket, no job or prospect thereof, some clothes jammed into an old handbag, and a bed in a tattered bookstore to call home. All things considered, I couldn't have been happier.

After George wished me a pleasant first night at Shakespeare and Company, I crossed back to the bookstore library. The young man was still at the desk typing, though now in a far less flamboyant manner. When he saw me, he leaned back in his chair and gave me an appraising look.

"So," he frowned. "You're a writer."

"A journalist actually. Some would say that doesn't qualify."

The dose of self-deprecation worked. The man's jaw muscles relaxed and he rose from his chair with a grin.

"Ha! I like that," he said, grasping my hand in an overly firm shake. "I'm Kurt. That's with a *K*, like Kurt Vonnegut."

With a flourish of his arm, this Kurt with a *K* stepped out from behind his typewriter and announced he would give me the official Shakespeare and Company tour. Once he was standing, I saw he was taller than I, a good few inches over six feet, and wore a heavy gray overcoat.

"The store's not heated," he said, catching me looking at his coat. "Get used to the cold."

To start, Kurt pointed to the books around us. This, he said, was the library. Nothing on this floor was for sale, only for reading at the store. There were more than ten thousand volumes in all, from Shakespeare's plays to presidential biographies, from nineteenth-century treatises on tropical birds to the most recent Julian Barnes novel. "Can you believe it?" Kurt asked. "How many businesses devote half their space to things that don't make money?"

Next, I was taken back out to the staircase and led up several steps to a landing. There was a wooden door, which I'd previously presumed gave onto a closet, but Kurt swung it open to reveal a stained porcelain hole in the floor with grooved footholds on each side. Though the air was foul, Kurt made me lean in to see a rickety faucet and a plastic bucket for flushing. This was the Shakespeare and Company toilet. George had even installed bookshelves here. With mild dismay, I noticed the pages of the books on the lower shelves were moist. I told myself it was humidity.

"That's for us. There's a good one upstairs in the apartment, and a bathtub, too, but those are saved for important guests and established writers," he said with some envy in his voice. "We don't get up there much."

Once back inside the library, he pointed to the pair of narrow beds covered with red velvet that ran along one wall of the front room. These were two of the thirteen official beds at what George liked to call "the Tumbleweed Hotel": one in the antiquarian room, two in the main part of the bookstore downstairs, six in the library, and four more upstairs in the third-floor apartment. Besides these beds, there were another half a dozen corners and cracks that could quickly be converted into sleeping spaces. According to Kurt, during the height of summer as many as twenty people stayed in the bookstore at one time. Winters were generally quieter, as the gray Paris rains discouraged the drifters who otherwise flocked to Shakespeare and Company. At the moment, there were just six people living at the store, including myself.

"You're lucky," Kurt insisted. "I got here at the end of December and the place was so packed for New Year's, I had to sleep on the floor for two nights."

Taking me to the narrow passage connecting the front and back rooms, Kurt opened another door. This time, it was in fact a closet, and an unsteady heap of knapsacks was piled beneath shirts hanging from a makeshift clothes rod. Kurt shoved my bag into this pile and leaned into the door to stop the contents from tumbling out.

"That's our storage space. Don't keep anything too valuable in there." Then, with a half smile, he added, "Strange things go missing here."

We moved past the cubbyhole, which, I was told, had been installed for a writer who'd dared to complain about the lack of actual writing space at the bookstore, and then into the room with the bunk bed and children's books. Kurt stopped beside the mirror with the letters and photographs taped to it. They had been sent from couples who had fallen in love at the bookstore. Myth had it that more than sixty people had met their future wives or husbands at Shakespeare and Company; Kurt said that considering what an aphrodisiac the store was, he guessed the number might actually be higher.

Passing through the next doorway, we entered the room where I'd previously stumbled upon the two men making soup. Kurt laughed at my description, saying the men were from Argentina and lived their own unique Nietzschean philosophy. They apparently tried to make every minute of their life as fulfilling as possible, in the belief that it might go on forever. "They were always sharing their food, their clothes, their wine, whatever," said Kurt. "Deep down, I think they're crazy."

The pair had left that morning, so the room now stood empty and I could choose my bed. I sat on the larger of the two and tried to get a feel for my new quarters. This was known as the fiction room, and for good reason. The shelves were filled with hardcover novels, and in an instant I recognized at least twenty books that someone at some time had insisted I read. Faulkner, Capote, Hesse, Camus, Richler—it was a comprehensive collection of the century's great works.

For furniture, there was a mirrored cabinet, as well as a wooden table with political magazines organized neatly on top. The second bed in the room was a feat of carpentry, tucked between two bookcases and measuring no more than five feet in length. Clearly, one of the Argentinians must have been either very short or very flexible. There was also a window in the room, but it shed sparse light, as it was obstructed with shelves of books. I could just make out thin lines of the fading day in the spaces where the books didn't come evenly together. It made the room slightly claustrophobic, but the air felt good, like the municipal library near my parents' home.

As I sat, Kurt fingered the spines of books, making it clear there was something on his mind. After the prerequisite throat clearing, he got to what was bothering him.

"Did George really say you could sleep downstairs in the antiquarian room?"

All I did was give a slight nod. This was the task George had given me while we ate our pepper soup. It concerned an enigmatic poet by the name of Simon. In the mid-nineties, George had offered this Simon a bed in the bookstore when the poet had no place else to go. George had expected him to stay for a week or two; instead, Simon had been holed up in the bookstore for more than five years. Now, George's enormous reserve of goodwill had been exhausted.

Early on, Simon had actually been a fruitful member of the bookstore family. He helped around the store, he counseled the younger writers, he gave readings of his work in the upstairs library. But George said things had changed. In the past few years, Simon had taken to bad habits: lifting from the till, refusing to unlock the door of the antiquarian room for customers, and hiding away from the world so he could stay in bed. The worst part seemed to be that he didn't even read good books. "Detective novels," George said, spitting the words out like putrid grapes. "He locks himself in and reads lousy detective novels."

Tired of this spiral, George had asked me to evict Simon in the most diplomatic of fashions and then take over the antiquarian room for my own living and writing space. He'd warned me, though, that the affair should be handled with discretion. Not being sure who knew what about the case of the strange old poet, I kept my silence.

"I wanted that room when it came empty," Kurt continued in a hurt voice, "It's the perfect place to write. . . ."

He shook his head and continued to fiddle with the books. Not wanting to upset my new living companion, I quickly assured him there were no set plans, that the whole situation was very mysterious and I'd only know more after I spoke to this poet myself. Kurt decided to accept the explanation and, like a swimmer shaking off a cramp, he regained his confident attitude.

"I guess that's just George. That's the whole Shakespeare and Company thing. You never know what's going to happen."

With the air thus cleared, he sat down beside me on the bed and we began to talk. Kurt was from Florida and his dream while growing up had been to make movies. He'd worked in video stores, watched practically every B movie ever made, and then studied film at university. A few years earlier, he'd packed up his things and gone to New York to try to catch his break. He'd been shopping a script called *Videowrangler,* the story of a young clerk in a Florida video store who finds a blackmail tape mistakenly slipped into the return slot one morning. But first there was no luck, then a string of decidedly bad luck, so he decided Paris might shake things up.

The change in countries didn't change his fortunes. There'd been a misunderstanding with the girl who he'd thought had invited him to stay with her; then he'd been mugged while taking his money from a bank machine. Making it worse Kurt had decided to take out almost all of his money on that one occasion to avoid multiple service charges.

"I should have gone for his gun," Kurt said ruefully. "I could tell it was a starter's pistol, but I just froze."

Left with few resources and no place to stay, someone suggested Shakespeare and Company and that's how he'd arrived at the bookstore. In such an environment, Kurt had smoothly switched aspirations and was now transforming his movie script into a novel. With the air of a determined young writer, he spent his days scrawling notes in cafés and pounding conspicuously at the typewriter in the bookstore library.

"I want to write another version of my biography for George," he said earnestly. "My life's totally changed since I got here. I'm a writer now. I feel it in my blood."

But no matter how hard Kurt tried to adopt this now literary posture, he still reeked of his old film ways. As we talked, he quizzed me on directors and constantly compared life to scenes from movies. My arrival in Paris, he said, was just like that scene from *Dead Man* when Johnny Depp arrives in that frontier town and finds himself with neither job nor money. Kurt was even physically marked by his devotion to movies. On his back was an enormous tattoo of spooling film. It descended from the tip of his left shoulder blade down to the base of his spine and then rose up to his right shoulder to form a giant V. His ambition was to fill the frames with the significant events of his life so he would have a permanent self-tribute etched in skin. He showed me the frames detailing New York and Florida and confided that soon there would be an image representing Shakespeare and Company.

"George, he's a great man, a great man," he repeated as he lowered his shirt to conclude the viewing.

Having lived at the store for the better part of a month, Kurt had discovered there was a minimum of structure. The official store hours were noon to midnight, but most days George opened earlier to accommodate the crowds. The major rule was that residents were expected to be out of bed in the morning to cart out boxes of books for the sidewalk display and sweep the floors before the customers arrived. Beyond that, George liked everyone to help out for an hour each day, whether it be sorting books, washing dishes, or performing minor carpentry chores. More idealistically, George also asked each resident to read a book a day from the library. Kurt said many chose plays and novellas to meet the quota, but he was still tackling novels. He fished out a dog-eared copy of *Tropic of Cancer* from his pocket to illustrate his point.

The other important detail was the store's closing hour. As Shakespeare and Company shut at midnight, residents were expected to be back beforehand to help bring in the boxes of books and lock the shop for the night. The closing time also served as a de facto curfew, because with the store locked, it was difficult to get back inside to one's bed. Kurt said you could arrange to be met at the door or toss stones at the window in hopes of rousing another resident. Or, best of all, he added with a gleam in his eye, you could hold the keys to the store.

"Right now, it's the Gaucho who has the keys."

The Gaucho was another Argentinian, who'd lived at Shakespeare and Company for three months and had gradually earned George's trust and the right to the keys. He made sure the residents kept in order, watched over the store, and occasionally helped with banking and other administrative tasks. Now this Gaucho was moving on to Italy to follow a woman, and his departure would leave a vacuum. Someone would have to fill the role of George's top assistant, and there was great speculation as to who would be given the ring of keys associated with the position. It was obvious that Kurt wanted them badly.

As he spoke, I fingered the keys in my pocket and wondered if they were the coveted ring. I didn't say anything though, not wanting to damage our budding friendship or, worse, earn an enemy in my precarious new home. Even if Shakespeare and Company appeared to be a happy commune among the books, it was clear there was still some sort of social hierarchy to be climbed.

Our talk was interrupted by a voice bellowing from below. I couldn't make out any words, but the sound was a cross between the call of a rutting caribou and a grizzly bear with its foreleg caught in a steel trap. Whatever this noise was, Kurt jumped to his feet and made for the stairs.

"That's the Gaucho now," he shouted over his shoulder. "We have to go."

Something about the voice made me hesitate, but still I followed, too unsure of this new world to do much else. Downstairs, there was a tall man with a goatee and a fedora tilted at a rakish angle. This, I gathered, was the Gaucho. He was leaning over and talking to a woman seated behind the clerk's desk. Kurt informed me she was a young actress by the name of Sophie. She was taking a year away from Oxford to study at the Jacques Lecoq school of movement in Paris. Like Pia, George had given her a job at the desk one day when he'd been struck by her abundant charms.

"Where have you been?" the Gaucho roared when he looked up and saw Kurt. "It's time for dinner."

Kurt hastily apologized and explained I was a new resident and he'd been showing me around the store. When the Gaucho heard this, he puffed up his chest.

"How long do you think you're going to stay for?"

"I'm not sure," I replied, puzzled by the question. "A while probably."

"A week," he said. "Nobody stays at the bookstore for more than a week."

I shrugged, uncertain. "George told me I could stay as long as I wanted."

The Gaucho grimaced. "Don't listen to what George says. He's too nice. If everybody stayed as long as they wanted, there'd be no space in the bookstore. You, you stay a week."

It was then that Kurt demonstrated his allegiances. After a soft cough to gain the floor, he reported that George had promised me the antiquarian room. Hearing this, the Gaucho growled and took an aggressive step toward me.

"And what do you think you're going to do about the poet?" he demanded, jamming his finger into my chest.

Just as the scene began a slow descent into ugliness, the door of the bookstore creaked open. It was the man with the black hair and French-Chinese dictionary I'd seen in the library the day of the tea party.

"You're here," he said, slapping me on my arm in a most friendly fashion. "Welcome, welcome."

The man introduced himself as Ablimit and then turned to Kurt and the Gaucho. "We miss the best food if we don't leave now."

The urgency of dinner trumped the Gaucho's rage. He slowly removed his finger from my chest and turned away. The three of them were half out the doorway when Ablimit looked back at me.

"Aren't you coming to dinner?"

I hesitated, but Ablimit smiled again and Kurt reached back to drag me along. Even the Gaucho nodded grudgingly. It seemed a temporary truce had been called.

9.

During the weeks of living cheaply at the hotel, I'd devised a series of ma neuvers to eat with little or no expense in Paris. There was a restaurant on rue de Clignancourt that served limitless plates of free couscous and vegetables on Friday nights so long as you ordered a half glass of beer. The large American Church in the seventh arrondissement had an almost-free all-you-can-eat pizza night with a minimum of sermonizing. Then there was the constant delight of the four-franc baguette and the endless cheeses that could be had so inexpensively at the city's supermarkets.

A particularly sublime discovery came from a teacher at the French school I'd attended. Anne was a graceful woman who took the job as language teacher after her husband died. She thrilled in introducing neophytes to the enchantments of Paris and by chance took an interest in polishing my rather rough crime reporter self. Anne suggested operas to see, offered books to read and, most wondrously, introduced me to the nutritious world of the Paris vernissage.

Vernissage is a derivative of the French word for varnish. In reference to the last shining coat that artists layered on their paintings the night before their shows, opening parties became known by this name. In an art-rich city like Paris, there was always some gallery launching some artist and they lured visitors with bottles of wine and plates of hors d'oeuvres. Though these pleasures were intended for the journalists and potential patrons, if one dressed correctly and knew how to behave, these events made for delicious meals.

Anne knew the best of the Left Bank vernissage scene, and while she toured these venues in search of new artists and old friends, I somewhat crassly focused on the food. The protocol was simple: Browse the art with an attentive eye, compliment the artist, then hover by the food table for long enough to gorge on a day's worth of calories. There was one night when a gallery on the Left Bank served hundreds of miniature spinach and salmon quiches; another time, it was sushi and rice wine on a boat moored in the Seine; my favorite was an event for a painter of Lebanese descent that featured hummus, tabbouleh, kafta, and a divine array of falafels.

Leaving Shakespeare and Company that night, Kurt and the rest dismissed my schemes as the work of an amateur. With everyone nearly broke and no proper cooking facilities in the lower part of the bookstore, the residents had become expert scavengers. They swore they would initiate me to their ways, and the lessons were to begin that very night.

We turned left out of the bookstore, crossed rue St. Jacques, and took rue de la Huchette. The narrow street had once been among the filthiest in Paris and home to a young Napoléon Bonaparte when he first arrived in the city. Now it was a garish tourist ghetto, filled with Greek restaurants that competed for customers with displays of skewered seafood and the scent of burning fat. Touts stood in the restaurant doorways, playing merry with the crowds and shattering cheap porcelain plates at the feet of the more promising herds.

Shakespeare and Company residents clearly weren't worth wasting plates over, so we negotiated the street with ease. Emerging at place St. Michel, we cut past the spouting stone lions, along the flower shops and trendy bars of rue St. André des Arts, then down boulevard St. Germain until we arrived at a dismal gray building on rue Mabillon. Two guards stood slouched at the front door, but Kurt told me to walk straight in as if I belonged. We climbed two flights of stairs and came to an enormous cafeteria with row after row of benches and a long snaking line at the food counter.

This was a student restaurant, one of more than a dozen in Paris. Subsidized by the government, a full meal cost fifteen francs here, just two American dollars. Technically, one needed a student identification card, but the line was full of other impostors like us: a family with three small children, a couple with shaved heads and scalp studs, a drunken man with a variety of stains across his shirtfront and down his pant leg.

In exchange for a colorful meal ticket, one received two bread rolls, a thick bowl of vegetable soup, a generous slice of Brie, half a boiled egg with a squib of Dijon mayonnaise as garnish, a main plate of grilled lamb, sautéed potatoes, and green beans, a strawberry yogurt and even a slice of honey sponge cake with sliced almonds for dessert. With each morsel of food added to my tray, the more inclined I was to agree with my companions: This was the zenith of the cheap Paris meal.

We sat at one of the long benches and while we ate, Kurt acted as spotter. Whenever a fellow diner left behind a tray with an untouched piece of cheese or a fair-size chunk of bread, Kurt raced out of his seat to grab the bounty. The objective was to collect enough abandoned food to furnish late-night snacks for the entire bookstore family.

"Watch him well," the Gaucho advised. "Next time, it's your job."

Throughout this strange meal, Ablimit asked questions about my work at the newspaper and freedom of the press in Canada. As the dictionary I saw him with that first day suggested, he was in fact from China, but not Chinese, he stressed. He was Ughur, an ethnic minority from the northwest of the country. For more than half a decade, he'd worked as a television reporter and documentary producer, but he became frustrated by the censorship and pressure to put a positive spin on the news. Two years before, shortly after his thirtieth birthday, he'd managed to get a visa and then headed west, stopping first at a kibbutz in Israel, then moving up to Paris and Shakespeare and Company.

"People just find themselves here," said Ablimit, shrugging.

As I ate, I felt bliss. Part of it was the simple pleasure of a full belly. I had always been thin of frame, consistently weighing 170 pounds for my six feet and one inch in height. But during that scant month in Paris, I'd nearly starved myself trying to conserve money, eating one meal a day instead of three, fasting entirely when I knew there was a promising vernissage that night. The week before, I'd passed a pharmacy that offered the free use of a scale and I'd availed myself of the service. The digital display read seventy-four kilograms, so the shock didn't come until I scratched out the conversion in my notebook. It translated to just under 163 pounds. Between the forced diet and the long hours of walking, I'd lost seven pounds I could ill afford to lose. Now, thanks to the combination of George's pepper soup and this plentiful cafeteria dinner, my body rejoiced in the sudden rush of salts and fats.

I was also coasting along on my bookstore high. It was nearly miraculous that I'd found such an exotic solution to my predicament, and I felt giddy that the fear of homelessness—or worse, being forced to beg for a loan from my parents—had been lifted. Of course, if I'd rationally analyzed my situation, I would have realized it was barely better than before: I still had no money, no job, no plans for the future, and the bed in the bookstore certainly wasn't the height of stability. But the day you move into an infamous old bookstore certainly isn't the day for rational thought. I was eating with three intriguing and gregarious men from three very different corners of the world, we were sharing stories and laughing like friends. It was all good.

And though I didn't tell anyone at the table this, I took special pleasure in that cafeteria dinner because it was my birthday. I had turned twenty-nine that day, and though I'd always shunned parties and dismissed birthdays as something that should be celebrated by mothers, I was happy not to be alone. If I hadn't found the bookstore, I would have spent the night in that dreary hotel room, looking forward to nothing more than another long walk the next day. At least at Shakespeare and Company, tomorrow offered the infinite promise of the unknown.

When we'd finished our dinners and Kurt had a hefty sack of leftovers, we treated ourselves to cups of two-franc coffee from a machine on a lower floor of the building. The three of them discussed their plans for the night: Ablimit was giving a Chinese lesson at a nearby café, Kurt had accepted an invitation for a glass of wine from a young woman who'd been browsing in the bookstore earlier that day, and the Gaucho had errands to run in preparation for his departure for Italy. Ablimit and Kurt left first, leaving the Gaucho and me together in the entrance hall of the student cafeteria. Once we were alone, the Gaucho turned on me with the same ominous tone as before.

"I'm still the boss here," he said. "You'd better learn that."

Despite my high spirits, I felt my hackles rise. I have a pet theory that all that is bad and good about men can be neatly divided into animal and human behaviors. The animal side represents the base instincts that make us want to strike out at strangers on our territory, mate with every female, and hoard food and belongings for ourselves. Our human side, the result of overdeveloped brains that allow us to predict the logical results of our actions, tells us peace with the stranger is a more efficient way to secure safety, a monogamous relationship better ensures healthy reproduction, and sharing resources among fellow members of a community protects individuals. As he stood before me, the Gaucho was nothing but a dog of a man eager to prove himself alpha male.

"I'm watching you," he warned. "Don't think you can get away with anything."

Before anything else could be said, he turned his back and disappeared into the Paris night.

10.

Though ruffled by the Gaucho, there were more urgent concerns as I retraced my steps to Shakespeare and Company. George had entrusted me with a most formidable task and I was eager to prove my worth. I also suspected that two birds might be felled with this single stone: If I could please George by properly expelling the poet, surely the Gaucho would be forced to back down. Though there were no hydra to slay or stables to clean, I felt a little bit like Hercules.

When I arrived at the store, the antiquarian room was empty. The shutters on the windows were open and the light was on inside, but the door was locked and there was no sign of my prey. Satisfied Simon hadn't returned, I crossed back to the main bookstore with the intention of sitting near the window so I could monitor the entrance.

At the desk was a dark-haired man with a pale face. He was meticulously dressed in a sharp black suit jacket, a blue shirt, and a black tie. His appearance reminded me of the mods of the eighties with their ankle-tight pants and thin ties, but this fellow looked far more sinister. As I went to say hello, the man recoiled to the back corner of the desk and raised an eyebrow suspiciously.

Quickly introducing myself in hopes of relaxing the air, I explained I would be living at the bookstore for the foreseeable future. The man left my hand hanging a touch longer than was comfortable before tentatively accepting my greeting.

"I've heard about you . . ." he began in an accent that had a strong dose of north London in it. He was still hunched defensively in the corner, but then, as if he just woke up and didn't realize where he was, he examined his posture, shook his head, and sprang upward in his seat with a grin.

"Oh, hello, old boy. I don't know where my head is these days." To emphasize his point, he violently whacked his left ear two times with his palm. "Something's gone wrong with my ear. I think its been affecting my equilibrium."

Waving me gallantly into the green metal chair beside the desk, the man continued: "Make yourself comfortable. Sorry I was a bit off there. You see, strange people come in at night and I'm always a tad . . ." He put a finger to his chin, searching for the appropriate word. ". . . apprehensive."

He then reached under the cash register and withdrew an enormous black flashlight with a menacingly long metal handle, the sort favored by security guards who don't qualify to carry more lethal weapons.

"I keep this just in case," he smiled, caressing the flashlight with real tenderness.

Well used to the inherent idiosyncrasy of everybody and everything associated with Shakespeare and Company, I merely said it sounded like a wise policy.

This was Luke the Night Man. He'd been on a purposeful drift for years—around Spain and Greece playing harmonica in a blues band, from New York to Rio with an old-school word processor and notes for a novel weighing down his backpack, up and down India and Thailand. He'd once worked in a back-alley London jazz establishment, but his last real job was as a muppet, one of the techs who set up the sound equipment and scaffolding at stadium rock shows.

"I quit when somebody dropped a wrench on my head," he said, rubbing his skull in memory of the pain.

Luke had arrived in Paris the previous April with three hundred dollars in his pocket and a vague idea of getting construction work. Instead, he happened past Shakespeare and Company on his second day in the city and decided to ask for a job. George gave him both the night shift and a bed in the store and he was set up.

A while back, Luke had found an apartment in the north end of the city, not too far from my old hotel, but he'd continued working at the store from eight o'clock until midnight, Monday through Saturday. One of the disadvantages of keeping the bookstore open so late was the rather unpredictable crowds it attracted, so along with straightening the occasional shelf and selling books to the surprisingly frequent late-night customers, Luke's major occupation was warding off the thieves, drunks, and raving madmen who began appearing at the store in increasing numbers the closer it got to midnight.

"There's one now!" Luke erupted, and sure enough, out front by the cherry trees, there was a lurching drunk screeching at the night skies and waving a near-empty bottle of cheap Bordeaux.

Peering through the window, I watched as Luke took the drunk gently by the arm, spoke a few words into his ear, and then led him away from the shop. The drunk grinned wildly, like a child being taken to the circus, and Luke returned a minute later, making an exaggerated gesture of dusting off his hands. "I call that one Godzilla."

Sitting with Luke at the desk of Shakespeare and Company turned out to be terribly unsettling, like watching a man cursed to live a perpetual case of lady or the tiger. Anytime the door creaked open, he would flinch backward into defensive posture. If it was a friend, an interesting tourist, or, better yet, a cute young woman, he would smile and show utmost hospitality. If it was one of the army of freakish night visitors, he would leap to his feet, arm pointing back out the door, and holler, "Out! Out! OUT!"

I genuinely liked this latest bookstore character. He had a subversive charm and was suave sitting there in his black suit. When Luke asked whom I was waiting for, I felt comfortable enough to confess my mission.

"That sounds like George," Luke said after digesting all I had told him. "He puts people in these awkward situations just to see what will happen. He's an anarchist that way."

———

According to Luke, Simon had been an alcoholic tumbling toward destruction when he moved into Shakespeare and Company back in 1995. He'd pulled himself together under George's watch, but it had been years since he'd finished with the drink and still he clung to the bookstore. It was a vicious circle: The longer Simon stayed, the more detached from society he became, while the more detached he became, the harder it was for him to leave.

Kurt and the Gaucho, the young lions of the bookstore, were the ones who were rallying for Simon's eviction. They neither liked nor trusted the poet. Simon was much older, mildly condescending, and massively eccentric. There was also something about his teeth; he was described as having a very English smile. It was the Gaucho who pestered George about Simon's alleged theft of money and regularly pointed out examples of his sloth. Luke admitted that he, too, was suspicious and was convinced the poet needed a healthy shove to get out of his rut.

"George never would have asked Simon to leave himself. It's against his nature—he doesn't like conflict," concluded Luke. "It makes sense he would ask somebody like you."

It apparently wasn't unusual for George to lay such responsibility at the foot of a stranger. Luke cited the case of one of George's oldest friends in Paris. In the 1960s, this man walked into the bookstore while George was minding the desk. George asked a small favor: He was going to run out for a moment and he wanted this stranger to watch the store. Though his only intention had been to buy an English novel, the man agreed. Four hours later, George returned, having gone to a book warehouse in the suburbs to place an order. This random customer had watched the desk the entire time and had accounted for every book sold and franc taken.

"You'll see with George. He gets a feel for people," said Luke. "He's not often wrong."

By this time, Luke and I had been speaking for more than an hour, so I decided to make sure this curious Simon hadn't arrived without being noticed. When I got outside, I saw that the books and benches had disappeared from out front of the antiquarian room, the shutters on the windows had been closed, and there was even a heavy wooden guard on the window of the door. Inside, however, a light still burned.

Astonished all this had been done without enough noise to rouse either Luke or myself, I knocked soundly on the door. Twice. The third time, there was a pained reply in a soaring English accent.

"Wha-aat is it?"

"Simon? I've just moved into the store, and George asked me to have a talk with you."

A long silence followed. "I'm really beat, okay?" he finally replied. "And I'm not feeling well. I had this terrible accident today. I'm just not up for it."

"Look, George was pretty insistent. Can't we just talk for five minutes?"

"Have a heart, won't you? I've had a horrible day. Come back tomorrow morning. Okay, mate?"

I slunk back to the main store, angry with myself for letting the poet slip so easily through my fingers. Luke just sat and nodded knowingly.

"I thought he might sneak in. He's been keeping a low profile since this all began. He's a sly one."

Seeing my chest fall further, Luke laughed.

"Don't worry, old boy. You'll have another chance tomorrow."

When midnight came, I helped Luke and the rest carry in boxes and close up the shop. Then, utterly exhausted by the day's events, I climbed the stairs and collapsed into my strange new bed among the books.

II.

I woke up straight. The instant my eyes opened, everything felt sharp and clear, as if I'd finished a wind sprint or stepped from a frothing sea. I'd always been one to play with snooze buttons, lolling in bed and rationalizing being ten, twenty, thirty minutes late for work or school. But that first morning at the bookstore, there were no slow degrees of consciousness or seductive fingers of sleep. I was alive.

In the gloom of the fiction room, it was impossible to tell the time of day. The bookstore was shivering, though, cold enough that my breath broke into fog. I dressed quickly, putting on an extra sweater and a toque I'd brought from home.

Ablimit was sitting at the desk in the front room, working on grammar exercises. As I approached, he put a finger to his lips and pointed to where the Gaucho lay curled and sleeping. I noticed there was an *E* and a Chinese symbol inked onto the skin between the thumb and forefinger of Ablimit's right hand. It was a ritual, he explained, to write either an *F* or *E* on his hand each morning to remind him what language to think in that day.

"You must train your mind," he said softly, tapping his finger against his temple.

It wasn't yet ten o'clock and George was still at the open-air vegetable market at place Maubert. Ablimit told me we'd open the store when he returned, so I went back to my room, found the light, and pulled a book from a shelf. It was *Lolita,* and the more I read, the more astounded I was that I hadn't come across this novel before. Reporting gross acts of pedophilia are a must for any city newspaper, so I'd long been versed in nonfictional accounts of child sexual abuse. On dozens of occasions, I'd sat through an accused man's courtroom testimony or interviewed the mother of the victim, but not until Nabakov had I heard the sickness described in such loving tones.

Shortly before eleven, George appeared, wearing a smorgasbord of clothes—a faded blue baseball cap that sat unfastened atop his head like a limp rag, a red blazer that was missing buttons, a bright purple shirt, and pants that stopped well above his ankles, revealing unmatched socks. In his hand was a canvas grocery bag overflowing with leeks.

"What are you reading?" he demanded, flicking at the cover of my book.

When I showed him, he nodded approval. "I prefer *Pale Fire,* but there's nothing like the great Russian novels," he said. "My favorite is *The Idiot.* I think I'm a little bit like Prince Myshkin, bumbling along in this world of my dreams, trying to do my best without any grip on reality."

It was time to start work, so while George deposited the leeks in his office, I hurried downstairs. Kurt was in the bed across from the stained-glass alcove, and the store's sixth and final resident, an Italian woman from Bologna, was asleep in the Russian section. I shook them both awake and told them Shakespeare and Company was opening for the day.

Out front of the store, the Gaucho was explaining he had parcels to mail and couldn't stay to help. Ablimit stood beside George, who was peering intently at the sky. It was the usual miserable gray.

"Everything out," barked George.

"But sir, don't you think it's going to rain?"

"Nonsense!" George jumped toward Ablimit and began slapping his back with the faded baseball cap. "What are you? A lunatic?"

Before Ablimit could say anything else, George hustled inside the store. At night, all of the boxes of books from outside were piled around the cash desk, along with the wood and crates used for the sidewalk display tables. George grabbed a long plank and teetered out of the store with it. Worried about his eighty-six-year-old body, I lunged to help, but he just swung it at me in disgust.

"What are you doing, you imbecile? Get the stools."

I found two battered stools inside and George placed the plank on top of them to form a shelf in front of the main window. Kurt, Ablimit, and the Italian woman were ferrying out boxes of cheap paperbacks, so I took the opportunity to check on the antiquarian room. The shutters were open and the wooden guard had been removed from the window of the door, but the room was empty. Simon had eluded me again.

In the meantime, Kurt had begun carrying out a complete set of the 1967 *Encyclopaedia Britannica,* which George insisted was going to sell if he left it in front of the store long enough. Ablimit pointed at this and then muttered in my ear: "George, he crazy sometimes. Who wants old encyclopedia?"

George, sensing dissent, bullied his way past and helped Kurt with the encyclopedia. On the way back, he made sure to bang volumes G through N into Ablimit's abdomen and then went off cackling.

Once the sidewalk display was in place and the store was swept and readied, the others dispersed. George sat at the desk, drinking coffee and reading the *International Herald Tribune.* He had long been a voracious consumer of the news and as a young man kept vast files of clippings regarding labor issues, poverty studies, and the political movements in the Soviet Union. Today, he only flicked at the newspaper and harrumphed that it was capitalist propaganda. It was quarter past eleven and as the bookstore didn't officially open until noon, Pia hadn't yet arrived for her shift.

"Is there anything I can do to help?"

He grunted and waved me away, but eager to make a good impression, I pressed on. "Maybe I could put away these books?" I pointed to a precarious pile of paperbacks that sat on the desk's edge. Not looking up, George made a motion with the back of his hand that suggested approval. I began to shelve the books but was almost immediately interrupted.

"That doesn't go there, you nincompoop!" He sent a hardcover whizzing into my chest. "Put this with the art books."

We worked like that for almost an hour, me shelving, George serving customers and yelling orders, until Pia arrived on her bicycle shortly past noon. She was wearing a pink silk scarf and her cheeks were flushed from her ride to the store. George grumbled about her being fifteen minutes late, but he was quickly mollified by a good-morning kiss on the cheek.

"Will you do me one small favor?" Pia asked once George had gone upstairs. "I had the most horrendous evening. Will you watch the desk for five minutes?"

Before I could answer, she was out the door.

Sitting at the desk of Shakespeare and Company is a bit like sitting at the prow of a large ship. The desk is at the front of the store and faces the window so the vast bulk of the store is behind you. This means that the customers flood past as they enter and then disappear into the rooms of books. The only way to monitor them is to twist painfully around in the seat and then lean awkwardly out over the desk. The upside to this arrangement is the view: From the desk, you can admire the passersby on the esplanade, the two cherry trees, and then, beyond that, the shadows of Ile de la Cité.

As soon as Pia left, I realized I had no idea what I was doing. The cash register was crusty from various hot and cold spilled beverages and the money drawer hung crookedly out, exposing wrinkled fifty- and one-hundred-franc notes. Adding to this financial chaos, there were coins scattered across the desktop and two more fifty-franc notes crumpled on the floor. As I experimented with buttons on the register, none of which seemed to have any effect, a customer approached.

"Can you tell me how much this is?"

A stern-looking woman was holding a new paperback copy of *A Moveable Feast*. George kept dozens on hand because so many tourists wanted to read about Hemingway's Paris. They also occasionally confused Sylvia Beach's original Shakespeare and Company, which has an entire chapter devoted to it in Hemingway's memoir, with its present-day incarnation. To George's great irritation, they sometimes even asked him to autograph the book.

After a thorough examination, all I could find was the American price. "It says twelve dollars," I offered uselessly.

The woman was digging into her purse for a calculator so we could determine the exact franc-dollar exchange when I noticed a square of white paper taped beside the register with the following equations: $ = 10, £ = 12. At this rate, the woman owed 120 francs, but she pointed out the official exchange rate was closer to seven francs to a dollar. I couldn't help but agree, and after some quick arithmetic she presented her credit card to pay the eighty-four-franc sum.

Thus began a frantic search for a credit card machine. I looked for a modern one with the magnetic reader and punch pad, but no luck. I dug under the desk to see if there was an old-fashioned sliding contraption with carbon imprints. Nothing. The woman was becoming impatient and only had sixty-eight francs in coins with her. Embarrassed, I accepted her money and rushed her out of the store before George could discover my ineptitude.

As I sat there wondering how I would handle the next customer, Kurt walked in.

"Pia is sitting down with a friend at Café Panis. She took you." He shook his head disapprovingly and announced he was going upstairs to write.

"Wait! Kurt!" I shouted before he could leave. "Do we take credit cards?"

He looked at me with a raised eyebrow. "Dude, Shakespeare and Company doesn't even have a telephone. Of course we don't take credit cards."

A weedy young man arrived next and bought a copy of *Love in the Time of Cholera,* thankfully proffering cash. I was only slightly staggered when he asked that the book be stamped. Remembering Eve on the day of the tea party, I found the ink pad and pressed the bookstore logo of a kindly eyed Shakespeare onto his page. As he left, a young couple stepped into the store. The woman held a guidebook open and scanned the page.

"This is Shakespeare and Company. They published *Ulysses* here and the owner is the son of the poet Walt Whitman," she said with authority.

The man only listened with bored eyes. I decided I should probably correct her, but the couple promptly left to see the next featured attraction, Paris's second-oldest tree, which was held up by concrete buttresses in the park beside the bookshop.

A half hour after she vanished, Pia returned with flowing apologies. "I had to have a coffee. You can't believe what's happening to me. It's all so exhausting."

Assuring me her crisis was far too complicated to explain, she fluttered her eyelids and took her place at the desk. My compassion her slave, all I could do was babble something about replacing her anytime she needed. Then, feeling a deep blush coming on, I hurried away.

Upstairs, Kurt was assaulting the typewriter again. Amid a savage clattering of keys, he scolded me for interrupting his writing, so I crossed the hallway and knocked on George's door.

"Is there anything else I can do?"

He was sitting at his desk with a book catalog, carefully filling out an order form with a dull pencil. He looked up at me as if he didn't understand my question.

"Go out and enjoy the city."

I stayed where I was. "I'd like to help if I can."

"Why don't you write?"

"I write at night."

He sighed and put his pencil down. "I'm so far behind on work. I want to be downstairs at the desk with the customers, that's where all the fun is, but instead I'm up here with this."

He waved a book catalog in front of me and then motioned me to come closer. "Isn't that awful?" he said, pointing to a list of books on promotion. "*The Art of War* listed as a business-advice book. What does that tell you about our society?"

Brushing aside the catalog, he reached into his pocket and withdrew a red two-hundred-franc note.

"If you really want to help, there's a Marks and Spencer across the river that has Cheddar cheese. You can't get it anywhere else in Paris. Get two blocks of the strong cheese."

He scratched his head and thought some more.

"There's an Ed's nearby. It's the cheapest store in Paris. Olives without the stones. And beer. They have cheap German beer in bottles, fifteen francs for a small case. Make sure you get the strong stuff."

The strong stuff?

"You know," he chastised. "The strong stuff. It's the same price as the regular kind. Go on."

I easily found the Marks and Spencer store on rue Rivoli near the Châtelet tower, but the cheese fridge was a greater challenge. There were six grades of cheddar, including "strong" and "biting." The way they were arranged on the shelves, it appeared that biting was stronger than strong. The question was whether George meant *strong* as a noun or an adjective. It seemed a daunting test, and I circled the aisle three times, trying to recall the exact inflection of his voice. Concluding George to be a man of extreme tastes, I bought two bricks of the biting.

Around the corner was the Ed's. It was a discount grocery store in the great global tradition of discount grocery stores. The products were still in their cardboard boxes, there were jumbo sizes and a long line at the checkout counter where you had to pay for your plastic bags. What was so unlike the North American discount stores were the products available: champagnes, no-name foie gras, frozen cuts of duck, seven types of mustard. The gourmet roots went deep here.

The olives were easy to find, as was the beer. The strong variety was clearly marked at 6.9 percent alcohol, compared with 4.5 percent for the regular kind. The only question that plagued me was if it was good for an eighty-six-year-old man to drink high-alcohol beer. Remembering how easily he'd swung the plank at me in the morning, I bought a six-pack of the strong.

When I handed George the bag of groceries with the receipts and proper change, he pulled out a brick of cheese. After inspecting the label, he winked at me in the most gratifying of fashions.

"I made your lunch," he said, bringing a homemade hamburger with grilled onions out of the kitchen.

He opened us each a beer and poured his into a glass half-filled with ice. As we ate, I described how I'd missed Simon the night before and promised to speak to him that day. George nodded approval and repeated that he wanted me to keep the antiquarian room open for customers during the day.

"Detective novels," he sighed.

I also told George of my half hour behind the desk, save for the discount I was obliged to give the credit card–wielding woman. He took a special interest in my tale of the tourists who'd been confused by the store's history.

It somewhat bothered George that his Shakespeare and Company was mistaken for Sylvia Beach's old bookstore, which had in fact published *Ulysses.* However, the confusion that the great poet Walt Whitman was his father could be blamed squarely on George. The poet is one of George's heroes, not just because of *Leaves of Grass,* but also for his efforts as a renegade publisher in Brooklyn at the turn of the last century. Walt Whitman is held in such esteem, there is even a portrait of him anchored to an outside wall to greet visitors. And when George first arrived in Paris in the 1940s, he often passed himself off as the poet's illegitimate grandchild, even writing a letter to his mother asking her to look into the genealogy. The rumor had even made its way into the pages of papers like the *New York Times,* the *Washington Post,* and the *Independent.* As George grew older and his age became more inscrutable, the rumor became bolder and named him as Walt Whitman's actual son—even though the poet died in 1892, twenty-one years before George was even born. Considering this, it was no great surprise that visitors occasionally asked if there was a family connection.

"Sometimes I say yes," George shrugged. "So what? It makes them happy to think he was my father."

And, of course, George wasn't really even lying. His father was indeed Walt Whitman the writer, but the author of science textbooks, not epic poems.

Finishing my plate, I stood up and thanked him for the meal. He motioned good-bye with his pencil, but before I got to the door, he called out to me again.

"Wait! Read this."

He pushed a dog-eared paperback toward me. It was a copy of *The Idiot.*

The rest of the day was spent stationed by the front window waiting for Simon. Dusk set, night fell, then Luke appeared for his shift.

"Still no luck?" he asked.

For the next hour or so, Luke and I talked, but every fifteen minutes, I got up to check the antiquarian room to ensure there wouldn't be a repeat of the poet's covert return. Around nine o'clock, Kurt came into the store and held out a bottle of red wine.

"Eleven-franc special," he beamed.

When I told him I couldn't join him upstairs for a drink because I was waiting for the poet, Kurt shook his head.

"I'll take Simon's things and chuck them onto the road if you want."

I assured him this wouldn't be necessary, and Kurt started to grouse some more about the poet. That's when I heard a slight scraping sound and dashed to the front of the store. There stood a tall man wearing a black-brimmed hat with a flowered cloth band, a seventies-style brown suede trench coat, and crooked silver-framed glasses. He had a drawn face and wild curls of white hair sprouted from underneath his hat. Startled by my sudden appearance, he tried to cover his distress with a smile. I noted that the few decayed and twisted teeth he had left were indeed very English.

"Simon?"

12.

"Simon?" I repeated. "We were supposed to talk this morning. I've been waiting all day."

The man was in the process of lifting one of the benches to carry it into the antiquarian room. Returning it to the ground, he straightened his back and brushed his lapels with considerable dignity.

"Oh . . . oh, hello, matey." His eyes were dodging about, as if he were looking for a place to hide. "I was about to go find you. I was closing up first. You know, the weather looks like it might turn."

It was the dark cloud of Paris night but otherwise there wasn't a hint of rain. Still, Simon held out long fingers, as if expecting the first drops of a deluge. Having little choice but to accept the explanation, I properly introduced myself and together we finished closing down the antiquarian room. Luke, standing in the main doorway to better watch the proceedings, gave me an encouraging nod as I followed Simon into his lair.

Once the door locked behind us and the shutters were secured with iron bars, the antiquarian room felt like a fortress. Tapping the solid wooden panel that protected the door window, Simon assured me he needed such defenses against the miscreants of the night.

"They're perpetually screeching and fighting until all hours of the morning. Once a drunk even urinated on the door and it ran in through the crack and puddled on the floor. Talk about a person you wouldn't mind watching wither away in a gas chamber while standing comfortably on the other side of the Plexiglas."

But with the room barricaded like this, there was a terrible sense of claustrophobia, not to mention the tang of musk associated with the cramped living quarters of men. I picked my way through the clutter of boxes and benches that were kept in the room at night and found a place in the stuffed leather armchair. Simon immediately began apologizing for the previous night.

"You wouldn't believe what happened. I was walking by the river and a woman on Rollerblades came whizzing along like a demon and knocked me over. Those things should be outlawed. They're so American. Why can't a person just walk? Why do they have to put wheels on their feet and go rushing about at a hundred miles an hour, knocking into innocent pedestrians and smashing them to the ground? I could have broken my arm!"

While he spoke, Simon shuffled papers among a series of orange and blue folders. Though he appeared to be moving items at random, I hesitated to disturb him.

"Look," I finally said. George wanted me to talk to you . . ."

At this, Simon turned a porridgy gray and put up his hand to stop me. Getting down on his knees, he searched wildly under his bed until he located a green cardboard box. Opening it with an immense sigh of relief, he withdrew a translucent brown glass bottle labeled Neo-Codion.

"I'm not feeling well, what with the monstrous weather," he said, nudging his head in the direction of the door. "This helps with the congestion in my chest."

He put his hand to his mouth and coughed slightly. It sounded rather forced. Then, hoisting the bottle to his mouth, he took a long swallow.

"Captain Cody's Midnight Rangers to the rescue," he said wiping his mouth with the back of his hand.

I'd heard talk of the wonders of legalized codeine in France, but this was my first direct encounter. In Canada, codeine is a common opium-based painkiller prescribed by doctors after minor surgery or to combat severe toothaches. When I was a reporter, my mentor, Woloschuk, would collect tablets of codeine-rich Tylenol 3 from girlfriends. When it had been a particularly bad day at the newspaper, we'd sit in his apartment, swallow a handful each, and watch the Cartoon Network for a couple of sluggish hours. It was a pleasant relaxant, but nothing extraordinary.

In France, however, codeine is an industry all to itself. Pharmacies sell six-ounce bottles of sweet codeine syrup or packets of twenty light blue sugar-coated codeine pills for twelve francs, a bit more than $1.50. A single pill or teaspoon has as much codeine as a Tylenol 3, and you don't need a doctor's prescription, though there is a state-imposed limit of one box or bottle of codeine a day, and the pharmacist generally scowls if you become too regular a customer. Still, with the flashing green pharmacy cross on almost every Parisian corner, it is easy enough to stockpile the drug, and there are many a surreal story about nights spent under codeine's sweet spell.

The theories for this bonanza are rampant. One claims that the government needed to provide a soft fix for all of the workers who returned to France after becoming addicted to opium and heroin in French Indochina. My favorite is conspiratorial: All this discount codeine is a cheap and sweet tranquilizer provided to keep a notoriously revolutionary population happily subdued. Simon certainly appeared calmer now.

"These Paris winters," he sighed. "The dampness gets in your bones. The old man doesn't like me running a heater in here because of the electricity bills."

He took another guzzle, grimacing slightly for effect, and then replaced the lid and put the bottle back under his bed. With Simon more composed, we returned to the subject of my visit.

"Look, I don't know much about the situation, but George says you've been at the bookstore too long," I said. "He wants me to move into this room. I'm supposed to make sure you leave this week."

"He said that? George wants to be rid of me?"

I nodded and Simon leaned back dejectedly, raising his eyes to the ceiling.

"You have a place to go, don't you?"

"I have friends, sure, I can find places to go, but not at short notice like this. I need time. It's the middle of winter. I can't just go out on the street. It's cold out there."

Taking off his hat, he smoothed his wild white hair. Gradually, his hand movements became furious and I worried he would rub tufts from his scalp. Finally, he slapped his hand on the bed in rage.

"You know what's happening, don't you? It's those kids from next door. That Gaucho and his pretty little flunky. What's his name? It's so odious. Kuu-rrrt. That's it. They march around like they own the place, and now they've got it into their heads that I should leave. They've poisoned George against me. Nobody understands how much I hate this civilization and the people produced by it."

Heated now, he thrust his hand back under the bed, rooted around some more, and pulled out what looked to be a can of beer. Prying open the tab, he tilted the contents down his throat. The can was emptied in one long swallow, like a pelican downing a fish.

"Don't worry, it's alcohol-free," he said, eager to show me the label. "It gives me the taste, but it doesn't even have one percent. I'll tell you, though, the stress is going to send me back to the drink. It's unbearable. You've got to help me."

Simon was looking at me so beseechingly that I didn't know what to say. Judging by the dire condition of his clothes and the fact he'd been forced to live in a bookstore, without access to shower or kitchen, for five long years, he didn't have an abundance of financial resources. And if my brief time with him was any indication, he wasn't the type of man who could merge seamlessly into the rigors of an everyday job.

"Couldn't you just buy me a few days?" he asked with real despair in his eyes.

It was at about this point that Simon began fiddling with his black waist pouch and took out a vial with a plastic screw top. He opened it and withdrew a generous lump of hashish.

"You don't smoke, by any chance? I usually have a little puff before I go to bed. I think I'll need it tonight."

Thus began a most convoluted evening. A dozen different trains of thought sped through Simon's head at any one time and he jumped between conversations like a CD on random play. The entire time, he adopted different voices and accents, switching compulsively between a middle-aged American woman, a nineteenth-century colonial officer, a postwar schoolboy, a sixties Rastafarian, a Cockney copper, and even the devil. Instead of listening to one man, I was treated to a throng of cockeyed stereotypes and cameos.

"I was listening to the BBC World Service the other day and they had this report on what police can do to monitor telephone calls. They could be listening anywhere! Not that I haven't had a few experiences with police, mind you, I lived in London in the sixties. Two thousand micrograms of acid in one go, it was like a million Mickey Mouses roaring through your head on a million tiny motor scooters. Oh, I knew the police and they knew me, but it was cordial enough. 'Hello Si. Up to no good again, are you? Oh, Constable Stephen. Out earning a little overtime tonight?' God, it feels like yesterday."

Another codeine swig.

"Paris has changed since I first knew it, too much noise, too many tourists, too many American people with their Rollerblades. Isn't it extraordinary those people with their whiny voices—'Randy, get the camera so I can take a picture of that Eiffel Tower, Randy, isn't that a sweet postcard of the boy with the baguette'—are descendants of fine English stock? Though the way the Americans cheated and butchered the Indians does old England proud. The apple doesn't fall that far from the tree. Just look at the atrocities we British are responsible for. We basically went around the world raping and killing and bringing the plunder back to Essex. I'm not immune. Where do you think my family got their money from? Some great-great-uncle who pillaged Burma, of course. Our family still has an execution sword he brought home as a souvenir, two hundred and seventeen notches on the handle for each of the heads it lopped off. You can feel the bad vibrations coming off that thing."

Another joint lit.

"It wasn't easy growing up in my family. My father, he was a special fellow, put me on horses every Sunday, and little Simon went galloping off, terrified for his life, hating the creature that was hurtling through the woods looking for a tree to smash little Simon's neck against. He wasn't a bad fellow, my father, but, well, yes, he was. He kept me hidden all those years, so I was living in foster homes and private schools, and not very nice things happen to cute little blond boys in those places. They should hunt down pedophiles, they should be stripped and hung from their toes and flayed."

It went on like that for a steady hour, bizarre tangent following bizarre tangent, until I was able to piece together the life of this crazy-eyed poet. He was born in London in the 1940s, the result of a wartime affair between an English military gentleman and a young Scottish nurse. Initially, he was named Rex. Renounced by his father, he was the unwanted child of a single mother, bouncing between foster homes and friends of the family, never sure of his place, never sure of anything.

After several years of such havoc, his father finally confessed to his wife and agreed to bring his illegitimate son into his legitimate home. Rex was suddenly renamed Simon, and this was actually one of the easier transitions. A new mother, a new brother, a new house, a new school, a new life—it twisted an already tortured head into fresh knots. Finally, when Simon was a teenager, the situation became too much for everyone and his father arranged a job for him at a London advertising agency to get him out of the house.

Simon had long had a flair for words, even winning school poetry competitions, so the work suited him. Up he rose, a young star making a name in a fanatically competitive business. But he also embraced the excesses of London in the sixties, and there was seldom a night when he wasn't filling his body with some combination of chemicals and cocktails. When Simon unexpectedly lost his job for designing a campaign that used propaganda footage of Hitler to sell German beer—"*Ein Volk. Ein Reich. Ein Bier*"—he made the smooth transition from being one who consumed recreational drugs to one who provided them for a growing circle of friends and acquaintances.

His little business boomed, but along with the ankle-length fur coats and Mercedes sport coupes came a rather unpleasant possession charge. Simon was spared jail, but the affair convinced him it was time to leave England. It was off to France, then Spain, then back to France again, teaching English to businessmen to earn his money, filling endless notebooks with poetry to ease the manic swirl in his head, and always, always drowning himself in drink.

By the time Simon reached his fiftieth birthday, alcohol had gone from pleasure to habit to disease. He found himself back in Paris with no job, no money, and an increasingly short list of friends. One day, he lost his apartment, and that's when he remembered Shakespeare and Company and the owner who'd once complimented his poetry. He was sure it would be only a temporary solution, but by January 2000, that temporary solution had been going on for five long years.

"I beat alcohol here. You don't know how hard that was. The old man was really good to me," he said with great fondness, and the mention of George brought us back to our present conundrum.

If Shakespeare and Company was indeed a writer's refuge, then this particular poet still wasn't ready to be jettisoned into the real world. I felt a shiver of disloyalty for not executing the eviction warrant to the fullest, but deep inside I was sure that if George had sheltered this man for so long, he wouldn't want his things unceremoniously chucked onto the road as Kurt had so boldly offered to do.

With the briefest of negotiations, Simon and I were able to agree on a plan. After shaking hands with mock solemnity, he showed me to the door and thanked me for the surprisingly enjoyable meeting. Then, just before locking up behind me, he thrust his hand through the crack and passed me one of the folders he'd been shuffling about earlier. It was filled with poems, each written in the most elegant of handwriting, each with faint sketches of animals and trees and birds chasing butterflies scattered in the margins.

"If you're interested, you could read this," he said with lowered eyes.

Back in the bookstore proper, Luke shook his head when I told him what had happened. The reaction I was truly anxious for was from George.

13.

Polly Magoo's was a dim tunnel of a bar with cracked orange vinyl booths and scarred wooden tables. Old French movie posters were painted onto the walls, one a flaking silhouette of an Ali–esque boxer, another the bar's namesake, the William Klein film *Qui êtes-vous Polly Magoo?* In the back corner stood the counter with bottles of brown liquor lining the shelf and a perpetually out-of-order pay telephone off to one side.

The bar had, as they say, seen the day. During the heroin rages of the seventies, management drilled holes in the coffee spoons to keep junkies from pocketing them; of the many establishments in Paris that claim to have been graced by Jim Morrison, Polly's was his drinking spot of preference when he lived at a hotel up the street; and word was the bartenders had bedded an impressive list of French actresses.

The modern reality was equally impressive. Polly's stayed open until the last decently paying customer was ready to leave, usually six or seven in the morning. In a city where the only other options for drinks in the depths of the night were discos with too-high cover charges and cafés with too-bright lights, this made Polly's a rare luxury. Many an evening, the crowd actually swelled out onto the street while pedestrians with the more innocent intentions of bed or late-night television were forced to wade through elbows and burning cigarettes on their way home. Yet despite this, the bar maintained an air of intimacy, a just-between-us feel. Mauro, the bar's fixer, always shook your hand when you arrived, and he watched over his motley clientele with the gruff love of an older brother. It was the kind of place where at three on any given morning you could enjoy a slow drink in the back corner with a lover or get raucously drunk out front with a friend.

The best part of Polly Magoo's, at least as far as the residents of Shakespeare and Company were concerned, was its location. Leaving the bookstore, it was twenty-three paces to the left along rue de la Bûcherie and then another forty-eight down rue St. Jacques to the front door. The distance was so inviting, it wasn't unheard of for someone from the bookstore to wander into the bar in their pajamas for a last drink before bed.

On this night, Polly Magoo's was the setting for the Gaucho's last party. He was due to leave Paris in the coming week, so Kurt had played it safe and organized the celebration early. For three months, the Gaucho had been a leading star in the Shakespeare and Company constellation, and most all of the regulars had come to pay their respects.

Considering the surly treatment I'd received at his hand, I was inclined to stay at the store and read, but Ablimit and Kurt had insisted I attend. By the time I arrived after my encounter with Simon, there was a teeming group around a front table. The Gaucho was at the center, a bottle of bourbon before him. His dark eyes flashed wildly as he told his stories, and for the first time I saw how richly he deserved his nickname: "the Gaucho"—the South American cowboy, the rugged man living on the fringes of society.

Splurging for a pint of beer, I sat down next to Kurt. As I'd already learned, he wasn't shy about showing off his tattoo, and that boldness extended to the rest of his body. He had an athlete's build, and on the slightest pretense of heat or discomfort, his clothes would begin to be shed, usually to the pleasure of some young woman or man in his company. At Polly's, he was down to his undershirt, feverishly working the table for free drinks. He flirted, he pouted, he flexed, until one after another they relented, their ardor measured by the beverage provided:

a half glass of beer from the vaguely amused, a full pint from the ones who felt he was genuinely sweet, and a tumbler of whiskey from those who thought they'd found that night's answer to their lonely ache.

Across from this hormonal spectacle was Eve, the girl who'd introduced me to the peculiar world of Shakespeare and Company by inviting me to tea. Her already-pink cheeks were flushed further by the heat of the bar and she pressed a glass to her face for relief. Realizing I now was a resident of the bookstore, she squeezed closer to welcome me properly.

The bookstore had become her home away, she explained. She was just twenty years old and had come from middle Germany to work in Paris for a year. Fluent in three languages, she'd had no trouble finding a job in the call center of a large European corporation. But the city was another challenge. Paris struck her as hostile and impersonal and she'd felt very much alone until she found Shakespeare and Company.

After meeting George, everything changed. Eve began taking meals at the bookstore and was gradually absorbed into the strange life among the books. With pride, she told me she now held the position of Tea Lady. This involved arriving at the bookstore every Sunday to boil huge pots of tea, distribute trays of custard cookies, and keep the guests happy. I was not, it turned out, the first to be invited upstairs for tea by Eve; another part of the job was to replenish the party with new faces.

"I love the bookstore, I do whatever I can to help," she told me. Then, with the giggle of one unhabituated to the bewitching grip of alcohol, she added in a whisper, "I adore George. He's the greatest man I've ever met."

Also there that night was the Italian woman from Bologna. She was my age and had run away to Paris when her marriage began to crumble. A friend told her that Shakespeare and Company was a perfect place to lose oneself, and she decided she wanted to be lost for a while. George welcomed her with his usual hospitality.

At the far end of the table was Ablimit. He was holding court and getting steadily drunker on Polly's watery beer. His talk swerved madly. First, he would deride Western culture as a whole. "You were monkeys living in caves when we had Silk Road," he'd roar. "While China great civilization, your ancestors hit each other with sticks." Moments later, the insults forgotten, this jaded child of Communist China would bang his fist on the table and declare capitalism the philosophy that would redeem humanity. Around him, the temporary children of George's neo-Communist bookstore rose loudly to disagree.

That night at Polly's, there were Italians and Argentinians, Germans and Chinese, Americans and English, all ablaze with the glories of life, all overjoyed to be in Paris. Between sips of beer and drags on cigarettes, the talk was of voyages to be had, films to be made, books to be written. Everyone had something close to a dream glittering in their eye.

This was the best of Paris. Dreams, like money, can be accounted for in simple terms of deficit and surplus. My hometown is a bureaucratic capital, the kind of place people leave: to Toronto or Montreal, or to New York, Los Angeles or London for those with a deeper thirst. Such exoduses leave a reduced population of those individuals with an insatiable ecstasy for life and an inexplicable optimism for the future. What is left behind is a lingering sense of compromise. Just like nobody ever dreams of being a payroll clerk at a software company when they are a child, nobody ever dreams of living in my city.

In a place like Paris, the air is so thick with dreams they clog the streets and take all the good tables at the cafés. Poets and writers, models and designers, painters and sculptors, actors and directors, lovers and escapists, they flock to the City of Lights. That night at Polly's, the table spilled over with the rapture of pilgrims who have found their temple. That night, among new friends and safe at Shakespeare and Company, I felt it too. Hope is a most beautiful drug.

It was nearing midnight and the bar was full and sweaty, the people spilling out onto the street like blood from a hemorrhaging vein. When

Polly's was this crowded, the normal lines that divided tables of drinkers were forgotten and people moved about the bar in a staggered version of musical chairs. If someone rose to go to the toilet or left for home, Mauro promptly squeezed a stray body into their chair, and thus our party morphed and grew.

Throughout, the Gaucho received a merry parade of good-bye kisses and poetic tributes. Simon's complaints still fresh in mind, I watched with a cynical eye and raised my glass halfheartedly to the many toasts. At one point, the Gaucho rose and strutted around the bar before coming to a stop just beside where I was sitting. He offered a smug grin and then sat down.

"Maybe you think I was hard on you before," he began. "Maybe you think I am a bastard. I don't care. I have to be this way to protect George. You'll see."

He pushed his fedora up on his head so he could press in close to my face. His breath smelled of bourbon.

"Go ahead. Ask me something. Everyone wants to ask the Gaucho something. Do you want to know about the time somebody tried to burn the store down? Or maybe you want to know if it's true George used to go to bed with Anaïs Nin? Go on. I'll answer anything."

The Gaucho presented this as a magnanimous gesture, but I didn't know what to ask. He obviously wanted to prove how much he knew about Shakespeare and Company, but I wasn't eager to take his bait. Instead, remembering that everyone at the bookstore was writing something, I asked the Gaucho about his work.

"My writing . . ." He looked perplexed, his menu of pat answers lost. Reaching for Kurt's beer glass, he drank heavily before continuing.

"People usually ask me about George. . . ." He hesitated again before continuing in hushed words.

"I was sending letters home to a friend in Buenos Aires and I told him my stories from traveling. They were letters, written like that, but my friend works with a publisher. He thinks maybe I should make a collection of them. . . ." He shook his head sheepishly. "I'm not a writer, though. I'd never call myself a writer."

And at that, he hastened to introduce himself properly for the first time. His name was Esteban; the Gaucho a nickname he'd picked up along the road. He told me how much he respected George, how maybe he'd start a bookstore of his own in Argentina one day, something like Shakespeare and Company, but not with quite so many beds.

It was as if a mask had dropped and he was Esteban the traveler again, not the Gaucho, the feared deputy at Shakespeare and Company. Our animosity melted in the humid air of Polly Magoo's, and though it may have been the magic of the alcohol, we raised our glasses to friendship.

The hour grew late. Some made a sortie back to the bookstore to help Luke close up shop, where a few remained, hoping to get a good night's sleep. Back at the bar, shoulder still pressed against shoulder, and another round of drinks arrived. Then, like an icy spray, it was Last Metro.

In Paris, the metro stops running at the early hour of one o'clock in the morning. For those far from home, this makes for painful decisions. One either has to abandon the evening and catch the last train or commit to a night of debauchery and accept a long walk, an expensive taxi, or the dangers of a night bus. At our table, watches were discreetly checked and the gathering lost more of its conservative members.

By three, the once-strong party was reduced to a handful. Among them was the beautiful porcelain-shouldered woman who'd asked me for a cigarette the day of the tea party. Her name was Marushkah and she'd moved to Paris from Poland after her mother married a rich Columbian oil executive. Though nominally attending university, she was mostly found in cafés or at the bookstore. Much of her night at Polly's was spent lamenting the fickle nature of Kurt's affections. She'd bought him a glass of whiskey.

By five, the bar was near empty, with a few pastis drinkers at the counter and two men vying for one woman's affection at a booth in the back. Outside, an early-morning dog walker peered through the window at the dregs of the night. Without really noticing how, Esteban and I ended up alone at the table.

There was nothing left but the leaving. Outside, the streetlights reflected off the damp paving stones, a crescent moon hung over Notre Dame, whispers of mist rose up from the Seine. We couldn't be blamed for thinking the world revolved around us.

Still not ready to end the night, we stood together on the esplanade out in front of the store, and Esteban told me why he was leaving. He'd fallen in love at the bookstore, the real thing, and he was going to marry this woman. They were moving to Italy together; she'd already found an apartment and was waiting for him.

Then, without any sort of warning, Esteban turned and touched me on the arm. "Did George give you my set of keys?"

Wondering how he had known, I placed the keys in his hands. He ran his fingers along the ring until he found a tiny ceramic icon. It was the Virgin Mary, red-robed on a blue background.

"George would have killed me if he'd known I'd put that there. He doesn't go for any of that."

In a melancholy voice, Esteban identified each of the six keys on the ring and explained what doors they opened and how they should be used. When he was finished, he returned them to my hand with a sigh. "I only gave them back to George yesterday. . . ."

Again he lapsed into silence. Somewhere, a bird awoke and to the east there were fingers of peach where the sun would rise.

"I think I'm leaving at the right time," he finally said. "Now, it's not too late. Everybody still loves the Gaucho. They'll remember me well. You, you'll be all right if George picked you. But take care. This place can change you."

The fatigue that had been creeping up on me now struck with its full weight. I was so tired, I could barely stand, but Esteban wasn't ready to move. Leaving him out in front of the bookstore, I used the keys to get inside and left the door ajar behind me.

14.

George had always been an unpredictable sort. Spurning job offers to walk to Panama, clinging to the underside of trains with Mexican *vagabundos,* letting complete strangers share his home. Then there was his penchant for disappearing.

A most memorable example of this occurred when he first arrived in Paris in 1947. He was taking the French civilization course at the Sorbonne and was also thinking of a studying psychology, having come up with a theory of personality that linked the libido and the death instinct. But mostly he became embroiled in the Paris bohemia. He circled the various literary salons, he had numerous girlfriends, he dined with Russian princes, he was invited to châteaus in the French countryside by the likes of the Countess de Godlewska. George even started writing poetry in French, such as *"Poèmes écrits dans l'après-midi,"* which included verses like:

> *La-haut une triste pluie creve*
> *Cette amourette*
> *D'une fleur, d'une fille*
> *Pendant que meurt*
> *L'après-midi*

It was such a frenzied lifestyle that many months passed without him contacting his family. Grace Whitman became so worried that she wrote the American embassy in Paris, asking them to look for her son. The embassy secretary conducted an investigation and wrote back to say that George was "apparently in good health" and it was "suggested that he communicate with you directly."

Even knowing this history, it was unsettling when George up and vanished the day after the Gaucho's party.

"Gone?"

"He run off after the mail came," Ablimit answered.

It was eleven o'clock in the morning, and while the rest of us moped groggily about the bookstore or lay prone in bed after the previous night's indulgences, Ablimit was the sole portrait of diligence. He'd been at the library desk since eight, an *F* inked on his hand and grammar books spread open before him.

"His face very strange after reading a letter," Ablimit continued. "He said to open store without him."

Ablimit assured me whole days passed without George making an appearance, and once he'd even left for a month in England without telling a single person staying in his bookstore. The clerks worked their shifts, the residents cleaned the bookstore, and Ablimit kept the bookstore earnings hidden away in a file folder.

"You must forget how to worry if you live here," he advised, turning back to an exercise on the use of the apostrophe.

When opening time came and we began carting out boxes of books and greeting the day's first customers, I was struck again by the faith George had in the inherent goodness of people. Here we were, a group of virtual strangers, running the famous Shakespeare and Company. Personally, I'd known the man for forty-eight hours and yet I had the keys to both his bookstore and his bedroom in my pocket. Coming from a life of police bulletins and home security systems, such trust seemed almost folly.

Once the store was up and running, I took my place in the antiquarian room. One of George's prime complaints was that in recent months

Simon had repeatedly locked the door during the day and refused to let customers inside. As part of our arrangement, I was to rectify this by spending the afternoons in the antiquarian room and welcoming visitors while Simon kept out of the way.

Simon was good to his word that first morning and had left the antiquarian room both empty and relatively tidy. As I settled behind the desk, I actually felt a flicker of relief that George had disappeared. The night before, I'd thought it obvious that the poet deserved a stay of eviction; in the sober light of day, this felt more like an obvious betrayal. George had asked me one thing in return for my bed—to rid the bookstore of the poet—and I had failed. Despite the keys in my pocket and the warm resolution with Esteban, there was the creeping fear that I would be the one banished.

At least working in the antiquarian room, there was no shortage of distractions. Every few minutes, the door swung open and there was a visiting American scholar searching for original translations of Zola, an ornithologist with a question about a rare seventeenth-century birding guide, a lost Australian physicist wondering how to get to the Panthéon so she could pay homage to the Curies. It was akin to hosting a running talk show with a never-ending series of eccentric guests, all of whom wanted to stay and talk for at least a little while. After the solitude of the hotel and my walks, I quickly embraced this social mayhem.

There was, however, one incident that left me troubled. Midway through the afternoon, a man dressed in a dapper black suit and a black cowboy shirt came into the room. His shirt was open at the neck and revealed a tattoo of a red heart with flames jetting from the severed aorta. In his hand was an unfiltered cigarette.

"Excuse me, sir," he said with the utmost politeness. "Do you happen to have a light?"

With a flick of his thumb, he demonstrated that his silver Zippo had run out of fuel. Using matches I found in the desk drawer, he lit his cigarette and thanked me, again in the most courteous of manners.

A short time later, there was a knock on the window and the man held another cigarette in the air. He was so gentlemanly that when he also asked if he might borrow a book to read while smoking on the bench under the cherry tree, I agreed without hesitation. After selecting a hardcover volume of Shaw dating from the 1920s, the man left with a gracious handshake. A short time later, I glanced outside and the man and the book were gone.

Now a tremble of panic set in. Not only was there my handling of the Simon dilemma to worry about, but I had also let a rare and expensive book go missing during my very first shift in the antiquarian room.

It was well past dark by the time I locked the antiquarian room. During the day, I had entertained dozens of visitors, answered a score of tourists' questions, and even sold three books. I felt a contributing member of the team. My only regret was that George hadn't passed and seen me hard at work.

Hunger voicing its needs, I climbed up to the front library to see if Ablimit and Kurt were making the trip to the student cafeteria. Finding the room empty, I crossed into the main stairwell, where I was startled to see the office door open. George was inside, leaning over his desk and peering intently at a piece of paper. When I knocked, he jumped slightly in his seat and quickly pushed this paper under a pile of invoices.

"What do you want?" he grumbled.

Sensing it wasn't the time to broach a subject as sensitive as Simon, I tried to retreat into the hall, but George would have none of it.

"I saw you downstairs. Does that mean the poet is gone?"

"Well, not exactly," I blundered, "but close, really close. . . ."

A raised eyebrow indicated George wanted me to continue, so I explained how I'd staked out Simon and surprised him while he was shutting down the antiquarian room the night before. This drew a chuckle, so I went through the rest of the story with great flourish, though careful to avoid mention of the substances consumed. I concluded by saying that Simon knew it was time to leave the store but needed at least a few days to raise some money. Meanwhile, the two of us would share the space, with me keeping it open for customers during the day and then writing there in the early evening and Simon sleeping there at night and doing his best to avoid being seen at Shakespeare and Company. I meekly expressed the hope that George wouldn't be too upset with the arrangement, then awaited the verdict.

"Did he show you his poetry?" George asked after a long pause.

During lapses between antiquarian room visitors, I'd gone through the folder Simon had given me. Though I hadn't read much poetry in my life and Simon's work was challenging enough that I had to read each poem at least two times, I'd admired it. There was a crispness to the images and several of his lines kept running through my head like stray echoes.

"Hah!" George exploded when I admitted that Simon had given me the folder. "He's bamboozled you! I knew you'd be friends with that character. Now he's got you under his spell and we'll never be rid of him!"

Shockingly, George didn't seem too upset by this prospect. Instead, he broke into a wide smile and repeated the story of Simon's arrival at Shakespeare and Company.

"A week! He asked to stay at the bookstore a week and he's stayed five years."

Leaning back in his chair, he looked me over as if seeing me for the first time. Then he reached under the pile of invoices for the paper he'd been reading and stood up.

"Why don't you come have dinner with me upstairs?"

15.

It was the first time I'd been up to the main apartment since the tea party. Free from the crush of Sunday visitors, the room was infinitely more serene. We were in a book-lined cocoon and the madness of the store felt much farther than just three floors away.

The apartment had long been the retreat of Shakespeare and Company. George spent countless hours here, cooking meals, reading through old letters, leafing through his books. The rich history of the store was reflected by the walls of framed photographs, the first editions of *Ulysses* and *Tropic of Cancer*, the mementos of travels past. George often boasted that with the apartment's grand bedroom, its lofty view of the Seine and Notre Dame, and its endless supply of great books, the best Parisian vacation could be had without ever passing beyond the door.

This apartment was also where George lodged his distinguished guests and closest friends. It was here that Allen Ginsberg caught his breath during his voyages to and from India, that Lawrence Durrell drank during the dizzy days of the *Alexandria Quartet*, that Margaux Hemingway dallied about while discovering her grandfather's Paris.

And, as I was soon to learn, this apartment was also the setting for one of the murkier chapters of George's personal life.

In the kitchen, the stove could have been a great work of Surrealism. The surface had been scratched clean from decades of constant use and there was no longer any numbering or gradations around the dials. A burner could just as easily be on high or low, the oven set to bake or grill. With an expert hand, George fiddled with several knobs until a frying pan of hashed meat and onions came to life. A large pot of potatoes was already bubbling at a slow boil and I was handed a fork and given precise mashing instructions.

"*Parmentier forestiere,*" explained George as the meat began to sizzle. "It's simple but it tastes good and is nutritious."

The food did smell appetizing, but I was slightly distressed by the state of the kitchen. Along with the dried cockroach husks I had seen the day of the tea party, there were now several live ones scurrying among the sticky jars and empty tins.

"Aren't those a problem?" I worried over George's shoulder.

"Bahh, they're nothing," he scoffed, and tried to swat a roach or two into the potatoes. "More protein for us. Are you crazy? Don't you like protein?"

While the meal cooked, George brought out a large bottle of beer from the refrigerator. It wasn't one of the discount high-alcohol beers I'd bought, but a Chinese brand, Tsingtao. George smiled when he caught me inspecting the label.

"This is what I really like, but it's more expensive," he said as he pulled two glasses from the shelf.

The beer was brewed not far from where George had spent his year in Nanking, and, in fact, he had a special love for most everything Chinese. The time when his father worked as a visiting professor in China was among the happiest of his childhood; then as a young man, he visited the country several more times when the freighter ships he rode docked at Chinese ports. Later, he became a keen supporter of Mao's politics, and to this day George preaches to all who will listen that Shanghai is the city of future. There was even a surprise visit to the bookstore from Chinese government officials in the 1960s. They'd known of George's Communist leanings and invited him to what was then Peking to open a branch of Shakespeare and Company.

"They were going to pay for everything, but I couldn't go. Too busy here, always too busy," he muttered.

When the dinner was ready, we sat at the table with our glasses of beer. George had brought a stick of butter with him, slicing off tiny pats and slipping them into his mouth as he ate. Having seen the condition of the kitchen, I was skeptical, but the meal was delicious and I quickly refilled my plate.

Encouraged by George's reaction to my bumbling of the Simon eviction, once the meal was done and another bottle of Tsingtao was brought forth, I dared to tell him of the man with the unfiltered cigarette and the missing volume of Shaw. Again, rather than being upset, he found the incident amusing.

"Do you know how many books get stolen here?" he laughed. "I'd give them all away if I could."

George told me that during his first five years in business, so many books were taken that it actually cost him money to run the store. Then, during the sixties and seventies, he barely hung on when a handful of Left Bank bookstores were bankrupted by a notorious band of thieves. And over the decades, dozens of Paris writers stocked their libraries courtesy of Shakespeare and Company. Perhaps the worst culprit was Gregory Corso. He had an international reputation for duplicity. Lawrence Ferlinghetti still remembers the time Corso smashed the front window of City Lights at two in the morning to steal from the cash register. Ferlinghetti had a policy of never calling the police, so when he arrived at the store and found that the officers had already dusted the register and found Corso's fingerprints, he took immediate action. After rousting Corso from bed at six that morning, Ferlinghetti recovered what money he could and then told the shamed poet to get out of town because the police were on to him. In Paris, Corso was no less audacious. He repeatedly stole books from Shakespeare and Company and then returned the next day in hopes of selling them back to George.

"The saddest thing is most of the thieves don't read the books they steal," complained George. "They just go to another bookstore and sell them to make some quick money."

Though some people's regard for humanity would have been shaken, George was unfazed. He took hope from the American man who'd mailed him a traveler's check for a hundred dollars a few years earlier. It was in payment for the books he's stolen from Shakespeare and Company while studying in Paris two decades before.

"This fellow who took the Shaw book, he doesn't sound so bad. At least he asked," George said. " 'Give what you can, take what you need'—that's what I always tell people."

I was instructed to keep a eye out for the man and try to find out a little more about him but otherwise not to worry. Another bottle of Chinese beer was opened, and though I prided myself on my Canadian thirst, I soon found myself struggling to keep up with a man sixty years my senior.

"You're drunk," George roared as he poured two more glasses, the beer foaming up and soaking the table. "You ought to be ashamed of yourself, drunk on a weeknight."

Perhaps I was drunk, perhaps we both were, for it was then that George pulled the letter out of his pocket and passed it across the table to me.

"We have a lot of work ahead of us," he said with a glimmer of conspiracy in his eyes.

The letter was written in French and was some sort of real estate notice. Considering the beer swilling in my head and my feeble grasp of the language, all I could make out was a reference to a property at 37 rue de la Bûcherie. It turned out to be an offer to buy Shakespeare and Company.

It was the work of a French businessman, George explained. The man already owned several apartments at 37 rue de la Bûcherie and wanted to buy the entire building and transform it into a four-star hotel. Located in the heart of the Latin Quarter and with its windows facing Notre Dame, the property promised a sure financial windfall.

This would-be hotel baron had already contacted the other tenants in the building and had agreements in place to buy them out at a significant profit. The only obstacle was George, the single-largest property owner in the building. He'd repeatedly turned down the man's attempts to buy the bookstore, but that morning a new offer had arrived, this one taking advantage of a quirk in French real estate law: the *acheter en viager*. Under this clause, the businessman offered to pay the money immediately but not take over the property until after George's death.

"It's not very good, is it?" George said as he took the letter back. "We could lose the bookstore."

In fact, I didn't see the problem. So long as George refused to sell, where was the trouble? The businessman couldn't forcefully take over the bookstore, so it didn't matter how high the offer or what clauses of French realty law the businessman invoked. The bookstore was safe, wasn't it?

"You don't understand, do you?" George burst out in exasperation. "If something happens to me, my wife will inherit the bookstore and she'll sell in a second."

His wife?

It always surprises me how quickly people are willing to confess their secrets to me. I attribute this to my talent for listening. Normally, a listener barely keeps one ear on the conversation while passing the time thinking about what he or she might say next or gazing at the attractive man or woman waiting at the bus stop. As a journalist, everything depends on opening the person up to talk. This means listening like a safecracker, waiting for those almost inaudible ticks that tell me I'm on to something precious, and then choosing my questions like surgical tools to persuade the person to talk more. It was clear from the moment George invited me to dinner in the apartment that he had something he wanted to talk about, and after enough beer and delicate prompting, he finally shared what was troubling him.

Throughout his years in Paris, there had been an abundance of young women attracted to George. He cut a dashing figure, he possessed romantic ideals, he lived a poet's life, and he was a handsome man. There had even been several engagements. In 1948, he wrote his parents about his fiancée, Josette, a lovely woman who, he insisted, despite her tuberculosis, would become their "new daughter . . . the mother of your grandchildren." More than a decade later, George again announced an engagement, this time to a woman by the name of Colette, the proprietor of an art gallery on Ile St. Louis. But despite such brushes with love, it wasn't until the approach of his seventieth birthday that George married for the first time.

In the early 1980s, a young British woman passed through Shakespeare and Company. She was beautiful, creative, well read, and incredibly feisty. Once, while walking to the bookstore, she was confronted by a raving exhibitionist. She promptly kicked the man squarely in his exposed flesh.

"Not everyone would do that," George remembered with admiration.

George took an immediate liking and this woman began sleeping in the upstairs apartment and worked on one of the Shakespeare and Company literary magazines. Even though she was twenty-eight and he was sixty-eight, they dated, fell in love, and married. The two were wed at a private city hall ceremony, where George's best man was a woman, his former fiancée Colette no less. Maybe it was choices such as these that doomed the marriage.

There were good times for the couple—travels through Australia, a trip back to the United States, the romance of Paris. But then Shakespeare and Company got in the way. Life in a communal bookstore became overwhelming, and George's wife resented the constant intrusion of strangers and the frazzled day-to-day existence. George said she even began to begrudge his devotion to the bookstore and couldn't understand why they couldn't have a life of their own.

"I was saving money to expand the library and she wanted me to buy a car," he said. "A car! Does that make any sense?"

Not in George's world, where a pack of real garbage bags was considered frivolous and every franc was saved to realize his Shakespeare and Company dream. Relationships require flexibility, but George was now past seventy and had never been a man susceptible to compromise. First, his wife left the bookstore and took a room in a hotel around the corner; then she moved from Paris altogether, their communication reduced to ping-ponging letters from their lawyers.

At the time of their marriage, George had signed over a third of the bookstore to her, and it seemed that if he were to die, the rest would automatically go to her as well. Considering her bad memories, George said it was likely that she'd simply sell to the highest bidder. This is why the French businessman's unrelenting attempts to buy the bookstore were so unsettling: If he was prepared to wait until George died, which, since George was eighty-six, wouldn't be forever away, he could well succeed in his mission no matter how often George refused his overtures.

"You mean Shakespeare and Company could end up a luxury hotel?"

George just nodded and fell into gloomy silence. The joyous beer-drinking mood had long since evaporated and now he stared off at the wall of framed pictures. The photograph of his old friend Lawrence Ferlinghetti, a picture of Richard Wright at the bookstore desk, and an almost formal portrait of George, a woman, and a young child standing in front of Shakespeare and Company.

16.

When I'd arrived, Shakespeare and Company appeared the answer to all my problems. A place to recuperate, time to calculate my next steps, an assortment of lost folk to camouflage my own disenchantments. Now it seemed my newfound sanctuary was in jeopardy, and with all the fervor of a new convert, I began to imagine ways of saving the bookstore.

I was convinced it would be an easy enough task. If George was right in saying that forty thousand people had slept at his store, this alone was a formidable army. Add to this the countless visitors who fell in love with the shop each day and George's list of famous friends, and it seemed we surely had the resources required to fight the hotel baron and secure the future of Shakespeare and Company. All we needed was the proper plan.

As I lay in bed that night, I was sure my journalism background could help. All reporters know how much the public loves a good tragedy, and if the plight is pathetic enough, the response can be enormous. On one occasion in my city, a man punished his dog for pooping in the house by tying the animal to the back of his truck and dragging it around the block at high speed. The pads of the dog's paws were abraded by the pavement, and when our paper ran photographs of the animal's bandaged legs, there were hundreds of offers to adopt. Similarly, when a Christmas Eve fire claimed all the presents for a family supported by a single mom, the fund-raising drive organized by my paper to help the family was such a success that one of the woman's neighbors faked a fire the next Christmas in hopes of netting the same windfall.

The morning after my talk with George, I was so preoccupied by a fantasy involving a random encounter with Oprah Winfrey and an international television campaign to designate Shakespeare and Company a French national monument that I went to unlock the antiquarian room without thinking. It was the most nonchalant of gestures, so it was with great alarm that I looked up and saw Kurt barreling toward me with intense hurt spreading across his face.

"Where did you get the keys?" he demanded.

With all that had happened during my two days at the bookstore, I'd forgotten Kurt's lust for the ring of keys. I mumbled an awkward explanation, but still his cheeks flamed.

"I don't get it," Kurt said as he turned away. "Doesn't George like me?"

We finished opening the store in an uncomfortable silence. When the work was done, Kurt declared he was going for coffee. Sensing a chance to mend our fragile friendship, I decided to momentarily postpone the Oprah plan and offered to treat.

Only a hundred feet or so from the bookstore, on the other side of the city park with the second-oldest tree in Paris, is a blissful spot known as Café Panis. Its waiters are stiff-backed and nattily tuxedoed, couples sit side by side at the neat row of tables out front, the menu is chalked onto the dining room blackboard at the beginning of each day. In brief, it adheres to all the grand traditions of a French café.

Partly because of this ambience but largely due to its inviting proximity, the café had been embraced by the inhabitants of Shakespeare and Company. When chores were done, the residents crossed the park for their morning coffees and then repeated the trajectory several times throughout the day. Rare was the occasion when there wasn't at least one of George's denizens propped at the Panis bar with a book in hand or pen at work.

In its own way, Panis had also embraced the misfits of the bookstore. The café offers a magnificent view of Notre Dame and, as a result, is buffeted by anonymous waves of tourists. Each day the hordes arrived with their cameras and guidebooks, asking the same questions about the menu, making the same jokes about the exorbitant price of a glass of cola. Faced with these nameless masses, the waiters at Panis understandably became attached to their regular customers.

For convenience's sake, these regulars could be divided into two groups. The first was composed of the sidewalk artists who worked out front of Notre Dame and on the stone walkways of the Seine. They were mostly embittered middle-aged men who'd arrived in Paris dreaming of masterpieces but now drew jiffy charcoal sketches of lovers and children for fifty francs apiece. They were generally a scowling lot: When it rained, they filled the café and complained of the weather; when it didn't rain, they filled the café and complained of the stinginess of the tourists; and on those sunny occasions when their sketches did sell well, they filled the café, got boisterously drunk, and started insulting the waiters.

Perhaps it was no great surprise, then, that the waiters unanimously preferred the second group. While the Shakespeare and Company residents were usually unshowered and apt to loiter for hours over a single cup of coffee, they were at least happy to be there. When Kurt strode in that morning, it was clear he was a particular darling. A busboy carrying a tray of omelettes saluted as he passed, while a waiter with an immaculately shaven head glided to the door to greet us.

"Monsieur Kurt! How are you today?"

Kurt struck a young Hemingway pose and made an offhand comment about the trials of writing, which was received with a sympathetic nod. At the bar, the counterman reached across to shake his hand while I was welcomed as "Monsieur Kurt's friend." Even an aging German Shepherd rose creakily to his feet so he could come and have his ears scratched by Kurt.

"That's Amos," he explained as the café dog settled contentedly at his feet.

Cheered by this grand welcome, Kurt was inspired to tutor me on café life. The fundamental rule was to sit at the bar in order to escape the two-tier pricing system of French restaurants. If you took a table in a café, you could expect to pay fifteen or twenty francs for a basic café express. The grand cafés like the Deux Magots or the Café de Flore charged as much as twenty-five francs just for the right to sit and drink a short cup of coffee. But if you stood at the bar, you generally paid half the menu price. At Café Panis, the coffee that cost fifteen francs in the dining room was just five and a half francs at the counter.

With these prices so attractive, the second lesson was to hawk for stools. Panis had four high stools facing its bar, where you could sit comfortably with your coffee. If you couldn't nab one, you were left leaning, which greatly diminished the joy of spending hours in the café. These stools were the subject of a constant struggle between the bookstore crowd and the street artists, and one had to be fast to secure a seat and remain determined to keep it.

But by far the most important thing I learned that day was the location of the downstairs bathroom. It was clean and spacious, with two shiny porcelain urinals and a separate room with an extremely comfortable toilet. There was also a large-basined sink with spigots for hot and cold water, a broad mirror, soap, towels, and even a hot air hand dryer. During the midmorning lull, it was relatively easy to make a quick scrub of your genitals and armpits, wash your face, shave, and dry up before another customer disturbed you. Considering the state of Shakespeare's common toilet and the lack of shower facilities, Café Panis was the place for morning ablutions.

As if this wasn't enough, the bald waiter, who was introduced as Nico, even gave us croissants that were left over from that morning's breakfast service. "They would have been put in the garbage," he assured me when I began to thank him a little too profusely.

We lingered for a pleasant hour and made ample use of the toilets, until the lunch crowds forced us to abandon our stools. Kurt had already shown a certain resiliency when it came to bookstore disappointments, and after our long coffee, he proved it again.

"George knows I'm the wild one," he commented as we returned to the bookstore. "I obviously can't be trusted with the keys. That's all right. Who needs the responsibility?"

All day, I tried to catch George's attention. Oprah, media campaigns, fund-raising drives, heritage status, and a thousand other helpful ideas spun in my head. But every time I approached, he kept waving me off, saying he had other things to do, behaving as if we'd never even discussed the problem the day before.

Confused and frustrated, I waited until Luke started work and then went to take a place in the worn green metal chair by the front desk. As I sat, Luke was in the midst of selling a book on the history of Ethiopian jazz. The customer was a Cuban musician who was in Paris for a week of gigs and it so happened that Luke had a special interest in Cuba at that time. He'd traveled through enough of the Third World to have questions about the way wealth was distributed across the planet. Now, working for George, who'd actually walked from Havana to Santiago after Castro's revolution, he was subjected to almost daily lectures on the glories of Cuban socialism. Suspicious by nature, Luke wasn't ready to believe anything, but he did think it might be worthwhile to spend a month or two in the country.

"Just to see for myself," he explained. "I just think there's got to be something better than this."

After a long discourse that wove between the cultural wonders of Havana and the general ambivalence toward Castro's government, the musician left and I was able release my angst.

"Uh, Luke . . ."

"What's bothering you, old fellow?"

Barely pausing to breathe, I told him everything. The French businessman, the luxury hotel, George's ex-wife. . . . It was all too bizarre to be true.

"Actually, that sounds about right" was Luke's nonchalant reaction.

"Everyone around here asks the same question: 'What's going to happen when George is gone?' "

From what Luke had gathered during his time at the store, not only was there nothing in place to protect the bookstore but George was also refusing to take any practical measures for the future. Luke said the plans were at best highly optimistic and at worst entirely ludicrous. One of the more bizarre plots to date had been a halfhearted attempt to donate Shakespeare and Company to the billionaire philanthropist George Soros.

George had long admired Soros's social crusading and, along with the likes of Noam Chomsky and Rigoberto Menchu, his photograph was on the wall of honor at the back of the store. Though the two had never spoken of such an arrangement—in fact, had never even met— George was confident that Soros would have such affinity for the bookstore's cause that he would protect the property from the clutches of the hotel baron.

A year or so before, George had put together an impressive dossier and then sent an official offer to the Soros Foundation. "He has money and imagination (two things needed to build an institution here) and that is a combination that most people lack," wrote George at the time. But before there was any response, more practical voices prevailed and he was persuaded against giving away everything he'd worked for to a complete stranger.

"You see, from a normal perspective it looks like an easy enough problem to solve," Luke finished. "But people forget we're dealing with George. He's not exactly your normal chap."

17.

Shakespeare and Company prides itself on being a socialist utopia, but it can't escape the pressures of a capitalist world. Along with the hotel baron who menaced the bookstore proper, all the residents suffered financial hardships and we wondered how we would survive the gray Paris winter.

Of the group, it was Simon who was pressed the hardest. Aside from George, nobody else living at the bookstore was more than thirty-five years old. For the younger residents, though poor and desperate, we could always rationalize our misery as youthful adventure. In our hearts, we knew we could return to the real world and find gainful employment if needed.

Simon, however, had recently celebrated his fifty-sixth birthday and thus was of an age where financial hardship becomes distinctly more disconcerting. Watching the poet unravel each night in the antiquarian room, it was hard to believe he could ever find stable ground. Simon himself was so depressed by his condition that he'd recently asked friends traveling to India to give offerings at a Hindu temple on the Ganges so his soul wouldn't be resurrected and he wouldn't have to suffer through life again.

After my discussion with George, I told Simon that there was no longer the danger of an immediate eviction, but this proved to be only the briefest of respites. The poet still had no money, still had no place to go, still faced the very real prospect of losing the only home he knew.

A job would have been the easiest answer, but Simon hadn't done any regular work for almost a decade. There were occasional menu translations for tourist restaurants and minor editing duties for a friend who worked at a pharmaceutical company, but this barely kept him in food and plentiful habit. The poet also knew that even under the best of circumstances, employers were reluctant to hire someone his age, and Simon was hardly in any best circumstance. Between the years of alcoholism and the years of living in a communal bookstore, the poet had become something of a Steppenwolf, someone who could never truly blend into society again.

All this was reflected in Simon's rather fanciful plans for his future. When seeking sources of money to leave Shakespeare and Company, his first idea was to sell a book of his poetry. An Irish publisher, Salmon Press, was interested in one of his manuscripts and Simon entertained notions of an advance.

"I might get a check by the spring," he said with hopeful eyes.

But we both knew this was the longest of shots with the lowest of rewards. Contemporary poetry was rarely a big seller, so even if the book were to be published, it wouldn't earn Simon more than a few thousand francs. This would be barely sufficient for a week at the old Hotel des Medicis up rue St. Jacques, let alone enough to start a new life.

A more realistic ambition was translation. Simon had built himself a minor literary reputation during his years at the bookstore and had recently translated a Céline play, *The Church,* for a California publishing house. His goal now was to win the contract for a novel by Claude Simon, the French Nobel laureate and one of the founders of *le nouveau roman.* Simon had already translated short stories by the author, and this project was worth 28,000 francs, close to four thousand dollars, a kingly sum at the bookstore.

"Maybe then I could get an apartment and finally be able to sleep without the paralyzing fear that the old man will descend from above like the Dark Angel and expel me from my humble abode," Simon pronounced one night as we shut down the antiquarian room.

As for the rest of Shakespeare and Company's impoverished residents, most of us didn't even have the right to employment in France. Ablimit had a special nonworking visa, while Kurt and I were beneficiaries of the automatic three-month tourist visa available to North Americans, but this forbade living permanently at one address, let alone finding a job. Thanks to the new European Union labor laws, the Italian woman could technically find work, but she had no interest in staying in Paris and was already planning a return to Bologna.

Ablimit was the most industrious, giving covert Mandarin lessons in the upstairs library. But this barely covered his daily meals at the student cafeteria and a monthly spin at the local laundry. Kurt had been reduced to living off his credit card, and after the binge at Polly Magoo's, I was in no better shape.

Thankfully, there were seams to this financial bind. Long ago, George had installed the wishing well in the main room of the bookstore to create a haphazard fund for the needy. The well was replenished each day by whimsical tourists and there was an open invitation to the neighborhood's homeless to scrape out a few coins for bread or bottle. The bookstore residents also made ample use of the fund, and if you didn't mind scraping among dirty coins, you could always gather enough centimes for a baguette and a round of Brie.

And if the well ran dry, Kurt and I once decided, we could always go cap in hand. We'd discovered there was a team of three Roma girls working the crowds in front of Notre Dame. They carried a plasticized multilingual card proclaiming them Bosnian refugees and used an infant child as a mercy prop. The baby was strapped into a harness and passed between the girls throughout their long begging shifts in front of the cathedral. One morning, Kurt and I watched them count out a cascade of five- and ten-franc pieces while they sat on the benches in front of Shakespeare and Company. Seeing their bounty, we were sure we could handle a few hours with our hands outstretched.

It was one of those jokes that wasn't really. I only had a few hundred francs left, and even if I kept the most modest of budgets, my money wouldn't last much longer than another week. Something had to be done.

My first work in Paris came courtesy of one of the store regulars. Nick was an accomplished street hustler and could often be seen skulking around the quarter. He kept a ponytail of brown hair and frequented Shakespeare and Company between the hours of four and eight, which happened to be the hours when Sophie, the lovely British actress, worked the desk. I first made his acquaintance when I found him sitting mooningly in the green chair, trying to induce Sophie to join him for a movie.

Nick had been raised in Yugoslavia with an Albanian father and a Serbian mother, and when things started going bad in the Balkans, they went particularly badly for him. He'd been a Goth as a teenager, the type who favored dark trench coats, dyed black hair and, for special occasions, painted fingernails. In October of 1991, after an all-night party at a Belgrade club, he arrived home in full Goth regalia and found four soldiers waiting for him in the lobby of his building. Like that, he was in the army.

Having already undergone his year of mandatory basic training, Nick was deemed ready for action as soon as they cut his hair and turpentined his nails. A few days after stumbling home from that club, he found himself creeping across a field with a dozen other young soldiers so they could attack a Croatian-held village. Unfortunately, a machine gunner was stationed on a hill to protect the village from just this type of assault. Nick remembers the gunner breaking into an expression of utter amazement when he looked up from his newspaper and saw the soldiers crossing the field in broad daylight while a large gun was trained on them. The next thing Nick knew, the boy beside him exploded into blood and three other soldiers fell screaming to the ground. The remnants of the unit ran back to their side of the field while the enraged captain spat and swore revenge the next day.

Nick thought that maybe this type of soldiering wasn't for him, so he approached the commander to see if there was any other work available. The next morning, he found himself standing on a football field with another soldier who'd dared to complain. They'd been given a special assignment. The field had been sabotaged with a special sort of land mine that detonated when touched by metal. Nick and his partner were given plastic forks, the type found at fast-food restaurants, and were told to cross the field on their hands and knees while poking the ground gently to locate the mines.

For an hour, Nick and the other solider solemnly poked and sweated profusely. When they saw a truck rumbling down a nearby road, the two young men looked at each other with the wordless understanding of terrified soldiers. The driver wasn't quite convinced they'd been given a leave of absence, so he asked them to throw their rifles and uniforms in a bush before giving them a ride back to Belgrade.

Nick left Yugoslavia shortly thereafter. Without the proper work papers or even official refugee status, he did the one thing he could: hit the streets. First, he sold bootlegged tapes and videos in London. Then he came to Paris and had so far operated a hair-braiding stand, sold tawdry beaded jewelry off a sidewalk blanket, and, at the time I entered the picture, defrauded a major department store with the consonant-rich name of FNAC.

The sweetest part of the job was that it involved only the barest of illegalities. There were about half a dozen FNAC outlets in Paris, and though they all sold the same products, they didn't have a central computer or pricing system. This meant music CDs in the twenty-five franc discount bin at one FNAC store were often still being sold for the full price of more than a hundred francs at another outlet. Having discovered this gambit, Nick spent his days scouring the discount bins and buying CDs that could be returned for a profit. All he did was peel off the discount sticker to reveal the original price tag underneath and then, taking advantage of FNAC's generous chainwide exchange policy, he presented the unopened CDs to a clerk at another outlet, saying they were an unwanted birthday gift.

He'd been working this angle for several months and had earned thousands of francs. The only problem was that now all the clerks recognized him, which is why he subcontracted the job out to the likes of me. The afternoon I agreed to work for him, we walked from the bookstore up to the FNAC outlet at Montparnasse, where he handed me a bag of four CDs with a combined sticker price of 460 francs.

"Whatever you do, just stay calm. You can't get in any trouble," he said.

Though Nick was trying to be reassuring, the fact that he thought it necessary to wear oversize sunglasses as a disguise while waiting outside the FNAC did make me slightly uneasy.

The CDs were by Johnny Hallyday, a pop star who'd been button-cute in the 1960s but was now all artificial dyes and tans, the French version of Las Vegas Elvis. The young woman at the exchange desk nodded compassionately when I said they'd been a gift but I didn't really enjoy that sort of music. She wrote me a credit slip that I used to buy a fifty-franc long-distance telephone card, and then I left the store with a fresh 410 francs in real money. Nick let me keep the phone card and one hundred francs. So, just like that, I had my first job since leaving the newspaper.

Unfortunately, any visions of a quick fortune were dispelled when Nick told me I couldn't work for him too often. "Your face, you have a very unusual face," Nick said, motioning to my prominent nose and shoulder-length red hair. "The clerks, they'll remember you."

But with frugality such a crying necessity, there was no better place than at George's side.

Having traveled around the world with little more than a change of shirt and a paperback book, George had long ago learned to live lean. While riding the rails during the Great Depression, he'd arrange to do yard work in exchange for a meal or would panhandle in the city square until he had enough money for an eight-cent can of beans. "Some of the others would go on begging until their pockets were full of coins," George recalled. "I was happy with my beans. What more did you need?" Later, one of the reasons George got his seafaring papers was because of the expensive berths on the ships. "My friends would pay two hundred dollars to take a boat to Europe and I'd get off the same boat with two hundred dollars in my pocket."

Once George opened the bookstore, these lessons proved crucial. He washed his clothes by hand, ate the most basic of meals, and shunned the cinemas or restaurants. With this regime, not only was he able to survive on the bookstore's paltry receipts but he also managed to provide communal meals and tuck away enough money to keep expanding the bookstore.

After seven decades like this, George could stretch a franc to unimaginable lengths. No piece of bread was too stale or rind of cheese too dry. Once, I was soundly berated for pouring the leftover pickle juice down the sink while washing the jar. "That's a delicacy! I can make soup with that. I used to drink pickle juice," George roared. "What are you? A Rockefeller?"

Watching him live was a daily lesson in parsimony. He would walk miles to save a few francs on green peppers, he bought the barest of staples from the discount grocery stores, he furnished his wardrobe exclusively through church rummage sales. In his kitchen, the same piece of aluminium foil was reused until it was blackened and tattered, while tea was bought in bulk because it was marginally cheaper than buying it in individual bags.

The practice of such discipline is how Shakespeare and Company survived, and how he was able to spend half a century feeding and housing people for free. George had discovered money to be the greatest slave master, and by reducing your dependence on it, he believed, you could loosen the grip of a suffocating world.

"People all tell me they work too much, that they need to make more money," George told me. "What's the point? Why not live on as little as possible and then spend your time with your family or reading Tolstoy or running a bookstore? It doesn't make any sense."

Under such tutelage, I found myself going whole days without spending more than a few francs. Still, George insisted I could do better. While I was cleaning up the kitchen, he caught me throwing away a crust of bread that should have been saved for soup croutons. Then, sin of sins, he noticed a plastic bag that I'd put in the garbage because it had been splattered with grease.

"What are you doing?" he asked, raising his hands to his head in despair. "We save these bags for customers. Wash it out, don't throw it away. When are you going to learn?"

It was coming, I told George. Day by day, I was beginning to understand.

18.

There was a blinding light and in the fog of sleep I imagined secret police, aliens, and even that famous tunnel to the afterworld. Then there was a familiar cackling laugh and I realized it was just another morning at Shakespeare and Company.

"Pancakes! Upstairs for pancakes!"

My eyes opened and George was standing over me with his flashlight on high beam and a wicked grin across his face. His mission accomplished, he scuttled off and performed a similar wake-up service for Kurt, who had by now taken Esteban's former bed in the front room of the library. As I felt for my clothes in the groggy dark of the fiction room, I could only wonder at this latest insanity.

"Lazy people!" shouted Ablimit when Kurt and I arrived at the third-floor apartment. "You finally wake up! Come, eat pancakes!"

This was another of the great bookstore traditions. Every Sunday morning for more than four decades, George had served his guests a pancake breakfast to ensure there was at least one common meal a week. Sure enough, this was the first time I'd seen everybody together in the same place since the night at Polly Magoo's. The only absentee was Simon, who, I was gruffly informed, hadn't bothered to wake up for a pancake breakfast in years.

Wearing flannel pajamas and well-holed slippers, George was in the kitchen stirring batter. There was already a panful of pancakes frying on the stove and a pot of freshly brewed coffee on the counter. In

France, many of the dairies package yogurt in tiny glass jars that the majority of consumers throw away afterward. George uses these jars for everything from paper clips to strawberry ice cream, and we now cradled them in our hands to absorb the heat of our morning coffee.

I sat beside the Italian woman, who was in the midst of telling Ablimit why George especially liked guests from Bologna. Not only was it home to the oldest university in Europe, she said, but it was a stronghold of the Italian Communist party. Ablimit was on the verge of arguing politics, but the Italian drowned him out by singing a rousing refrain of "Ciao Bella," that George accompanied from the kitchen by banging pots to the rhythm.

The song done, George emerged and began slapping pancakes onto plates. They were tapioca in color and had a lumpy appearance. To go with these pancakes, there was a metal pot of syrup, but not syrup that would have come from any maple tree. George watered down molasses because it was less expensive, and he now spooned it onto my plate and urged me to eat up.

Pushing the pancake once with my fork, I tried to prepare myself. I had never been an enthusiastic morning eater and this breakfast didn't look desirable, no matter the tradition. The Italian woman cut into her pancake as if dissecting a frog while Kurt elbowed me discreetly. "These can be pretty nasty," he whispered. "Sometimes George uses the same batter for a month."

I bit. It wasn't that it tasted bad, only so very different from any pancake I'd previously encountered. There was a cloying sweetness from the molasses, patches of salt where the batter hadn't been mixed thoroughly, and the general taste and texture of clumpy flour paste. Yet while I forced myself to finish the one pancake, Ablimit was happily munching a second, then a third.

"We live like kings!" he burst out as George finally joined us at the table with a pancake of his own. Despite the questionable nature of the meal, I don't think anybody disagreed.

Sunday was the busiest day at Shakespeare and Company, and George asked the residents to give the store a thorough cleaning before the crowds arrived. Kurt was ordered to vacuum the entire bookstore, Ablimit's job was to wash the windows, and the Italian woman had to straighten the shelves of books. I was to scrub the tile floor at the front of the bookstore, a job in which George took a special interest. He insisted that over the past fifty years nobody except for him had ever done the job properly.

"You have to get down on your knees and scrub, really scrub," he said, handing me a bucket, a beaten wire brush, and a tin of scouring powder.

It was a challenging assignment as the floor was filthy from a week's worth of grime and the rust-and-cream tiles were so old that both colors were closer to gray. It didn't help that the few bristles left on the wire brush sagged more than they scrubbed, but still I sweated for half an hour, cleaning harder than I'd ever cleaned anything in my life. My craving to please was accentuated by the competitive side of my nature, which made me keen to outdo George. When I was finished, the floor didn't exactly shine, but I was confident it couldn't look any better.

"Look at that!" George grunted as he inspected my work. Pointing to a corner under the cash desk where a shadow of dirt remained, he got down on his knees, scrubbed it cleaner, and then stood up.

"Ha! You people today don't know how to do things," he said, and went humming off to continue his inspection.

With the store open, I went to take my usual station in the antiquarian room, but when I opened the door, I found Simon lying comatose in bed.

"You mean I overslept?" he groaned when I told him George was already at the desk next door.

He spoke in a slurred voice and had such trouble coordinating the movements of his limbs that I worried he wouldn't be able to dress and get away before being discovered. But Simon was prepared. Each night, the last thing he did before returning to the bookstore was order a double espresso to go from Panis. He kept the plastic cup a hand's reach from his bed in order to kick-start his mornings.

As I watched, he downed the cold coffee in a single swallow and then, Popeye after his spinach, the poet leapt to his feet and flung on his clothes. During his exile from the bookstore, Simon had been spending his days at the various libraries and museums in the city, places where you could both stay warm and read in peace. Putting on his hat, he told me he was off to library of the Centre Pompidou.

"I don't envy you," he said as he hurried away. "Sundays are impossible here. They descend in swarms. Swarms."

Indeed, there was such a constant rush in the antiquarian room that for the first time I understood why the poet occasionally locked himself away. The door kept swinging open, the cold air kept rushing in, the absurd questions kept showering down. "Did William Shakespeare really live here?" asked one particularly misinformed customer.

At one point, George came in and introduced a gentleman as an editor at the *Paris Review*, saying he had once lived in the store. The man said hello and George left him to browse through the books. Minutes later, Kurt burst in with several typewritten pages clutched in his hand.

"Is the *Paris Review* guy here?" he demanded. I realized what was about to unfold and kept quiet in hopes of preventing the imminent scene, but to no avail. There were two men in the antiquarian room and Kurt grabbed the closest one.

"Are you the editor?"

The man, a German tourist, shook his head in a frightened manner, while the actual editor shrank farther into the back corner. Kurt swooped like a hawk on a gimpy rabbit.

"I want you to publish this," he said, thrusting a chapter of *Videowrangler* into his hands.

The editor appeared pained and said he was overwhelmed with submissions but would try and give it a read. After receiving half a dozen hearty slaps on the back, the editor quickly fled. I wondered aloud if Kurt didn't think he'd been presumptuous.

"How else am I going to get my break?" he scoffed.

My vigilance at the desk was later rewarded when a sparkly girl by the name of Gayle appeared at the door with a basket of freshly baked bread. With the residents' reputation for poverty, it was common for people to deposit spare baguettes or even bags of groceries at the front desk. No contribution was anticipated more than Gayle's. She was chef at the New Zealand embassy and, as the bread attested, a master of her art.

Another pleasant surprise was the identity of Gayle's boyfriend. He was sitting outside on the bench under the cherry tree, reading a book about bullfighting and smoking an unfiltered cigarette.

There is a certain discrepancy of view when it comes to a bullfight. Some consider it a tremendous sport that pits man against beast; others contend it is cruel to taunt, torture, and kill an animal for the pleasure of a supposedly civilized human audience. Rare is the individual with no opinion at all.

The classic bullfight as seen in Spain or Mexico has three parts. The first involves the angering of the bull, where a picador on horseback circles the bull and stabs bright ribbons into the animal's neck with a lance. By the end of this procedure, the blood is streaming down the bull's flanks and the ribbons are a sticky red. The second stage is the famous one, where the matador brandishes his cape and encourages the bull to charge, then steps aside and ushers the beast past. After the bull is exhausted, the final stage begins. Here, the matador approaches the bull, looks it in the eye, and plunges a sword between the animal's shoulder blades. The bullfighter then takes his bows while the bull is dragged away by a team of oxen, the corpse leaving a wet trail of blood across the sand of the arena.

After a few moments of conversation, it became evident that Tom, Gayle's boyfriend, appreciated this sporting tribute to man's struggle against animals.

The only professional bullfight I'd had the pleasure to witness had been in Portugal and this left me of the opinion that the sport could be enjoyed without the slaughter. There, the first two parts are the same, but the final stage is one of the most gripping events I have ever seen.

Once the matador leaves the ring, thirteen men dressed in white enter and confront the angry bull. The men, all of whom wear white caps except the leader, whose cap is bright red, form a line opposite the bull and then creep toward it like a slithering snake. When the bull charges, the man with the red hat leaps onto its head in an attempt to land between the horns and block the animal's vision. The second man in the line then runs behind the bull and yanks on its tail to slow the bull's forward progress while the other eleven men wrestle it to the ground. Once the bull is on its knees, it is considered vanquished. In thanks for its troubles, a herd of lovely cows is then ushered in and the bull is allowed to sniff their genitals and follow them out of the ring.

That moment when the man is about to leap onto the bull's head is as intense as a World Cup shoot-out. The day I spent at the Portuguese ring, there were six bulls on the bill. Three times, the bull was successfully subdued on the first leap, twice it took two attempts, and the final time the line of thirteen men had to approach the bull four painful times and the red hatted man was barely able to walk after being thrown on his first three tries. Blind courage, in my mind, is defined by a man who will stand before a charging bull and jump onto its head.

Tom had not been familiar with this more humane offspring of the bullfight and, perhaps won over by my animated reenactment of the event, agreed it a worthy thing to consider. A gentleman's bond of debate thus formed, I inquired if he had enjoyed the Shaw play. To my delight, he withdrew it from his jacket pocket, thanking me profusely for having let him borrow the book. Feeling petty for my concerns, I offered Tom a seat inside the antiquarian room to escape the wind.

One of the most remarkable features of this man, especially considering the breakfast I'd been served that morning, was his last name. Tom went by Thomas Pancake and held true claim to the name. As he told it, his father was baptized Sperry Pancake and had even been photographed for a box of General Mills instant pancake mix when he was a baby.

Tom had left Portland the year before with his guitar and a plane ticket to the Czech Republic, where he had a job teaching English. After a salary dispute with the head of the school escalated into arson, Tom headed south to Morocco. There he learned Arabic, adopted a stray cat, and received an offer from a fellow traveler to live free at a house outside of London. He was on his way to England when he stopped over in Paris to stretch his legs after more than sixty hours on the bus.

That first night in the city, Tom slept under a bridge on the eastern part of the Seine and at dawn his guitar case was stolen. He was in the habit of sleeping with his instrument, but the case had been filled with clothes, toiletries, and several cartons of cigarettes he'd bought cheap when leaving North Africa. For Tom, who smoked two packs of unfiltered Lucky Strikes a day, this was a devastating blow. In deep distress, he walked along the Seine and passed Shakespeare and Company. Tom thought the bookstore would simply be a place to warm his bones for a few hours, but instead he ended up moving in, Moroccan cat and all.

That was in December, and since then the cat had run away and Tom had fallen for Gayle. A few weeks before, he'd moved out of Shakespeare and Company after receiving a gracious invitation to live with her at the New Zealand embassy.

"I'd always thought she was easy on the eyes," Tom said, winking.

The devil having been spoken of, Gayle reappeared after distributing bread through the rest of the bookstore. Her mood bright, she invited us both for coffee. At Panis, we snagged stools, chatted with Nico, and Gayle even had a crumb of bread left over to feed to Amos the dog.

When I returned to the store, the tea party was well under way. Eve was passing out custard cookies and stirring the cauldron of tea, there was the woman with the one-eyed dog, and many of the other exotic characters from the week before. The handful of new visitors could immediately be identified by their wide-eyed countenances. Watching their bewilderment, I couldn't believe only a week had passed since I'd come to Shakespeare and Company myself.

Once the last guest had left, I helped Eve wash the cups and tidy the apartment. George, who rarely appeared at the tea party itself, came upstairs shortly after and offered us dinner, a feast of chicken, ratatouille, and Chinese beer.

As we ate, George fussed over Eve, filling her glass and making sure she received the choicest morsels of chicken. "She's my little Nastasya Filippovna!" he said with a glowing smile. "She's the only one who really loves me."

Eve responded with a kiss on his cheek. It was the first time I'd seen an eighty-six-year-old man blush like a little boy.

With George in such good humor, I was tempted to raise the subject of the bookstore's future, but I decided it was futile. George was clearly a man who did things at his own pace, so I decided just to sit back and enjoy the evening. At one point, George pulled an electric organ from one of the couches and, with us all well under the influence of Tsingtao's touch, we sang the official Shakespeare and Company song.

If you ever come to Paris
On a cold and rainy night
And find the Shakespeare store
It can be a welcome sight

Because it has a motto
Something friendly and wise
Be kind to strangers
Lest they're angels in disguise

More beer was opened, more cheeks were kissed, and George put his arm around my shoulder. "Comrade," he said, "I'm glad you came to my little bookstore."

19.

Over the years, there has been many an offer to help secure the Shakespeare and Company legacy. Some were from those passing through like me, awed by the bookstore and thunderstruck it could be lost. Others were the work of do-gooders who devote their lives to preserving such troves of literary history. But the most serious attempts came from two men dear to George, his younger brother, Carl, and his old friend Lawrence Ferlinghetti.

Carl Whitman is the youngest of Grace and Walt Whitman's children and the last living member of George's immediate family. Because of the eleven-year age difference between the brothers, there was a certain distance growing up. Carl admired his older brother, but there was never the deep bond that might have been established if they had been closer in age. Beyond this, there was another subtle rift, the result of the religious discord between the Whitman parents.

George's father was the son of New England farmers and his fierce intellect propelled him to study at a university and then go on to work as a professor and textbook author. Walt was a man of books, a student of history, and a world traveler. And, perhaps most importantly, Walt was ambivalent about religion. Not that he was a declared atheist; he was just so caught up in science and the wonders on earth that he didn't have time to contemplate more heavenly pursuits. Grace Whitman's life was a stark contrast to her husband's. George's mother was raised in a wealthy family that had chauffeurs and owned one of the first Rolls-Royces on the East Coast. But greater was the spiritual divide: Grace was a staunch Presbyterian, a woman who devoted herself to the church. She convinced her children to give themselves over to Jesus—George signed a document when he was thirteen years old that stated, "Trusting in Lord Jesus Christ for strength, I promise that I will strive to do whatever he would have me do"—and she generally frowned upon her husband's ways. By their later years, Walt had retreated to the third floor of the Whitman house and began living among his books and journals.

It is no surprise that in such a household the children tended to choose sides. George and his sister Mary were drawn to their father's path. Mary was ambivalent about religion and followed her father into academia, earning a doctorate in philosophy at Columbia and then working as a professor, first at Wellesley, then at Vassar. George, meanwhile, declared himself an atheist from the moment he first read about the doctrine of disbelief and dedicated his life to the written word. But Carl embraced his mother's world. He picked his own church as a child, after not getting along with the family pastor, and had been a devout believer ever since.

It seemed that Carl always had a foot in both worlds. He attended Cornell for engineering and then got pulled into the navy during World War II. He was actually on the way to serve at Pearl Harbor when the atomic bombs were dropped on Japan and the war was declared over. Back home, he felt torn. He read of George's adventures in letters to the family and had been convinced by many of his brother's socialist sermons. But his parents insisted it would be better to get a teaching position and strive for a greater stability. Always having looked up to George, Carl first tried a spell on the road himself to see if it fit. He hitched across the country, working in coal mines, laying rails, unloading crab boats. On one occasion, when he and his mother visited Paris in the 1950s, he even took a trip to Russia at George's urging.

In the end, perhaps to no one's surprise, Carl chose a middle road. He became an academic and an activist. When he got his master's, he was the first white student at Fisk University in Nashville, an institution that was founded in 1866 to educate freed slaves. After first taking a job as a professor at Fisk, he later moved to Florida A & M University, where he was involved with the campus union and worked with refugees who came north from Central America. It was at this time he also started volunteering with Witnesses for Peace, the Christian group that fights oppression and poverty in Latin America. He became so committed to the group that he eventually served on the organization's board of directors.

The brothers' lives further diverged when it came to family. Carl remained close with his mother and later got married and had four children. George, meanwhile, seldom had the time to go home, missing such crucial events as his father's funeral and Carl's wedding. The family became so worried about George's distant ways and his decision to open a bookstore in Paris, Grace even withheld his portion of the inheritance for three years after his father's death in 1952. She hoped, as she had hoped with his tramping and his communism, that this was just another phase and George would one day return to the United States.

Yet, if anything, family relations became worse. On the upsetting occasion when his sister died, George even remained out of touch for more than a week after receiving the telegram. By the 1950s, Mary Whitman was teaching at the University of Buffalo. One evening, while entertaining a guest at home, she choked during dinner and retreated to the bathroom. Her airway became clogged by a piece of steak and by the time her friend came to help, it was too late. George's sister died in 1956 at the age of forty-one. When George eventually wrote the family, he explained the delay as the result of a motor accident and apologized for being so distant.

I suppose that, as a family, we tend to be negligent in vital situations— For years I have understood certain facts about Mary & the family—in fact, ever since she came into the Taunton Book Lounge in 1946 I realized she was desperate & yet because of my passive nature I failed to give her sufficient encouragement. . . . I just didn't have enough brotherly love to see her through a difficult period & thrash out her problems with her. Because after all a psychoanalyst is just a crutch for what the family doesn't provide.

Between the missed funeral and George's resentment at having his inheritance delayed, his relationship with his mother suffered. In his later years, he would carry a deep resentment for her, accusing her of everything from refusing to breast-feed him as a child to biting him as punishment when he was an infant. It was no surprise to anyone, then, that when Grace Whitman died in 1979, George was unable to attend that funeral as well.

But George and Carl were clearly beneficiaries of the same extraordinary vitality. After retiring from the university at the age of seventy, Carl tramped the jungles of Nicaragua and Guatemala, investigating atrocities and helping poor villagers as part of his duties for Witnesses for Peace. That winter I was at the store, Carl was seventy-seven and continually on the move, touring Africa, Asia, and Eastern Europe with his wife, a traveling professor for an international education program.

As the years passed, the two men made efforts to build a friendship. Carl wrote regular letters to George and began staying at the bookstore whenever he passed through Paris. It was on one such visit that he came up with an idea to help the store.

Carl knew of the uncertain future ahead of Shakespeare and Company and thought the best option was to set up a nonprofit foundation that would both protect the bookstore after George was gone and cement its historical standing. This could be done, he reasoned, by selling the bookstore's archives and using the money to start a nonprofit foundation to manage the store.

The Shakespeare and Company archives were sure to be cherished. Among the many boxes and files were the papers concerning the start-up of the bookstore and correspondence from five decades of authors including a piquant collection from Anaïs Nin, letters from the likes of Howard Zinn and Max Ernst, and even a brief note from J.D Salinger. There were also posters heralding the hundreds of readings and book signings held at the store, first editions and rare books, such as two of the original copies of *Ulysses* he'd inherited from Sylvia Beach and volumes from Graham Greene's personal library, items that George had managed to buy when the author died.

The archives also contained records of the various literary magazines that had been run from the store, including Alexander Trocchi's *Merlin* and Jean Fanchette's *Two Cities*. Trocchi's battles with heroin and his work with Jean Genet, Henry Miller, and Samuel Beckett are well chronicled, but George remembers the soft-spoken Fanchette with more fondness. A psychoanalyst from the island of Mauritius, Fanchette conspired with George to publish *Two Cities* from the upstairs library of the bookstore for more than half a decade. During that time, George introduced Fanchette to Lawrence Durrell who would go on to become the Mauritian's friend and adviser.

The finishing touch to these archives was the autobiographies from forty years of bookstore visitors. Stashed around the store were the scribbled stories of everyone from Allen Ginsberg to John Denver and they gave tantalizing glimpses of the thousands of people who passed through Shakespeare and Company. Astonishingly, the themes kept repeating themselves: people disillusioned with mainstream culture, looking for a place to lick their wounds, yearning to make the world a better place. In fact, according to George, the only major difference between his first guests in the 1950s and 1960s and present-day guests was the status of their families. "You didn't see so much divorce then," he told me. "Today, everybody seems to be from a broken family."

Carl had already talked to Boston University about these archives and there was a great amount of interest. He even had a meeting with an attorney in Paris to discuss the project. Yet the idea was rejected by George. The archives first had to be properly organized—not a slipshod job by a temporary resident of the bookstore, but a proper cataloging by a qualified librarian. A professional archivist had offered to come from the United States to do the work and had even told George he would live in the store to reduce the expenses. There would still be a fee of twenty dollars an hour, though, and forever frugal, George balked at such an expense.

The idea of an official foundation still remained a possibility. A state-recognized foundation with a board of directors and a constitution would mean the bookstore's future would be assured. This is what Ferlinghetti had done with City Lights and this is what George's old friend was encouraging him to do with Shakespeare and Company.

After receiving his doctorate from the Sorbonne, Ferlinghetti left Paris in 1950, the year before George opened Le Mistral. In 1953, Ferlinghetti, with his partner, Peter Martin, created the City Lights bookstore in San Francisco. Ferlinghetti's hope was to create a home for "a running conversation between authors of all ages, from ancient times to modern."

Ferlinghetti did just that, fostering a literary community around his bookstore, installing a mail rack so writers with no fixed address could receive letters, and starting City Lights Publishing. He went on to produce almost two hundred books, including work by Jack Kerouac and Paul Bowles. When Ferlinghetti was brought to trial on obscenity charges for publishing Ginsberg's *Howl*, City Lights became synonymous with creative freedom. Ferlinghetti also earned acclaim for his own work, most notably his collection of poems, *A Coney Island of the Mind*, which was one of the best-selling volumes of American poetry in the 1970s.

Born in 1919, Ferlinghetti was seven years younger than George, but he had already faced up to the question of the future. The city of San Francisco had helped set up the City Lights Foundation, a nonprofit cultural and educational organization dedicated to nurturing literacy and the literary arts. Ideally, this is what George needed to do in Paris. As Shakespeare and Company and City Lights were sister bookstores, there was even talk of George joining Ferlinghetti's foundation.

"George didn't want his ex-wife to inherit the store. There was a great enmity to it," recalled Ferlinghetti. "I supported the idea. I thought it would officialize our status as sister bookstores."

But there were several obstacles. First was the system of accounting at Shakespeare and Company. George had never done well in such business matters; not surprisingly, he had received *F*'s both times he attempted the

Advanced Accounting Theory course in his university years. The book-keeping at the store consisted largely of fictitious pencil scribbles in green account ledgers and there was no proper method of tracking income or expenses. The accountant who did the store's taxes, a woman George warmly referred to as "Mrs. Gingerbread," helped keep the bailiffs at bay, but a certified accounting system would have to be adopted before the store could receive status as a nonprofit foundation. This alone promised to be a mountain of a chore, and when City Lights' lawyers examined the paperwork, they quickly advised Ferlinghetti to postpone any decision.

More unsettling was the hundreds of thousands of francs' worth of repairs and renovations that would be required before Shakespeare and Company could gain any official sanction. The electrical system was the prime suspect, as evidenced by the major fire in July 1990 that destroyed more than four thousand books and whose soot still blackened the beams in the library. The writer Christopher Sawyer-Lauçanno was staying at the store at the time. Having already published a successful biography of Paul Bowles, he was researching his book *The Continual Pilgrimage*, which was about American writers in Paris after World War II. He was in George's office when the fire broke out in the library and witnessed the gushing black smoke and the mountain of smoldering books on the esplanade in front of the store. He also remembers George standing out front of the bookstore, rallying people with Joe Hill's famous words: "Don't mourn—organize!" The loss was devastating, yet amazingly, despite such a traumatic warning, no efforts were made to assure the store met city safety codes. Officials complained about everything from the width of the front door to the lack of a fire exit.

And what proved to be the biggest hurdle to any foundation was George himself. He'd spent half a century building Shakespeare and Company and had a very particular view of how things should be done. He wasn't ready to cede control to anybody, whether it be his old friend Ferlinghetti or a foundation's board of directors. Shakespeare and Company was his passion, his life, his child. In the end, just days before he was to transfer money to Ferlinghetti in order to start work on the dual foundation, George decided to go it alone.

20.

It was during a visit to the Sandwich Queen that I learned of the bookstore's newest resident.

Kurt was continuing to school me in cheap Parisian food, and that afternoon was my introduction to the glories of the discount sandwich. As we left the store, he jovially informed me the tuition fee was the price of his own lunch. Though financially in no position to be so magnanimous, I couldn't bring myself to refuse, so off we went on another culinary adventure.

"Trust me, it's worth it to you," he insisted. "These sandwiches are legend around here."

Around the corner from the bookstore, on rue St. Jacques, just a few doorways before Polly Magoo's, was a narrow storefront that most people passed without noticing. Though the space was no wider than the average arm span, an ingenious craftsman had turned it into a sandwich counter. Here, a round Cambodian woman stood behind a glass case of cellophane-wrapped baguettes. This was Tuee the Sandwich Queen, a regular stop for the low of budget on the Left Bank.

After an appropriately royal greeting, Tuee rummaged among the stacks to show off her wares. There was chicken, fish, Camembert, fake crab, and, of course, the omnipresent *jambon fromage*. Though all the meat was a hue or two from normal and there was the occasional speck of blue-green mold on the bread, it was only twenty francs for a pair of foot-long sandwiches and a canned beverage of choice.

"You can go a whole day on this," Kurt advised as we tried to gauge which sandwiches were the closest to being bacteria-free. "Eat one now for lunch and the other later for dinner and you're set."

Sitting under the cherry trees with our sandwiches, Kurt wondered if I'd met the new arrival. As he told it, a young woman had been browsing through the books that morning and Kurt had struck up a conversation about the marvels of Shakespeare and Company. An hour or so later, the woman had returned with a suitcase in hand and asked George for a bed.

"I told her she should read *Tropic of Cancer* and she bought a copy," Kurt said, grinning.

Kurt was a notorious flirt and kept watch over the many attractive young women who passed through the store. He believed that if a woman bought a book by either Henry Miller or Anaïs Nin, she was interested in immediate sexual intercourse, and in hopes of testing this theory, he constantly hovered around the fiction section. Apparently, an unsuspecting subject had just stumbled into his laboratory.

"I think you'll like her," he said with a coy wink.

Unsure of how fit Kurt was to judge such things, I concentrated on my egg and tomato sandwich. The bread was stale enough to make for rigorous jaw exercise, but otherwise it made for a filling meal. Once again, I was obliged to thank Kurt for his teachings.

That evening, there was a reading at the bookstore, so after closing the antiquarian room, I found a seat among the crowd. An Irish woman was going to recite Joyce and Wilde while performing an erotic dance routine, and the room was brimming with curious eyes.

Readings have been organized at the bookstore since the doors first opened and everyone from William Saroyan to William Styron has held literary court in the upstairs library. Shakespeare and Company's reputation for attracting quality readers and discerning ears was once so great that in Mordecai Richler's *Barney's Version*, a young writer is humiliated when he fails to impress the bookstore audience. But as this

Irish woman careened lewdly around the library, screeching lines from *Finnegans Wake,* I suspected there might have been an easing of standards since the hallowed days when Ginsberg and Corso performed regularly at the store.

After an uncomfortable moment where the audience sat unsure whether to applaud, the show was declared over. The room quickly cleared, but a woman with long braids and olive complexion stayed behind and sat with Ablimit near the window. She had dark hollows for eyes, and I found myself wondering where the line was between her pupil and iris.

Ablimit helpfully introduced us, which somewhat made up for my gaping. The woman smiled hello, but my tongue was jelly. Slurring some excuse about a bathroom and a book, I fled the room. This was Nadia, the newest resident of Shakespeare and Company.

The following day was market day, and I had the pleasure of accompanying George on his rounds. Every morning of the week, open-air markets operate in different parts of Paris, selling fruit, vegetables, fish, cheese, and most everything else considerably cheaper than at the grocery stores. While the most celebrated of these markets was at Bastille, there were less expensive and more unruly versions at Belleville, La Chapelle, and place d'Aligre. We at Shakespeare and Company were fortunate enough to have a small market just down the street at place Maubert.

Three times a week, George roved the stalls, haggling for an extra pound of zucchini, negotiating down the price of carrots when the stalls were about to close, asking for an extra onion to be slipped into his bag. The great secret was that once the market shut at the end of the morning, all the produce that wouldn't make it through another day was thrown into empty crates and left behind. With a minor amount of scavenging, one could find most anything, and there was an entire community who waited for the markets to close so they could begin their shopping. That day, along with the vegetables we'd purchased, we found half a bag of apples suitable for stewing, some barely bruised eggplants, and, nestled alone in the gutter, a blessed potato.

Toting the bags back to the bookstore, I decided it was an opportune time to ask about Nadia. George only looked at me suspiciously.

"Her biography was very good," he said. "Why, do you like her?"

"Of course not," I replied in my most sincere voice. "I'm simply interested in the newest member of our little family." The matter so dropped, we carried the groceries upstairs to the third-floor apartment and George began preparing lunch. He was making the dumplings to go along with the vegetable stew when he suddenly slapped his hand to his head.

"I forgot the salt downstairs in the office. Will you get it?"

There was a fine-looking box of salt on the shelf in front of him, but George insisted this wasn't the right kind, so I hurried downstairs. It was easy enough to find the second box of salt in the miniature kitchen, but what really caught my eye was a piece of paper on George's desk. It was Nadia's biography.

Nadia was born in Romania under the horrors of the Ceaușescu regime. Though only a girl at the time, she remembers when much of Bucharest's historic downtown was leveled to build "the People's House," the dictator's warped Communist lingo for his presidential palace that would become the second-largest building in the world after the Pentagon. When Ceaușescu was overthrown in 1989, Nadia's parents managed to get visas for the United States and settled in Arizona. Nadia was in junior high school at the time and the move was a complete culture shock—a new language, a material decadence, a general optimism, and a brightness foreign to Eastern Europe.

It was no surprise she didn't fit into small-town American life, and after an unhappy bout with high school, Nadia resolved to get away. Her escape came when she won a scholarship to study fine arts at Columbia University. Surrounded by the chaos and diversity of New York, things started to make sense again and she felt something akin to happiness.

Though her professors admired her work, her scholarship wasn't renewed and Nadia was forced to transfer. Seething, her art became darker, her outlook cynical, and suddenly she was looking for another place to go.

That was when she thought of Paris. She moved to France to write and paint and hopefully just be. Her first step was a hotel near the place de la République and a plan to find some sort of under-the-table job to pay for the room. Instead, work wasn't forthcoming, and the money was running out when she passed through the bookstore and Kurt told her of George's generosity.

When I later saw her with a collection of Kafka's short stories, I pounced on the opportunity for conversation.

"I thought you were reading Henry Miller," I said, hoping she wouldn't notice the tremble in my voice.

"Who told you that?" she demanded.

Flustered, I mumbled something about Kurt having suggested the book to her. Nadia only gave a sarcastic laugh.

"He pushed *Tropic of Cancer* on me, for God's sake," she said. "I only bought the stupid book because I needed a place to stay and I thought it might help me get into the bookstore."

Afraid of incurring further wrath, I left her to "A Hunger Artist" and sulked away.

Visiting Café Panis for bathrooming the following morning, Kurt asked what I thought of the new resident. "Beautiful and smart," I answered, "but definitely a tad corrosive."

"You think so, too?" Kurt snapped. "She cuts down everything I say. You have to be careful with women, they'll tear you up."

Everyone has a good heartache story and it was clear that Kurt was no different. As we sat and nursed our coffees, he shared the real reason he had decided to leave New York.

It'd been his first love, back when he was still in Florida. From Kurt's telling, she was incredibly wild, incredibly beautiful, and had worked as a model before they'd met. Together, they became small-town restless and left for New York to make their way. Kurt's dreams collided painfully with big-city reality as his script for *Videowrangler* stalled and he was forced to work two jobs to pay the rent. Day by painful day their love became infected by his malaise.

His girlfriend's odd hours made Kurt suspicious. He began trailing her when she left the apartment, and one day he followed her to the lobby of a hotel, where another man rose to meet her. They kissed like familiar lovers, and she followed him to the elevator. Kurt was devastated but tried to play the scene with class. He went up to the front desk. He calmly asked for the room number. He sent up a tray of strawberries and champagne with a signed card. And then he left.

It was a good story and I could've sworn there was a trace of a tear in Kurt's eye when he finished. Still, I was somewhat unsettled when he squared his thumb and forefingers to frame the imaginary shot of him walking out of the hotel.

"Just like a Cary Grant movie," he insisted.

21.

For a lifelong Communist, George had a canny business sense. His first foray into the world of commerce came when he was a boy in his hometown of Salem. The man who lived across the street from the Whitmans was a gregarious alcoholic who worked shifts at a local bottling factory. At the time, rare was the house that kept a bottle of wine in the cupboard, so the drunkard was a neighborhood curiosity, and young George inevitably struck up a friendship with such a character. One particularly hot summer, the two came to an arrangement where George bought cases of orange, lemon, and sarsaparilla soda at a discount from the man's factory and then sold individual bottles on street corners. Later, George switched to selling Health-O products door-to-door in his neighborhood, but this enterprise was also abandoned when he decided to enter agriculture and filled his parents' basement with manure to start a mushroom farm.

In high school, George started his first genuine business, the Whitman Multiple Products Company, and his letterhead announced the sale of "office supplies, novelties, boats, gliders, radios, household appliances, motorcycles, books, toys, printing and all general merchandise." As an adult, George was drawn to the book business. He ended his military service during World War II by working nights at an army hospital in Taunton, Massachusetts, and during his spare time he opened the short-lived Taunton Book Lounge, a combination bookstore and reading room. Later, before departing for Europe, George started a mail-order book company, The Lost Phoebe, based in Salem. And when he arrived in Paris, before discovering the cherished spot across from Notre Dame, he first tried his hand at an English bookstore on boulevard de Courcelles, near Parc de Monceau.

Bookselling isn't the surest road to riches, and George needed every morsel of his business acumen to keep Shakespeare and Company alive. He printed postcards to sell to tourists, he bought secondhand books for cheap prices at church sales and then marked them up substantially for resale, he sneaked decent-looking used novels among the full-priced new editions, he kept the doors open until midnight to eke out every last sale. When all this wasn't enough, George actually went selling door-to-door. His greatest boon was when *Tropic of Cancer* was banned in the United States. George visited the residences of the American students in Paris and offered to sell them the licentious book. He seldom failed to make a sale.

It wasn't that George was especially proud of his business intuition; he just realized there was no other choice. Until the revolution arrived, he was forced to live in a capitalist society, so his solution was to participate in the economy in the least harmful fashion. For George, one of the major problems of the profit-driven system was that people were rewarded for doing harm to their fellowman. Food companies increased sales by loading their products with sugars and salts; manufacturers lowered their costs by closing union factories and cutting health benefits; oil companies raised their stock value by paying lobbyists to block environmental legislation.

"I'd rather have a free lending library, but I can't escape the fact that I run a business," George rationalized. "At least by selling books, I know I'm not hurting anybody."

All this business experience was about to come in very handy. Once I was settled into bookstore life, George began regularly inviting me into his office on the pretense of finishing a book order or filing papers, but usually it was just to talk. When there was something especially urgent to discuss, he would search me out and demand I immediately accompany him upstairs. But of course, George being George, this was never done in a direct manner.

Typical was the occasion when he found me at the front desk, chatting with Pia about the Chinese New Year's party she was organizing for the bookstore. Pia, like George, loved all things Chinese and had traveled the country extensively when she was helping her mother, a former Ford model, prepare a book on the historical quarters of Shanghai. With an eye to dealing in contemporary Chinese art, Pia was even taking Mandarin lessons from Ablimit and could maintain a rough conversation in her new language.

That February, it was going to be year 4697 by the Chinese calendar, the Year of the Dragon, and Pia was in the midst of describing the celebration that would be held at Shakespeare and Company, when George appeared in the doorway. He listened for a while, then began shuffling books, then complained about the sorry state of the bookstore. Finally, he turned to me with a look of exasperation. "You look thirsty, comrade," he muttered.

The sign thus given, I bade good-bye to Pia and trudged upstairs to the office to see what he had to tell me. Once the door was closed, I learned George adhered to the philosophy of the best defense being a good offense. With the hotel baron breathing down his neck and the future of the store as murky as the Seine, he'd decided that the appropriate thing was to expand the bookstore.

There was a vacant apartment in the Shakespeare and Company building, just across the hall from George's beloved third-floor retreat. This apartment had the same view of Ile de la Cité, as well as large eastern windows that looked out to Ile St. Louis and beyond. George had long dreamed of turning it into an extension of the bookstore library, where conferences could be held and political activists lodged.

"There will be doctors from Médecins Sans Frontières and aid workers from the United States staying at Shakespeare and Company on their way to Africa," he predicted.

Over the years, George had been scrupulous in monitoring the apartment. When the previous owner died, it was left to her children and had remained empty, but with real estate prices in Paris soaring, the apartment would be coming on the market. If George could buy it, he was certain his temple of books would be complete and he could finally feel at peace with what he had accomplished.

"It would be the jewel of the bookstore," George said. "Can't you see how perfect it would be?"

Perfectly illogical, I thought to myself, but George wasn't one to worry about niggling issues like logic. Not at all concerned about diverting his energies, his only question was whether he could beat the French businessman to the apartment. George was confident his bid would be preferred so long as he could raise the money and get his offer in first.

"I only need two million francs," he declared with a broad smile.

Now, two million francs was more than $300,000, a considerable sum, but George wasn't daunted. He announced he was going to raise this fortune by publishing a best-selling book. Nothing too fancy, a simple accordion-style laminated leaflet with photographs and an essay on Shakespeare and Company. He thought he could sell 100,000 copies at twenty-five francs apiece and this windfall would be enough to buy him the apartment.

It actually wasn't as far-fetched as it sounded. George had a long history of successful publishing. In high school, he produced and edited *The Reflector,* a magazine that included sections like the "Poet's Corner," and also contained half a dozen advertisements for the Whitman Multiple Products Company. At Boston University, he was advertising director for the *Boston University News* and then started his own breakaway paper, *The Campus Critic.* Once he had the bookstore, it was publishing bedlam. In addition to the literary journals he'd supported, George started *Paris Magazine* in the 1970s and sold ten thousand copies of the first issue. When the fire devastated the store, he produced *A Biography of a Bookstore in Pictures and Poems,* and a few years later he put out *Angels in Disguise,* a collection of autobiographies that remains the best-selling book at the store. Even the postcards he'd printed brought in a constant tinkle of coins.

For the current project, Luke had already been recruited to help. He'd recently bought a new computer and had downloaded pirated copies of all the latest software. Pleased to be part of the Shakespeare and Company publishing tradition, Luke had volunteered to design the booklet. If I agreed to help with the editing, that meant the only cost George would incur was the printing of the book, but he was sure he could get that done for 100,000 francs.

Even though I was flattered to be taking part in such an auspicious venture, I couldn't stop from brooding about the other problems at the bookstore.

"Wouldn't it be smarter to use that money to set up a foundation like Ferlinghetti's?" I finally mustered the courage to ask. "Something to protect the store?"

"What are you talking about?" George snapped back. "Whose side are you on? Do you want to help or not?"

The answer was yes, so I held my tongue.

As much as I tried to accept the general chaos and uncertainty of the store, I couldn't escape the worry. Even as I began to help George on his quest for the apartment, I had a nagging suspicion there was something he wasn't telling me, some reason why he hadn't created his foundation or at least anointed a trustworthy successor. Sure enough, one afternoon, while scrounging about under George's desk on my hands and knees, I found the answer.

One of George's colossal woes was that he continually misplaced his keys. Sometimes they were forgotten behind a pot of beans in the kitchen, sometimes they were left in the gap between Amis and Atwood on the fiction shelf, sometimes they slipped off the back of his desk and became wedged against the wall. This is where I was in the process of looking—and I'd already found four crumpled two-hundred-franc notes, half a baguette, three spoons, and a silk Hermès tie when I came across a postcard with an English stamp and a note written in an adolescent scrawl. It was addressed to George, but to my astonishment it started "Dad."

"What's this?" I asked as I poked my head out from under the desk.

"Give me that!" George shouted, and grabbed the card from my hand. "That's none of your business."

Turning his back to me, he stared at the card for a long time, all the while sighing heavily.

"It's a long story," he finally said.

George had an heir. In the very early days of their marriage, he and his wife had a baby girl. It was one of the greatest wonders in George's long life, not to mention a remarkably virile act, considering he was sixty-nine years old at the time he fathered this child.

His daughter was born in 1981, on the first of April, the day for fools, and she was glorious with curly blond hair and George's blue eyes. They named her Sylvia Beach Whitman in honor of the founder of the first Shakespeare and Company, and thus began an unusual life for this little girl. Living in the third-floor apartment, the family shared their home not only with thousands of books and a German shepherd named Baskerville but also with the constant crowds of eccentric visitors who slept on the couches and attended the Sunday tea parties.

It was a kaleidoscope existence. Sylvia grew up with authors and actresses as baby-sitters. The poet Ted Joans took a special interest in her development, encouraging her to write poems and perform them aloud. Meanwhile, George was reading to her from first editions of *Alice in Wonderland* and *Winnie-the-Pooh* before she went to bed each night, and during the days, she sat on his lap while he served customers. She became something like the fairy princess of Shakespeare and Company. From the very beginning, George believed Sylvia was destined to take over the bookstore.

But then the marital problems began and the stress of living in a communal bookstore became too much for the family. It unnerved

George's wife to raise her daughter amid such chaos and she was especially disturbed when Sylvia began breaking into tears whenever one of her temporary "aunts" or "uncles" left the bookstore to continue his or her travels.

When Sylvia was six, her mother decided enough was enough and she took her daughter and left Paris. They moved back to England and custody and alimony disputes became standard fare. George had lived austerely for so long that he believed everyone was capable of existing on almost nothing. His wife thought a young girl should enjoy some comforts while growing up and she constantly pressured George to pay more child support. Thanks to George's oft-cluttered ways, the couple also began fighting about the promptness of these support payments. Soon the regular visits George had been promised became less regular and a summer vacation at the bookstore for Sylvia was canceled altogether. As recently as that winter, there'd been a letter from lawyers demanding George make a greater contribution to Sylvia's university education.

As for Sylvia herself, there had been a card from her the previous Christmas, and the postcard I'd found under the desk had been sent two years before. But George grimly explained that he hadn't actually seen his daughter for five years.

"Once, she happened to be in Paris and put her head in the store, but she ran away after five minutes," George remembered sadly.

Yet George still dreamed his daughter would take over Shakespeare and Company. This was why he'd delayed starting a foundation, this is why he hadn't joined forces with City Lights, this is why he wanted to expand the bookstore.

"She has to fall in love with this place," George said. "Her mother wrote that Sylvia wants to become an actress. Well, Shakespeare and Company could be the greatest stage in the world."

Finally, I thought I understood. And finally I thought there was something I could do to help. Contact Sylvia, bring her around the bookstore, let her fall in love with all her father had built.

"We can't do that, you ignoramus," George said with a dismissive wave. "Her mother is poisoning her against me. She might use my daughter as a Trojan horse to get control of the bookstore. My wife would ruin the place. Forget I ever said anything about it."

Of course. What was I thinking? Instead of starting a foundation to protect the bookstore, we were going to wait for his daughter to come take over, which George would never let happen, so instead we were buying an apartment. It was all was so obvious. We were through the rabbit hole and into the world of Shakespeare and Company, where down is up, white is black, and nothing is ever normal.

22.

It was the beginning of a most industrious time at the bookstore. George was gripped with the idea of finishing his booklet before Easter so he could take advantage of the summer tourist rush and quickly raise money for the apartment. Long days were spent sifting through files in search of photographs, and George was at his desk until late at night, scratching out drafts of his essay with a dull pencil. When George came up with an idea for a page, he would mock it up using paste and scissors and then there would be endless trips to Luke's apartment to scan in the photographs and print out sample layouts.

With his daily whims and ever-changing instructions, George was the most demanding editor I'd ever worked for. He always wanted a picture a shade brighter or a title in a different font, or, sometimes, history altered altogether.

There was a decades-old photograph of him sitting at the desk that he thought should be included in the booklet. After several hours of searching, the photograph was located, but to George's dismay it included a cigarette dangling from his fingers. George had smoked for years and his old hotel room on boulevard St. Michel became known as the "Old Smokey Reading Room" because of the dense clouds emitted by George. He even admitted as much in a letter home to his father, whom he called "the Governor." "I might as well start with the worst scandal of all and that is the fact that I pay $150 a year for cigarettes," he wrote as part of an attempt to get his father to forward him more money. Health concerns finally convinced him to quit, and he now was an ardent antismoker, routinely lecturing bookstore residents and even crushing any stray packages of cigarettes he found around the store. To bolster his credibility, he was doing his best to erase any evidence of his own dalliance with tobacco. This meant Luke was ordered to take the damning photograph home, scan it into his computer, and then carefully eliminate the cigarette with the magic of Photoshop.

This fervor of activity infected everyone. One morning, Simon donned an impressive suit jacket and hurried off to deliver his translation proposal to the French publisher. A friend had even given him an old cellular phone so he could wait for a response.

"I'm a regular Richard Branson now, aren't I?" he said while peering at the tiny buttons on the phone. "Maybe I'll get a briefcase and start reading *Le Monde Economique* in the mornings."

Up in the library, Ablimit had pushed aside his grammar books in favor of a calculator and business plan. Having grown up in China, he was now reborn an ardent capitalist and was working to get a visa that would allow him to go to the United States. While he waited, he'd hatched a scheme he was sure would make him a minor fortune.

In France, chicken producers cut off the birds' feet and discarded them before processing. Chicken feet were a common foodstuff in Asia, so Ablimit was negotiating to buy several tons cheaply so he could ship them to China. He was trying to determine how many chicken feet he would have to sell to make a reasonable profit once he'd paid all the expenses and given a cut to his investors.

"Money, it rules the world," he insisted while breaking down the cost per cubic foot of refrigerated shipping containers.

Kurt and I were inclined to agree. We were both almost at zero and despite the bounty of Tuee's sandwiches, many days our stomachs weren't entirely full. Having already thinned considerably before I arrived at Shakespeare and Company, I was now down to 155 pounds and was forced to punch new holes in my belt with a nail and hammer so my pants would stay up. Although we tried to convince ourselves that living the poor artist's life in Paris was romantic, it was hard to erase the lurking unease that occurs when one's bank card stops functioning.

Kurt had already tried a most optimistic ploy to make money. He had a collection of flattering pictures of himself, so he compiled a modeling portfolio and made the rounds of the agencies. Though he returned dejected after being told that at twenty-five he was too old, his looks did net him some plums. A young German fellow also named Kurt fell deeply in love with our Kurt about that time. This German Kurt began hanging around Shakespeare and Company, treating Bookstore Kurt to expensive lunches and even buying him a snazzy fedora similar to what the Gaucho had worn. The episode climaxed when German Kurt treated Bookstore Kurt to a weekend at an expensive Bavarian spa, plane tickets and all. Though the German Kurt had been discouraged when Bookstore Kurt refused his advances, it was a pleasant enough time.

"Hot springs," our Kurt advised afterward, strutting about with his skin freshly softened from a strawberry seed and clay facial. "They do wonders."

Still, this didn't put any actual currency in Kurt's pocket and our destitution continued. There were ways to earn money without papers in Paris: under-the-table kitchen work in restaurants, giving English lessons at an hourly rate, baby-sitting the children of the seventh arrondissement. But that must have seemed far too practical, because Kurt and I entertained more elaborate visions.

The most tantalizing possibility involved the stream of tourists who visited Shakespeare and Company. The bookstore was listed in most every guidebook to Paris and visitors burbled into the store in happy droves. They were intoxicated by the books and the bohemian writers who lived among them, all the time spending large sums of their holiday money.

Kurt and I began to watch these tourists like hungry jackals eyeing a herd of plump wildebeest. Many wanted to believe that every writer staying at the bookstore was another Hemingway in order to add that certain flare to their vacation. In truth, of the hundreds of poets and writers who pass through the bookstore every year, only a handful ever publish. But, with such bare pockets, Kurt and I saw no reason why we couldn't indulge the fantasies.

Upstairs in the library, there was an old metal typewriter and battered wooden desk with enough scars to give it character. Our plan was to set these up in front of the store and offer to sell short stories for ten francs a page. As we sat dreaming of our fortune, Nadia found us and demanded the right to join. As her contribution, she agreed to paint our sign. After a shared bottle of wine, we came up with our slogan: "Stories for Sale, 10 Francs a Page, Typos Free of Charge."

As the paint was drying, George wandered past. "That's highway robbery!" he declared. Then, gesturing at Nadia, he added, "The only one worth paying for is her. She's going to be the best writer of any of you."

George cackled some more while Nadia blushed a most attractive shade of pink.

The next afternoon, we set up the desk in front of the store and erected our sign. After days of wet gray skies, the clouds were mostly white and there was even the occasional break of sun. We thought it augured well.

Kurt volunteered for the first shift, and soon enough two Australian women who were on a tour of Europe approached and wondered what this handsome man was doing on the sidewalk with a desk and a typewriter. Kurt needed all of fifteen seconds to convince them to buy stories, then began ferociously banging out several pages of lustful Paris romance. After earning a quick sixty francs, he abandoned the desk when one of his clients offered him a beverage at a bar around the corner.

As I took his place, I immediately began to panic. What if I froze? What kind of short story could I write on the spot? I began to hope nobody would stop, and if it hadn't been for that ting of competitive spirit, I would have packed up altogether. As luck had it, the first person to approach was Fernanda. I hadn't seen her since my long walk to the store, and she was delighted that George had let me stay at the bookstore.

Fernanda insisted on buying a story and I readied myself before the typewriter. We'd bought carbon paper so we could keep track of what we'd written, and my fingers were smudged blue from the efforts to get it into the machine. I was terrified nothing would come, but then I looked across to Notre Dame and remembered Fernanda's prayers for me. I wrote a story about a man waiting in the cathedral after eye surgery. It was the day the doctor had told him he could remove his bandages and he wanted the beauty of Notre Dame to be the first thing he saw. After Fernanda read the story, she gave me a long hug.

It was the first time since moving into the store that I'd remembered there was life beyond Shakespeare and Company. I'd become entirely absorbed in George's strange universe, never going much farther than Café Panis or the student cafeteria, never leaving the store for more than an hour at a time. I hadn't even called my family to tell them my life had temporarily righted itself. Before Fernanda left, we made firm plans to meet at the Louvre later in the week to help reintroduce me to the real world.

Faint from the exertion of this one story, I was convinced this was the hardest money I'd ever earned. Thankfully, Nadia found me then and, after mocking my decrepit state, took over the story desk with gusto. In the next two hours, she wrote nine dazzling short stories with a myriad of characters and voices, and her customers praised her efforts to no end. At one point, a distinguished gentleman who turned out to be Dr. Z, *Sports Illustrated*'s top football writer, bought two stories from her. For one, he even gave Nadia the first line to use, which happened to be the first line of the novel he'd always wanted to write.

Nadia was the star of the story desk that day and Kurt and I suffered severe ego bruising. In this state, we slunk away and felt more than justified in buying a comforting bottle of wine with our earnings.

23.

If this hasn't been made clear, Shakespeare and Company is an extremely difficult place to keep clean. It begins with the simple fact of age. The bookstore is on a road that has been in continuous use since the year 400 and was officially made a street of Paris in 1202. Even the name has ancient roots, rue de la Bûcherie deriving from the word *bûches,* French for logs, from the time centuries ago when the area was known as "port aux bûches" and all the wood for Paris arrived by boat just feet from where the bookstore stands today.

According to George, the Shakespeare and Company building rests on the foundations of what was a sixteenth-century monastery and he compares himself to the monks who used to live on the same spot, a *frère lampier* who keeps a light on to welcome strangers and cares for old books and lost folk with semisacred devotion. In the early 1700s, the monastery gave way to apartment blocks and 37 rue de la Bûcherie itself was constructed as part of a housing boom to meet the needs of a growing Paris.

During its three hundred years, this six-story building has borne witness to many of the great dramas of Paris. Napoléon surely trod past the building when he first moved to the city as a young soldier and lived a half block away on rue de la Huchette. The Germans took residence in the quarter during the Franco-Prussian War and again, less than a century later, during World War II. And until it was razed in 1909, the annex of the Hôtel Dieu hospital was just across the street from number 37 and was used as a holding area for terminal cases. The corpses flowed out of the hospital by the hundreds, filling rue de la Bûcherie with the stink of death as they were taken around the corner to St.-Julien-le-Pauvre for burial ceremonies.

But these same three hundred years have taken their toll on the building. The wood beams sag, the plaster crumbles, the pipes leak. It leaves the bookstore with an air of perpetual decline and this is just the start of the bookstore's sanitary concerns. On any given week, thousands of people visit Shakespeare and Company, slamming doors, bumping shelves, tromping the pollution of Paris through the store. Then there's the grime inflicted by the men and women who sweat, sleep, and eat among the books; a close inspection of any bookstore blanket will reveal a DNA bank's worth of hair samples. Little Kitty does her part, too, with constant shedding and her habit of dragging semidecomposed birds and mice into shop corners. There was even a running rumor of bedbugs but though the residents were an itchy lot, George swore it was slander.

"Once! Once in fifty years we had bedbugs!" he declared. "Some reporter wrote about it to spice up his story and now everybody thinks we're infested."

All of this means that the bookstore weaves a thin line between romantic tumble and filthy sty, and the delicate balance is forever endangered by the fact that George's financial modesty extends to bookstore maintenance. He uses guests with a passing knowledge of plumbing or carpentry to execute repairs, he recycles wood and shelves from the neighbors' garbage, he shuns the rainbow of supermarket cleaning supplies in favor of cold water and old newspapers. Even on the day of the great library fire, George showed an eye for savings. In an attempt to help the cleanup efforts, the writer Christopher Sawyer-Lauçanno ran to the local supermarket and bought a package of heavy-duty garbage bags. When he returned to the store, George took one look at the purchase and soundly chastised him for wasting francs.

It was thanks to such economies that George was able to shrug off the chains of contemporary business culture, but it certainly wasn't the most efficient method of cleaning. One respected magazine editor who'd been invited to stay in the third-floor apartment lasted all of a quarter of an hour before fleeing to the sanctuary of a hotel. The cockroach scuttling across his pillow served as an early warning; a moldy bowl of stewed apples on the counter proved to be the coup de grâce.

Of course, I, being a sturdy young Canadian with absolutely no other options before me, would never have noticed or complained about the state of the bookstore hygiene except that I was suddenly feeling extremely self-conscious. It had to do with Nadia. It seemed I was falling in love.

Part of this was her cavern eyes; part of it was her feisty spirit, that had punctured Kurt's advances so cleanly; part of it was her genius with words that day we sold stories. And, it must be said, a final part of it was that like desperate men the world over, I sought salvation in a woman's arms.

Despite the kindness I'd received from George, I still hadn't worked out any of my problems. I hadn't pursued any real job, I hadn't made any actual plans for my future, I hadn't asked myself why I'd made the sort of life decisions that led to death threats and police investigations. But with the exotic and beautiful Nadia before me, I suddenly didn't have to think about any of the nasty business I'd left behind. After all, I would woo her, win her, love her, and then we would pass blissful lives together before dying entwined in each other's arms at the age of 102.

I was sure the only thing that was keeping this from happening was the fact that I smelled liked a rotting moose carcass. It'd been close to three weeks since I'd left the hotel near Porte de Clignancourt and moved into the bookstore and it'd been just as long since I'd had a decent shower. There'd been a few quick scrubs in the Panis bathroom but nothing else. My nails were dark with dirt, my hair hung in oily strings, and I was painfully aware of the ripe odor emitting from my crotch and armpits.

Cleaning up would have been easy enough, except for Shakespeare and Company's bathroom. For those living in the main part of the bookstore, there was only a cold-water sink on the first floor and the aforementioned cramped toilet on the communal stairway that was so rank with urine it made one's eyes water just to step inside. There was the small tub in the third-floor apartment, but this, alas, was reserved for George and the more established guests who were invited to stay upstairs.

All this meant getting creative in one's bathing, and according to Kurt, there were two solutions. Many of the visitors who came to the store were sympathetic to the residents' plight and often showers or bathtubs were offered. Kurt himself was a frequent beneficiary of such luck. One night, we'd been sitting by the cash desk, arguing over the Bukowski books. Luke kept the store's expensive Black Sparrow editions of Bukowski's *Ham on Rye* and *Post Office* high on a top shelf to prevent mucky fingers from cracking their spines and soiling their pages. Kurt was nonetheless trying to wheedle a copy to read, when a young woman walked in and agreed Bukowski was a fine poet. Sensing an opportunity, Kurt donned the air of impoverished poet and in less than half an hour was invited back to the woman's hotel for room service and a long, hot bath. Another time, the offer was from a very pretty red-haired girl. But to my surprise, Kurt tactfully declined this invitation.

"Dude, she was fifteen years old!" he explained. "I don't want to pull a Polanski!"

The alternative to these intimate bathing opportunities was the public showers. Since the only girl on my mind was staying at Shakespeare and Company, I chose the latter route.

Paris has an admirable array of services for the homeless, or the SDF—*sans domicile fixe*—as they're referred to in France. Each arrondissement features official soup kitchens along with a network of charities that provide meals and operate roving vans that dispense food and supplies to street people. There are also government-run shelters with clean beds, state-subsidized apartments, and a great emergency room at the Hôtel Dieu hospital.

Of all of the services, the most pertinent for those living at Shakespeare and Company were the public showers. Scattered throughout Paris are more than a dozen city-run bathhouses, each with dozens of meticulously kept shower stalls free to the general public. The bathhouse closest to the bookstore was part of a grim concrete sports complex on rue du Renard, almost directly behind the Centre Pompidou. The rainy afternoon I walked there, I felt a twinge of embarrassment: Never before had I availed myself of social welfare of any kind, and now I was just another filthy body without a centime to his name and in dire need of a wash.

As luck had it, the bathhouse was staffed by two of the warmest people I'd come across in Paris. One half of the tandem was an enormous Senagalese woman who kept exploding in laughter when she heard my mutilated French; the other was a short Algerian man who made a determined effort to remain serious. Seeing how anxious I was about my visit, the woman immediately began teasing me about my dirty hair. As the man pushed my shower ticket toward me, he waved his finger at me, "You wash well."

The shower area was in the basement and had a main waiting room with a clean tile floor, off of which were separate wings for men and women. As I stood in line, there was a corner drunk ahead of me and a family with three children behind me. One of the boys kept tugging on his dad's jacket and asking, "How much longer? How much longer?" Not much was the answer. There were a dozen stalls in each wing and the wait was no more than ten minutes. When my number came up, an attendant gave me a towel and led me to a stall. After showing me inside, he wrote the time in a erasable marker on the door so he would know when I'd had my allotted quarter of an hour.

Locking behind me, I found a small bench for my clothes and a gymnasium-style shower. The only irritant was that in order to get the shower to work, you had to press a small button that only gave a minute's worth of water at a time. Luke later told me that he specifically took a butter knife with him to the public showers to jam into the button in order to keep it depressed. But that day, I was forced to push again and again as I showered. Still, it was a minor detail. There was an abundance of almost-hot water and the grime sleeted off me. I scrubbed myself raw, basking in this luxury of clean.

Upon returning to the bookstore, I hurried to find Nadia to see if she would notice my freshly washed self. I discovered her upstairs in the library along with Kurt, Marushkah, and a few visitors who'd been kind enough to bring a bottle of wine.

Among the crowd was a young Mexican named Kenzo, who was in Paris working a three-month contract as a runway model. I am sure he was a fine fellow, but I immediately loathed him. Not only was he sitting next to Nadia, he was paying her courtly attention. Worse, where I was proud to be fresh from the public showers, he was coiffed and cologned and dressed in silky designer fabrics.

"Dude, you have it bad," Kurt said once he noticed my distress.

24.

Suspicions arose that I wasn't the only one suffering from such a malady of the heart. At around this time, Eve began making more frequent visits to the store, and whenever she appeared, George immediately halted all activity. Whether he was at the desk serving a customer or up in his office working on his beloved booklet, he would leap up to embrace his little Nastasya Filippovna and then run to fetch her a cup of hot coffee or a yogurt jar of strawberry ice cream or a nub of marzipan. Once, George became so inflamed by Eve's visit that he insisted on treating both of us to lunch.

An old Alsatian restaurant near place St. Michel had won a place in George's heart because it sold a large plate of sauerkraut and sausage, a glass of beer, and a slice of pie for only forty-nine francs. As if this wasn't merry enough, throughout the meal George kept fishing into his bag for presents. For him and me, these were film canisters of hard alcohol. George loved to get drunk in restaurants but abhorred restaurant prices. Before we'd left the store, he'd filled a dozen empty film canisters with vodka and now he slipped them from his bag a pair at a time so we could flip off the lids and down quick vodka shots when the waiter wasn't looking.

The presents for Eve were of a more tender nature. Vials of hand cream, samples of perfume, a diary with a bronze clasp. Every time she received a present, she gave George a kiss on his cheek that left him giddy.

"Why are you always bothering me about work?" he asked with mock rage. "Aren't I richest man in the world? What's worth more than the smile of a beautiful girl?"

It's true that right about then I would have given most anything for a decent smile from Nadia and it so happened that fate conspired to help me on this front.

Shakespeare and Company's Monday-night poetry-reading series dates back to the bookstore's days as Le Mistral, but as George's energies waned, the schedule became less organized and instead of a Lawrence Durrell book signing, you often got an Irish woman reciting Joyce while convulsing against a shelf of books. And whereas, before, the readings had been arranged months in advance, now it was often the Thursday morning before the Monday-night reading and there was nothing planned.

It was such a Thursday morning that Nadia admitted she was working on a short story and wondered if she might fill the slot. Even though this offer elicited dubious glances from Ablimit and Kurt, I enthusiastically seconded the idea and selflessly volunteered to help her prepare.

Nadia's story was about a young woman with a strange creature growing between her lungs that began to control her thoughts and behavior. That night, we sat on a bed in the back fiction room. Nadia read through her story several times, trying different voices, getting her mouth around her written words. It was a compelling piece but not particularly uplifting. Clearly, Kafka had gotten inside Nadia's head.

"You think it's morbid?" she asked.

"In a good way," I insisted. "In the very best-possible way."

We sat close together on my narrow bed and worked together until well after midnight. When we were done, I stuttered on awkwardly while Nadia gathered up her papers to return to her bed downstairs in the Russian section. Then, as we said good night, she raised herself onto her toes and, with a mischievous smile, gave me the briefest of kisses to thank me for my help. I fell asleep in the highest of spirits.

When the days were mild, I began accompanying Simon on his afternoon walks through the Jardin des Plantes. The park was only a fifteen-minute walk down the Seine and Simon had taken an annual membership to the small zoo tucked into the corner of the grounds. During the dark days when he feared immediate expulsion from the bookstore, he'd spent long hours with the animals and had even taken to saying they missed him when he wasn't there to say his daily hello. Once, he actually quarreled with a mother who was letting her young son pelt stones at a glumly caged ostrich. Simon, who'd spent so much of the past five years on display in the window of the antiquarian room, empathized.

On these walks, we'd stop at one of the garden benches and I'd listen to Simon give impromptu lectures on everything from the battle of Sebastopol to the relationship between black holes and life on earth. For decades, he'd read four or five books a week and it was only recently he'd veered toward the more pulpy genres.

"I don't know why George goes on about me reading detective novels," Simon complained. "I've already read everything else."

As a result, the poet's head was crammed with an epic assortment of information. I was learning much about the world on these excursions, though part of me wasn't completely convinced it was wise to be getting lessons in history and sociology from such a disjointed professor.

When finished with his deconstructions of European influence in postcolonial Africa, Simon would read his poems aloud to me. Encouraged by the Irish publisher's interest in his manuscript, he'd begun to write again after a long dry spell. He was rapidly filling a spiral-bound notebook with scrawled verse and sketches of the cherry trees in front of the bookstore. As we sat, he would pull out this book and give me sonorous renditions of his new poems.

"You really liked it? Really?" he'd ask over and over when he was done.

I did. I was having poetry read to me by a wild-eyed Englishman in one of Paris's most beautiful gardens. Like everything else then, it felt a touch enchanted.

What with Nadia's short story, Simon's poetry, and Kurt's oh-so-public efforts to finish his novel, I was feeling the urge to write again. Granted, writing the two books I'd already had published hadn't been the most pleasant experiences. They were quick true-crime books, the type my friends joked were sold in better gas stations everywhere. The first was written during a three-week vacation from the newspaper, with workdays that began at eight o'clock in the morning and didn't finish until well past midnight. For the second book, I took a five-week writing sabbatical, but the days were just as long and by the end it physically hurt to sit in front of the computer and churn out the pages. Still, inspired by Shakespeare and Company, I decided to try again.

When I was alone in the antiquarian room, I began sketching out a novel about a young man who gets a death threat and is forced to reevaluate his life. Not overly concerned by my overt lack of imagination, I typed away, dreaming the same dreams of Paris literary fame that Kurt and so many others had nurtured before me. Seven published novels had been written at Shakespeare and Company and a thousand others begun. The bookstore was catnip for idealistic writers and I was succumbing to the drug.

Whenever George found me like this, he'd stand over me and harrumph at my efforts. "What's that about?" he'd cry, pointing at some clichéd turn of phrase. "You have to use words like cannonballs if you want to move people."

In his day, George had made his own efforts at fiction, receiving rejections from the likes of *The New Yorker* and *The Nation*. His oeuvre also included a collection of short stories narrated by a man who was following an alligator across the Sahara. Those manuscripts had been lost or stolen, depending on the day George told the story, but there was one published sample of his work. After the great fire that destroyed the upstairs library in 1990, a book titled *Fire Readings* was published to raise money for Shakespeare and Company. Included in its pages was a story George wrote in the 1940s. Entitled "Joey," it was about a Mafia kid who ends up killing a man. "When Angelo was ten yards away I filled him with lead," the story climaxed. "He crouched on his hands and knees and then collapsed when my last bullet spun his head around. A shooting star fell through a break in the clouds. It rattled me for a moment."

George even admitted that one of his great regrets in life was never having written the novel that was in his head.

"I'm not going to tell you the story," he said in a surprisingly serious tone. "It would be one of the greatest books ever written. You'll just steal the idea and use it for yourself."

The night of Nadia's reading arrived with much anticipation. We'd put posters up around the store and had invited all the bookstore regulars to see her read. Word had spread of her Stories for Sale accomplishments, and since George continued to boast of her talents, there was a considerable crowd eager to gauge her work for themselves.

All this made Nadia nauseous. In the hour before her reading, she made three trips to the Panis bathroom, and it required four yogurt jars of wine before she could be persuaded not to cancel. By the time eight o'clock struck and the reading was due to commence, she was knee weak and the library was standing room only. Tom Pancake and Gayle were seated at the back, Pia and Marushkah were beside Kurt and Ablimit, even George was there, standing in the hallway with Eve, peering through the crack in the door to watch the goings-on. More unfortunately, the Mexican Model was admiring Nadia from a front-row seat.

Though the pages trembled in her hand at first, Nadia read with an actor's flare. The audience laughed when the black humor allowed it, cringed at the more morose passages, and erupted in applause when she came to a finish. With well-wishers milling about, she triumphantly announced she was going to Polly Magoo's and invited all to join her.

Promises of free drinks ringing in the air, Kurt and I followed, ready for a night of celebration.

At the bar, I ended up sitting with Kurt, Tom, and Gayle. Tom was trying to convince us that it was man's biological destiny to become breatharians. He insisted it was possible to use energy as efficiently as plants and said that one day he would be able to exist using a human form of photosynthesis, with his body extracting nutrients provided by water and the sun's rays. Though I found his theory somewhat implausible, I could barely muster a proper rebuttal, as I was far too distracted by the events unfolding at the other end of the table.

Nadia was perched on a stool between the Mexican Model and Marushkah, maniacally keeping two conversations going at the same time, radiant from her postperformance high. My shower now days old, I noted again the superior cut of the Model's suit jacket. As I watched him flirt with Nadia, the confidence bestowed by that midnight kiss melted away.

"Don't worry," Kurt whispered. "You're the John Cusack character in this one. Trust me."

By midnight, the festivities were on the verge of breaking up, but Nadia wasn't ready to end her night. One of the great perks of Paris is that corner groceries sell decent bottles of red wine for less than twenty francs and with a friendly wink these bottles can be had as late as three or four o'clock in the morning. It was quickly agreed that we would pool our remaining francs for a wine run and reconvene beside the Seine. Marushkah spurned Kurt's invitation to join us and my heart soared when the Mexican Model, debating whether he should try to get some sleep before his morning shoot, was told by Nadia to get a taxi home. It would be an intimate party of three.

*

25.

February nights by the Seine tend to be cold and damp, but these dis-comforts are more than compensated for by the solitude. The crowds who clog the river quays on summer evenings disappear during the gray winter months, and for those who brave the chill, vast stretches of waterside can be found blissfully deserted.

This was the case as we descended the stone staircase to the Seine. There wasn't another person along the river and our footsteps echoed back from the stone wall of the opposite quay. A light rain was falling, so we took shelter under the Pont-au-Double. Through the gaps in the metalwork on the underside of the bridge, the stone face of Notre Dame loomed over us, while a few feet below where we sat, the Seine rushed blackly by. For one surreal moment, hundreds of slices of baguette swept past after a restaurant upstream dumped a flotilla of stale bread at closing time.

We used Kurt's army knife to open our wine and passed the bottle. Drunk on alcohol, drunk on Paris, drunk on our sudden new lives, we felt for all the world like the best of friends. And like this, we started telling our stories.

Nadia talked of her adolescence, saying how she'd arrived in the United States scared and shy and knowing barely a word of English. She was isolated and alone in a strange American high school, all of her attempts to fit in rejected with the cruelty unique to teenage social law. At home, there was an ever-widening chasm as she tried to adapt to her new country while her parents became more and more introverted, clinging to their language and their memories.

The tensions between daughter and parents turned the house into a tomb. Days, then weeks would pass without a word spoken. For one terrible summer, Nadia was forbidden to leave the house at all. By the end, she simply stopped talking and the family lived in silence. Nadia had been swallowed by this darkness for so long, she felt almost mute when she finally got away to New York to study art.

"I don't think I'll ever understand what normal is," she told us in a quiet voice.

Our thoughts cast backward, Kurt also spoke of his home and his youth. In all the time I spent with him before and after, I always detected some layer of false bravado, a mask he donned to impress others or just hide away from himself. That night was the only time I knew for sure he was being absolutely honest.

Kurt was sixteen and working for a suburban supermarket. He was gathering stray grocery carts in the parking lot one Saturday afternoon when a white sports vehicle pulled up beside him. The tinted window hummed down and inside was a woman with tears flooding her mascara. "Kurt I'm your mother" is all she managed to say before speeding away.

This is how Kurt discovered he was adopted. Until that instant, he thought his life ordinary, his parents true. Later that afternoon, after composing herself, his birth mother returned to the grocery store. She told him he was left behind because she was just a teenager herself when she gave birth, that there hadn't been any other choice, that he was always in her heart.

Kurt's world changed that day in the parking lot and he still hadn't fully grasped how it had affected him. He was never able to escape the sense of abandonment. Maybe this is why a man who appeared to have everything—good looks, athleticism, charm—was forever trying so hard.

He was pale and empty standing there after he was done with his story. I was surprised he'd revealed so much, but I understood. A rainy night under a bridge in a city a long way from home is an ideal place for confession.

I, too, had my past to contend with, a skeleton that refused to stay in its closet. When I was fifteen years old, I was arrested for assault. It was late at night and, in the grips of powerful chemicals, I broke into a house. In a state of frenzied panic, I pushed and beat the neighbor I'd awakened.

It was a shock for everyone. I was an honorable student at high school, I had a part-time job at a local market, I had friends who were interested mostly in baseball and board games. Nobody expected something like this.

I spent the night in a police cell and the next morning, with my mother and father in the front row of the courtroom, I was remanded to the youth wing of the local jail. By chance, a boy from my Little League team was awaiting trial for robbing a convenience store at knife point. We sat in our cell and reminisced about the year we almost made the play-offs.

Because I didn't fit the profile of a violent offender, I was transferred from the jail to a psychiatric hospital for evaluation. There was a ward bingo game that I repeatedly won because the other patients were heavily sedated and couldn't keep track of their numbers. I also remember petitioning the doctors to break a "no daytime television" rule to watch the first Montreal Expos game of the season on television. My father and I had a tradition of going to Olympic Stadium together for the home opener and it was the first time in a long while that we weren't watching the game together.

I went through a battery of tests, the most crucial of which was the urinalysis. When strong traces of methamphetamines were found, it all but assured I would be spared jail. I ended up being sentenced to community work and probation.

The incident left me forever changed. My crime hung over my family, dark and unmentionable. Even though under the conditions of the young offender act, my name hadn't been made public, the assault was common knowledge in our community. I was scared to look anyone in the eye, certain they knew, certain they condemned me.

I guess this is why I was always trying to get away, to escape the past. I worked two jobs during high school and left for Australia when I was nineteen, but I ended up returning home after less than a year. I thought journalism would be my escape and I dreamed of working in Hong Kong; instead, I received that remarkable job offer from my hometown newspaper. At one point, I even volunteered to act as an unarmed bodyguard in East Timor. This meant living with the politicians and priests who were fighting for independence from Indonesia, the rationale being the militia was less likely to commit atrocities when a Westerner was present.

It seemed something was keeping me from leaving my city until I dealt with what had happened. Acceptance came slowly. I mentioned a few minor details of the crime to a girlfriend and she didn't reject me. At the courthouse, while covering a criminal trial, I saw the lawyer who'd defended me. It'd been a dozen years, but we recognized each other immediately. I was terrified he would give away my past or express some disgust. Instead, he congratulated me on the success I had found. Then, finally, I got the courage to phone the victim of my crime to apologize. It was the hardest phone call I have made in my life. But it made things better.

Back then, I'm not sure I'd have described myself as broken, but it's obvious now I was in need of some mending. I'd struggled to come to terms with my past, not always choosing the best avenues, too often relying on the distraction of my work and the anesthesia of drinking. These kinds of bad choices were part of the reason I ended up alone and scared in my apartment that December night, an angry man on the phone threatening me, my life in chaos.

Only once before had I told the full story of the assault to anyone. But that night beneath the bridge, feeling safe at the bookstore and among my new friends, I confessed everything. They understood because they knew we all had our demons, that we all wanted help to beat them away, and we all needed a place like Shakespeare and Company to do it.

There is something more to this story, something that to this day makes me wonder about the line between coincidence and destiny. I said I had told this full story only once before, but I didn't say to whom. It was to the man who sent me hurtling off to Paris by making that threatening phone call that dark December night.

Having already betrayed him once by using his name when I shouldn't have, I will give only the briefest details. He was a few years younger than I and grew up in what can be described as a poorer part of town. He took to crime early and developed into what police liked to describe as a "hardened criminal." In street terms, he was "solid," a man of his word who didn't rat to police and was a reliable partner for thieving. He drank, he womanized, he brawled. He also sponsored foster children in Africa and slept with a rosary under his bed.

Every so often, this man flirted with the idea of going straight, and in exchange for his help on my second book, I promised to help him register a small business. On the day we drove down to city hall, he was unusually quiet and answered my questions curtly. Finally, he confronted me.

"There's something I gotta ask you."

Okay.

"Did you do time for a sex beef?"

It is known that sex offenders are the most despised of criminals, and in prison settings they have to be put in protective custody to prevent beatings from other inmates. For someone solid like this man, it was considered poor form to be seen in such company. When he asked this question in the car, there was a nervous clutch in my stomach and I pulled to the side of the road.

"No. Absolutely not," I said. Then, for the first time, I explained all that had happened when I was fifteen years old and how distortions and rumors had been floating around ever since.

After listening to it all, the man looked at me carefully and then broke into a brilliant grin that will never leave my memory.

"Jesus, why didn't you say so before?" he exclaimed, and began pounding me ferociously on the back. "That's okay."

He absolved me; he was the first person to make me feel somewhat normal about myself. And despite our problems, despite my betraying him in print and his threatening me on the phone, I will always thank him for this.

26.

Using my ring of keys, we slipped back into the bookstore, careful not to wake Ablimit, who was asleep in the front library. Kurt got into bed with a silent good night and without a word Nadia followed me to the fiction room where until that night I had been sleeping alone.

After, I kissed her neck softly. We didn't speak of the river, but I did admit that earlier in the evening I had been jealous of the Mexican Model. Nadia only looked at me oddly.

"Him?"

Playing with my lip, she said there was something she needed to tell me. She'd been attracted to somebody at the bar that night, but it wasn't the Model. It'd been Marushkah. She'd found every excuse to be near her, to touch her arm.

"You're okay I told you that, aren't you?" she asked.

I laughed and said of course, and in truth I was relieved. It was considerably less of a threat to one's ego when your rival wasn't of the same sex. I could always save my esteem by blaming my anatomy.

"You know, you might even be able to win her heart from Kurt," I whispered.

She smiled at the thought and purred like a cat in my arms. We fell asleep like that, cramped onto a narrow bookstore bed with the walls of novels around us.

By then, hardly a day passed without George rushing toward me while wielding a hardcover like a meat cleaver. Giving me a stiff whack in the shoulder with the book of the day, he would insist it was essential reading if I wanted to understand anything about the world. Thanks to these subtle suggestions, I had already read my way through more than a dozen classic novels and another dozen books on political history and the roots of socialism.

When working as a journalist, I'd always tried to read as much as my schedule would allow, but that wasn't nearly enough. I managed a few pages before I fell asleep each night and found a few hours on weekends, but that was about all. Worse, I chose my books in such haphazard fashion that only random corners of the literary universe were illuminated, and thus I never grasped the fuller harmony between authors and their times.

Now, I was almost keeping up with George's ordinance of a book a day, and thanks to his recommendations, I gained a comprehensive overview of the history of literature. All of a sudden, my once-dark universe was being illuminated in enormous swathes and I swung between dizzy confidence at my new knowledge and doleful embarrassment that it had taken me so long to acquire it.

My relationship with Nadia only added to the luster of my education. One afternoon, we were walking past a shop on rue Dante that featured bright cartoon postcards by Keith Haring in the window. Nadia was shocked when I admitted I'd never heard of the graffiti artist turned Warhol protégé, so she decided to give me a crash course in art appreciation. I still remember her voice ringing with passion the night she told me how Marcel Duchamp changed everything in 1914 by presenting as art a plain metal bottle rack he'd bought at a store.

"It was the start of the ready-made movement," she exclaimed. "Can you imagine what a genius he was? Can you imagine breaking all the old rules like he did?"

I said yes, but frankly, I was just happy to be learning these old rules and left such dreams to her.

Toward the end of February, Tom Pancake left Paris to continue his journey east. When he'd quit the United States, he'd been aiming for Egypt and a few months before, while still down in Morocco, he'd made plans to meet friends in Cairo. At the time, he wasn't aware he would fall in love with Gayle, so an otherwise glorious departure was tinged with sadness. Tom dallied and the trip was twice delayed, but eventually the two bid a melancholy good-bye.

His absence meant Gayle spent more time at the bookstore. Even though she was younger than all the residents, she played big sister to Kurt, Nadia, Ablimit, and me. She would arrive almost daily with home-baked cookies and exotic sandwiches, while on special occasions she would risk inviting us to the embassy for dinner.

Back in Auckland, Gayle had cooked her way up through various kitchens and ended up at a popular downtown bistro. When she saw the advertisement for the job of personal cook to New Zealand's ambassador in Paris, it was a pinch-me-I'm-dreaming kind of moment. There was official skepticism about hiring somebody in her early twenties, and Gayle's short spiked hair didn't help the negotiations, but in the end she was hired. The job came with a plane ticket to Paris and an apartment on the top floor of the embassy. Suddenly, Gayle found herself in the glamorous world of European diplomacy.

The embassy was in a building that France had given to New Zealand as a gift for their help in liberating France during World War II. It was off of place Victor Hugo, a few blocks from the Arc de Triomphe and far enough from Shakespeare and Company to make it a most strenuous walk. With no budget for the eight-franc metro tickets, this meant that whenever we received Gayle's kind invitations, we were obliged to start stealin' trains, as Kurt called it.

The ease with which the metro could be hopped was another of the things that made being poor in Paris so tolerable. There were entrance doors you could pry open, low turnstiles you could jump, slow-closing gates that allowed you to sneak in behind a paying customer. Catching these free rides was made simpler because the clerks who worked in the ticket booths belonged to a different union than the metro controllers and refused to police the turnstiles out of respect for their colleagues' job security.

Once past the gates and into the belly of the metro, there were rare occasions when you stumbled onto a spot check, but this was never much of a problem. I started picking up a discarded ticket from the floor and chewing it for the duration of my metro ride. This saliva-damp state made the controllers reluctant to check the ticket's validity and made for many a safe passage. But even when I was caught, it wasn't a tragedy. When you declared you had no money, a notice of a fine was mailed to you at a later date. For those of us blessed with no fixed address, that later date never came.

It was the 4 line to the 1 line to the 2 line to get to place Victor Hugo and then there was a strict protocol for the Shakespeare and Company crowd to follow. First, we had to loiter down the street from the embassy so as to better conceal our grubby appearances from the security cameras. Then, on a special signal from Gayle—she insisted it was the call of the kiwi bird—we would rush to the front door so she could sneak us onto New Zealand territory when the ambassador was elsewhere in the building. Finally, we hurried to the giant kitchen in the bowels of the building, a service-only area, where the masters of the house never deigned to set foot.

Safely in the kitchen, Nadia, Kurt, Ablimit, and I would chop and grate and stir, all on Gayle's precise orders. One time, while washing lettuce in the sink beside her, I noticed a long scar running up one arm.

Kitchen accident?

"Nah, back home I lost control of my motorbike. I tore into the side of a bridge. Nearly died."

Ahh.

When the cooking was done, we'd take the service elevator up to her apartment on the top floor of the embassy. After eating, we would take turns using Gayle's bathroom to wash and shave. Some nights, there were more than a half dozen bookstore refugees up there, muffling our conversation and walking without shoes so as not to disturb the building's official residents.

A favorite day was when Gayle prepared a reception for the New Zealand All Black rugby team. The ambassador's wife was so terrified of their sporting appetites, she ordered an outrageous amount of food: mango and duck salad, roast cherry tomatoes with feta, salmon sushi, prunes in bacon, smoked trout, lamb tarts, tray after tray of calorie-rich delights. But when the players arrived, they were groggy from celebrating their victory over France the night before and left vast amounts untouched. We descended on the embassy with ravenous hunger, and there was still enough left over to take platefuls back for George.

Luke and I were becoming closer with every page of George's booklet. Enduring his irrational requests and fluctuating moods had brought us together like two students who suffer the same eccentric schoolteacher.

"Monday, George wanted the picture tinted yellow, Tuesday, he wanted it tinted purple, Wednesday, he wanted it tinted orange," Luke complained one Thursday night. "Now he wants it tinted yellow again. Can you believe it?" Of course I could. During those same four days, I'd watched George rewrite the same sentence eleven times.

Despite these mild annoyances, Luke was becoming addicted to the project. Like everyone in the bookstore community, he was at Shakespeare and Company because he wasn't quite sure where else he should be. Sometimes the idea of Cuba was strong in his head and he wanted to open up an English-language bookstore in Havana. Sometimes he remembered the vampire novel he'd conceived while living in Brazil and he wanted to write gory thrillers. Now, high on the thrill of the booklet, sometimes he wanted to become an underground publisher.

Luke was an avid reader and possessed such a critical eye that he was constantly asked to review the short stories written by residents of the bookstore. Seeing firsthand how easy it was to record a little bit of bookstore history, Luke imagined starting a publishing company that would record all of the stories and autobiographies written at the bookstore.

If he went through with this, Luke wouldn't become the first rogue publisher at Shakespeare and Company. There had been Trocchi with *Merlin* and Fanchette with *Two Cities* and George with his myriad of efforts. More recently, there'd been Karl Orend, the night manager before Luke. During his years at the bookstore desk, he'd founded Alyscamps Press and published a range of translations and poetry.

"I don't think it'd be difficult to get started. I even have the name for it," Luke said, pointing across the river.

"You're going to call it Notre Dame?" I asked.

Luke only rolled his eyes. In front of the cathedral was a metal disk that marked the starting point for all the distances measured in France. If you passed Lyon and saw a road sign declaring it was 459 kilometers to Paris, it meant it was 459 kilometers to this exact little spot in front of the cathedral. Hence, this disk was called Kilometer Zero, and where Luke and I were sitting at the bookstore desk was actually in Kilometer Zero of France.

"Kilometer Zero," I agreed, "is a pretty fine name."

It was now March. I had been at the bookstore more than a month, but it felt like time had barely passed. Without the normal barometer of a workday or a fixed schedule, life had become fluid. It was hard to keep track of the hours and days at the bookstore, everything came and went in pleasurable waves of evenings and mornings and afternoons.

In the criminal world, there is a term, *hard time,* which refers to difficult prison sentences in maximum-security facilities or under some form of protective custody. This is for the dangerous convicts, the murderers, the sex offenders. Hard time goes slowly and painfully and leaves a man bitter when eventually he does get released into the world.

At the opposite end of the spectrum were the medium- and minimum-security facilities, which were designed to rehabilitate offenders. Here there were libraries and weight-training rooms, high

school–equivalency classes and floor-hockey tournaments. One institution I visited had a farm inside the barbed wire where the inmates
worked the fields and provided fruit, vegetables, and eggs for the
prison. Another prison had a baseball team that toured the region,
playing in a community beer league. This was known as *soft time,* time
that went easily, time that was a pleasure to do.

Time at Shakespeare and Company was as soft as anything I'd ever felt.

27.

Since I'd been at Shakespeare and Company, there'd been a regular flow of people sleeping at the bookstore: the married Italian woman who'd left with nary a word; an ecowarrior from Canada who spent a week trying to convince George to convert to fair-trade shopping; a young trumpet player from Idaho who practiced beneath the bridges of the Seine each day of his stay; a Jesus freak from Oklahoma on her way to Lourdes after discovering God while watching her boyfriend do bong hits and play Game Boy; a young socialist who submitted a biography that began with this sentence: "When my father was twelve, his father gave him a copy of the Bible; when I was twelve, my father gave me a copy of the Communist Manifesto."

This all made the bookstore feel like a running sleepover party with revolving bedmates, but it also distorted one's normal sense of human relations. I'd wake up to see a stranger getting dressed in front of me, and I learned to think nothing of it. I'd return to the bookstore after a coffee at Panis to find a new body drooling on my pillow, and I would just offer him another blanket. Often, I'd just learned somebody's name by the time they'd moved on, another destination beckoning or the bookstore's accommodations simply too despairing.

There were, however, two arrivals of note during this time. The first was a young man named Scott, an aspiring writer from Boston with dark hair and a boundless sense of humor. He was traveling through Europe courtesy of a Watson Fellowship, and George was so impressed with his research that he was offered an indefinite stay at the bookstore.

Scott's project was to trace the paths of Walter Benjamin, the philosopher who'd come through Paris after being hounded out of Nazi Germany. He was hoping to write a book that juxtaposed their two lives, a young man following a philosopher's faded footsteps and reflecting on the contemporary value of his wisdom. He'd already spent months researching in Berlin and was now on the trail of Benjamin's Paris. Scott's trip would climax in the spring, when he traveled to the remote mountain pass in the south of France where the philosopher had taken his life after Nazi agents had discovered him crossing the Pyrenees into Spain.

Early in his stay at Shakespeare and Company, it became clear Scott was somewhat obsessed with his subject. Not only was he a running faucet of Benjamin anecdotes, not only did he convince George to order *Introducing Walter Benjamin; Walter Benjamin: Selected Writings*, volume 1, 1913–1926; *Walter Benjamin: Selected Writings*, volume 2, 1927–1934; and *Walter Benjamin: The Colour of Experience*, but Scott even thought the philosopher was suitable material for romance. Though he had a girlfriend teaching English in Japan, the terms of their separation were blurry and it seemed heavy flirtation was allowed. If ever a potentially amorous situations arose, Scott inevitably brought out the Benjamin.

When a striking Danish woman came to the store for a weekend's stay among the books, Scott was particularly smitten. He even had the luck to find himself sitting alone with this woman on his bed late one night. But in this most intimate of settings, his only thought was to read to her from *Illuminations*.

"I think she was a bit confused," he admitted afterward.

The other new resident was my old friend Dave. During my time at the bookstore, we'd been exchanging letters and he wanted to see Shakespeare and Company for himself. One March day, he appeared on the shop's doorstep with his knapsack and George graciously welcomed him.

Dave was especially curious about the bookstore because he, too, had thoughts of writing fiction. There is a cliché about journalists being frustrated novelists, and perhaps there is some truth to it, because Dave was convinced he could leave business reporting behind and become another Bret Easton Ellis.

"Why not?" he said. "You have to dream, don't you?"

He'd come to the right place, then. Dave adapted quickly to the life, reading his quota of a book a day, sharing breakfasts of muesli and fruit with Nadia and me, telling stories under the bridge by the Seine when we gathered there at night with our bottles of wine. To Dave's credit, he didn't even complain when George asked him to do the foulest chore of all, the twice-yearly washing of the stairway bathroom with bleach.

"Paying the dues, I guess," he said, as he flaked stale urine from the wall.

Dave's presence was a mirror for me and we were both surprised at how much I'd changed since that January morning in front of Sacré Coeur. Thinner, clothes frayed and on the dirty side, a skittish eye from lack of sleep. But happier, he said. Better.

With no warning at all, a red Citroën van stopped in front of the store one morning and a ruddy-faced man began flinging cardboard boxes of books onto the esplanade. There was quickly a pyramid taller than the average basketball player and still the boxes kept coming. The whole while, a spunky black dog with a shock of white fur on her chest raced between the van and the boxes with joy.

This was John, the traveling book salesman. He lived in the south of England and had connections that allowed him to buy bargain books in bulk. All the big English publishers had tens of thousands of unsold books returned to them from bookstores each month. Instead of going to the cost of sorting and refiling them in their warehouses, the publishers put these boxes of returns onto pallets and auctioned them off. John would buy the books sight unseen for as little as a few pennies a pound. Opening them was a constant surprise. Sometimes there would be hundreds of celebrity weight-loss books; other times, there'd be copies of a popular novel like Alex Garland's *The Beach,* which had an overly ambitious mass-market run. But mostly, there'd be a strange collection of art books and history texts and first novels, whatever had been scheduled for pulping the day after the auction.

With these books loaded into his red Citroën, John hit the road with his trusty dog Gwen. He drove a circuit from Barcelona to Nice to Paris to home, visiting English-language bookstores, setting up tables at school book fairs, and always stopping at Shakespeare and Company on the way home so he could sell a few thousand books and drink a few bottles of Chinese beer.

George tore into the boxes like a castaway on a coconut. The wares came in three price ranges—five, ten, and twenty-five francs—and he would rip open a box and hold books aloft so John could spit out the appropriate price. The ones George wanted would be hurled into piles on the bench, with John scurrying to keep a running tally of the purchase. All the bookstore helpers—Kurt, Nadia, Ablimit, Scott, Dave, and I—ferried the books inside, racing to get them onto the shelves before the inevitable rain started.

A man standing at the cash register could only gape in amazement. "It's like they're throwing garbage pails of books in here," he said.

Hearing this, George chuckled. "But look at all those boys and girls working together like that," he replied. "It's amazing to see everybody pitching in around the bookstore."

The next step in this venture was the frantic search for money. John's bill usually came to more than ten thousand francs, so George would be forced to dig into his various stashes around the store. He'd long had a habit of shoving bundles of francs between books or hiding them under his pillow, and he would furiously seek them out while John waited downstairs. Once, he found his favorite hiding place had been colonized by mice. They had shredded stacks of two-hundred-franc notes to make a nest worth more than three thousand dollars.

"At least it's not the books." George shrugged. "One time, the mice ate through my collection of *Les temps modernes.*"

After the money was found and the accounts settled, the table was set for all who had helped. There were pots of vegetable stew and fresh baguettes and the omnipresent beer. George would offer the discount bottles for the helpers and keep the prized Tsingtao for John and himself. After years of experience, the bookseller had learned to refuse a refill often enough to minimize his hazards on the road back to England.

Every day there were surprises like this at Shakespeare and Company. If it wasn't John the Bookseller, it was an English woman who'd stayed at the store in the 1960s or a Hungarian journalist hoping to conduct a radio interview with George.

All these distractions meant that what should have been a very attainable goal—finishing George's booklet before Easter—was turning into a colossal feat. Whenever we gained a smidgen of momentum, there would be a knock at the door and somebody asking to stay for a few days, or tourists wanting to have their picture taken with George, or some magnificent sight out of the office window that we absolutely had to stop and appreciate. One afternoon when I was coaxing George to finish his essay, he glanced out the window and saw a father and his three children leaving the bookstore. They wore matching rain slickers and were trotting off toward Café Panis.

"It looks like a family of ducks, with the children trailing behind their father like that." George sighed. "That's one of the most beautiful things I've ever seen at the bookstore."

As he stared after them, I thought of his own daughter and the long years that had passed since they had lived together. Ever since I'd learned about Sylvia, I had noticed tributes to her throughout the bookstore. Her photograph was on the cover of his collection of biographies, another book George had published was credited to her, there were dozens of pictures chronicling her upbringing at the store. Could it be, despite the literary institution he had created, the thousands of lives he had changed, the celebrity Shakespeare and Company had brought him, that George regretted his decisions and longed for the simple joys of family life? Just as I was wondering if I should raise the delicate question, George dismissed me for the afternoon and returned his gaze to where the man and his children had been.

Getting anything accomplished was made more difficult by George's substantial fear that the store was being infiltrated by American agents. There was a standing rule that we could never work on the booklet with the office door open, and Luke and I were forbidden to discuss the project with anyone. There were spies about, George told us, spies who were all too eager to sabotage his efforts. If this had come from anyone else, it would have sounded simply mad. George, however, had seen more than a few undercover agents in his day, and once bitten, he was thrice shy.

As a declared Communist after World War II, George says he was marked as a potential troublemaker and the U.S. government tried to block his visa for Europe. Things got worse when he opened the bookstore and began preaching against the American military economy and the fictions of the Cold War. According to George, during the 1960s, CIA agents routinely visited the shop, listening in on lectures, making reports on his running protest against the Vietnam War. George even guesses that it was American influence that caused his bookstore to be shut down in the 1960s. The French authorities forbade Shakespeare and Company to sell books, on the pretense that George hadn't filled out the correct paperwork as a foreigner operating a business in France. George's answer was to bully his way through, running a Marxist lecture series at the store, keeping the library open, housing radicals of all descriptions, writing an open letter to André Malraux, who was then the French minister of culture, asking him to expedite the paperwork. Finally, after persevering for more than a year, he conquered the bureaucratic mazes of French administration and secured the proper business license.

Having seen George's files from the 1960s, I could fully imagine him being the target of CIA investigators in those paranoid days. But now?

"Are you naïve?" George demanded, and went on to name a woman who had long frequented Shakespeare and Company. She was routinely about the store, attending the tea party, telling people how much she respected and admired George. I thought she was a nice woman, as she occasionally bought me a coffee at Panis, but George only shook his head.

"Where do you think she gets her money from?" he chided. "The American government! She's CIA!"

But what slowed down work more than anything else was Eve. One morning, I found George penciling away at a paper on the office desk. I'd hoped it was the final draft of his booklet essay, but when I peeked over his shoulder, he tried to shoo me away. He was so obviously flustered, I pressed on, and finally George admitted he'd fallen in love with Eve.

"Love?"

"I didn't start it. She did!" George insisted. "She was always looking at me with her pretty smile. It just happened."

When I pointed out that Eve was just twenty years old, sixty-six years his junior, George scoffed. He wasn't interested in a sexual relationship, he said; he was too old for that now. He just wanted a loving companion. His grandfather had had a young nurse at the end of his life and George believed it was dignified to spend one's final years with a charming young woman at one's side. Then, pulling out the piece of paper, he announced he'd written something special. It was called "Evelina."

I wish I was a pretty girl like you
Flowers in her hair and miniskirt askew

I would use my smiles like artillery
To make victims of men like me

I would sing and sigh
I would laugh and cry
I would let you see every part of me
From my dimples to my anatomy

But if you said I loved you I would say goodbye
And find some other man to mystify

When George asked with hopeful eyes whether I thought she would like it, I assured him she would be thrilled. I knew Eve basked in George's affections and adored Shakespeare and Company. Maybe something could work out. I couldn't be blamed for my optimism. I had Nadia. I believed in love. I believed in bookstore miracles. Anything could happen.

28.

One Saturday, Kurt was sent to Ed's for groceries and one of the items on the shopping list was sugar for the upcoming tea party. When Kurt returned, it was with a box of sugar cubes, and George was frothing mad.

"It costs thirteen centimes more when you buy it cubed instead of powdered," George yelled. "You imbecile! Don't you know anything?"

Yet for a man who could lose his temper for the want of thirteen centimes, he often lost thousands of francs through sheer negligence. Along with the mice who ate through small fortunes, George forgot bills between the pages of books, or had bundles of money slip through the holes in his pocket, or saw the cash register emptied by thieves after he'd wandered away from the desk and left the drawer hanging open.

When George and I were eating together one night in the upstairs apartment, he took off his jacket and several bundles of one-hundred-franc notes tumbled from an inside pocket. Alarmed to see such a concentration of money, I hurried to collect them, but George only laughed and jammed what was close to a thousand dollars' worth of francs underneath the foam cushion of the couch.

"If you get too attached to these sorts of bagatelles, it'll ruin your life," he declared.

There was an especially curious incident when George and I were looking for old photographs to use in the booklet. As we rummaged through a file box, George discovered an old wallet of his with fourteen hundred francs inside. He handed it to me, and, thinking I was meant to hold it only while he continued his search, I attempted to give it back to him once he was done. Waving his hand at me, he said to return it later. I assumed he meant that afternoon, but when I tried again, he looked at me as if I were a fool. I'm not sure George realized how broke I was, though I guess the ludicrous story-selling business was a good indication, but it seemed he wanted to help me.

I put the pouch in my pocket, grateful that I would be able to do a load of laundry, buy a decent lunch, and rest easy for a few weeks. This was the first of two times that George gave me money.

One day, Nadia came running back to the store from the local Internet café with a pleasant bit of news. A sculpture of hers had been selected for an exhibition of young artists being held at a Brooklyn gallery. It was a prestigious affair and she'd decided to push her credit card to its maximum in order to fly back for the opening.

"This could be my break," she said as she fluttered around the bookstore bestowing celebratory kisses on Ablimit, Kurt, and, I couldn't help but notice, Marushkah, who happened to be keeping Pia company at the front desk.

The sculpture was a series of hatbox-size cubes with the sides covered with a photograph of a man or woman's body part. There were hairy backs, thin elbows, voluptuous thighs, wrinkled penises. It was a participatory work and spectators were urged to assemble a being of their own sexual creation.

Nadia took devilish delight in such possibilities, and I was beginning to enjoy dating a woman with such a fluid idea of sexuality. The afternoon she left for New York, she gave me a kiss and a crumpled note. It read, "The man in me loves the woman in you," and I fell a little deeper.

It seemed everyone was off on some adventure, as Kurt announced he was going to spend seventy straight hours on a ratty bus to Morocco.

Ever since Nadia and I had begun our intimacies, Kurt had been behaving strangely. Unhappy that the rowdy days of the boys were over, he started relentlessly flirting with the many women who came to the store, searching for a girlfriend of his own. Kurt ended up choosing a young French woman with a degree in astrophysics, a semishaven head, and a taste for body piercing.

"She's my Femme Nikita," Kurt told me when he made the introduction.

With his new girlfriend in tow, Kurt decided to take up a standing invitation from a bookstore regular to travel to the seaside city of Essaouira. Chris Cook Gilmore was an aging beach hipster who kept his gray hair long and most always wore sunglasses inside. In the 1970s, he'd made a name for himself as a writer while incarcerated at the Rebibbia Prison in Rome for smuggling five kilos of hashish into Italy. During his seventeen months behind bars, Gilmore wrote a series of short stories, which his mother showed to a literary agent in New York. The result was a book contract and an acclaimed first novel, a rum-running adventure called *Atlantic City Proof*, which was made into a BBC radio play and translated into Italian.

Since that first success, Gilmore had written twenty more books, some published, others not, and spent his time living in three countries, depending on the season. In summer and fall, he lived with his mother in Margate, a city on Absecon Island, off the coast of New Jersey. His home was a block from the beach and a few miles down from the Atlantic City casinos. Winters were spent in Essaouira, the walled city on the northwest coast of Morocco where Jimi Hendrix used to play. And for the spring, it was Paris—or more precisely, the third-floor apartment of Shakespeare and Company. When he'd been through the bookstore on his way down to Morocco in January, Chris had extended an open invitation to join him at his hotel, and now Kurt longed to join the old writer in Africa.

"This guy used to hang out with Paul Bowles," Kurt said, as if no further reason for the expedition was needed.

With the Femme Nikita helpfully subsidizing the bus tickets, Kurt left for Essauoira not long after Nadia went to New York. After I saw them off from the Gallieni bus station, it struck me that life at the bookstore was suddenly extremely quiet.

As may be obvious by my indulgences that first night in the antiquarian room with Simon and my investment in a growing operation back in Canada, I am not adverse to recreational drug use. In fact, I even credit marijuana for nudging me along the road to salvation.

During the darkest days at the newspaper, I had taken to a troubling amount of drinking, and there was no more bitter memory of my alcoholic discontent than the night I crashed my 1977 Lincoln Continental.

It was the dream car I'd bought as a present to myself when hired full-time at the newspaper. Baby blue with glimmering chrome and the original eight-track player, the Mighty Lincoln was longer than two economy cars put together. It had a fifty-dollar-a-week taste for gasoline, didn't start in the rain, and was prone to expensive breakdowns, but I loved every bit of it.

On the night in question, I was driving home, agreeably inebriated after a friend's bachelor party, when I spotted traffic pylons in the middle of an intersection just a block from my apartment. These pylons were the traditional indication of freshly painted street lines, so without hesitation, I tore ahead. After coming to a squealing stop, I looked through my rearview mirror and noted with pride that I'd managed to smear a decent bit of paint and knock down all the pylons save one. Just as I was about to flip into reverse to complete the task, I happened to check over my shoulder. There, idling at the curb, was a patrol car.

I sped away. The police car followed. Barreling toward my parking lot at fifty miles an hour, I swung wildly into my spot without braking. My precious Lincoln ricocheted off an oak tree and came to a stop at a drunken tilt. The police car pulled in after me with considerably more control.

Stumbling out my car, I took two gentle steps away from the police car and then dived headfirst into a thick hedge. A dash down an alley and two jumped fences later, I arrived at the side entrance of my building. Safely inside my apartment, I hid under a pile of dirty shirts in my closet while the phone rang and rang and the door buzzer buzzed and buzzed. I didn't emerge until the morning.

My beloved car suffered a tragic gash along the passenger side and the beautiful chrome had been scraped to tinsel. Though the police had tracked me to my apartment a few minutes after the accident by running my licence plate, they didn't have a search warrant to come inside. Only the technicality that required a drunk driver to be caught behind the wheel saved me from arrest and spared my good standing at my newspaper.

And that was a rather mild night of drinking.

I likely would have been at a loss as to how to combat this destructive tendency had it not been for a girlfriend I met while working as a crime reporter. She was a tranquil soul and a regular smoker of marijuana, and it was through her that I came to appreciate the calming effects of the drug. Before, getting high was always something I did between beers; with her, I smoked as an alternative to drinking. I was more relaxed, my appetite for alcohol shrank considerably, my evenings out were less violent.

These revelations didn't come as a total surprise to me. Working with the police as a reporter, I'd learned that alcohol was among their least favorite drugs, that officers universally preferred dealing with a whimsical pothead than a raving drunk. A prison warden I knew even confided that he turned a blind eye when marijuana or hash was smuggled into his jail, because it had a soothing effect on inmates. But if an illegal alcohol still was uncovered, it meant an immediate thirty days in solitary.

The change in my personality became so great that my friends soon began referring to the eras of pre- and postmarijuana, and they unanimously preferred the latter. After all I had been through, it was an easy decision to bring marijuana into my life until I developed better coping mechanisms.

It so happened that Dave shared my enthusiasms, though more out of a search for life's rushes as opposed to any deep form of therapy. Together again, and with Kurt and Nadia gone, it didn't take us long to recollect fondly about our old habits and it didn't take much longer for us to hit the streets.

The best open-air drug market in Paris is at Les Halles, the municipal park just north of Châtelet. It used to be an enormous fruit and vegetable market, and there is a scene in *Tender Is the Night* where a band of revelers rides into Les Halles on top of a carrot wagon as dawn breaks over the city. Unfortunately, in the 1960s, a property developer was allowed to dig a huge pit under the market and turn it into a sunken mall. Now, hundreds of clothes shops, CD stores, and reeking fast-food outlets descend beneath the earth like Dante's rings of hell.

Above this shopping center, the city built the park now known as Les Halles. Here, a few old men play boules, a few brave au pairs stroll with their charges, and a few dozen dealers sell a variety of products, including one-hundred- and two-hundred-franc chunks of Moroccan hash.

Dave and I went to Les Halles early one afternoon and, using the universal language of such transactions, circled the park to see who would try to catch our eye. Two young men making such a purposeful tour were obvious clients and soon enough several dealers were vying for our attention. We stopped at a seller near the Matisse sculpture of a hand cradling a head.

"*Tu cherche?*"

We nodded and the man produced a thimble-size morsel of hash. I picked it up and was alarmed by the large sum of money demanded.

"*C'est un peu petit,*" I muttered in my bastard French, then returned it in hopes of negotiating. The man proceeded to punch me in the head.

Staggering backward, I managed to avoid another blow, while Dave had already scuttled away, his arms waving wildly in the air.

"What are you doing haggling?" he demanded, checking over his shoulder to make sure we weren't being followed. "We don't know how it works here!"

Rubbing my temple, I agreed it had been presumptuous. We made another circle of the park and this time chose a man in an Adidas jumpsuit. His hash was cut into spaghetti-thin sticks and wrapped tightly in cellophane, so we couldn't give it a decent sniff. Still, after the previous experience, we weren't about to complain and I walked away, feeling quite contented with my first drug transaction in Paris.

A few days later, Dave left for a relative's farmhouse in the Austrian hills to write his great novel, so I was left lonely again. Sitting on the bench under the cherry tree one night, I was envisioning my happy reunion with Nadia, when Simon approached, distraught with worry.

"I think Kitty's dead," he said in a hoarse voice.

Kitty was the subject of a covert tug-of-war between George and Simon. George believed Kitty should acquire a survival instinct and only fed her every second day so the cat would learn to hunt birds and mice in the nearby park. But Simon rebelled against turning a domestic animal into a savage, so he sneaked Kitty into the antiquarian room each night and discreetly fed her tins of wet food. Each man was confident his approach was the right one and each was equally confident that deep down the cat preferred him.

Pulling me by the hand, Simon led me down rue St. Jacques to near where Tuee the Sandwich Queen had her stand. Under a truck was the stiff body of a black cat that had been struck by a car. We crouched beside the body, unsure if it was really Kitty. It had the same fur, but something seemed wrong. Finally, Simon reached out and felt the dead animal's tail to see if it had Kitty's telltale kink. It wasn't there and we breathed deep with relief. Still, with the two of us sitting there hunched over a dead black cat, I couldn't help but think it was an ominous sign.

29.

Since arriving at Shakespeare and Company, I'd graced a privileged rung of George's informal hierarchy. I'd been given the keys, I'd been invited upstairs for dinner, I was his chosen confidant when he wanted to talk about buying the apartment, the future of the bookstore, or the love he had for his lost daughter. But suddenly, I was usurped.

From the outside, Scott looked like everyone else at Shakespeare and Company. He hadn't showered in a week, he was red-eyed from lack of sleep, he had bulging pockets of notes for his Benjamin book. But somehow, in just a few short weeks, he'd replaced me as George's assistant of choice. It was Scott who always managed to be the first one awake to open the store, it was Scott who filled in at the desk whenever Pia or Sophie had their afternoon coffees, it was Scott who spent his free hours alphabetizing books in the fiction section.

George watched over it all like a proud father and never missed an opportunity to herald Scott's accomplishments. Depending on the hour of the day, George would tell visitors Scott was a distinguished scholar, a soon-to-be-famous writer, or simply an all-around swell guy. Scott soaked it up with unfailingly modest smiles.

Something close to jealousy began to tickle inside me. I'd never really worried about my standing at Shakespeare and Company, but now doubt began to claw. I remembered Esteban and his reaction when I'd arrived. I wondered if I wasn't feeling the same way about Scott.

When George was preparing to travel to London for the annual book fair, I won points days before his departure when he lost his train ticket, his accreditation for the fair, and his passport. Having grown accustomed to George's regular losing places, I was able to find the vital documents mixed in with a pile of invoices from Penguin. Proud of the feat, it stung doubly when George invited Scott to sleep in his bedroom while he was in London.

"He's a serious writer, he needs a quiet space to work," George reprimanded when he saw my distress. "You rabble-rousers spend too much time drinking by the river anyway."

Perhaps that dead black cat was bad luck. After weeks of waiting, Simon's cellular phone finally rang, but it wasn't the answer he needed.

"They're going to give the contract to somebody with more experience," he told me glumly. "These people don't care about art. They know I'm the best person to translate Claude Simon, but they want somebody with a reputation and a degree they can parade around their fêtes."

We were sitting at the Panis bar, but there was no cheer to be found in the café, either. Simon noticed that Amos was lying prone on the floor and couldn't even get to his feet to greet us. One of the waiters said there had been blood in the dog's feces and that the café's owner was going to have to call a veterinarian.

Between the sick dog and the lost translation contract, Simon was despondent, but even this dire state was trumped by his fear when he learned I'd fallen out of bookstore favor. George hadn't mentioned Simon's leaving Shakespeare and Company since we'd come to the arrangement to share the antiquarian room. The poet gratefully attributed this stay of eviction to my charms, and now he worried again that he might lose his home.

"I think they'll find my body floating in the Seine if that happens," he muttered.

———

I'd hoped for succor on Nadia's return from New York, but things immediately went sour. The cold bookstore nights, the lack of sleep, and the careless diet had left my body vulnerable and I succumbed to a wretched bookstore virus. Reeling from flu, I barely managed to get to the airport at all, let alone get there on time. Nadia was initially upset that I was late and then completely underwhelmed by my sickly lack of enthusiasm for our reunion.

There was also a sense of distance created by Nadia's trip back into the real world. Though the gallery show had been a success, it reminded her how the art world hummed along on contacts. She felt numbing pressure to build her own network and questioned what she was doing living in a bookstore. Though Nadia admired the camaraderie and spirit of Shakespeare and Company, there was never space or time to be alone and actually create. I at least had the luxury of the antiquarian room during the days and evenings, while Kurt thrived in the goldfish-bowl world of writing in the bookstore. For Nadia, who needed artistic solitude, the communal life was becoming suffocating.

Theft was a continuous problem, as George's carelessness with money gave Shakespeare and Company a stunning reputation among neighborhood villains. Dozens of thieves came in on regular visits, searching through books for francs forgotten by George or lying in wait for him to stray from the cash register. Rare was the week when there wasn't a successful strike.

There were apocryphal stories of the great bookstore larcenies: a young Belgian finding thirty thousand francs behind volumes of a encyclopedia and going climbing in Nepal for a year; a pair of Spanish heroin addicts who'd supported their habit through George's left-about money for five straight years; an American poet of marginal acclaim who hid under a table of books when the store closed at night so he could hunt for the caches of francs once everyone fell asleep.

More sadly, there was also internal theft. George not only trusted strangers to sleep in the store but also to fill in at the desk. With no accounting system and a majority of buttons on the cash register short-circuited, the odd bill could be nipped with impunity. As one former resident put it, it was easy to stretch the meaning of George's personal proverb, "Give what you can, take what you need."

And, as I discovered one terrifying night while talking books with Luke, there was occasionally theft of a more violent sort.

Luke was in fine form, dressed in a sleek black suit and reviewing the merits of Nelson Algren's *The Man with the Golden Arm*. Algren grew up in Chicago, served in World War II, had a famous affair with Simone de Beauvoir, and, most importantly, wrote dazzling prose. *The Man with the Golden Arm* was the first American book about hard heroin use and it depicted a violent edge to Chicago street life. According to Luke, when Hollywood turned the book into a film, the producers cast Frank Sinatra as the lead, and after Algren deemed him too soft for the role, the writer got kicked off the set for belligerence.

In the midst of this story, Luke realized it was near closing time and went upstairs to make sure there were no customers left in the library. He'd only been gone a minute or two when four young men bulled their way into the store. One of them lifted up his shirt to reveal a knife with a long curved blade tucked into the waistband of his sweatpants. The man then pointed to the cash register and withdrew the knife.

I screamed like a little girl.

And then I ran.

"Luke! Luke! LUKE! There's a knife in the store," I hollered, sprinting back to the German section.

But in what I mark as one of the great acts of courage in my life, I stopped and decided I should try to protect the register. As I turned back toward the front of the store, I noticed that a writer who'd recently shaved his head was browsing through the art books. It made the man look like a death-squad agent, so, in a moment of inspiration, I dragged him with me to the front of the store, where the young men were prying at the till with the knife.

"Get back!" I screamed, this time with considerably less little girl in my voice.

Whether it was my sudden reappearance or the ghoulish face of the bald writer, the young men actually stepped back. As they stood there unsure of what to do, Luke burst through the front doorway, having raced down the main stairway to trap the intruders inside the store. He was brandishing a very large plank of wood.

"Where's the knife?" he scowled.

The men quickly decided this wasn't the store to rob and fled into the night. Though we were a little shaken, we all puffed out our chests and complimented one another on our manliness.

When George returned from London, things actually got worse. One afternoon after lunching with Eve, he approached me in a fit of rage.

"Why did you tell her the bookstore was almost robbed?" he demanded.

Because it was a good story, because it was exciting, because I thought the fact that I went back to confront the thieves made me look like a pretty courageous guy.

"That was stupid. Stupid! Now she'll be too scared to come live here," he yelled, and then went stalking off.

A few days later, George caught me writing to friends back in Canada. I was using his Shakespeare and Company postcards and by chance I'd misspelled a few words and torn up one effort. George, who despised all waste, found the pieces and became furious.

"Don't you know we don't have many postcards left? Don't you respect anything?"

But the worst was the morning when I was shelving an order of poetry books. Scott was at the desk and had already been given a cup of steaming coffee and an almost-fresh doughnut, while I'd been entirely neglected. When George finally remembered I was working in the bookstore, too, it was only to come examine my work.

"You've put things all in the wrong order," he said. "You're messing it all up."

I tried to tell him that the job was only half-done, that Blake and Browning were next to the two Hugheses only because Eliot and Frost hadn't been shelved yet, but George refused to listen.

"You don't care about this place. You're trying to ruin me."

I think most people have a threshold where they can no longer manage their anger, and perhaps mine is unusually low, for I exploded. For the first and only time, I yelled at George.

"Why don't you show some patience?" I shouted. "If you don't like my work, do it yourself."

Slamming the door of the bookstore behind me, I walked around Ile de la Cité three times, cursing George and his bookstore. My anger eventually subsided, only to be replaced by a sickening sense of crisis. I was in such a precarious position that if I lost my place at Shakespeare and Company, I would have only three choices: sleep on the street, go to a shelter, or phone home and ask for money. I couldn't decide which was worse.

In such a state, I left on George's desk a slice of his favorite lemon meringue pie as a peace offering and went to consult Ablimit. Amazingly, he laughed when I told him what was troubling me. George, he explained, always preferred new faces to old friends. Their inevitable infatuation with Shakespeare and Company, the enthusiasm and energy they brought to the store, the tantalizing blank canvas of an unknown person. It wasn't that the permanent residents of the bookstore fell out of favor; it was just that they were less shiny than the bright new arrivals. George was a man who liked a little shine.

It had even happened to Ablimit. When he'd first arrived at the bookstore more than twelve months before, George had treated him like a prince, regularly cooking his meals and letting him sleep upstairs in the third-floor apartment. For eight weeks, Ablimit had lived in perfect accord with George, but one day, Ablimit sensed a note of disapproval on his brow and a sharp edge to his voice. Without being asked, he moved downstairs, kept out of George's way, and resigned himself to eating at the student cafeteria.

"George, he doesn't say anything. You just have to know," Ablimit advised. "The new people always get the best of him, but old friends like us, we get to really know George."

They were comforting words, but my sense of security had already slipped.

30.

Redemption began with a visit from an Irishwoman. It was a chilly evening in early April and I was writing at the desk in the antiquarian room. Since my falling-out with George, I'd been racing to finish my little novel, thinking that if I could sell it for a few thousand dollars, I would have enough money to escape George's manic mood swings. It was in the middle of such reverie that there was an urgent tap on the window.

Opening the door, I discovered a short woman who claimed to be an attaché for the Irish embassy in Paris. In her hand was an extremely important message for Simon. Was this where the poet lived?

Inviting the woman in to sit, I learned some most wonderful news. Simon was being invited to read at a literary festival in Dingle, a small town in southern Ireland. In fact, the festival was to begin in less than two weeks time and the organizing committee, having already publicized that Shakespeare and Company's poet in residence would appear, was frantically trying to reach him. Three invitations had been sent by post, but what the organizers didn't know was that mailing a letter to the bookstore was only barely more effective than putting a note in a bottle and flinging it into the Irish Sea. At the store, letters got misplaced or forgotten or even waylaid by George's curious eyes.

According to the Irishwoman, there would be a travel subsidy as well as room and board in Dingle if Simon agreed to read. She admitted it was terribly late notice but hoped the poet could accept. Dingle would be most fortunate to have a man so talented, she said before disappearing out the door.

"I can't believe it," Simon beamed. "The land of the poets! I've never even been to Ireland, I've never had the courage after all the horrors we English inflicted on those long-suffering people."

The invitation was the work of another poet, a man who'd passed through the bookstore the year before and had appreciated Simon's work. Though confident in his poetry, Simon had until now been convinced he would get his rightful due only after he died. But with an offer to read at the Dingle festival, where guests would include both the Irish chair of poetry and the man who published Samuel Beckett and Henry Miller in England, the possibility of a living reputation dangled before him. Suitably elated, Simon cracked open the codeine and alcohol-free beer to celebrate.

This good mood lasted almost a full day before the pressure began to gnaw. Simon had never before given such an august reading and his nerve faltered. Was he ready for Ireland? The land of Oscar Wilde and William Trevor? The country that had a portrait of James Joyce on its ten-pound note and didn't make poets pay income tax?

To complicate matters, Simon wasn't at all sure how he was going to make the journey. Dingle, whose population numbered fewer than two thousand people, lay on the raw southwest corner of Ireland and was mostly known for a friendly dolphin that swam in its bay. The cheapest plane ticket to the area was more than twice Simon's travel allowance and he started using this as a possible excuse for not attending. And once Simon was besieged by the full fury of angst, he even decided he should refuse the invitation as a safeguard against his tumbling back into the bottle.

"All those drinkers in Ireland, it's practically a nation of alcoholics," he said. "I can just imagine being with all the other poets while they belly up to the bar. How will I make it?"

It was then that we realized a whole flock of birds might be felled with this one poetic stone. I needed time away from George, I yearned for a literary escapade like Kurt was having in Morocco, I was once again in great need of money, I wanted to help Simon seize this grand stage that had been offered him. Despite my murky departure from my newspaper, I still had some good relations with certain editors, so I proposed an article about Simon's odyssey for the weekend magazine. The money I'd earn could help subsidize Simon's trip and I would be by his side to defend against Irish temptations.

When we told George we would be leaving for a week, he was taken aback. No matter how gruffly he might treat his guests, George never likes to see friends leave. In the past, he had actually confiscated plane tickets and passports to prevent departures. With Kurt already gone, the prospect of losing two more familiar faces, even for a week, didn't sit well.

"Layabouts," he grumbled. "Off to Ireland on a junket. That's writers for you."

But deep down, George was thrilled by his obscure in-house poet's sudden rise to fame. George was fastidious in tracking the success of those he had taken under his wing and kept a file of all the newspaper and magazine articles that celebrated his store. With the prospect of Simon's acclaim and my article chronicling it, George took to calling Simon the Literary Colossus of the Latin Quarter.

Before we left, George gave me a brief lesson on packing. He'd traveled the world with only a change of shirt, a toothbrush, and a book in his pocket. What more did you need other than the coat on your back?

"That's the way Ferlinghetti does it, too," he told me as he removed such unnecessary items as spare socks and a bottle of shampoo from my travel bag.

The date of our departure was Easter Sunday and Simon was awed by its potential significance. Perhaps, Christ-like, he would rise from the ranks of the literary dead. Before we left to catch our train, George treated us like soldiers going to war. Along with a markedly tastier version of the regular Sunday-morning pancakes, there were eggs, bacon, sausages, potatoes, and fresh juice. To end the meal, George proposed a toast to Simon and we all raised our glasses high. Then, with the Easter bells pealing across the river at Notre Dame, I received a sweet good-bye kiss from Nadia and then Simon and I tramped off to the metro to begin our journey.

We were getting to the festival by the elliptical combination of a train to Cherbourg, in the north of France, an overnight ferry from France to Rosslare Harbour in Ireland, a bus to Cork, and then a second bus to Dingle itself. The entire trip, though almost forty hours each way, would cost only a hundred francs more than Simon's travel grant.

Things began well enough, with the metro to Gare St. Lazare peaceful in the early Easter Sunday hours and the seats on the train easy to find. As we rolled north, Simon was transfixed by the fields of yellow flowers. "Those are van Gogh colors," he said. "You know, in a way, I'm a little like van Gogh—miserably poor, unappreciated in my lifetime."

When we got to Cherbourg, there was a three-hour wait for our ferry and Simon paced impatiently in the terminal. After staring out into the gray waters of the English Channel, he spun around and began digging in his travel bag.

"I need a drink," he declared.

Simon withdrew an alcohol-free beer from among the six-packs and codeine bottles he'd crammed into his luggage. Clearly, George hadn't reviewed the poet's packing technique. As he gulped back the beer, I noted with some alarm that it was still before noon on the first day of our journey.

The *Normandy* pulled into dock and it was a massive vessel. Eleven decks, twenty-eight thousand tons, room for a thousand passengers. Simon and I had booked the cheapest cabin and found it on the seventh deck, just above the cars and well below sea level. Simon looked around at the cramped room with its narrow bunk bed and opened another can of alcohol-free.

The next morning, we arrived at Rosslare Harbour, a rut along the cliffs, to catch the bus west. The company had given Christian names to each of its buses and ours was called Simon. "This must be a cosmic joke," Simon muttered as we boarded.

Westward we rolled, amazed by the infinite greens of the country-side. After changing buses again in Cork that afternoon, the hills be-came more rugged, and even though we had been on the road for more than thirty-five hours at this point, we both actually wanted the bus to go slower so we could better savor scenery. Shortly after eleven that night, more than thirty-nine hours after leaving the bookstore, we ar-rived at the Dingle bus station.

Our room overlooked the bay and from our window we could watch the fishing boats come in with their nets each morning. The town was small enough that one could walk from one end to the other in less than a half hour, never ascending more than three or five blocks from the bay. I mostly wandered the hills or sat in pubs with Guinness pints and seafood chowder while Simon spent his time worrying about the reading. His codeine supply ran short, so, claiming a toothache, he went to the festival organizer. An ever-efficient host, the man saw that all was quietly arranged with a local pharmacist.

Alone in our room, we talked late into the night and I learned more about Simon's life, his broken loves, his family regrets. I also heard of his alcoholism. Not a bad drunk, but self-destructive. Once, in Spain, he'd stumbled off a cliff in the dead of night and lay broken on the rocks for twelve hours. It was a questionable accident.

I tried to take note. I'd had my troubles with alcohol, my brushes with police, my desperate arrival at Shakespeare and Company. Listen-ing to Simon, I wondered if he wasn't something of a Ghost of Christ-mas Future.

The festival began with suitable flourish. A blind poet of Irish renown performed. Jigs were played. There were ample trays of wine and beer. Throughout, Simon kept his resolve, drinking deeply from his private supply of alcohol-free.

The night before Simon's reading, he pent himself up in the hotel room and brooded about the task before him. He opened and closed the window, he gulped his beer, he flicked incessantly with the television remote. He even twice called back to France to ask a former girlfriend which scarf he should wear for his performance.

Looking through a copy of the festival brochure, Simon realized there were three other poets on the same slate as he was. Scanning their biographies, he became unnerved.

"They have books; they have names. I have nothing."

Then, a surge of confidence. "No, I have my work."

The reading was scheduled for two in the afternoon and it was on the other side of town, which meant the shortest of walks. Still, twice along the path, Simon ducked into pubs and downed alcohol-frees. He'd discovered a Guinness brand with the frisky name Kaliber which was only a hair away from being 1 percent alcohol. In the last pub before his reading, he held the bottle to the shaft of light that crept in through the window.

"I'm going to pretend this one is fourteen percent."

As we approached the bookstore where the reading was to be held, Simon picked up his pace and steamed directly past the front entrance. I caught up to him and pulled him to a stop. He was whispering distractedly to himself.

"Help me, Jesus, in my hour of need. . . ."

"Simon, are you praying?"

"The religion in me comes out at times like this," he said with a shake of his head.

About sixty people were waiting to hear Simon read. There were mothers with babies on their laps, a cluster of high school students, other writers from the festival, and, in the back corner, a handful of publishers and journalists.

Simon took his place at the front of the room. Someone familiar with the wonts of writers had left a tall glass of wine for him at the podium. He looked at it for an extended moment and then waved to the bookstore's owner.

"Can you get this away from me, please?"

And so he read. His deep English accent massaged his words and drew the audience into him. He chose four short poems, and there was a murmur of disappointment when he announced he would read one last poem. He ended with a piece he'd written about the cherry trees, which had started to blossom in front of Shakespeare and Company before we had left.

Smelling faintly of woodscent
outside my door all through the long winter
two country girls in bark and brown kimonos
arms raised ready to dance

In one more day not even one more week
they will become rich geishas
flicking open their fans of white and pink
cherry blossom while my eyes are elsewhere

First the last winds of March will blow
then I shall turn around astonished
Am I seeing snowfall in Spring?
Or did they throw
their fans on the ground?

When he finished, there was thunderous applause. The other writers nodded their approval. The Irish chair of poetry clapped him soundly on the back. A journal editor approached and asked to review his work. A correspondent from Irish radio wanted to talk to him. Everyone had a kind word.

Simon's smile engulfed him. His face radiant, he removed his glasses to wipe away a tear. Then, disappearing amid the crowd, he was swept out into the streets of Dingle.

31.

As shameful as it is to admit, the thing that made me the happiest upon my return from Ireland was to find that Scott had fallen from favor.

I immediately noticed a coldness between Scott and George, and this was soon confirmed when Scott confided that they had stopped talking altogether. Fearing eviction, Scott asked me to find out what was going on.

After a brief investigation, I concluded Scott had made the critical mistake of becoming too friendly with Sophie. Though he insisted it was just friendship, Scott spent untold hours at her side while she was working at the bookstore desk and had even begun using his Watson Fellowship money to invite Sophie to expensive dinners.

It was hard to blame Scott for his fascination; along with Nick the Street Hustler, there was a handful of admirers who regularly visited the store to court the young English actress. But the others who had lost their hearts to Sophie didn't live at Shakespeare and Company, and I discovered that for residents of the bookstore, becoming involved with a clerk was something of a taboo.

George kept a close watch over the string of beautiful women who worked at the store, and he didn't appreciate any of the residents paying them too close attention. Part of it was a paternal gesture, as he wanted to protect his wards from the emotional ravages of bookstore romance. Many times, true love has bloomed at Shakespeare and Company, as evidenced by George's running count of the marriages between people who'd met at the store. But many more times, bookstore affairs ended in ruin. Once, I sat for a tea with George and a lovely Korean woman who'd come back to visit the store a decade after she had worked the front desk. With her was a beautiful young girl, the product of a bookstore romance with a writer who'd long since disappeared.

Yet there was something more to George's protective instinct. He was also the aging wolf, trying to mark his territory in the face of bounding cubs. For fifty years, he'd been the center of attention at the bookstore and he was at times reluctant to share the spotlight. Sophie and Scott hadn't taken any measures to conceal their friendship and the fact that it was platonic didn't really matter.

When I asked George if he was angry, he only grumbled that Scott was preventing Sophie from getting any work done by entertaining her at the desk all day. I interpreted this as a warning and told Scott that he should avoid being seen with Sophie.

It was as if I'd passed another of George's misty tests by suffering through his preference for Scott and still returning to his side. We ate dinner together again, we once more conspired about the future of the store, we conducted another raft of changes to his booklet. He even took me aside and said it wasn't everyone who could endure his peccadilloes.

The strength of our friendship was proven the day I got into a nasty fight with a new resident. It was one of George's greatest talents to judge the hearts of people in a brief moment and protect Shakespeare and Company from bad seeds. Considering more than forty thousand people had slept among the books, there had been relatively few violent or fanatic incidents. Though, of course, there were the occasional lapses in judgment.

George once told me of the murderer who'd stayed at the store in the 1990s. He'd pegged the fellow for an unusual sort at first sight but gave him the benefit of the doubt. Then one day, George heard screaming from the third-floor apartment and ran upstairs to find the man strangling a young woman who was staying at the store. George had to threaten the man with a wine bottle before he would let the woman go.

"He didn't want to rape her, just kill her," he told me. "His eyes were filled with the worst hatred I've ever seen."

Years later, an English police detective came through Paris and stopped by the bookstore. He had a photograph and asked if George recognized the face. George explained what had happened when the man stayed at Shakespeare and Company and the detective nodded grimly. It turned out this man had stalked and killed a woman in London the year before and the police had tracked him all the way to Russia to make the arrest. The detective was vacationing in Paris and, remembering that the murderer had spoken fondly of George, thought he'd pass on the news.

"I was really surprised by that one," George admitted.

In the case of this new resident, a Sri Lankan woman from Cambridge, it wasn't that she was an attempted murderess, just that she was so damn aloof. She was studying for exams and had written George in advance to ask to stay. For once, George had been organized enough to send off a postcard of confirmation and the woman arrived one sunny morning in late April.

The two of us were immediately on the wrong foot. George had agreed to let her stay in the third-floor apartment so she could have peace to read and revise. The Sri Lankan woman had brought two heavy suitcases and demanded that I carry them upstairs for her. Taken aback, I nonetheless hefted the bags.

During the woman's first week, she never once helped out in the store. Not in the morning to open the doors, not at night to take in the books, not when there was a major delivery in a pouring rainstorm and the customers helped run boxes inside. She even had the gall to beg out of Sunday chores, and I just didn't get it. How could she ignore the store's traditions? Why wasn't she doing her part? I finally confronted the woman, and after harsh words became reckless screaming, she ran upstairs in tears.

Afterward, I worried George would be angry with me for losing my temper, but instead he took me into his office and explained how sometimes we have to give the least deserving people the greatest allowances.

"I've always agreed with what Walt Whitman said, that there's a touch of genius in everyone, that everyone can be special," George said. "It's not too late for her. We can help her. It's the people like this we need to win over."

Huddling close to the gas heater one cold night, we were fantasizing about the tropical humidity we'd enjoy at Luke's Cuban bookstore, when the door banged open. Just as we were about to curse the cold, Kurt burst in. He was wearing the same gray overcoat he always wore, but he had a crisp tan and a bright blue head scarf in the tradition of Maghrebian nomads.

"I'm back," he announced with arms spread.

Any misgivings about his headgear were washed away by my relief to see him again. After almost four months in Paris, Kurt was one of my closest friends, and I looked forward to relating all that had passed while he was away. Kurt, too, had his tales and launched into descriptions of the red deserts, a rooftop hotel room costing a few francs a night, the mosques with their calls to prayer. But he saved his highest praise for Chris Cook Gilmore, the man he now reverently called "the Captain."

"He's an inspiration," he said, brandishing his notebooks. "I've finally got *Videowrangler* done."

Kurt said Chris would be coming through Paris in a few days and would be staying at the bookstore. I carefully noted his arrival date. For the most part, the writers who'd stayed at Shakespeare and Company during my sojourn there were on the first steps of their ambitious journeys. It would be edifying to encounter someone who had actually published.

I loved Nadia as much as ever, but things were becoming increasingly strained. At the time, I blamed the cramped quarters, the constant filth, the lack of any real time alone together. But really it was me. Living in a subversive old bookstore makes one feel like a ready-made bohemian, but I still had a couple of decades of middle-class upbringing in my bones. I discovered I couldn't really handle such an unconventional young woman.

The breaking point came one story-time evening. Ever since Kurt, Nadia, and I had spent that first intimate night by the Seine, the gatherings had become a loosely organized event. Once or twice a week, we would meet by the river with bottles of wine and people would take turns telling stories, usually feeding off a line thrown to them at random from the others.

A woman named Claire walked into the store during the afternoon and Kurt, having dispatched of the Femme Nikita after Morocco, set upon her with voracious charm. He ended up introducing her to everyone, and when Claire met Nadia, there was instant spark. Kurt had already told of the session by the Seine planned for that evening, but when Nadia repeated the invitation, Claire immediately accepted.

Nadia and I had been invited to the studio of a fellow Romanian artist that night, so we shared an awkward dinner in a garage filled with juggling clubs and rolls of fabric. Nadia was on edge, too quick to laugh at jokes, always with an eye on the clock. On the metro ride back downtown, she raised the prospect of an open relationship for the first time. Kurt and Claire were already down by the Seine when we arrived and Claire leapt up to give Nadia an enormous hug. Once the bottles of wine were opened and passed around, Kurt took the storyteller's position at the quay's stone wall. Using a first line about fire, he wove a story about homeless men burning books for warmth under a bridge and coming to a copy of *Don Quixote*.

As soon as Kurt left the spot, Claire flurried into place. She took a first line about love and told a choppy story about a girl's first lesbian encounter. Though Kurt and I were breathless with titillation, the whole time she looked only at Nadia. At the peak of the story, Claire yanked off her shoe and threw it in the Seine. Nadia was so taken by the gesture, she brought her hands to her face and gasped.

Oblivious to the undercurrents, Kurt removed his own shoe, knelt before Claire, and placed it on her stockinged foot. Very pleased with his chivalry, he stumbled back to me.

"I think she really likes me," he whispered, his bottle of red wine already mostly empty.

Meanwhile, Nadia had taken the spot underneath the light. Without waiting for a first line, she burrowed into a story about a crush she'd had on an older girl in high school. Kurt kept elbowing me in the ribs to demonstrate his excitement, and when Nadia finished, she was flustered and blushing. Claire suddenly announced she had to go to the bathroom, and though Kurt rose to escort her, Nadia immediately blocked his way.

"Get more wine," Kurt shouted after them as they disappeared up the stairs to street level.

It was then that I told Kurt there was a strong possibility the two weren't coming back. At first, he refused to believe me, but after I pointed out the similarities in their stories, their rapid escape together, and the fact that Nadia had told me she was attracted to Claire, he finally seemed almost ready to accept the rejection.

"But I gave her my shoe."

For the next hour or so, we stayed at the river in case the two returned, but my initial feeling of adventure was turning into a desperate sense of abandonment. I thought I loved Nadia and enjoyed having her as my girlfriend, yet as I sat on the cold river's edge, she was in the arms of someone else. Around three in the morning, we finally gave in and returned to the bookstore. After Kurt passed out in his sleeping bag, I went back to the fiction room and found Nadia and Claire in the bed that, until that night, we had been sharing. I skulked downstairs and lay awake in the Russian section until the first light of dawn.

32.

Near April's end, George received word that the cherished apartment was finally coming on the market. With this news, all the bookstore's forces were mobilized and the expansion campaign moved into full throttle.

George had the name of the agent who was handling the sale and decided to use one of his favorite tricks to better his chances at winning the apartment. He'd long been the type of man to run afoul of neighbors, city officials, and other authority figures and was often called upon to account for his infractions. After enough of these encounters, George discovered a clever way to soften the blows: Whenever a meeting was held to sort out problems with the store or his unruly guests, he would claim illness and send one of his employees, most always a woman of considerable beauty, to take his place. The combination of sick old man and enchanting young woman was usually more than ample to win clemency.

For the real estate agent, George chose a variation of this technique. Sophie was to visit his office, find out when the apartment would be officially for sale, and use her skills as an actress to ensure that George got a bid in before the hotel baron. George was so confident he'd get the apartment, he asked Nadia to make blueprints for the renovations. Under his guidance, she sketched pastels of the view from the windows, the sleeping benches, and, over and over again, the bookshelves.

"If I get this apartment, I'll have done it all myself," George said with no small pride. "I bought the bookstore. Even Ferlinghetti didn't do that. He rented the space for City Lights and then the city bought it for him."

As Kurt promised, the legendary Chris Cook Gilmore arrived from Morocco and installed himself in the third-floor apartment with an elaborate hookah and a lovely lady friend named Anita. The pair built a nest upstairs, where they cooked potato and leek soup, bought a different variety of French bread each day, and regularly invited all the residents up to share their meals. It was on these nights that Chris taught me the expression "You fly, I buy," and we spent long nights drinking beer, with either Kurt or me whisking off to the nearby grocery store when supplies waned.

Chris was a born storyteller and he was especially gifted at recounting the extraordinary events of his own life. His father, Eddie Gilmore, had been a reporter for the Associated Press. He'd left his wife and baby Chris behind in America to take a job reporting in Moscow during the 1940s. There, he fell in love with a teenage ballerina at the Bolshoi. The two were married and then spent a decade trying to escape Stalin's Russia, until they finally slipped out of the country on a fishing boat in the dead of night. Eddie Gilmore even wrote a book about the story, which was made into a Hollywood movie, with Clark Gable in the role of Chris's father. But to Chris's disappointment, he wasn't even mentioned in the memoir, so to this day, whenever he finds a copy in a used bookstore, he inscribes it: "Dad, now I'm finally in your autobiography. Your son, Chris."

Chris was full of such stories: how his family tree could be traced back to the legendary Captain Cook who discovered Hawaii and was murdered by natives for being a false god; how he'd lived in Mexico with a teenage hooker and was arrested for carrying a gun; how Jimi Hendrix had helped him tune his guitar in a Moroccan hotel room back in the sixties; how he'd met George by ducking into the bookstore to escape the police and the tear gas of the May 1968 riots; how he'd had the world's most dangerous girlfriend when he lived in Cambodia during the country's civil war.

Sometimes I couldn't help but wonder if Chris wasn't using a touch of poetic license in the telling of these incredible stories. This doubt was erased the day I discovered him in the third-floor apartment with a very powerful machine gun.

I'd gone upstairs to fetch a bottle of beer for George and had found Chris in the kitchen. He was behaving a little unusually, a little too quick to laugh, a strange gleam of sweat on his brow. Sure enough, after a few minutes of awkward small talk, he waved me closer.

"If you can keep a secret, I'll show you something really neat."

Chris led me to the back of the apartment, and there on the master bed was a slick black machine gun set up on its tripod. Chris gleefully ran down the specifications: It was one of four hundred thousand MG42 machine guns produced by the Germans during World War II, it weighed twenty-five pounds, it was capable of firing fifteen hundred rounds a minute, it was generally considered the greatest machine gun ever constructed, and it cost just four thousand francs if you knew the right antique-gun dealer in downtown Paris. "They called it a 'burp gun,'" he said as he passed it over so I could heft it. "That's because it fired so fast, it made a burping sound. *Burrr-burrr-burrr-burrr-burrr.*"

After that, I put more faith in Chris's stories. When you see a man holding a machine gun, all of a sudden all his other wild tales become a little more credible.

With the apartment now in sight, work on the booklet was in its final sprint. George found one of his favorite pictures, a black-and-white photograph of a mother and child reading a book on the store's inside steps, which were painted with the words LIVE FOR HUMANITY. It had been taken by Pia's mother during a trip through Paris, and for George it represented the essence of Shakespeare and Company. We fussed over the photograph for two days, making sure the tint and contrast were perfect. Once the proper font had been chosen for the text, the booklet was done.

As happy as I was that Luke and I were on the verge of sending the files to the printer and in a few weeks would be touching paper, I was troubled when I saw the final copy of George's essay. It was to be the centerpiece of the booklet, but it flitted between hopeful beauty and somber foreboding. It began:

> Looking back at half a century as a bookseller in Paris it all seems like a never ending play by William Shakespeare where the Romeos and Juliets are forever young while I have become an octogenarian who like King Lear is slowly losing his wits. Now that I am coming into my second childhood I wonder if all along I have just been playing store on one of the back alleys of history, putting obsolete books on dusty shelves. . . .

I could have dismissed this as George's modesty, but then I read what followed. After writing of how he'd meant to spend seven years walking around the world, he said it was his biggest regret not to have completed the journey. Then he intimated that he might try to finish it now:

> . . . I may disappear leaving behind me no worldly possessions—just a few old socks and love letters, and my windows overlooking Notre Dame for all of you to enjoy, and my little Rag and Bone Shop of the Heart whose motto is, "Be not inhospitable to strangers lest they be angels in disguise." I may disappear leaving no forwarding address, but for all you know I may still be walking among you on my vagabond journey around the world.

> Amitié Sincère,
> George Whitman

When I read this, I was alarmed enough to ask George if he really was thinking about leaving Shakespeare and Company behind.

"I don't want to become a burden for this place," he replied with a sigh. "I want to be able to make the bookstore nice enough so my daughter will want to run it. That would make me happy. Then maybe I really will go back on the road."

We were already nervous as we waited for the decision on the apartment, and things became more tense due to an inexplicable series of thefts. The stolen items were mostly letters and diaries, but also the occasional alarm clock, stick of deodorant, and even a train ticket. One young art student from the University of North Carolina had her travel journal taken from beside her bed and was so unnerved, she left the store the next day.

Kurt had warned me of this when I arrived: Strange things went missing at the bookstore. Certain items, such as cameras or wallets, could be attributed to the usual thieves. If they didn't find money in the books downstairs, they'd come up to the library and rifle under beds and in the closet. But articles of clothing and writers' notebooks?

When I returned to the store one afternoon and found two of my shirts missing, I cursed the instability of Shakespeare and Company life and started toward Panis for a consoling coffee. I must have been visibly distressed by the loss of the better part of my wardrobe, because one of the homeless men stopped to inquire after my well-being.

This man's name was Richard and he was cleanly dressed and had dark hair. Though in his fifties, he showed only a few of the life bruises that usually marked the people of the street. There were stories of him having fought in Vietnam for the French and withdrawing from society shortly thereafter, but whatever the case, he spoke five languages fluently and a smattering of others.

Richard was philosophical about his situation. There were enough shelters in Paris that he could have a bed each night if he wanted, and every so often a woman fell in love with him and attempted to move him into her apartment. But he'd decided he was meant for the street, his addiction to alcohol and his years of rough traveling making it impossible to live a confined life.

His days were spent sipping beer in front of the park beside Shakespeare and Company, sometimes in the company of other men and always with a scraggly black dog. One could gauge his mood by the strength of beer he drank. The stores of Paris sold a standard selection of six varieties of half-liter cans of beer. There was the green Heineken for the well-to-do drinker, a 4.5 percent alcohol Kronenbourg for moderate drinkers of limited means, a 5.9 percent beer called 1664, which we at the bookstore favored, and then three levels of high-alcohol beer: a red can with 8 percent alcohol, a black can with 10 percent, and a special dark green can with 12 percent. Richard was drinking a red can that day, which meant he was fairly well disposed to the world.

"They stole my shirts," I explained to him. "All I have left is this dirty one I'm wearing."

Richard nodded sympathetically and admitted that many of the men who slept on the street knew the bookstore was a jackpot of left-about money and travelers' knapsacks. Promising to keep an eye out for my shirts, he dug into his pocket, withdrew a scrap of paper, and wrote down several addresses.

"This church will give you clothes for free," he said.

Then, looking down at my feet, he jotted down the number of the closest Emmaus, a nationwide chain of charity shops founded by the Abbé Pierre and operated exclusively by homeless men trying to take a step back into society.

"They always have good shoes," he told me.

I was greatly cheered by his decency, and Richard became a regular conversation stop. He drifted from an extremely clean and well-spoken state to the mumbling depths of an alcohol binge and back again. Sadly, a month later, I found him with bandages over his hands and legs. He and a friend had been sleeping in a doorway a few blocks south of the bookstore one night when someone set their sleeping bags on fire.

As May arrived and the weather grew warm, Paris was changing before our eyes. More sun, more blooming flowers, more Disney-clean, more busloads of tourists. At the bookstore, there was a temptation to begrudge this cosmetic transformation, to deride these waves of spring sightseers as mere transients who didn't know the real Paris like we at the bookstore did.

This, of course, was youthful folly, but Kurt and I soon learned there were concrete disadvantages to the surge in moneyed tourists. Watching the hordes of people traipse up and down rue St. Jacques with their expensive cameras and guidebooks, Tuee the Sandwich Queen decided she could squeeze a few more francs out of these moneyed customers. Woe of woes, the price for two sandwiches and a can of soda went up from twenty francs to twenty-four. Kurt and I immediately arranged a bookstore-wide boycott and wondered what had become of the Paris we knew and loved.

33.

George's first steps toward communism came after seeing the ravages of the Great Depression. In his opinion, there had to be a better way, a system where the world's wealth wasn't concentrated in the hands of a precious few and where people were more than just cogs in an economic system that forced them to work and buy, buy and work.

At Boston University, George discovered the great socialist writers and then, while working in Panama, he saw firsthand the exploitation, environmental devastation, and corruption associated with modern business. It was at this time that he announced his belief in communism to his family, an announcement that wasn't particularly well received.

"Are [Communists] not people who have never succeeded anywhere, the flotsam and jetsam of society?" Grace wrote to her son. "There is one trait in human nature that Karl Marx does not take account of and that is the lust for power."

George was undeterred. After World War II, when the geopolitical games between Russia and the United States turned *communism* into a dirty word, George was horrified. For him, communism was the great social experiment that was bound to come, the simple doctrine of "the stronger the community, the stronger the individual." George thought that, unlike capitalism, which measured its success by looking at the most privileged members of society, a system should be judged by how its least fortunate individuals fared.

"Look at the poor people, look at the single mothers, look at the prisoners," he said. "These are the yardsticks of a civilization."

Living with George at Shakespeare and Company and reading the Noam Chomsky essays he showered upon me, it was easy to believe all he told me, to see the flaws of modern existence. But at the bookstore, I was also faced with the direct drawbacks to communism. Nadia had repugnant stories of growing up under Ceauşescu, and Ablimit never missed an opportunity to deride the Chinese government.

Considering all I had been through at the bookstore—negotiating Esteban's hostility, peacefully settling the Simon situation, listening to George's troubles with his wife and daughter, recovering from the falling-out over Scott—I now felt entirely comfortable with George. I was ready not just to listen to his ideas but to challenge them. So one day, I asked the obvious question: If Communism was so good, why were there so many bad stories from their regimes?

George sat up in his seat and his eyes became alert. Pushing back the papers on his desk, he stood up and closed the door so we wouldn't be disturbed.

The first thing George did was to explain that there had never been a true communism in the world. Stalin was a violent fraud and Castro's once-beautiful idealism had become corrupted by his love for power. What were needed were more governments to experiment with Marxism and socialism, to experiment with a system where money and resources were directed to education and families, not to designing yet another multibladed razor or creating weapons of greater mass destruction. But few modern leaders had the courage to try because the global business community would raise the interest rates on a given country's national debt and shut the country down with a hammer blow to its economy.

"Think of the rich oil companies, the wealthy dynasties like the Bushes, the cowboy entrepreneurs like Bill Gates. Why would they want to change the rules of the game? They're winning and they don't care that everyone else is losing," George explained. "With all this entrenched power fighting ideas like communism, it's no wonder the ideas get a bad name."

According to George, while stories about Ceauşescu's human rights abuses and the leaky boatfuls of refugees from Cuba were rampant, members of the world media, who earned their money from a capital-based economy, weren't particularly eager to spread stories of Communist successes.

"Take Cuba," said George. "Under Castro's communism, Cuba enjoys the highest rate of literacy in South and Central America, has twice as many doctors for every one thousand people as in the United States, and unlike the United States, provides paid maternity leave for mothers and free health care for everyone. In fact," George added with an emphatic thump on his desk, "the average man in Cuba lives longer than the average man in America.

"Sure, Cuba's hospitals and schools have fallen behind in recent years but that's because the economy has been devastated by the American-led embargo," said George. "Cuba's not perfect, but the country's got a lot of things that work and a lot of things that work better than they do in America."

Not satisfied, George launched into the tale of the Indian state of West Bengal. Here, the economy had grown at twice the national average, schools and hospitals were ahead of the rest of the country, and the quality of life was among the best in all of India. "The Communists have done this," roared George. "The Communists!"

George explained that in the 1970s, the Communists broke up the land monopolies and redistributed property so poor families could run farms and own homes. With state administration and Marxist ideals, the economy has been so healthy and the people so happy that the Communists have won six straight elections. "Do you read about that in the *Herald Tribune*?" George demanded. "Of course not! It's all American propaganda."

"Communism just means thinking about the community first," said George, who believes a group of people are stronger together than alone and that it's worth it to sacrifice the riches a single person can amass in order to provide a higher quality of life for the general population. Although the world hasn't found utopia yet, George is convinced we have to keep looking.

"Look around you. Look at how rich the planet is, but look how a few people in Europe, North America, and Japan end up working all the time and enjoying all the benefits, while rest of the world is poor and hungry and without clean water," finished George. "Is that right? Most people out there aren't even asking the question. At least I believe a fairer world is possible."

After brooding for days, I decided it was time for a serious talk with Nadia. With due propriety, I invited her for a walk along the Seine. I explained I loved her, I believed in her art, I thought she was a great woman. But I told her I wasn't sure I could handle this sort of open relationship, and maybe we didn't make the most perfect couple, and perhaps we weren't destined to die entwined in each other's arms at the age of 102.

I went on like this for a good ten minutes, with plenty of banal apologies and sweeping conclusions about nature of love, until Nadia finally pulled me to a stop.

"Why are you getting all serious like this?" she demanded. "All I wanted was to have a little fun in Paris. What did you think? I wanted to get married?"

Nadia left the bookstore shortly after that humiliating walk. By luck, she'd met a photographer who was leaving for a lengthy assignment in Milan. He'd offered her the free use of his apartment, and in early May she moved out of the store with little fanfare, anxious for quiet and peace and a shower of her own.

While it was the worst of times for me, George was enjoying the best. Eve's visits to the store were practically daily now, and Luke and I noted a corresponding change in George's appearance. Gone were the stained jackets and mismatched socks. Now he wore sleek suits, along with shirts he'd actually had dry-cleaned.

One morning, George and I went to a church rummage sale on

avenue Georges V, which was a ritzy part of town off the Champs-Elysées. This was part of his regular hunt for cheap used books, and I was honored to be appointed the official bag carrier. On this trip, George was also hoping to find some pretty secondhand dresses that he might offer to Eve when she came to the store for dinner that night.

"She told me she feels like crying when it comes time to leave the bookstore," he said as we walked up to the Hôtel de Ville metro station. "See, comrade? Once in a while, things work out around here."

It was a good thing George was feeling so hearty, as we had quite a day ahead of us. On the metro, there were two young boys, no more than seven or eight years old, working the train and trying to steal from tourists. They noticed George's shirt pocket was wadded with francs and they lunged for the bills. Together, George and I were able to ward them off and force them out the metro doors before they could get any money. Then when we got to what I thought would be the friendly confines of the church, we were instead met with scorn. George had a reputation of frequenting the rummage sales and buying up the best books. The priests at this church were offended he would sometimes resell their books at a profit, and they actually tried to hide items from him. At one point, George and a priest got into a tugging match over a hardcover copy of *Anna Karenina* and the priest began cursing at George in a salty mix of English and French.

"I thought you were supposed to be kind and loving?" I snapped as I helped George pull the book out of the priest's hands.

George only laughed the encounter off and continued on his way. Nothing could faze him as he went humming off into the clothes racks in search of flowery skirts for Eve.

This fresh verve of George's was given a further boost by the return of a familiar face. Tom Pancake was back in town, drawn from Egypt by his love for Gayle. He'd moved into the New Zealand embassy again and had visited the bookstore shortly after his plane had landed.

Along with his stories of Cairo and a fresh tattoo on his right arm,

Tom bore a tremendous gift for George. Among his many attributes, Tom possessed a most divine sartorial eye: He always dressed in sharp suits and vintage shirts and had an admirable wardrobe for a traveling man. Among his collection was an exquisite pinstriped zoot suit from the 1930s. It was one size too small for Tom, so he offered it to George.

The next afternoon, I found George in his apartment, preparing for Eve's daily visit. He was wearing the suit Tom had given him and was sitting at the front table with a mirror and a candle. This was George's method of trimming his hair, one he saved for special occasions. He would put the flame to his head, light his hair on fire, and then bat out the flames once the hair burned down to the desired length. It stank the air to no end but was amazingly effective. With a fresh trim and Tom's zoot suit, George looked absolutely dapper.

Sitting me down for a glass of beer, George reviewed all the encouraging things that had passed between him and Eve in recent weeks: how she loved the bookstore, how she adored the poem he'd written for her, how they laughed, how they read together on the couch.

"I know people will say I'm crazy when they find out how much I love that little girl, but I can't help it," George said.

I understood. New love is the greatest drug of all, and he'd been in the Shakespeare and Company vortex for so long, he couldn't kick the habit. During his fifty years at the bookstore, there had been endless affirmation from women who arrived and fell head over heels for George and the romantic world he'd created. Such a constant rush of love can be dangerously addictive, and George still yearned for it, even at eighty-six years of age.

Considering all of this, I was about to assure him of his sanity, but then he did something that made me reconsider my assessment. George reached into his pocket and pulled out a ring.

"I'm going to ask Eve to marry me."

34.

The only thing that surprised me more was that Eve didn't say no.

This came to light a pleasant spring afternoon when George declared we would have a group lunch in front of the bookstore. It was a warm May day and he'd set up a long table with a dozen chairs and stools outside the door of the antiquarian room so we could feast in the open air.

Almost everyone was there: Kurt, Ablimit, Marushkah, Gayle, Tom, Scoot, Sophie, Simon. The guest of honor was Eve, who sat proudly at George's side, though it didn't seem anybody realized the meal was a tribute to her. A free dinner had been offered and the hungry hordes had descended without question.

George served chicken and rice stew, a dozen baguettes, big pots of potato salad, yogurt jars of homemade strawberry ice cream, and plenty of the cheap high-alcohol beer. As we ate, customers continued to flood in and out of the store, many stopping to take pictures of this impromptu party. We sat like this for hours, the afternoon warmth dimming into a chill dusk. No stool or chair was empty for long as friends came and went, and George even pulled the occasional stranger down to share in our bounty. It was toward the end of the meal, when George and Eve started holding hands, that I noticed she was wearing the ring.

When the meal was done and I was carrying chairs back up to the third-floor apartment, I found Eve alone in the kitchen, washing the dishes. As I helped dry, I asked her what the ring on her finger meant and she was surprisingly happy to have somebody to tell about her growing intimacy with George.

She did, in fact, love him. He was the type of man she'd always dreamt off—kind, mischievous, romantic. Granted, she'd never thought her dream man would be quite so old, but she was gradually coming to terms with their age difference.

"Besides, he's still an attractive man," she insisted.

I had to agree. George was definitely the sexiest eighty-six-year-old man I had ever met. When I said this, Eve started giggling.

"You know we've kissed, don't you?" she said.

"You've kissed George? On the lips?"

She blushed. "Sometimes, just before we go to bed. . . ."

"You sleep in the same bed with George?"

"Oh, I wasn't naked or anything. I was wearing my bottoms." Eve blushed redder and giggled more. "He's such a sweet man."

Eve was flattered by the ring and wore it proudly. She hadn't technically said yes to George's suggestion they marry, but she was going to take some time to think about it. For now, she was going to come stay at the bookstore to see what it was like to live with George.

That week, Eve moved into the upstairs apartment. She and George started going to movies together, holding hands at dinner, and generally behaving like love-struck children.

"Dude, this is so *Harold and Maude,*" Kurt said when George returned with a semi-crumpled bouquet of carnations for Eve.

Though it was tempting to be critical of George for seducing a woman nearly seven decades his junior, I saw a poetic side to the romance. He wasn't doing it for sex or for status; he was doing it because he genuinely loved Eve. Having lived such an extraordinary life and having run such an extraordinary bookstore, wasn't he entitled to one last extraordinary love affair?

George had always believed in love. His first was a woman named Gwen. They'd been members of the same Communist cell in Berkeley and fell for each other at first glance. Gwen's mother disliked George and he could only see Gwen by hiding outside her house and whistling a secret code. They decided to travel to Mexico together and arranged to meet in a town close to the border, but while hopping trains on the way down, George was picked up by police for being a suspicious person and was actually in jail the day of their rendezvous. Once freed, he tracked Gwen down to a restaurant where she'd found a job as a waitress and their adventure began—on foot through the Sonoran Desert.

George remembers them walking at night to avoid the hot sun and then arriving at the estate of a rich Mexican near the Yaqui River. The young couple were given a room and the Mexican even offered George a magnificent gift. An old boat had sunk in the river, and if George dredged it up and repaired it, the man said, he and Gwen could continue their journey by water. A few weeks later, they were drifting down the river together.

They were eventually separated, first when George made a trip home, then by the war. The last George heard, Gwen had returned to Mexico and married. She'd had several children but hadn't been happy. It seemed her husband followed the tradition of keeping a wife to raise his family, while mistresses sated other appetites. On certain days, George would even say he should have married Gwen, one of the great what ifs of his life.

There had been other women, too. Laura de Los Rios, a classmate of his sister's who'd fallen in love with George after reading the letters he sent home from Panama and of whom he wrote, "Among the visions which my memories trace/There is one brightest star, one face." The Russian woman who took him to Saint Petersburg but got angry when all he wanted to do was stay home and read the Russian books in her library. His fiancées Josette and Colette. The shadowy Anaïs Nin. His ex-wife.

These were the important women in George's life, and he rarely pursued the temporary indulgences that his bookstore offered. If he'd wanted, he could have had a new girlfriend every week, but instead, he kept on falling in love.

"I wasn't like Henry Miller and the rest of them, running around, do-ing their things," George explained. "I liked being in love with my girl-friend. I liked writing her love letters up here at my desk and giving her presents that made her cry. I guess I'm a bit old-fashioned that way."

Still, it was tempting to replace the word *old-fashioned* with *childlike* when describing George's approach to love. He was eternally captured by his romantic visions, and in all his years he was never able to build a mature relationship. Perhaps it was because of his lingering anger to-ward his mother, but when it came to women, George was a Peter Pan, his spirit forever that of a young boy.

It was also difficult to judge George, as my own behavior was far from exemplary. With Nadia gone and my heart splintered, I gorged on the sugar high of Shakespeare and Company romance.

With so many young men and women eager to explore the world and press their limits, and with Paris's reputation for romance, the bookstore was a bastion of sexual indulgence. In the four months I'd seen Kurt at the bookstore, I would have needed to use my fingers and toes to count his various girlfriends, and from what Luke told me, one could always find a Kurt or two around the store. Newly single at Shakespeare and Company, for the first time in my life I was actually refusing offers of intimate companionship, and this had turned my sexual psychology upside down. Previously, I'd been somewhat typical male, conditioned to believe I should have an insatiable sexual appetite and bed dozens of women if I were to be a proper man. Even when I reached my twenties and had plenty of lovely girlfriends and sex be-came more easily accessible, I always felt lacking, as if I wasn't living up to the sexual conquests expected of a man of the *Details* generation. With this doubt, I often made poor decisions, partaking of intimacy for no other reason than the intimacy itself.

This brings to mind my mother's favorite dog, Daisy. She is a Brit-tany spaniel that was bred in a puppy mill, where the owners viciously abused and starved their dogs in order to maximize the per-puppy profit. The dog managed to escape into the woods, and when she was finally found and taken to the animal shelter weeks later, she was a frail skeleton and there were still scabs on her legs from where the owners of the puppy mill had stubbed out cigarettes as punishment for misbehavior.

Even after she had been adopted by my mother and regained her weight, it was embedded in Daisy's mind that she was starving, so whenever there was food about, she ate. The veterinarian said if left alone with enough food, Daisy might actually eat herself to death. In fact, she tried to prove him right on several occasions, once working through the better part of a ten-pound sack of potatoes, another time devouring a box of twenty-four candles.

Like the dog, I still had unexorcized fears of sexual starvation, and thus the bookstore could be a dangerous place. Though I wasn't as promiscuous as Kurt, I made rash choices after Nadia left me. A particularly doomed relationship involved a German woman I'd met in the antiquarian room. One day, she invited me to the woods of the Bois de Boulogne for a picnic. She'd made a red pepper salad and there was wine and fresh bread. We found a secluded spot among the trees. She declared immediately she wouldn't have sex with me and I agreed we shouldn't cloud our friendship, but we decided we could kiss a little.

It was a pleasant situation until in the middle of such a kiss, we heard the cracking of a broken tree branch. We looked up and saw a man standing about thirty feet away and masturbating fiercely. More alarming still, we noticed on the other side of the glade, perhaps eighty feet away, a second man leaning against a tree. He, too, had a busy hand in his shorts. I picked up a stick and chased the two men off.

The German girl and I sat for a few moments, laughing nervously about what had happened. Then she started to kiss me again, this time with unstaunched passion. And then she demanded, *"Cherches le préservatif."* That relationship likely would have been consummated if there hadn't been more cracking of branches a few minutes later. This time, the main masturbator was just fifteen feet away, leaning in and leering horribly at us. There were two more men in the woods this time and they formed a triangle of self-pleasure around us. I later found out this section of the Bois de Bologne was divided into strolls for men of various interests and that the German girl and I had inadvertently ended up in the middle of a prime cruising spot.

With the help of such episodes, it didn't take me long to conclude I was more like George than Kurt when it came to sexual adventure. Thanks to the wondrous Chris Cook Gilmore, I met a girl I could safely fall in love with.

With Eve moving into the bookstore, Chris and Anita were heading back to Atlantic City so that she and George could live alone in the third-floor apartment. Before he left, Gilmore gave his traditional po-etry reading. During the thirty years he'd been staying at the bookstore, he'd composed an epic poem called *Paris Blues* and performed the ever-growing masterpiece each time he passed through.

On the Monday night of Chris's reading, Kurt and I were setting up the room and inviting people upstairs. We saw a trio of beautiful women passing the store and decided they would make good guests. Babbling something about a reading and a bookstore, I led them up-stairs before they could say no.

They were all Italian and all working in Paris as au pairs. Young women from around the world come to France to watch the children of rich and upper-middle-class families, and these three all had part-time baby-sitting jobs, which gave them free apartments in Paris, pocket money, and a lot of time to experience the city.

Soon enough, I was dating Trudie, a woman with a scorpion tattooed on her left arm which she refused to talk about. As part of her baby-sitting job, she had a small room on rue Daguerre, and this be-came my escape from the bookstore. After months of constant late nights and sleeping in cramped and cold beds surrounded by strangers, I was perpetually exhausted. Trudie and I would sit beside the Seine or make dinner and then she would allow me to collapse into her bed. Bliss.

When Chris left, I thanked him for his unwitting help on this front and the old writer just laughed.

"You know, if you're going to be a writer, you have to love life, and there's nowhere better to love life than Shakespeare and Company," he told me. "You can meet just about anybody here, you can read books here, you see beautiful women here. Appreciate places like this, because there aren't enough of them in the world."

It was sad to see Chris walk off to catch his train to the airport. One of the great things about the bookstore he didn't mention was that people like him were there—writers who'd been around, who weren't necessarily rich or famous, but who had lived sensational lives and made people like Kurt and myself believe that maybe we could, too.

Spring was full on us and the store stumbled smoothly along. It was almost as if we were all holding our breath, holding the moment. Sophie had visited the real estate agent twice and we expected word about the apartment any day. The booklet was ready for the printers. All we could do was wait.

We began passing the sunny afternoons in the parks, and the story times by the Seine became more popular as the nights warmed. I was happy with Trudie, I was writing my little book, and I was with incredible friends. Everyone else felt pretty much the same way. The time was so soft and good that Ablimit wasn't even too upset when his chickenfoot exportation business proved financially unfeasible.

One fine May day, Gayle organized a picnic to celebrate Tom's return. Sitting in the park, enjoying the sun, the wine, and a decadent spread of lunch, nobody wanted to leave. A group of Algerian men were kicking a soccer ball around beside us and we challenged them to a game. We were a ragtag team who were mostly drunk and largely unathletic to begin with. The Algerian men passed and dashed around us, quickly taking a lead of 13 to 0. As the sun was beginning to set, we suggested that we should play next goal win, and the Algerians were confident enough to agree.

For another ten minutes, we sprinted and slid and struggled, and amazingly the Algerians didn't score. Then, through some spasm of co-ordination, I passed the ball up to Kurt, who edged it nicely between two defenders to where Luke was running at full pace toward the opponent's net. In one fluid motion, Luke took the ball and stroked it cleanly past the diving goalkeeper. It was a moment of heart-bursting joy. Kurt and I chased Luke around the park, collapsed on him, and then hefted him onto our shoulders and carried him back to our picnic area.

We lay panting and aching and reveling in our victory until long after the sun had set. We all agreed everything was going to have a happy ending. Maybe it was hubris.

35.

Within a week, Ablimit was in the hospital, the apartment was lost, I've stopped wearing George's ring, and a man was dead.

It started with Ablimit. Tom appeared one day and, with the bookstore bursting with customers, suggested a beverage at Polly Magoo's. Afternoons at the bar were a perfect place to lull away the time. The beer was cheaper in the day and just enough light filtered into the bar from the open front doors to erase any guilt one might otherwise feel at drinking the hours away inside. There was never a crowd, so there was enough space to read a newspaper or, better still, take advantage of the playing cards and chessboards stashed behind the bar. Most afternoons, there was at least one backgammon game under way, the competition a degree more than friendly, with stakes of a franc a point and doubling allowed.

When I got back to Shakespeare and Company, Sophie was pale at the desk and Kurt slunk down in the green metal chair, drained of his usual spark.

"Dude, Ablimit's sick."

Ablimit had been at his French teacher's home in the country that morning and his face had begun to grow numb. By afternoon, he couldn't close his left eye or move the left side of his face. When he returned to the store, he'd gone across the street to the emergency ward at Hôtel Dieu and was now in the neurology unit at the Pitié-Salpêtrière hospital near Gare d'Austerlitz. The talk was of a stroke.

The next day, Kurt and I formed a makeshift visiting committee and walked up to the hospital with magazines and assorted not-too-stale treats from George's refrigerator. We attempted gaiety as we passed Simon's animal friends in the zoo of Jardin des Plantes, but it was hollow. As much as we embraced our bohemian life, we were forced to recognize the reality of our predicament: We were all nearly penniless, mostly homeless, and without proper residence papers or health insurance in a foreign country. Though the whiteness of our skin protected us from the harassment North Africans and other more visible illegal immigrants suffered, one major accident or brush with police and our fairy-tale lives in Paris would come to an end.

We arrived at the hospital and continued in our roles of carefree young men, flirting with nurses, scampering through the gardens and halls of the eighteenth-century hospital. But the closer we got to the ward, the harder it became to treat this as just another Shakespeare and Company adventure. We found Ablimit alone in a hospital room, laid out on a blue bed with an IV drip and bandaging over the left side of his face. Kurt knocked on the door hopefully, and after an unnaturally long pause, Ablimit turned toward the door.

"What are you doing here?" he asked in a slurred voice.

Kurt grinned. "I was going to ask you the same thing."

Ablimit struggled up in bed and waved us over. With a lopsided smile, he urged us to sit down. There was a plate of uneaten hospital food beside his bed and he pushed it toward us.

"I get as much as I want here. Eat, eat."

Ablimit had suffered what doctors believed was a minor stroke triggered by stress and exhaustion. The left side of his face was still partially paralyzed. The doctors said it could go away in a few days, or gradually worsen, or maybe just stay the same. Understandably, Ablimit had lost confidence in the medical profession and had begun to buttress the physical medicines with prayer.

"A sign," he said with effort. "A sign I should change my life."

It was true he'd been pushing himself hard. Since leaving China three years before, he'd traveled across Asia, worked on a kibbutz in Israel, and then moved to France. In Paris, he'd been living amid the nonstop parties and social politics of Shakespeare and Company for more than a year. Ablimit had maintained his rigorous study regime throughout and had indeed become fluent in French and English, but the efforts had caught up with him. Surprisingly, he was glad for it.

"It's a message from God," Ablimit repeated. "From now on, I spend more time living, less time working. More time with friends."

As we relaxed in the hospital room, Ablimit told us we could use the private shower in his room if we needed. After a minor protest for the sake of decorum, I took the longest, hottest shower I'd had since moving into the bookstore. No people waiting outside the public shower stall, no girlfriend or friend standing in the next room while I was overly conscious of things like hot water tanks and electricity bills. Just an endless supply of steaming hospital water. As we got up to leave, Ablimit invited us back anytime.

Without Ablimit's studious presence, the bookstore felt more frivolous, and in the next days I realized it was becoming concretely so. In Europe and North America, the university and college students were starting their summer vacations and trainloads of backpackers began to descend on Paris. Shakespeare and Company was in all the travel guides and the store began to fill up with thirty-second tourists who wanted to check the bookstore off their must-see list. A smaller number had heard of the bookstore's residency policy, and George seldom said no to the frequent requests to stay.

In the winter months, there were never more than seven or eight people staying at one time, and often it was just Kurt, Ablimit, and me in the main store and Simon next door. Now, it seemed every day there were two or three new faces, and one night there were so many bodies, half a dozen people had to sleep on the floor. The bookstore spilled over with dozens of young people feeling the reckless excitement of first adventures.

Amid this chaos, I stopped writing. There was too much distraction at the bookstore, a constant buzz of people wanting to ask a question or drink wine or go to the Seine for another night of storytime. Even the relative tranquillity of the antiquarian room was becoming a rare luxury as my arrangement with Simon faltered. His status raised by his success in Ireland and with George preoccupied by Eve, he no longer feared expulsion and seldom left the room empty for me. He now declared himself the official writer in residence at the bookstore and told me he needed the space for himself.

Whereas just a few months prior, I had been loath to leave the bookstore even for a few hours, I now sought excuses to spend time away. Tom Pancake had discovered the French game of boule and it made the perfect afternoon escape. Boule is a game of accuracy, where participants toss heavy metal balls at a smaller target ball a few feet away. Boule involves lots of standing around, interrupted by walks of no more than ten or twelve feet and it is ideally suited to warm afternoons and cold cans of beer. Gayle or Tom would make sandwiches at the embassy kitchen and we would meet in the park around the corner from the bookstore to toss boule until a security guard chased us away for not playing at an authorized city ground.

George made it clear my absences weren't appreciated. One day, I returned to the bookstore and found my cupboard ajar and my belongings rifled through once again. My old laptop computer was missing, along with fifty thousand words of my interrupted novel. I couldn't believe it was a thief; the computer was an old Radio Shack word processor, more than a decade old and worth nothing. I searched the bookstore, depressed and bewildered. With no other ideas, I went to George. Though he denied knowing anything, twenty minutes later I found my laptop on a desk in the library.

"It's a lesson for you. You should keep your things locked away," George muttered.

I now had a suspicion as to the identity of the bookstore thief, and the next time George left his office, I conducted a thorough search. I found one of my shirts that had gone missing the month before, several letters addressed to Shakespeare and Company residents, and two diaries belonging to girls who'd stayed at the store.

"I don't know how the shirt and letters got here," George insisted when I confronted him with my discovery.

But the diaries?

George blushed and heaved his shoulders in a what-can-you-do fashion. He'd once written in an essay that he thought the ideal human situation was that of a seventeen-year-old girl in Paris in the springtime, ready for her first love. It appeared he wanted to experience these situations vicariously.

"You wouldn't believe the time I spend searching around for the diaries of the girls who live here," he said with a sigh. "They're my favorite reading."

One Sunday morning after a pancake breakfast, George was leaving the third-floor apartment when he saw the door across the hall swing open. There was the hotel baron, grinning broadly and holding the keys to the apartment in his hand. The sale had gone ahead and the hotel baron had gotten his offer in first. Everything came crashing down.

"He was like a troglodyte coming out from his cave," George said, pressing his fingers to his temples. "It's the worst feeling of my life."

George then locked himself in his office and didn't reappear for three days.

When George finally did emerge, he moped around the bookstore in a foul mood. He condemned himself for destroying Shakespeare and Company, saying if he'd been younger and more alert, he would have ensured that the apartment was his.

Sophie didn't understand what had happened. The agent had assured her George would be given first notice, but instead, it was the rich businessman with his millions of francs. Though George didn't blame her outright for this, he did become increasingly short-tempered with Sophie. Several days after the apartment was lost, Sophie twisted her ankle while dancing in front of the store. She was practicing movements for an upcoming exam at the Jacques Lecoq school. George fired her for wasting time on her shift.

Scott was especially affected by Ablimit's hospitalization. He was proving to be something of a paranoid fellow at the best of times. One evening early in his stay, Scott had been trying to sleep, when he heard an incessant ticking. While most others would probably have assumed it was a forgotten alarm clock, Scott decided it was a bomb. Just as he was about to throw himself out the window to save his life, the Danish girl awoke, calmed him down, and insisted he spend the rest of the night in her bed to help further ease his panic.

Such neurosis was fertile ground for hypochondria, and Scott was a textbook case. Shortly after Ablimit fell ill, Scott discovered a swelling in one of his testicles and became convinced it was cancer. He nearly sprinted over the bridge to the Hôtel de Dieu, where a nurse put him in the waiting room reserved for the less urgent cases.

Scott spent almost eight hours at the hospital, getting various X rays and having various doctors squeeze his glands. When a doctor finally returned with the results of his probe and said there was nothing to worry about, Scott still wasn't convinced. That night at the bookstore, he grumbled about the great history of medical misdiagnoses and insisted he would follow up with a specialist when he went back to the States.

Not too long after Sophie was fired, Scott decided he'd had enough of life at the bookstore. Too many of George's mood swings, too many people fighting for beds, too many microbes waiting to infect him. One fine blue-skied morning, he left for the south of France to find the mountain pass where Walter Benjamin had committed suicide. Upon leaving, he praised George and Shakespeare and Company, but there was a shimmer of disillusionment to his words.

———

But the one who took the brunt of George's despair was Eve. Though at first she had been treated with pomp, her life at the bookstore became increasingly difficult. George retired early, often before nine o'clock at night, while Eve enjoyed the late nights and social whirl of the bookstore. George grew irritated they weren't spending more time together and resented her absences.

What had at first seemed like a romantic lark deteriorated further as George began complaining that Eve wasn't reading enough, that she left the upstairs apartment in chronic disarray, that she wasn't running the tea party properly. At the root of it, George was frustrated that Eve wouldn't commit to marriage and he was making life miserable for her.

Crying, she came to me one day, not understanding what had happened. Eve had arrived in Paris an awkward young girl from a conservative German family. At Shakespeare and Company, she'd found a place where she felt she belonged. All of these feelings were connected to George and she did love him, but he was pressuring her to do something she really didn't want to do.

"I'm going to go home. I can't take it anymore," she said with a trace of tears in her eyes. "I can't marry him."

The next day, she returned George's ring and then packed her things and went back to Germany. A perpetual gloom descended on the bookstore. George even fell ill, coughing thick mucus and losing his appetite. I brought him fresh-roasted chickens from the butcher on rue de Seine, but he waved them off and complained he was getting too old and that he didn't know how he could go on after these bitter disappointments.

They were dark days. Gone were the sharp suits and haircuts, gone were the lunches in front of the store. I tried to cheer him with beer or stories, but he would have none of it.

"Just leave me alone," he asked. "There's nothing to be done now."

36.

It was a Monday night in May, the fifteenth to be precise. As tradition demanded, after the poetry reading at the bookstore, there was a midnight session of storytelling by the Seine. The evenings had become popular as word spread and the weather got warmer. That midnight, there were more than a dozen people sitting on the bank of the river, cans of beer and bottles of wine on the cobblestones before them.

Kurt was there and Luke had showed up for the first time. Having been convinced to attend by our constant tales of story time, he was dressed in his black suit and fedora and sat skeptically to the side. There were also a few writers who wanted to be part of a growing literary event. But the crowd was mostly inflated by young women and men passing through the bookstore, congratulating one another on how splendid it was to be young and free in Paris.

When I surveyed this assembly by the river, I felt a bad vibe. Story times had always been a personal affair. In the intimacy of the first nights, we had all cleansed dark memories, and we did it with trust in one another and an optimistic belief we were doing something special. This night, there was an animal edge in the air, the spring pheromones driving like mad.

The riverside was filled with strolling tourists, and many stopped, curious about such a large group of English speakers. We also attracted the attention of the various men who spent summer nights ambling along the river with hash cigarettes and cans of strong beer.

I talked with Kurt about moving the event someplace quieter, and we began asking people to start walking down the river, closer to the Jardin des Plantes. There was a butting of heads, as some of the people were expecting friends to arrive. I bristled at the presumptuousness of these strangers who'd invited others to our night.

It was at about this time that a young Algerian man approached. He was in his early twenties and had a short, stocky build, pimpled olive skin, and a light goatee. In the tradition of Paris street culture, he wore a Sergio Tacchini track suit with the cuff of one pant leg jammed into his sock and the other cuff rolled up to just below the knee. He also wore the required white Lacoste baseball cap slightly askew. More importantly, his pockets were filled with bottles of beer and he carried another three or four squeezed under his left arm. The man was drunk and looking for women, friends, or trouble, with no real preference for what he found. We were an obvious stop.

At first, he was just leaning in, talking to girls, asking their names, and we barely noticed. He tried to sit too close to one woman and she got up and moved, but again we weren't too bothered. The trouble started when his beers began to slip from under his arm and crash to the pavement. From a distance, it appeared sinister when the second bottle smashed.

Kurt and I rose to confront him. The young man became offended when we asked him to leave. Another beer bottle hit the ground, this one perhaps not accidentally. Kurt pushed the man backward. The man spat and Kurt swung, striking him above an eyebrow. He came back in a rage and pushed Kurt so hard that he fell against the stone wall. Then all of us were into it, stepping between the two of them to prevent further blows. The man's neck veins bulged and he strained, trying to break our hold on him. I hate to admit that I suggested throwing the man into the river, thinking the cold water would sober him up.

It was then two Frenchmen appeared. They were older than the fellow who was giving us trouble, but of the same general character. Track pants tucked into socks, chains around their necks, hash cigarettes waiting to be lit. Perhaps they had a genuine sense of civic duty, because they interrupted us and asked if they could be of help. We explained the situation and they offered to take care of the problem. The last thing we saw was the young man being dragged away.

The violence of the episode added to the savage feel of the evening. Kurt was talking loudly about his desire to fight while everyone gossiped furiously about the incident. Moving the crowd along, we found a space between two boats about fifteen hundred feet down the Seine. As people sat, Kurt began jostling with another man to see who would start the storytelling.

Part of me wanted to be up in front of the crowd too, claiming their approval, but part of me wanted to be a long, long way from there. I thought of how beautiful those quiet February nights beside the Seine had been and I saw the decadence before me. Without saying good-bye to anybody, I slipped away, Kurt's voice fading into the hum of the night.

I went back to Trudie's little apartment on rue Daguerre, feeling vaguely depressed. I slept for twelve hours and woke up tired. It was night again when I finally dragged myself back to the store.

"They've got Kurt in jail," Luke said in an empty voice.

The police had been by the store. A man had been murdered by the Seine the night before, beaten up and thrown into the river. He'd either been unconscious when he hit the water or couldn't fight the undercurrent; they wouldn't know for sure until after the autopsy. Whatever the case, they'd pulled the body from the river and were looking for answers.

The dead man was last seen talking to a group of English and American tourists. The bookstore had been an obvious place to start an investigation and someone had not only volunteered our names but had also told them we had been in a fight with the dead man. There were now written orders demanding that I, too, report to the police station for questioning.

When I went upstairs to the library, George pulled me aside and chastised me for being away from the store the night before. Not only was the bookstore now mired in a police investigation but he'd been awakened at five in the morning by people screaming in front of the store. He'd issued a warning to the Shakespeare and Company crowd. He was going to clean house and invoke a midnight curfew.

"I'm tired of this foolishness," George told me. "It's going to have to stop."

Slowly, I pieced the night together. After I left, the story time unwound in unruly fashion. No structure, much drinking, and then a large group of people returning to the esplanade in front of Shakespeare and Company. A fellow by the name of Jonny had been staying at the store. He was a writer, with a tattoo of an anchor on one shoulder and his family motto, If Not Peace, War, on the other. He and Kurt ended up squaring off in front of the store to play punches. They took turns, one man standing chin straight while the other landed his blow. Jonny had been knocked down in the third round, but Kurt had his eyebrow cut open and his eye swollen. All of this had been witnessed by George and had fueled his fury.

Kurt finally appeared late that next night. The police had kept him in a cell or a holding room for hours, trying to make him think he was the suspect. They kept asking how he'd received the cut over his eyebrow and what he was doing fighting beside the Seine the night before. They returned him to a cell over and over to make him worry.

Eventually, the officers admitted they had witnesses who'd seen two men push the Algerian into the river. The police told Kurt that the face of the corpse had been covered in bruises to suggest there had been a fight prior to the murder, which explained why they had taken such keen interest in Kurt's facial wounds. Once he realized he was no longer a suspect, Kurt started to worry that the interrogation would lead to some problem with his status in France, but the police dismissed this as an issue for immigration and sat him down with a digital artist to try to sketch out the faces of the suspects.

The next day, I heeded my summons and went to the police station on avenue du Maine. Once the detectives assured me my residency status in France wasn't an issue, either, I began to enjoy myself. I'd spent many hours speaking with murder police in Canada and I liked to talk about crime. I explained my reporting past and we talked openly about the difficulty of the case. The witnesses had been only able to describe two men in their late twenties with dark hair. This matched about a thousand people on the quay that night and hundreds of thousands in the Paris area. I looked at a few books of mug shots but couldn't recognize anybody.

The incident caused a brief stir at Shakespeare and Company. It was written up in *Le Parisien* with a huge photo of the police boats dredging the river. George even kept a copy for his archives. Kurt spun the tale for a few store regulars and then typed out a short story entitled "Trading Fists with Jonny Diamond." Ever proud of his work since his return from Morocco, he showed the story to Luke, who took a fierce pencil to it and told Kurt bluntly that it was no good. Kurt was spitting afterward.

"You know, I'm getting sick of these Shakespeare and Company critics. At least I'm doing it, at least I'm writing. I finished *Videowrangler,* didn't I?"

Ablimit was still in the hospital, Scott was gone, Kurt was thinking of leaving, too. The bookstore wheezed under the strict new curfew, with the residents sweating and chafing while the night hummed on the other side of the window. Shakespeare and Company suddenly felt like a less good place to be.

At about this time, a criminal lawyer friend of mine wrote and suggested I tour Spain with him. I'd met Will while working the police beat at the newspaper. His practice was successful enough that he'd saved a substantial sum of money and he wanted to do good, perhaps buy land in Costa Rica and open a hospital or some other charitable venture. In order to learn Spanish, Will had enrolled in an intensive language course in Barcelona and we were to drive across the country once he was done. Though I was cleared of any implication in the murder, I still savored the prospect. Like many young journalists, I considered Hunter S. Thompson's *Fear and Loathing in Las Vegas* to be a touchstone and I enjoyed the fact that, like Hunter, I would be traveling under a rogue criminal lawyer's halo of protection.

For three weeks, we took a lazy tour around the country, driving through Valencia and Granada, up to Madrid, and then back to the coast. On the last day of the trip, we found a quiet cove and went for a swim. I noticed a wasp skim too close to the surface and get swallowed by the sea. I swam toward it and tried to lift it out of the water, but I was frightened I would be stung. Twice, I flicked the wasp into the air, only for it to fall back into the water. I still couldn't bring myself to cradle it out and I watched the wasp drown before me, its yellow-and-black corpse sinking beneath the waves. That's me, I thought as I returned to shore. Always well intentioned but never quite doing enough.

37.

There was hardly anybody left when I got back to Paris in June. Kurt's father had suffered a heart attack and Kurt had flown home to Florida to be with his family. Ablimit had left for a town near Dijon and a two-month Christian retreat. Scott was in the south of France.

Luke still worked nights and Simon still called the antiquarian room home and of course George still tramped about, but otherwise I didn't recognize the faces when I returned to Shakespeare and Company. It felt strange and dislocating when I saw new people amok among the books and I felt a pang of resentment. It was my bookstore, I wanted to tell them.

Tom and I once had a long discussion about signs. I argued there was a message to be had in them, that one could determine one's path by keeping an eye out for omens such as snarling dogs or smiling girls. Tom felt this was an internal process, that every minute of life was surrounded by a thousand potentially meaningful incidents and a person interpreted them as he or she was inclined. With my logic, if one was feeling nervous about an upcoming challenge and crossed paths with a snarling dog, it would be a sign to give up the endeavor; Tom would say that on the same corner as the snarling dog might be the girl, and if one wasn't so nervous of the dog, one would notice her smile and believe it to be a charmed day.

Either way, the arrival of an apartment was a significant indication it was time to leave Shakespeare and Company. I was standing out in front of the bookstore one day when a woman approached me and wanted to know if I was looking for a place to live. As the woman led me through a warren of streets to rue Dauphine in the sixth arrondissement, she explained her situation. She was German and this apartment was the hideaway she and her French lover had shared two decades ago. The two were now married and living in Germany, but they kept the apartment for trysts and rented it out when they needed money. The woman had come to Paris for the summer, but a consulting project had arisen unexpectedly in Berlin and she wasn't going to be staying after all. In fact, she was leaving the next morning and immediately needed a tenant for four months.

We mounted seven and a half flights of stairs, but I was so pleased by this miracle that I didn't notice the dizzying climb. The apartment had been decorated in the seventies and featured black-and-silver velvet wallpaper and a mirrored wall beside the bed. The ceiling slanted with the slope of the roof and there were exposed wooden beams, but best of all were the two windows, seven and a half stories over Paris, with red clay chimneys and slate roofs stretching forever across the city.

The woman wanted ten thousand francs for the four months and would accept whatever I could pay up front. I still had a bit of money left from my article on Ireland and it was enough to get me this apartment in Paris.

It was destiny and I didn't change my mind even when I found out Simon had specifically directed the woman to me, as he knew of my desire to leave the bookstore. With a quiet good-bye to George, I moved out of Shakespeare and Company the next day.

For weeks, I did little but sleep and read. After the scattered emotional existence at the bookstore there was nothing left in me. Once a day, I would gather the courage to descend to the street to buy bread and cheese, then drag myself back up the stairs and into a bed strewn with half-read books, where I would drift in and out of sleep and wonder at the time. Trudie would make the occasional visit to check my vital signs, but aside from that, I saw nobody.

By July, my spirit returned and I found pleasant afternoons sipping beer with Tom and Nick, my old friend from the FNAC scam. The CD exchange business had petered out, so Nick had set up a henna tattoo corner near Les Halles. He'd found cheap powdered hair dye that approximated henna and had entered the business of drawing dragons and flowers on people's bodies. The price was between fifty and one hundred francs, depending on the size of the tattoo. Alone, Nick could make one thousand francs in a few hours, and with Tom on a second stool, another six hundred could be taken in. The work consisted of sitting in the sunshine and waiting for customers, and I would bring cans of beer by in the afternoon and keep the two company.

With rent payments looming, I, too, needed money and fell into the luxury-goods business. The job involved Louis Vuitton handbags and a niche market that could only be filled by the likes of me—young, white, English-speaking, and financially distressed.

At that time, Louis Vuitton bags were incomprehensibly popular in countries like Japan and Korea. The bags were also several times more expensive there than they were in France, and in limited supply. For the many Asian tourists in Paris, that meant stopping at the Louis Vuitton store to pick up the handbags for a fraction of the price back home, a mere four or five thousand francs for a regular-size purse.

The twist was that Louis Vuitton seemed reluctant to sell its bags to Asian people in Paris. My theory was that the company didn't want to dilute their image as a European luxury brand, so they made it difficult for certain customers to acquire their products. On any given afternoon, at any given Louis Vuitton boutique, there was an enormous lineup of people waiting to be allowed into the store, and the vast majority of these people were of Japanese or Chinese origin. Not only were they forced to stand outside for hours, but once inside, I noticed the clerks treated them like a virus, sniffing at their accents and allowing them to buy only two items, a handbag and a change purse.

Meanwhile, the richest Europeans were given private appointments to buy their Louis Vuitton apparel, and if you were white and chic enough in dress, you could bypass the line and purchase whatever you wanted. From this disparity grew a raging black market. Middlemen paid people like myself to infiltrate the boutiques and buy Louis Vuitton bags on behalf of their clientele.

My black-market contact was a lovely young woman from Shanghai by the name of Flora. A friend of mine had been introduced to her one day after a French class. The teacher had asked the students to prepare an oral presentation on what they wished for. My friend said she'd like enough money to visit her parents. After the class, a fellow student approached and said she could earn enough for the plane ticket in a single afternoon. This was how Flora got her runners.

It was marvelous job. The first day, I dressed in a blue velvet jacket I'd bought secondhand and waited on the Champs-Elysées to meet Flora. She arrived with fifteen thousand francs in cash and a store catalog. I was shown what bags to buy and directed to a boutique a few blocks away on avenue Montaigne. At first, I thought it incredible that a stranger like me was being trusted with so much money; then I noticed a blue minivan drive slowly past me with its side door open. Three men were filming me with a handheld video camera.

Unsettled, I went to the store and bypassed the eighty or so Asians standing bored in line. Inside, I found the prettiest clerk and explained my problem. I was in Paris for a gig with my band. At this point, I stopped to ask if she'd heard of my group, which I claimed was the Tragically Hip, a brilliant Canadian band just obscure enough in Europe to ensure I would never actually be identified as not being a member. Later on, some of the clerks actually pretended to recognize me.

I then explained my dilemma: I had promised to buy my mother some Louis Vuitton bags while in Paris and I couldn't understand what the line outside was all about.

It was hot knife on butter. That first day, I bought two large handbags for fourteen thousand francs and delivered them to a smiling Flora. My commission was 12 percent of the total bill, so I walked away with more than sixteen hundred francs in cash, almost my entire rent for the month. The game became more difficult, though, as the stores tracked purchases and passport numbers to crack down on the very black market that I now was part of. This meant you could only hit a particular Louis Vuitton boutique once and had to be ready for surprise questions about visits to other outlets.

Over the course of my brief career, I hit all five Louis Vuitton stores in Paris and gained such a reputation that I was sent on the road. On one occasion, accompanied by Tom, who was always looking for money schemes, we were given a car, forty-eight thousand francs in cash, and another twenty thousand francs in traveler's checks to drive to Lille and Brussels to make buys at the stores there. Throughout the day, we had to stifle the urge to keep driving on to Budapest or Istanbul for a rather comfortable vacation.

My one regret from that run was that I never claimed the bounty of a Hermès bag. The Hermès boutiques were harder to crack than the Louis Vuittons and there was a two-year waiting list for their hypercoveted purses. But legend was that the stores always kept one or two on hand, just in case that suitably celebrated or wealthy client came in to shop. If you could buy one of these bags, it netted you five thousand francs. One time, Tom and I were in the beach resort of Deauville, hitting a Louis Vuitton outlet, and Tom tried his luck at the Hermès. His showman's swagger worked and the five-thousand-franc bonus was practically in our hands before we realized we didn't have the money to make the purchase. A Hermès bag went for twenty-seven thousand francs and we hadn't been provided with enough ready cash. That was as close as I ever got to the brass ring.

At the end of July, there was an E-mail from the man who'd made the threatening phone call to me in December. He wanted to pass along some important news. He was getting married and I was invited to the wedding.

A brief flicker of doubt made me think it was a trap, but then I read on. He'd fallen in love and moved to Toronto to be with the woman. He'd even taken a straight job, using his hustler's charm to make a very decent living as an electronics salesman. And amazingly, he thanked me. I had long counseled him to leave the city, where he was so entrenched in crime, and by disclosing his name in that book, I'd put a little more pressure on him to leave. It was a straw, perhaps not the backbreaker, but he wanted to tell me things had worked out. He still wasn't happy about our misunderstanding, but it was forgotten, or at least pushed to the back of his mind.

A weight lifted, but in its place came a sense of despair. If I was no longer on the run, what exactly was I doing?

Life drifted along that summer, but at times the idleness began to weigh. One humid August night in Trudie's apartment, she admitted that she was feeling restless and unfulfilled with her life in Paris. It had been a great adventure, a great romance, but she'd never intended to spend her life minding other people's children. She made inquiries about a university in Italy and found it wasn't too late to register for the fall term. We left with promises to write and perhaps even visit if our love wasn't diminished by distance. You could only stretch a daydream so far.

As the summer passed, I started returning to the bookstore to see George. At first, I worked in the office, helping organize biographies and compiling book orders. We also got back to the booklet and George decided to go ahead and publish it once he'd made edits to reflect the loss of the apartment to the hotel baron. One of the new passages even read like a call for help.

When I opened my bookstore in 1951, this area in the heart of Paris was a slum with street theatre, mountebanks, junkyards, dingy hotels, wineshops, little laundries and thread and needle shops and grocers. Back in the 1600s in the middle of this slum our building was a monastery with a frère lampier who would light the lamps at sunset. I seem to have inherited his role because for 50 years now I have been your frère lampier—the lamplighter who is hoping that someone else will come along and carry on his mission.

The booklet was finally published and it had opposite effects on its creators. After raising a glass with George to toast the arrival of the shipment, Luke was encouraged enough by our work to plunge into the world of publishing. He wanted to go ahead with his plans for *Kilometer Zero,* and we decided to work together. Between my hours at the bookstore and my hours beside Luke as we began our little venture, I had the semblance of a real life.

But with the booklet out of the way, George slumped and became preoccupied by death. Most of his contemporaries were gone and he struggled to stay in touch with the friends he had left. George said that even Ferlinghetti was mad at him because there'd been a mistake with a distributor and the store no longer carried City Lights books.

One afternoon, he told me about Tolstoy dying alone. Locked in a train car, he refused to let his wife, who was weeping on the platform, inside to say good-bye. George then quizzed me about Marx's funeral.

"How many people do you think were there?" he asked.

I guessed a few hundred, but George shook his head glumly.

Seven.

"I don't know what it all means." He sighed. "Nobody has the answers. I don't like people who pretend they do. Life is just the result of a dance of molecules."

George even looked different. After Eve left, he became scattered and absentminded, he went to bed earlier, his energies waned. He kept telling me he didn't know how much longer he could manage Shakespeare and Company, and as if to prove his worries true, he fell tremendously ill in August. His body became so weak, he could barely raise himself from his bed and he began vomiting blood. He couldn't even keep solid food down, and the protein drinks I brought from the grocery store did little good.

There were appointments at the hospital, but George kept forgetting to go to them. And then his eyes started bothering him and he told me he needed a cataract operation. All of a sudden, he really seemed eighty-six years old and I wondered where my friend had gone who had swung planks and gotten me drunk on high-alcohol beer.

As September broke, there was a cold snap and George fell sick once more. Again, he retreated into his bedroom; again, I could hear his cough echoing in the staircase. With the cold damp winter ahead of us, for the first time I worried that he might not make it through to another summer.

My father's favorite book is *A Prayer for Owen Meany*. In it, the miniature Owen is driven to practice the same basketball shot, an assisted dunk, where he springs off his friend's hands to reach the net. He practices this shot manically, perfecting it for no real reason, as he does not wish to play the sport. As an older man, his destiny comes when he is in an airport and a terrorist grenade is left near a group of children. Using this shot, he is able to throw the bomb out of a raised window, and suddenly he knows why he was compelled to practice that shot for so long.

I had spent five years perfecting the skill of tracking people down while working as a crime reporter. Now, what had largely seemed a wasted talent when used to find the ex-wife of a man who'd committed suicide after being charged with drinking and driving, had sudden pertinence.

In early September, I booked a train ticket to London and told George I was going there on business. I didn't specifically say anything about my mission and he certainly didn't ask. However, the day before I left, he gave me money for the second time. He put a fifty-pound note in my hand and told me to take somebody out to dinner, then recommended a Chinese restaurant that overlooked the Thames.

38.

The Eurostar is a great experiment in claustrophobia. You whiz along at a startling speed, getting closer and closer to a great body of water that, against all logic, the train is going to pass under. Images of terrorists packing plastic explosives into the body of the Chunnel dance through one's head as the train descends into the darkness. After twenty very aware minutes, the train emerges in England, clunks onto the lower-gauge rail system, and chugs into London. It gives the sweat just enough time to dry. The grand joke for French riders is the name of the arrival station, Waterloo, one of the unhappier moments in France's military history.

London is physically larger than Paris, has more houses than apartment blocks, and simply isn't walkable. Here, one is relegated to the underground, and I noted glumly that it was much better protected than the Paris metro, with guards monitoring the entrances and exits. Precious sterling pounds were spent just crossing town.

The city also felt different. London was all rush and money, like New York or Toronto, with everybody looking past you as they talked, making it clear they had someplace else they'd rather be. Coffees were consumed while walking at a brisk pace and there were no sidewalk cafés in sight.

George had received a card the year before from Sylvia and the return address was a student residence at the University of London. The office at the residence refused to release any details due to privacy concerns, but I chatted up a janitor who remembered the girls on the floor from the year before. He thought that Sylvia was studying in the school of Slavic and East European Studies.

At this school, the secretary also claimed privacy but I managed to find one of Sylvia's professors. I explained the delicacy of the situation and George's declining health and he agreed to help. Classes hadn't begun yet, but he explained students were in and out of the building, registering and preparing for the academic year. I left Sylvia a note with him and then posted small written messages around the building, asking her to contact me. All I could do was leave my E-mail address, so I spent the rest of the day wandering along the Thames and making frequent visits to Internet cafés.

The next morning, I went back to the university, checked with the professor again, and posted another round of notes. I sat in the lobby of the school, watching the crowds for three or four hours before tiring. That afternoon, after pacing the National Gallery, I found a web bar around the corner. There was an E-mail from Sylvia with a number for a cellular phone. I sprinted to a phone box and dialed. With her phone cutting in and out, we made plans to meet outside a tube station near Bloomsbury that night.

I arrived at the planned corner half an hour early and started after every young woman, but it would have been impossible to miss her. She was a blonde with a bright smile, but what gave her away were her eyes—pale blue, just like her father's. I had told her only a little on the phone, so she was curious about the reasons for my visit and was worried about her father. We found a nearby pub and she ordered two pints of beer for us.

"I'm just going to tell you the truth," I began.

I explained how I'd ended up in Paris and how her father had taken me in and helped me set my life straight again. I said he spoke of her often and missed her terribly. Now he was seriously ill and, with the future of the bookstore uncertain, George wanted Sylvia to visit Shakespeare and Company again and to mend their relationship. I told her that no matter what had happened in the past, it was important to know her father. He was getting close to ninety, and if she didn't seize the opportunity now, it might be lost forever.

Sylvia was mostly confused. Over the past five years, she'd sent cards and letters, but there'd never been a reply. She assumed he didn't have time for her, especially as her mother had described the mad bookstore life and George's habit of drifting away from people he loved. When she was in Paris a few years back, she had mustered the courage to visit the bookstore, but she remembered the encounter very differently from the way her father did. She went into Shakespeare and Company, a little intimidated by the store and the residents. George didn't seem to have time for her and feeling sad and humiliated, she walked away.

After we talked a little longer, Sylvia, though she wasn't sure what her mother would think, decided she wanted to see her father again.

It was a Friday night and I was scheduled to leave the following day. Sylvia was acting at the time, having already had roles in school productions of Tom Stoppard, Oscar Wilde, and Shakespeare. At the moment, she was rehearsing Chekhov's *The Cherry Orchard,* but she said she would try to juggle her schedule and visit in the coming weeks. Worried she might change her mind or be delayed further, I suggested she return with me for at least a day or two. She flipped through her agenda and finally agreed it would be possible to leave for Paris on Monday and stay at the store a few days. I wanted to buy her a train ticket right then, but she had a rehearsal, so we made plans to meet the next morning at the train station.

As we left the bar, I asked her permission to take a few photographs. The most recent pictures George had were of Sylvia as a young girl and I wanted to take him something to prepare him for his daughter's visit. In the dim evening light, she laughed while I took out the disposable camera bought expressly for this purpose and snapped away. With a wave, she told me she'd see me in the morning.

That night, I was torn between the joy of meeting Sylvia and the deep fear she'd change her mind and skip our meeting. I slept a few hours at the hostel and then made my way to the train station. To my surprise, Sylvia got there before I did. I bought her a Eurostar ticket, carefully noted the hour of arrival in Paris, and then said good-bye.

39.

I arrived back in Paris late that Saturday afternoon and when I got to the bookstore, George was so sick, he'd gone to bed hours before. I returned to the store early the next morning and, forgetting it was a Sunday, I walked into a pancake breakfast. George thrust a plate in my hand and I sat at a table of groggy residents. I didn't recognize anyone and listened to familiar comments about the quality of the pancakes and the bizarreness of the Shakespeare and Company experience. The photographs of Sylvia were in my pocket and I just wanted everybody to leave so I could tell George the news. I was eager for his affirmation, like a boy waiting for his mother to come home so he could show off his straight-A report card.

There was a young man who sat removed from the table and ate his pancakes in begrudging silence. I couldn't help but take note of him, due to his unusual appearance. He was gaunt, about my height with a pale complexion and black-rimmed glasses. The most striking feature was his hair: shoulder-length, like mine, and of an orange-red hue, also like mine. His name was Adrian and he'd just arrived at the bookstore. As I didn't often see men who looked like me, I couldn't help but think this was more than a coincidence.

After an interminable breakfast, chores where divided and the residents scattered. I followed George to the back room and said I had something important to talk about. He looked exasperated and sat on the bed.

"I saw Sylvia. She's going to come to Paris tomorrow."

George winced. "I knew you'd do something stupid like that. I don't want her to come here. I don't want her to see me like this. I'm sick. It's too late."

He stood up and began straightening books in his bedroom. "The store is a mess, it's a disgrace. She can't see it in this state."

I noted she wouldn't be arriving until the next night, which would give us a day and a half to clean. He sputtered something about being disappointed in me and my having ruined everything. I gave him the pictures and he sat back down to go through them, smiling despite his efforts to remain angry. I said he could keep them and he thanked me and put one especially beautiful photograph of Sylvia on the night table beside the bed. I asked if I could do anything to help clean up and he waved me off again.

"You've done enough," he said, keeping a cantankerous edge to his voice. But as I got up to leave, George grabbed me by the arm.

"Come back tomorrow. You need to meet her at the station with me."

I could see the happiness somewhere in the back of his pale eyes.

When I returned to the bookstore the next day, it was obvious George had been working the residents. The floor shone and the front window display was an elaborate mixture of flowers and glossy art books. The organization of the shelves was even more impressive. It turned out Adrian was a cunningly efficient character who'd studied literature at Oxford and was unnaturally adept at sorting out the chaos of books.

Upstairs, the apartment where Sylvia would be sleeping was vacuumed and polished and the refrigerator stocked with an amazing collection of food. George was looking his best in the pinstriped blue zoot suit Tom had given him in the spring. He hurried about in a panic and pulled me along with him on his inspection.

"I've told everyone it's my daughter's friend who's coming. Her name is Emily. Everyone has to call her Emily."

I suggested Sylvia might be disturbed if everyone at the bookstore called her by the wrong name, but he insisted it was necessary to protect her from the attention her arrival would bring.

"It'll be a fun game," he said, rushing upstairs with an armload of clean sheets for Sylvia's bed. "She's an actress, isn't she?"

That night, we took the metro up to the Gare du Nord to meet the Eurostar. The train was running late and George insisted she probably wouldn't come, wondering for the fifth time if I had the arrival time right. I was terrified that something would go wrong at the last minute and that I'd raised George's hopes for nothing.

The train finally pulled in and George craned his neck to find his daughter. When they saw each other, Sylvia ran forward to give her father a hug. Train station reunions and partings are the stuff of lore for good reason; amid the sound and fury of the Gare du Nord, their embrace resounded.

It was late and the occasion special enough that I asked George if maybe we shouldn't splurge for a taxi. Before he could say anything, Sylvia answered for him, proving to be every bit his daughter.

"A taxi? Why would we go to that expense when we can take the metro. That's silly."

George just beamed.

As we rode back to the store, we talked of the Eurostar and the weather. Sylvia gasped when she saw the warning sign for children to be careful of the automatic doors. It was a pink cartoon rabbit nursing a throbbing hand and she traced its ears with her finger.

"I remember that from when I was a little girl."

We arrived at the bookstore near eleven and though George was exhausted, he put out plates of food and glasses of beer and we had a light dinner to welcome Sylvia. She was introduced to everyone as Emily, and though most people were confused that George would devote so much attention to an unknown acting student from London, nobody suspected the truth. As it neared midnight, dinner ended and I excused myself to let George and Sylvia negotiate the end of their night in peace.

The next evening, I returned for another dinner George had planned. By now, word had leaked out that Emily the Actress was really Sylvia the Daughter, but he didn't seem to mind. Sylvia was glowing and George floated around her, trying his best not to be too happy but failing miserably at the task. During a pause before coffee, they sat close beside each other and Sylvia let her head rest on her father's shoulder.

It was my task to accompany Sylvia back to the train station the following afternoon. "I'll be back," she said as we arrived at the Gare du Nord. "Maybe next month—as soon as my rehearsal schedule lightens and I have time away from classes."

There was a full silence between us as I walked her to the train, as if we both knew there was so much to say, it was pointless to begin. She hugged me and then returned to London.

I suddenly felt very tired. I actually dozed off on the train back to the bookstore and missed my stop, so I had to walk back to Shakespeare and Company from the Jardin du Luxembourg. When I arrived at the bookstore, I found George in his office. He pretended to be angry with Sylvia. He wanted her to commit to coming back the next summer to manage the bookstore. She hadn't agreed to any of this yet and it was a disaster and . . . and even he couldn't keep up the charade of disappointment for long and chuckled happily when I told him how happy Sylvia was to be returning next month.

He had two Tsingtao beers chilling in the fridge and we drank them together in the third-floor apartment while watching the setting sun change colors on Notre Dame. He had a faraway look in his eye, an expression that I remembered from the first time I saw him and I said again how lucky I'd been to find Shakespeare and Company that rainy Sunday in January. George stopped me from saying anything else.

"You know, that's what I've always wanted this place to be," he said. "I look across at Notre Dame and I sometimes think the bookstore is an annex of the church. A place for the people who don't quite fit in over there."

I understood. We sipped our beer until the sun set and then sat awhile longer. When George's head became heavy with sleep, I promised to see him again soon and then left the bookstore.

Afterword

I am writing this from Marseilles. It is the second-largest city in France, a rolling Mediterranean port in the south, and about as far from Paris as you can get while staying in the country. I came down here for love and it is a decision I shall never regret. There isn't the gloss that comes with the museums and monuments and tourist dollars of the capital, but among these twisting hill streets, I sometimes think I get a truer scent of the human spirit.

It has been four years since I left Shakespeare and Company and I am only now coming to terms with what that time meant to me. The things I learned from George will likely keep me from ever returning to the sort of life I knew before. I still read the books he sends me, and though I'm not a sworn Communist by any means, he's shown me a path I'd never before contemplated.

George is ninety years old now, still dreaming of utopias. He continues on his quest to buy the apartment, hoping the hotel baron will come to realize Shakespeare and Company will never be dislodged. A foundation is, as always, in the works, and the legacy seems to have no end. I take hope from George's optimism. He continues to house wayward visitors, he continues to host tea parties, he continues to dole out radical books for his guests to read. A walk through the bookstore sees new Kurts, new Nadias, new Jeremys. It is a walk through hopeful eyes.

I remember that, but barely. I had gone to Paris from such dark things, I was ready for anything, ready to believe in anything. I found Shakespeare and Company and embraced it with everything I had.

Shortly after returning from London, I ran out of money and moved into Luke's apartment. It was under renovation, so there was no rent, but also no water or electricity for long stretches of time, and I slept on a dusty floor. Still, after the bookstore, I could cope with anything.

Luke and I ended up with our little publishing house and the foolishness bubbled and grew. We left his apartment for offices in an art squat, a year passed, then two, and the Paris dreams continued. Luke eventually quit his job at the bookstore and then, tired and burned-out, he moved to Italy, where he now teaches English and writes. Kurt went back to Shakespeare and Company after his father recovered from the heart attack, but as hard as he tried, he couldn't re-create what once was. He circulated *Videowrangler* and received a heap of rejections but wasn't dissuaded, and he still counts on being published. Ablimit is in Toronto now and routinely sends me E-mails with snide comments about Canadian politics and glowing references to his Christian faith.

The last time I saw Simon, he'd come from the aisles of Dolce and Gabanna. He had a pair of pants, a shirt, and a jacket, all of which had cost more than he used to spend in three months at the bookstore. His mother had died and the inheritance allowed him to finally move out of Shakespeare and Company. He's thinking of buying an apartment now, maybe in Lisbon, maybe even getting into the book business himself.

And just the other night, I was on the telephone with the man who threatened to kill me. We laugh about it now. I admit I overreacted a little; he admits he did get pretty angry with me on the phone and visited my apartment unannounced, hoping to surprise me. We thanked each other again when we talked. That blowout sent him to the woman who is now his wife and together they have a child and a beautiful home. Without that phone call, I might have never been dislodged from my city and I certainly wouldn't have found Shakespeare and Company.

I probably sound sentimental, but the bookstore neighborhood just isn't the same. Amos, the dog at Café Panis, died and then they replaced the luxurious toilet with a model that has no seat. I rarely recognize anybody if I sit at the bar for a coffee these days. Around the corner on rue St. Jacques, Polly Magoo's closed, as the building that housed it was turned into a three-star hotel. There were many rumored last nights, but one evening it was actually true and the next day the bar was gutted and the building cordoned off. Worse, a new Polly Magoo's opened half a block away, all clean and proper, but soulless, oh so soulless.

As for Shakespeare and Company itself, things go well there now. My instinct about the red-haired Adrian proved correct. He became day manager of the store and his rabid work habits hoisted much of the weight from George's shoulders. He, too, ended up leaving, but only after Sylvia came to live at the bookstore.

And maybe this is the best part of this whole story. As promised, Sylvia returned to Paris for a week that fall and then made another visit in the spring. She passed an entire summer at the store, as George had wanted, and each day she worked the desk between four and eight, learning a little bit more about the bookstore. She adapted well to the life and even found time to organize a production of A *Midsummer Night's Dream* on the esplanade in front of the store.

Now, she's graduated and taken over managing the bookstore full-time. George is still there, of course, overseeing everything his daughter does, complaining that he did it better in his day. This isn't my story to tell, but I can say things are good. The shelves are full and clean, the bookstore is organized, and George seems generally happier. It is with mixed feelings, however, that I report that the store now has a telephone and takes credit cards. Not a bad thing, I guess, just not the Shakespeare and Company I knew.

When I'm in Paris, I see George for a meal and to catch up. Once, about two years after I left the store, we had an interesting afternoon. George and I received subpoenas from the police. They had reopened the murder case and we were the only two people who were still in Paris. The suspects had never been found and the victim's family was loudly wondering why the case had been dropped. The police were reinterviewing as a formality.

There are few men I admire more than George. Though far from perfect and rife with idiosyncrasies, George, with all the hope and optimism of a child, still believes he can change the world and change the people he takes in at his store. In an age when it is so tempting to be cynical, this is enough to make him a hero in my eyes.

Looking back at those months, I realize everyone living at the bookstore had a ghost lurking somewhere not very far behind them. Probably that's why we all stayed at the bookstore together for so long. I think back to what George said about the bookstore being an annex to Notre Dame and I think it is very true. In the end, yes, it is a famous bookstore and, yes, it is of no small literary importance. But more than anything, Shakespeare and Company is a refuge, like the church across the river. A place where the owner allows everyone to take what they need and give what they can.

Living with George at Shakespeare and Company has changed me, made me wonder about the life I left and the life I want to live. For now, I sit, I type, I try to be a better man. Life is a work in progress.

Acknowledgments

Few things can be as alarming for a parent as a child's declaration that he or she intends to write for a living. Trapeze artist or treehouse designer must seem more stable career options. Nonetheless, my parents, Ross and Patricia Mercer, have always supported and loved me, and for this I thank them no end. As for Sonia and Jean Michel de Robillard, who treated me like a son during that long and impoverished year in Marseilles, they hold a special place in my heart.

While the task of writing is daunting, more daunting still is the business of publishing. I offer fathomless gratitude to my agent, Kristin Lindstrom, for selling this book, and equally fathomless gratitude to my editor, Michael Flamini, for buying it. The meticulous Carol Edwards, who ferreted out a gaggle of typos and errors, deserves high praise and a place in the Face-Saving Hall of Fame.

To Eric Perier of the In Fact squat in Paris, for giving me an extra atelier to write in. To Simon Green, Colin Freeze, and Julie Delaney for helping me in especially dire moments. To Sparkle Hayter, whose tenacity and creativity are a constant inspiration. To Carl Whitman, for taking me into his home. To Lynn McAuley, who paid me to follow a poet to Ireland. And to those who read the book and helped make it better—Luke Basham, Adrian Hornsby, Buster Burk, and Musa Gurnis. Thank you for your help and friendship.

The Inforoots Association—www.inforoots.org—helps the children of Noailles learn to use the Internet, and also hapless writers whose computers swallow nearly completed manuscripts. Then there's the amazing Quinn Comendant, who not only provided a replacement computer but gave that computer the power to love.

Finally, a word for the woman to whom this book is dedicated. Without her, it simply could not have been written. The sacrifice was too great.